RAIDER

OF THE

SCOTTISH COAST

RAIDER
OF THE
SCOTTISH COAST

AN AGE OF SAIL NOVEL

BY

MARC LIEBMAN

www.penmorepress.com

ISBN-978-1-950586-49-3(Paperback)
ISBN 978-1-950586-48-6(e-book)

BISAC Subject Headings:
FIC014000FICTION / Historical
FIC032000FICTION / War & Military
FIC047000FICTION / Sea Stories

Editor: Chris Wozney
The Book Cover Whisperer:
ProfessionalBookCoverDesign.com

Address all correspondence to:

Penmore Press,
920 N Javelina Pl,
Tucson, AZ 85737

or visit our website at:
www.penmorepress.com

Books by Marc Liebman

Big Mother 40
Cherubs 2
Render Harmless
Forgotten
Inner Look
Moscow Airlift
The Simushir Island Incident

"I wish to have no connection with any ship that does not sail fast; for I intend to go in harm's way."

Captain John Paul Jones wrote these words in a letter to Mr. LeRay de Chaumont dated 16 November 1778, while he was in France waiting for a new command.

Earlier in the year, commanding the *Frigate Ranger,* Jones raided the Scottish town of Whitehaven. He also captured *H.M.S. Drake* and brought it and other prizes to Brest, France. Jones was ordered to remain in France for another command that turned out to be the 42-gun *Bon Homme Richard.*

TABLE OF CONTENTS

Dedication
Author's Confession
Chapter 1—Successful Immigrants
Chapter 2—Two Midshipmen
Chapter 3—Passing in the Night
Chapter 4—First Battles
Chapter 5—Privateer or Not?
Chapter 6—A Fast Ship in Harm's Way
Chapter 7—Nova Scotia Tourist
Chapter 8—Lieutenant Squadron Commander
Chapter 9—Back at It With *Alfred*
Chapter 10—End of a Crew
Chapter 11—Making of a Hero
Chapter 12—My Enemy Is Now My Friend
Chapter 13—Training and New Guns
Chapter 14—*Scorpion's* Sting
Chapter 15—Battle in the Bermuda Triangle
Chapter 16—Golden Prize
Chapter 17—More Than a Wee Bit O' Burnin'
Chapter 18—Three Versus One
Chapter 19—Battle With the Bird
Chapter 20—Elusive Prizes
Cast of Main Characters by Ship
Royal Navy Ship Rating System
Ships of *Raider of the Scottish Coast*
Timing of Watches and Ships Bells

DEDICATION

Raider of the Scottish Coast is dedicated the men and women who came before me to make the United States Navy the greatest navy in the world, and to the Royal Navy from whom we learned so much.

AUTHOR'S CONFESSION

When Michael James, Penmore Press's president and CEO, suggested during dinner on September 25th, 2018, that I ought to consider writing an Age of Sail series, my mind began to race. I grew up reading C.S. Forester, Alexander Kent and Patrick O'Brian, who wrote books about Royal Navy officers fighting the French during the Napoleonic Wars.

I envisioned a story about an American in the Continental Navy fighting the British during the American Revolution. Follow-on books with the same characters could take place during in the Quasi War with France (1798—1800), the fight against Barbary Pirates (1800—1805) and battling the Brits in the War of 1812.

The more I thought about writing these tales, the more excited I became. And so did Michael.

Officially, the Age of Sail began in 1571 at the battle of Lepanto off Greece when ships of the Holy Roman Empire, pushed through the water by sails, defeated Ottoman Empire galleys powered by oars. It ended in 1862 during the American Civil War when two ironclad steam-powered ships —*U.S.S. Monitor* and *C.S.S. Virginia*—pounded away at each other in Hampton Roads.

Until I started writing *Raider of the Scottish Coast,* all my published books and those yet to be written had military and/or counter-terrorism/espionage plots that took place after World War II. Eagerly, I sat down at my MacBook and began writing a story concept for what started as three and is now four books. A rough outline of the plot and the timeline for the series sailed out of my laptop as fast as I could touch the keys.

When the writing began, I had no inkling of the amount of research needed to make the story tactically and historically correct. For example, sailing a square-rigger is very different from sailing a sloop with a fore and aft sloop rig. Some of the terms and steps are the same, but tacking a square-rigged ship is far more complex. One's mind can explode with the nomenclature, so describing how a square-rigger is handled was a challenge. For some readers, there aren't enough descriptions of pulling yards around and sheeting home sails and other square rigged ship evolutions. For others, there's too much and their eyes roll back into their heads when they encounter these passages.

During the American Revolution, we were not yet a nation, so technically the designation *U.S.S.* for *United States Ship* can't be used. According to the U.S. Naval Heritage Command, ships in the Continental Navy were referred to in official documents by their type and name, i.e. *Frigate Alfred* or *Sloop Providence*. Up until President Teddy Roosevelt issued Executive Order 549 in January 1907, there was no standard designation for U.S. Navy ships. He made the U.S.S. designation standard.

The book has a mix of real and fictitious ships. Those that are "made up" are based on real vessels from the era.

The other challenge was how different life was back in the 1770s. The pace was a lot slower than it is today. Smart phones, the Internet, computers, cars, trucks, malls, supermarkets, interstate highways, trains, weather forecasting based on satellites, running water, indoor plumbing, and electricity did not exist. What we do in fractions of a second today, back then took weeks or months. Before they deployed, all warship captains were given written sailing orders that provided strategic direction but were vague on specific actions. Tasking was based on intelligence several months old, or broad national goals. It took months for the Admiralty to send a letter to a ship at sea and receive a reply, leaving the captain on his own to decide what to do. Depending on the situation, he could be a diplomat or a warrior.

The English language has changed since the 1770s. Rather than use the diction and syntax of the period, the characters use modern speech patterns with a smattering of terms from that age.

Philip Allan, a fellow Penmore author who patiently answered my questions and pointed me in the right direction on many occasions, deserves a special thank you.

There's plenty of action and a love story in *Raider of the Scottish Coast*. Enjoy the read, or should I say, sail!

Marc Liebman

Chapter 1

Successful Immigrants

Salkehatchie, SC, May 1715

Looking up from where he knelt behind a large oak tree, Caidin Jacinto could see the different shades of green on the leaves made by the sun striking through the forest. The ground was a quilt of shadows mixed with shafts of light.

Ten yards in front of him, the land dropped five feet into a small, slow moving creek that fed the Salkehatchie River. The ankle-deep water made it the narrowest and best crossing for a mile or so in either direction and it was on the shortest route to a nearby Yamasee Indian village.

Caidin was one of 60 South Carolina militiamen waiting to ambush a Yamasee war party that had killed the men on two family farms and taken prisoner the women and children. Their mission: free their fellow South Carolinians. Earlier in the day, they'd leapfrogged the Indians to set up this ambush. This would be Caidin's first action as lieutenant in the South Carolina militia.

One of his two long-barreled muskets rested on his thigh, the other lay on the ground. Both had powder in their pans. When he pulled the trigger, the hammer would slam forward, scratch the flint and send sparks into the black powder that would, if all went well, propel the lead ball down the length of the smooth-bore barrel.

Besides the two long guns, Caidin had a brace of pistols in his belt and a tomahawk. Strapped to his right leg was a long hunting knife with a 12-inch blade. While this was his first formal battle, it was not his first time fighting the Yamasee. His experience did nothing to quell the tightness in his stomach or his fear of dying or not rescuing the hostages.

Jacinto had arrived in Charleston from the Netherlands in 1708, as an ambitious 18-year-old with commissions for both the Dutch East and West India Companies, along with one from their British competitor, the British East India Company. None of these firms thought Charleston was worth a paid employee, so in lieu of a salary their contracts offered Caidin generous commissions. The executives reasoned that if Caidin brought them valuable cargos they would profit handsomely. If not, the agreements cost them nothing. What his employers hadn't realized at the time was that South Carolina's forests were full of oak which the English needed for the Royal Navy, and which the Dutch needed to build merchant ships. With his commissions, young Caidin bought land, something his family had been forbidden to own in the Netherlands, or generations before in Spain. Before he bought any of what was offered for sale by the Royal Governor, he explored each tract of land to make sure the trees could be cut for lumber and the ground farmed. Now he owned 5,000 acres, with a warehouse on the waterfront in Charleston and a small house in town. At 25, he was considered one of the seaport's most eligible bachelors.

A few years ago, on one of these surveying excursions, a five-man Tuscarora scouting party had attacked him. He'd fired his musket, taking one down. He'd killed another with his pistol, then fought off the other three with a long knife in one hand and a hatchet in the other. In the end, three Tuscaroras lay dead or dying. Caidin had watched the two injured survivors disappear into the forest. He'd cleaned the

2

cuts in his arm and side in a nearby stream before sewing them closed, and considered himself lucky to make it back to Charleston alive.

The faintest rustle of green caught his eye and his heart rate increased. Now, it felt as if it was trying to beat itself out of his chest. Then there was nothing, but Caidin kept his eye on the crossing and the forest on either side. His vigilance was rewarded when a Yamasee scout edged into the open by the crossing.

From his position, Caidin could see the men under his command nestled amongst trees and rocks that overlooked the crossing. Their mission was to pin the Indians down while the other group of South Carolinians under Captain MacCleod rushed the column and freed the captives.

A second Yamasee emerged from the forest and knelt next to the scout. Caidin watched as the scout said something to the second man, who waved. More Indians appeared, taking cover behind trees at the edge of the stream.

Jacinto had ordered his men to not to shoot until he fired or if the Indians attacked. If anyone fired early, he was afraid the raiding party would melt back into the forest, taking the captives with them. Caidin eased the musket in his lap to his shoulder.

As three forward Yamasee scouts crossed the stream and started to climb the bank, their companions led two women, three boys, and two girls, all of them gagged and tied, down onto the bank where there was a cleared area at the crossing. Caidin aimed at the man holding the rope linking the captives together.

If there was a command to fire by MacLeod, Caidin didn't hear it. He heard the crack of a single musket, and then a ripple of others. The Indian scout in his sights crumpled to the ground, so he shifted his aim and fired. The man spun around as the musket ball ripped his shoulder apart. Without looking down, Caidin picked up the second musket, stood, aimed, fired—and missed.

Musket balls ripped through leaves, breaking branches that deflected them away from their targets. Enough thudded into human flesh to kill or wound many of the Yamasees. Gunsmoke, trapped by the leaves, formed a gray-white cloud that obscured his view.

Spinning around, he saw he was the American closest to the captives. *I have to save them before they are murdered by the Yamasee.* Dropping the musket, Caidin raced toward the captives, who had all crouched down and huddled together, but a Yamasee was closer. One woman spread her arms over a little boy and girl. The little girl covered her head with her arms. Caidin leaped over the water to close the distance and yelled as loudly as he could to get the Yamasee's attention.

It worked. The raider turned on him with a hatchet in one hand and a long knife in the other. Caidin fired one pistol point-blank into his chest and the man went down. He dropped the pistol, drew the second and fired at another Yamasee, who staggered from the bullet in his belly but didn't fall. Still, it gave Caidin time to draw his tomahawk and embed it in the man's neck. The blade lodged in the bones, and it took a hefty yank to pull it free.

The woman protecting the two children watched him with wide-open, bright blue eyes. Their eyes locked and he could see the defiance in her eyes as she held tight to the young children. She nodded in recognition of his actions, and Caidin felt a pang of sorrow for what she and the children had endured.

He heard a war whoop and turned to see a Yamasee charging him, swinging two tomahawks in lethal circles. He threw one at Caidin, who ducked awkwardly. While he was off-balance, the Indian tried to bury the other tomahawk in his shoulder and rush past.

Fear, adrenalin and anger made Jacinto determined to kill his opponent. Caidin caught the arm and held it long enough to redirect his attacker, who tumbled to the ground but sprang back to his feet, tomahawk swinging menacingly in his hand. It gave Caidin time to draw his knife.

For as long as he lived, he'd remember the smile on the Yamasee's face as he charged. Caidin wasn't sure if it was overconfidence or acceptance that he was going to die and didn't care.

A sweeping strike from the tomahawk slashed Caidin's left side. He stared at the Indian, not wanting him to let him think the cut was serious or that it hurt, and feinted a lunge with his knife. The Indian's parry gave Caidin the opening he wanted. Pirouetting away to the Indian's left, he swung back and buried his tomahawk's wide blade in his opponent's lower back.

The man screamed in pain and staggered. Caidin grabbed his shoulder and drove the double-edged knife into his throat, cutting the scream short. Blood gushed as he yanked the blade out and let the dying Indian fall to the ground.

Throughout the clearing and forest, knots of men struggled, fought with knives and bare hands. He could hear the grunts from the effort and the howls of pain as men struggled to kill each other.

Caidin helped the two women to their feet and used his bloody knife to cut their bonds. The young boy—Caidin guessed was about six—and the even smaller girl clung to the dress of the woman with ice blue eyes and long brown hair. The other woman looked around wildly for potential attackers, drew to her the other children, none of whom looked to be older than eight.

The violence stopped as quickly as it started. One South Carolinian was dead, three more, including Caidin, had wounds. But there were 18 dead Yamasees, including the leader of the war party. How many had escaped into the forest no one could say. It was time to reload muskets and pistols and head back to Charleston.

The woman with ice blue eyes tore a section of her dress off so she could use it to wipe the blood off Caidin's side and bandage it. Her name, she told him, was Ester de Castro. Three days ago, Yamassees had raided the de Castro's farm. They had killed her husband, Jacob de Castro, and taken her, their son Ezra, and daughter Dolce prisoner. She had fully expected to be forced to spend the rest of her life living in a Yamasee village as the concubine of one of the males.

Back in Charleston, a family took in Ester and her two children.

Six months later, Ester Cordoso de Castro and Caidin were wed, and he adopted Ezra and Dolce. Ester bore him two sons, Javier and Gento, and a daughter, Yona. Sadly, Dolce died from smallpox in 1717 and Ezra succumbed to scarlet fever in 1727.

By the time the Seven Years War broke out in Europe in 1753, Caidin's South Carolina Colony Import and Exports, Ltd. was the largest business of its type in Charleston. When Caidin died in 1770 at the age of 80, six years after the death of his beloved wife, the family owned 100,000 acres of land along the Carolina coast, and north and west of Charleston.

Charleston, 1768

The open roof of the small structure behind the synagogue was covered with palm leaves, and children were playing tag in the large yard. 10-year-old Jaco Jacinto and his best friend, Eric Laredo, were standing off to the side, watching. Anyone who knew the two boys knew enough to expect them to get into mischief—if their older brothers weren't around to restrain them.

One of their favorite pastimes was teasing their younger sisters, Shoshana and Reyna. Both girls were eight, and very competitive. Their unofficial motto was anything their brothers could do, they could do better. It didn't matter if it was hunting, shooting, sailing or riding a horse; anything their brothers did, they set themselves to master.

Dark gray clouds hovered overhead, and the merriment of children was punctuated by an occasional clap of thunder. Without warning, heavy rain started. Most ran for the covered patio, but the boys were out in the open and quickly became drenched.

When Eric made fun of Shoshana's rain spattered dress, she threw a handful of mud at him. Eric responded in kind. Soon all four—Reyna, Shoshana, Eric and Jaco—were hurling handfuls of mud at each other in a boys versus girls battle. It must have looked like fun, because other children joined in.

In a moment of inspiration, Jaco took two handfuls of mud, snuck up behind Reyna and pressed the gooey mass into her long black hair, raking his muddy fingers through the strands. Infuriated, Reyna whirled and threw what she had in hand at Jaco, screaming as she chased him, "I'm going to get you for this!"

She ran after Jaco, who was laughing, until she slipped and fell face first into a puddle. When Reyna got up, the front of her best dress was soaking wet and covered in mud. If looks could kill, Jaco Jacinto would have been vaporized.

Gosport, England, 1768

The Smythe family house was a stone structure right by the Gosport road that ran along the harbor. Across the bay was the Royal Navy base at Portsmouth. From his second story bedroom window, young Darren could see the frigates and ships-of-the-line entering and leaving the harbor. Every chance he could get, he would dash out of the house and to the docks to watch the ships come in. He would listen to the officers shout orders, and imagine himself on the quarterdeck giving commands to the crew as the ship navigated the channel to the anchorage.

When his parents couldn't find him in the house, they knew he was perched on a large rock watching Royal Navy ships depart and return. Even when he was supposed to be doing his chores or helping with the family business, Darren Smythe would bolt for the door whenever there was a ship in the channel.

One morning, Lester Smythe followed his son to his favorite rock and watched silently from behind as the boy stared avidly to sea until the ship's anchor splashed into the water. The lad was oblivious to his presence until he sat down on the rock next to him and put his arm around his son's shoulder. Silently, they listened to the waves slap the wooden posts of the docks, the voices of sailors, and the cry of the seagulls that arched and swooped overhead. Finally, Lester asked, "So, do you want to be on one of those ships?"

"Father, I do. I want to be a Royal Navy captain and sail to far away places, like the Caribbean, Canada and Minorca. Maybe even India."

The elder Smythe was happy his son paid attention to geography lessons. His teachers said Darren was a bright, dedicated student, but easily distracted by anything to do with the Royal Navy. "So, you do not want go to university and learn to be an engineer or a doctor or a solicitor?"

Darren looked at his father with the intensity of a 10 year-old with his mind made up. "No. I want to be an officer in the Royal Navy. I know I have to start as a midshipman. Father, can you help?"

Gosport, June 1773

Rain that had pounded the streets for hours suddenly stopped, and clouds drifted apart. Warm spring sunshine began heating the cobblestones, and soon tendrils of moisture were rising into the already humid air.

A lieutenant, resplendent in royal blue frock coat with gold buttons and white breeches, walked up the two steps to the offices of Smythe & Sons, Ltd., a company founded in 1610 to make surgical instruments and knives. The two sailors accompanying him waited on the street when he rapped smartly on the door.

Inside, 15 year-old Darren Smythe turned to his father and they shared a hug. Lester held his son and said, "Remember, son, no matter what happens, we love you. Godspeed, and do your family and your country proud."

"Father, I will." Darren Smythe wore a white collar patch insignia on his blue frock coat, signifying he was a midshipman of the Royal Navy. He put on his tall round hat. His naturally curly blond hair stuck out over his ears and neck.

Lester opened the door, and the officer introduced himself as Lieutenant Roote from His Majesty's Frigate *Deer*. Roote spotted Smythe's waiting sea chest and directed the two sailors to pick it up.

"Sir," he said politely to the erect, elder Smythe, "we'll take good care of your son."

All Darren could think about was that he was on his way.

Philadelphia, September 1775

City Tavern on South 2nd Street had not been hard to find, nor the third floor room. Sixteen year-old Jaco Jacinto paced back and forth, trying to formulate answers to possible questions in what could be a life-changing interview.

His father had written a letter to pave the way for this interview, but Jaco himself had done the real work of preparation.

Each summer since he was twelve, Jaco had shipped on a merchant vessel carrying South Carolina Import and Export company cargo to and from Europe. He had worked for four different captains and was comfortable handling a sailing ship. His father had insisted he start at the lowest level and learn each position's skills.

His first trip had taken him to Brest and Lorient France, where they'd unloaded a cargo of logs. The ship then sailed down the Bay of Biscay to Bordeaux, where the hold was filled with barrels of wine. The next summer, the merchant ship carried cotton to Liverpool for the nearby English mills. It returned to Charleston loaded with bolts of fabric and other manufactured goods. When he was fourteen, the ship went to Amsterdam loaded with cotton and dried corn. On the way back, it stopped first in England for tools and finely crafted furniture, and then again in Bordeaux for wine. The last trip before the war started, Jaco rode the ship to Cadiz in Spain where wood was unloaded and the ship filled with casks of Spanish wines and barrels of gunpowder.

Jaco was built like his grandfather: stocky but not fat, well muscled and athletic. He had inherited his grandmother's ice-blue eyes, which contrasted with the olive-brown skin of his Spanish ancestors, sun-darkened by summers at sea. His jet-black hair was long and straight, which made it easy to tie into a ponytail.

Nine days ago he'd set out from home. In three days a fast schooner that carried passengers and mail up and down the coast had brought Jaco to Philadelphia, where his father, Javier Jacinto, was a part of the South Carolina delegation to the Second Continental Congress and a member of the Marine Committee. For the past five days, Jaco had been at his father's side, silently watching the Congress attempt to manage a war against the most powerful nation in the world. In the evening, with the light from candles creating shadows on the wall, the two would sit and discuss what Jaco had observed.

The main problem, Jaco had learned, was money, or the lack of it. The Continental Army and Navy were short on everything. Most of the funds came from donations, often with strings attached, or loans from the Dutch, French, and Spanish governments. Even so, the Continental Army and Navy barely had enough money to function.

Javier Jacinto donated money specifically to convert merchant ships to warships, as well as build new, purpose-built warships.

The second problem was munitions. Foundries had to be built to cast cannon, factories to manufacture muskets and gunpowder. The three gunpowder mills in the colonies couldn't make enough. More had to be built and protected from the British. The Jacintos and their fellow merchants used their contacts to buy powder and shot that was smuggled in from France, Spain and the Dutch West Indies, but it was never enough.

Ships, their supplies and crews, were the third problem. Shipyards that had built sloops, brigs and small frigates for the Royal Navy now turned merchant ships into warships for the Continental Navy, but this was a slow and expensive process. Manning them was a separate problem. Consortiums holding letters of marque from the Congress or colonial legislatures could authorize ships' crews to sail as privateers to capture British ships. Because of the lure of prize money, privateers found it easy to recruit men, but finding skilled sailors willing to leave their fishing boats was harder. And finding men who could transition from thinking like merchant captains to acting as commanders of warships was harder still.

When the war started, Jaco had wanted to join his best friend, Eric Laredo, on the Charleston-based privateer *Duke*, but he'd agreed with his father to instead apply for a commission as a midshipman in the Continental Navy. Javier's back-up plan was to join *Duke* or its sister ship, *Duchess,* both of which were converted merchantmen built for speed as well as their ability to carry cargo.

The interview ahead would determine his course.

The door latch clanked open, and Jaco turned and faced the opening. A man wearing white breeches and a dark blue coat with gold trim stood in the doorway and announced, "Mr. Jacinto, Captain Saltonstall and Lieutenant Jones will see you now." Jaco crossed the threshold to what he hoped would be his new life.

On board H.M.S. Deer, *November 1775*

It was five days after leaving Portsmouth and the weather was getting warmer as the frigate approached the waters off Maderia Island. Supper had been served and the first bell of the second dog watch had just rung, signifying that it was 6:30 p.m.

Able Seaman Symon Truckee was sitting at the table, nursing his mug of beer and finishing the last of his duff pie. The other seven men in his mess had already cleaned out their bowls and put them away. Only Truckee was still at the table, which had to be stowed before the men could hang their hammocks and sleep.

Bosun Mate Owen Hammersby, who was from Berwick-on-Upton, a small town on the North Sea just south of the English-Scottish border, was making the rounds as part of his duties and saw Truckee and the unstowed table. "Symon, laddie, let's finish up so your mates can get their hammocks out. You're all assigned to the first watch which goes on at midnight."

Truckee, who was burly and pugnacious, had been offered a choice by a Royal Navy recruiter two years ago: stay in jail and finish a sentence for assault, or join the Royal Navy. He'd chosen the navy, but never shed his surly disposition.

"Leave me alone while I finish me beer and pudding."

Not wanting to get into a confrontation with the truculent Truckee, Hammersby kept his tone even. "Your mates want to sling their hammocks. They can't while you sit at the mess table."

"Too bloody bad. When I get done I'll be done and not a moment sooner. Nothing you say will make me go faster. In fact, you're slowing me down."

A crowd was gathering. Truckee was defying Hammersby, and by extension, Captain Tillerson's authority.

"Truckee, me boy, be a good lad and finish up. I'm going to finish me rounds and when I come back, I want to see you finished and this table stowed properly."

The bosun's mate nodded to Truckee's messmates and walked forward on the berthing deck. Everything else was as it should be. When he returned to Truckee's mess, however, the man was still sitting there, and neither beer nor pudding had been touched.

"Let's go, Truckee, finish up," the mate said firmly.

Truckee came to a boil. "I'm not done, Hammersby, so go your way. Leave me the hell alone!"

This flagrant challenge to the mate's authority, the captain's policy and navy regulations was not acceptable. "Yes, you are." Hammersby reached for the half-full mug and plate, but Truckee grabbed his arm.

"Fuck off, Hammersby!" Truckee flicked his mug and the beer splashed into Hammersby's face. His next move was to swing at Hammersby, expecting to catch him off guard. But Hammersby was not only strong from his years at sea hauling lines, he was also quick. His hand caught Truckee's fist. The two men grappled, surrounded now by 20 men.

Midshipman Smythe was on his way to the main deck when heard a commotion. He immediately changed course to see what the hubbub was about and forced his way through the sailors until he reached the two men. By now, Hammersby had Truckee face down on the table with his arm pulled up behind his back.

"Both of you stop, immediately. What is going on here?" Smythe demanded of Hammersby, who gave an accurate report of what transpired.

"Able Seaman Truckee, is that what happened?"

"He reached for my beer. No one touches me drink."

"So you splashed it in the bosun mate's face and took a swing at him?"

Truckee was silent. He narrowed his eyes at the young midshipman and clenched a fist.

Smythe turned to the sailors. "Is that what happened?"

No one spoke in Truckee's defense. *I have no choice but to charge him.* "Hammersby, put Truckee in irons on the orlop deck. I'm going to write him up on Article 22." Smythe wanted to avoid an Article 21 charge, because if Truckee was found guilty, death was the only sentence allowed under the Articles of War.

* * *

The next morning, Captain Avery Tillerson held the trial. It was something he hadn't expected to do so soon into *Deer's* voyage. He shot a glance at his bosun's mate and newest midshipman. It was obvious to him that they had downplayed the event to minimize charges.

The punishment meted out for an Article 22 offense was either confinement on bread and water for an extended period of time, or flogging. There was no place on *Deer* to house Truckee in isolation except by chaining him to a rib in the hold, where he would be bitten to death by the rats. That left flogging. How many lashes were enough for a challenge, albeit an indirect one, to his authority?

All hands mustered amidship to witness punishment. Truckee was led to a grating; his shirt was removed and his wrists were tied the base of the shrouds leading up the main mast. A rag was stuffed in his mouth to muffle his screams.

Tillerson read the charges and announced the sentence: six lashes. "Bosun Farley, do your duty."

The smack of the cat-o-nine-tails on Truckee's bare back carried over the deck. Smythe, standing at attention along with the rest of the officers, forced himself to watch as the welts on Truckee's back turned to bloody gashes. The sight made Smythe sick, and he vowed he would find ways to avoid flogging a sailor if he could.

After the lashes were administered, seawater was splashed on Truckee's back and he was taken to the surgeon, who would sew up the worst of the cuts.

* * *

Bright blue skies and 70-degree temperatures of the western Atlantic nor' nor' east of Santo Domingo were a welcome relief from the damp, raw winds of the English Channel. Overhead, an albatross soared over the clear water.

It was on days like this Darren wished he was a lookout stationed on a masthead. He loved standing on the platform searching the horizon with a spyglass as the wind hissed past and he absorbed the motion of the ship. On *Deer*, the main mast platform was 75 feet above the deck, and when the ship heeled on a beam reach, if he jumped he would land in the water well clear of the deck.

At the Royal Navy Academy, Darren had learned how to walk along the foot ropes, holding onto the spar with one hand and using the other to furl or unfurl sails. The prospective midshipmen performed every task needed to sail or maneuver a ship. When the ship changed course, they hauled on the braces to bring the yards around, or adjusted the sheets to trim the sails.

Sometimes, as he climbed the ratlines, Darren remembered a fellow student screaming as he fell from a topsail yard. The 13 year-old had bounced off the ratlines, but that had not been enough to brake his fall, and his head had split open on the deck. Darren had been one of the students tasked to scrub away the blood. The accident had been a brutal reminder of how dangerous life at sea could be, even during peacetime conditions, which these were not.

Today, Smythe was the officer on watch, and his station was on the quarterdeck. Like most of the men, Smythe was tanned and barefoot. He wore only a cotton shirt, open at the neck, and breeches, formerly white, that had turned light gray. As if to compensate, the sun had bleached his sandy blond hair almost white.

Overhead, *Deer*'s main, top and topgallants, along with jib and forestaysail, were taut, filled out and slightly angled to starboard, taking full advantage of the 10-knot Trade Wind. The 683-ton *Alarm* class frigate plowed through Western Atlantic swells, averaging six knots, on the prowl for privateers. The commander of the West Indies Squadron had assigned *Deer* to patrol off the Bahamas, Turks and Caicos Islands. With 32-guns, she was too formidable to be an easy target for a privateer, and her very presence in the waters helped safeguard the trade between England and her Atlantic colonies—the ones that were not in revolt.

H.M.S. Deer was Avery Tillerson's third command. As a lieutenant he had assumed command of a sloop-of-war taken as a prize during the Seven Years War; later he'd been made commander of a 20-gun frigate; now he was captain of *Deer*.

Her keel had been laid in 1770. Thirteen 12-pounder cannons ran along the port and starboard gun decks, with two 6-pounders as bow chasers. Four 6-pounders were on the quarterdeck, two on each side.

"Deck ahoy! Sail ho, three points off the port bow."

"Deck, aye." Midshipman Smythe took a spyglass from its holder on the quarterdeck and rested his elbow on the rail to steady the brass tube, then scanned the horizon 20 degrees to the left of *Deer*'s course.

"So, Mr. Smythe, if you were in my shoes, what would you do?"

The 16 year-old turned and looked at his captain, "Sir, if we want to catch this ship before dark, we need to increase our speed. In these light winds, I'd unfurl our royals and fly main and mizzen staysails to gain one or two knots."

"Are you sure about the increase in speed?"

"Yes, sir."

"You base that answer on what?"

Smythe brushed a lock of hair from his face. "Sir, experience. You had *Deer* sail under different configurations while crossing the Atlantic and I kept a chart with wind direction and strength, sea state, courses, sail settings and the resulting speeds in my journal. I believe I mentioned this to you, sir."

"Aye, you did that, Mr. Smythe. Well done, lad." Tillerson turned to the ship's master, who stood behind the quartermaster. "Mr. Hyde, call the watch and send 'em aloft to spread the royals, th' mizzen and main staysails."

Hyde, a Royal Navy veteran with a scraggly salt-and pepper beard, grinned. Young Master Smythe was always peppering him with questions. Some he had difficulty answering. "Aye, aye, sir."

Smythe watched the barefooted seamen climb the ratlines to the yards. When he'd first joined *Deer*, if he was not on watch he and Albert Crenshaw, *Deer's* other midshipman, would go up the masts to help the sailors furl and unfurl sails. It was done to earn the crew's respect more than to demonstrate their skills as topmen. *Deer*, due to manpower shortages, only had two midshipmen on board instead of its normal complement of three. Smythe was assigned the mainmast, Crenshaw the foremast, and a bosun mate to the mizzen.

Glancing up, he remembered how cold and stiff the canvas had been in the North Sea in winter, just like the midshipman handling it. Today the canvas would be warm to the touch.

With the royals out and the stay sails sheeted home, Captain Tillerson turned to Smythe with a look of inquiry that said, "Midshipman, what do you do now?" One of a captain's responsibilities was making sure his midshipmen were learning what they needed, for they would become the navy's future officersHe also had a duty to assess their skills and make reports to the admiralty.

"Sir, we need to wear the ship to a more westerly course."

"I agree. Master Hyde, alter course to west by nor' west."

They could feel the 120-foot-long frigate pitch slightly down and surge forward as the wind pushed against the additional canvas. "Carry on, Mr. Smythe. Stay on the quarterdeck until we catch this mysterious ship. You have the honor of guiding us through this chase, so think through your moves carefully before you recommend them. Master Hyde can adjust the watch bill, if needed." With those words, Captain Tillerson left the quarterdeck.

Smythe turned to Lieutenant Roote, the second lieutenant on *Deer* and, by definition, the third most senior officer on the ship. Roote was grinning. "Not bad for a Royal Naval Academy graduate. What next?"

Many in the King's Navy were of the opinion that Royal Naval Academy graduates did not become good officers. Smythe was determined to prove them wrong. Darren had finished at the top of his class of 40, which meant he would be eligible for promotion to Lieutenant in four years instead of six. "Sir, I'd like to wait until after five bells for this watch and then cast the log to confirm our speed. I believe we will be making close to eight knots."

The ring from the fifth bell died away, signaling it was two and a half hours into his watch; ashore it was 1030 in the morning. At Smythe's command, the quartermaster's mate picked up a triangular shaped piece of wood attached to a spool of twine that had knots 47-feet, three inches apart. He twirled the wood over his head, making sure it didn't catch in the rigging, and tossed it from the aft leeward corner of the quarterdeck into the frigate's wake. As soon as the wood hit the water, the bosun's mate on watch turned over an hourglass that would empty in 28 seconds as sand drained from from the upper bulb into the lower. The quartermaster's mate counted the knots as the twine played out between his fingers. Each knot that went through his fingers represented one knot of speed. When he was finished, he re-wound the line around the spool, retrieving the triangular piece of wood.

"Mr. Smythe, you can tell our good captain that His Majesty's frigate *Deer* is making eight and a half knots."

"Splendid! I'll ask him to note it in the ship's log."

Upon his return to the deck, Darren went back to looking at *Deer's* quarry, wondering if it were a rebel ship and what it might be worth as a prize.

The day wore on. When eight bells rang through the ship, signaling the end of the forenoon watch, *Deer* had closed the gap by about a third.

As the ringing of the last bell died away, Darren raised the glass to his eye. The unknown ship had changed course.

Darren called out to the bosun mate, who was coiling a line on the quarterdeck, "Handley, there." When the sailor looked up, Darren continued. "Pay my respects to the captain, and ask him to come to the quarterdeck."

The mate put the back of his hand to his forehead by way of salute. "Aye, aye, sir."

Smythe was working out an intercept course when he heard Captain Tillerson's footfall on the deck. He kept his eye on the mystery ship as he reported, "Sir, our quarry has changed to a more westerly course. Based on our position when I came on watch, the Turks and Caicos are 30 miles to our west. If she gets amongst those islands before dark, it will be difficult and dangerous to follow her."

"Concur. Mr. Smythe, what do you recommend?"

Before the midshipman could reply, a voice called out, "Ahoy, quarterdeck! Spars in the water, three points off the 'larboard beam."

Smythe handed his spyglass to his captain and took another from the rack. Through the narrow circular field of view, Darren saw bodies and flotsam floating 300 yards from the ship's port side. A man in the water raise his hand and feebly waved.

Tillerson gave orders. "Bosun, slack all sails. Mr. Hyde and Mr. Smythe, keep an eye out on our prey; I don't want her to come back and surprise us. Mr. Crenshaw, take a boat and find out what we have here. Then we will resume the chase."

Albert Crenshaw, the senior midshipman by a year, was on the main deck looking up at the quarterdeck. He put the back of his right hand to his forehead in acknowledgment of Tillerson's order.

Deer had two identical stacks of three boats, one between the fore and main masts and the other between the mainmast and the mizzenmast. The top boat was a 15-foot cutter with pegs for up to four pairs of oars. In the middle was a 20-foot pinnace that could have six pairs of oars, and it was nestled in a 25-foot long boat that could be propelled by 12 pairs of oars; all three could be rigged with a single mast and sailed as a sloop.

Tackles attached to the main and foremast stays were rigged on the port side end of the masts' mainsail yards and hooked to the cutter. The other end was attached to the mainmast's and mizzenmast's tackle pendants, connected by the triatic stay. Three sailors tied the ends of a rope to iron fittings on both sides of the cutter's bow and stern.

The tie downs were released and sailors took up the slack in the stays. At the command "walk away with the stays," the cutter rose and was eased over the side. When it was clear of the gunwale, the bosun mate yelled, "Lower away."

Three sailors clambered down the ladder from the main deck, freed the oars from their lashings and held the boat against the hull to allow Midshipman Crenshaw and three sailors to climb down and board.

Masts and yards groaned and creaked as *Deer* wallowed in the blue-green water. The heavy canvas sails, freed from their sheets, rustled and flapped in the wind. From the quarterdeck, Smythe gazed at the wreckage in the water; it looked like not one but two debris fields.

The boat crew hauled four men onboard. Smythe studied the face of one and turned to his captain. "Sir, that is Midshipman Drew Rathburn. I knew him at the Naval Academy. He was assigned to *H.M.S. Temptress*."

"When he is dried out, find out what happened."

Four exhausted men were assisted over the bulwark, then sprawled on the deck, gasping with relief. The cutter moved slowly through the debris to search for more survivors. Finding none, Crenshaw started bringing bodies to *Deer*. The sailmaker, alerted that there were sailors to bury, laid strips of sailcloth in a row on the main deck. When Crenshaw climbed back on board from his last trip, 12 bodies lay in a neat row.

It was a somber business. The ship's doctor and his mate sewed the canvas coffins up, after placing two 12-pound cannonballs at the feet of each man. When they had finished, Captain Tillerson read the Royal Navy's funeral service. Six Marines fired a volley salute as each body was brought to the side of the ship and placed on the plank. One by one the corpses slid into the Atlantic.

The grim work done, Captain Tillerson ordered the sheets taken in, and *Deer* heeled over on a starboard tack. With the ship underway again, Tillerson said to Smythe, "Turn over the watch to Mr. Roote and go see what Midshipman Rathburn has to say. Meanwhile, we will head in the direction the mystery ship was last seen. If we are lucky, we may catch sight of her before the sun goes down."

Smythe found Rathburn sitting in the gunroom on the berthing deck. Rathburn's skin was shriveled from the salt water and his face sunburned, but someone had provided him with a dry set of clothes to wear, and he was sipping a glass of His Majesty's port.

"It is good to see you, Drew. I am glad we found you in time."

Rathburn nodded. "Aye. Several ships passed us, but none spotted us."

"What befell your ship?"

"A hurricane overtook us. The captain thought he could outrun the storm. The lubbers were terrified by the waves, and even the old hands thought we were doomed. The wind was so strong, the raindrops felt like we were being hit with hammers. The foremast was carried away and the wind whipped it around like a bloody cricket bat. It took out the mainmast at the maintop."

Rathburn shuddered, recollecting how the 700-ton, *Amazon* class frigate had been tossed about like a cork in 25-foot seas. "We were thrown about like dolls. I think half the crew was hurt when the mizzenmast came down. Soon after, the ship capsized."

The young midshipman started crying, and Darren put his arms around his Academy classmate to comfort him. Between wracking sobs, Rathburn described crewmen clinging to the mizzenmast's spars as the wind and waves buffeted them. The bosun had gotten tangled in half-submerged ropes and drowned. When the storm abated, only 20 of his shipmates were still alive. For five days, as the sun rose and burned across the sky and set, one by one, men were overcome by thirst or exhaustion, and drowned.

Rathburn fell silent, and Smythe helped him into an empty bunk and waited until he fell asleep before going up on the quarterdeck.

Later in the day, with Rathburn's tale fresh in his mind, Smythe watched lightning flare amidst storm clouds on the western horizon. The sight made Rathburn's tale even more real.

Off the Turks and Caicos, *Deer* was battered by rain driven by high winds. Thunder sounded like the rolling fire of cannon, and lightning, brighter than any Smythe had ever seen in England, briefly and spectacularly illuminated the lowering sky. Tillerson had already sent his top men aloft to reef in the main and topgallants, so only the mainsails and jib were out to maintain steerageway. With the storm passing to the east, Tillerson sent the sharpest-eyed men were sent aloft, but there was no sighting of any other ship.

During the night, thunder boomed and flashes of lightning momentarily turned the darkness into daylight. The on-duty watch tried to stay dry on the gun deck; the helmsman and officer of the watch wore rope harnesses tied to a railing stanchion.

After standing the midnight to four a.m. middle watch, Smythe left the quarterdeck and made his way to his berth in the dark. By now now he was accustomed to the motions of the ship, each deck with its own smells and pitches. You could have put him blindfolded in any part of the ship and he'd have known instantly where he was. He was soaked and exhausted, but strangely exhilarated by the sights, sounds and scents of the storm. They were completely unlike anything he had known growing up in London or at the Royal Navy Academy. He had weathered storms before, but only North Atlantic storms, where the cold made a midshipman's fingers so numb he could barely grip the ropes. Until now, he'd never in the warm waters of the Caribbean. He wondered if the island sea gulls were different from those of England; he knew some of the birds and fishes were spectacularly strange.

He rolled into his hammock, wondering what it would like to be a sea monster arrowing through blue-green waters, with birds with bright feathers flying overhead. He fell asleep almost instantly. When he awoke the sky was clear, with the storm clouds on the eastern horizon.

On board Frigate Alfred, *November 1775*

Winter hadn't arrived and already Jaco didn't like Philadelphia weather. Dark gray clouds brought cold rain, then hung around dismally for days. The sun was a rarity, and cold, raw winds penetrated anything he wore like a knife.

First Lieutenant John Paul Jones had assigned him to follow ship designer Joshua Humphreys as he inspected modifications that turned the merchant ship *Black Prince* into the frigate *Alfred.*

They entered the forward hold and Humphreys gestured towards the lantern in Jaco's hand. "Hold that out so I can see, lad." The shipwright went to the forward end of the hold and examined the extra bracing pegged into the original ribs on the starboard side. Jaco followed him, taking care that neither man's shadow covered the area Humphreys was examining.

After the forward hold, the pair moved to the expanded and still empty magazine, then the after hold. Satisfied that the work had been done properly, Humphreys studied the extra rib stiffeners installed on the berthing deck and gun deck. In response to Jaco's questions, Humphreys provided clear, easy to understand answers about what had been added, and why.

A cold gust greeted both men as they emerged from the gun deck and onto the main deck. Jaco shivered noticeably.

Humphreys noticed the discomfort of his assistant. "Just wait until January, and you'll think this warm."

"Sir, I fear I never will stop shivering in this damnable climate. I don't know how you live here."

"We stay inside by a fire as much as we can!"

"Aye, sir. I hope we sail south to where the sun shines and it is warm."

The booming voice of Captain Saltonstall, standing on the quarterdeck without a wool overcoat, reached them. "Mr. Humphreys, is everything in order?" The tails of the captain's waistcoat flapped in the wind.

Humphreys took several steps aft. "Yes sir, everything is to my satisfaction. We need to finish the rigging, and you can finish loading the cannon. *Alfred* should be the equal of anything its size sailed by the Royal Navy."

Saltonstall looked off to the pier and then back at Humphreys. "I shall keep that in mind when *Alfred* is exchanging broadsides with one of His Majesty's frigates." Saltsonstall addressed his midshipman. "Mr. Jacinto, aren't you supposed to be with Mr. Reasoner on the gun deck?"

Damn, I forgot. Today we start training the gun crews. Gladly, Jaco ran down the ladder to the gun deck and out of the biting wind.

When he'd first met Harry Reasoner in October, Jaco could barely understand the man, his Massachusetts accent was so broad. Reasoner had learned his trade on a British frigate during the Seven Years' War; as the ship's gunner, he was a member of the officers' mess as a warrant officer.

Reasoner was tall; he had to stoop to avoid hitting his head on the beams supporting the main deck when he walked to the mainmast in the middle of the gun deck. From the men gathered around who had already reported aboard, Reasoner randomly picked six men for each nine-pounder.

Five days ago, Gunner Reasoner had taken Jaco to the cannon foundry to learn how the cannon were made. It was also a chance for Jaco to practice the loading drill and fire the guns under Reasoner's critical eye. Only half of *Alfred's* allotted twenty 9-pounders had been ready. Each new gun was fired three times with a double load of powder to make sure they were structurally sound. Once he accepted the cannon, Reasoner scribed his initials and the date on each breech. Two days later, the cannon and carriages had been hoisted aboard.

Since *Alfred* was tied to a pier, only the five guns installed on the seaward or port side were used for training. Reasoner picked the port number three cannon as the weapon he would use to demonstrate to the gun crews the six positions.

The 1st Sponger stood closest to the bulwark on the starboard side of the gun carriage. The 2nd Sponger was two steps inboard by the rear wheel or truck of the carriage, while the 1st Gun Captain stood behind the breech on the same side.

On the port side, Reasoner placed the 1st Loader by the gunport, the 2nd Loader at the midpoint of the cannon, and the 2nd Gun Captain opposite the 1st Gun Captain.

Next, Reasoner assigned men to positions on the remaining port cannon He looked up and down the port side to make sure the men of all five crews were in place before he issued the first command. "Cast loose and provide."

Each 1st Sponge Man and 1st Loader unlatched the heavy oak port and pulled the rope on his side. Once the gunport was raised, the ropes, made of quarter-inch Manila hemp, were wrapped to a cleat on the inside of the bulwark.

With the gunport open, each gun crew released the ropes holding the gun carriage in position so the cannon wouldn't roll around the deck. The loaders removed the wooden muzzle plug called a tampion, while #2 Gun Captain pulled off the touchhole cover. Both went into racks on the bulwark. The 1st Gun Captain held the powder horn in one hand and the long needle used to prick the cartridge in the other. The 2nd Gun Captain made sure the slow match, lashed to an iron rod in a wooden tub, was within reach. In combat, he would use it to fire the cannon.

The carriages were pulled back on the gun deck so there was room for the 1st Sponger to insert the wide sponge, secured to a long stick, into the barrel. Reasoner walked up and down the row of five guns to make sure they were properly cast loose and each man was in the proper position.

Reasoner, in command voice, said, "Sponge your guns."

Each 1st Sponger stuck the 10-foot long handle of the sponge out the gunport so he could insert the dry sponge into the eight-foot long barrel. Once it was in position, the 1st Gun

Captain placed his hand over the touchhole of the cannon while the sponge was shoved down the barrel and withdrawn. This created a vacuum that would extinguish any sparks. For real firing the sponges were wet, but for the purposes of this training session the water buckets were empty. The 2nd sponger did the same, then both spongers stepped back into position.

"Load cartridges."

Since the boys who would serve as powder monkeys were not yet on board, Reasoner nodded to Jaco, who put a single powder cartridge behind each gun, along with a wooden box containing felt wads that would go between the iron cannon ball and the powder. Reasoner had prepared five dummy cartridges made from wood and canvas that the crews could use for practice. The powder cartridges were shoved down the barrel by the 1st Loader, who stepped aside to let the 2nd Loader ram a rod into the barrel to push the cartridge as far back as possible.

"Load ball."

The 2nd Loader picked up a nine-pound cannon ball and a felt wad and arranged them so the wad would be wedged between the cannon ball and the powder cartridge.

"Ram Round." The 1st Loader used his rammer to push the ball into the wad and against the powder cartridge. He pulled the rammer out and shoved it down the barrel hard to make sure the ball was seated. A second thrust made sure of the positioning.

"Run Out." The loaders and sponge men grabbed the rope pulleys and pulled the gun carriage forward until it was against the bulwark and the long nose of the cannon projected from the ship's side. The 1st Gun Captain sighted along the barrel and used the elevating screw to raise or lower the barrel. Satisfied that it was aimed at hull of the target—a ship anchored in the Delaware River—he pricked the cartridge with the long needle and shook the empty powder horn to simulate filling the touchhole and the small tray above the breech.

"Fire as your gun bears." The 2nd Gun Captain touched the wand with the slow match to the top of the touchhole.

Reasoner observed all five crews. Until they went to sea, walk-throughs were all that they could do. Satisfied with the first walk through, he let the gun crews go through the process six more times before he started making changes to the teams. Besides training the gun crews, Reasoner was looking for the men who would make the best gun captains.

* * *

At dinner that night in the gunroom, Jaco asked Lieutenant Jones what he would do if he were *Alfred's* captain. "I would take her right into England's home waters, particularly the North Sea. Why? Ah, there are prizes aplenty off the Scottish coast that can be quickly taken to Amsterdam, where Dutch merchants will be eager to pay for captured ships and cargo. The Royal Navy views France as its natural enemy and regards the North Sea as a British lake. Its ships are based primarily in southern England, so they can quickly blockade French Atlantic ports such as Brest, Cherbourg and St. Nazaire. It leaves the east coast of England north of London unguarded. Does that answer your question, Mr. Jacinto?"

"It does, sir. If your assessment is true, an audacious captain could raid Scottish ports and send a message to King George that the Continental Navy is a force to be reckoned with."

"Aye, young man. And, given the right ship, that is just what I intend to do."

Chapter 2

Two Midshipmen

On board Privateer Duke, *November 1775*

Captain Richard Glenn stared through the windows of his cabin at the wake of his ship. The six-foot swells of the North Sea made it feel as if *Duke* were bounding through the gray blue water as its bow and stern rose and fell. There was a faint, rhythmic rattling sound as loose items inside the drawers of his desk shifted with the movements. The desk itself didn't shift, because it was bolted to the port bulwark, and the extra chairs were lashed to the starboard bulwark so they wouldn't slide around.

As captain of the ship, he had a decision to make. *Duke* was headed so' west by west on a beam reach pushed by a strong wind from the nor' west. Within a few hours, *Duke* would be within 20 miles of the English coast. Would he chance taking his ship through English Channel? He been sailing on merchant ships in these waters for 10 years and more, and knew that wind direction in the English Channel this time of year was unpredictable. If he was lucky, a nor' west wind would push him right through in two days. But tacking back and forth against an adverse wind between the French and English coast could take four days or more to claw through the Straits of Dover, past Brest and into the Atlantic Ocean. Or he could sail around Scotland and into the Atlantic. From their present position, it was an easy three days, unless they ran into a storm.

The two tons of gunpowder in *Duke*'s hold was desperately needed by the Continental Army. Time was of the essence, but so was avoiding capture.

Duke was the ideal ship for this mission. It was designed and built as an armed merchant ship to carry high priority cargos. Sixteen 9-pounders provided enough sting to fend off small warships and pirates, while the long, narrow hull gave *Duke* enough speed to outrun Royal Navy frigates.

There was a third element to consider. *Duke* was a privateer; that meant its owners expected to profit from prizes Glenn and his crew took. On the way from Charleston to Amsterdam, they had not taken any prizes. Now, if *Duke* were lucky, they might find a prize and make their owners, not to mention his crew, very happy. Shipping in the English channel was closely guarded, but English merchant ships plied the North Sea waters without escort.

Decision made, Glenn walked out onto the main deck, looked at the gray sky and climbed up to the quarterdeck to address his lieutenant. "Mr. Laredo, get ready to wear the ship and head nor' by east."

* * *

That night, high winds forced Captain Glenn to sail *Duke* within a mile of the Scottish Coast, sails reefed to reduce the strain on the masts. Dawn revealed a merchant ship two miles ahead of *Duke*. The sun peered over the eastern horizon around 7:30, and First Lieutenant Eric Laredo, standing the forenoon watch, gazed appreciatively at patches of blue sky. In the east, a rain curtain shimmered silver grey.

Through his spyglass, Laredo watched as the distant ship's crew worked to loosen the mainsails. Their leisurely pace indicated the captain was not in a hurry, unlike *Duke,* which had been under its mains, tops and topgallants since first light. As Eric began calculating how long it might take them to overtake the merchant ship, he saw his captan approaching.

"Mr. Laredo, do you have a name yet?"

"Aye, Captain, I do. Her name is *Majestic,* and she is flying the flag of the British East India Company. I don't see any indication of her using her pumps, so perhaps she riding low because her hold is full."

"So, Mr. Laredo, what are your recommendations?"

"We have about an hour before we are alongside, when we must decide whether or not to show our colors and reveal our intent. We can always sail away if we do not like what we see. However, if we decide to try to take her, we must be prepared for a fight. We ask *Majestic's* captain to strike and if she doesn't, we open fire. She has gun ports, as do most British East India ships, but we don't know if she has a big enough crew to man them."

Glenn studied the ship through a spyglass. "And where would you take *Majestic?"*

"Amsterdam is two days from here, and the Dutch know us. They will give us a fair price for the cargo and the ship."

"I agree. Mr. Suffern shall be given a chance to see if he can command a ship."

Eric looked down at the deck, then to his commanding officer.

"Captain, our cargo gives me pause. One lucky ball from *Majestic* and we all meet God!"

"Mr. Laredo, we think alike. Well, we have time yet to decide. At five bells man the guns, quietly. Have the muskets loaded and kept hidden. No drums, no men in the rigging other than the lookouts."

"Aye, aye, sir."

When word was passed to man the guns, *Duke's* second lieutenant Grant Suffern asked Lieutenant Laredo, "Ball or chain shot?"

"Ball, Mr. Suffern, ball. We want to send a message, not cripple *Majestic* so we have to spend half a day or more repairing her rigging."

Suffern waved in acknowledgement and went down the companionway to the gun deck. Eric stood alone. This would be his first action. As the ship's First Lieutenant, he would be on the quarterdeck, out in the open.

The privateer's bowsprit was sliding past *Majestic's* quarterdeck when Captain Glenn handed Eric a large speaking trumpet. "Do the honor of telling them what we are about, Lieutenant. I'll tell Mr. Suffern to run out."

Eric nodded and put the small end of the trumpet to his lips. "*Majestic, Majestic,* this is the *Privateer Duke.* Haul down your colors, heave to and prepare to be boarded. If you resist, we will take you by force."

A portly man came to the starboard aft corner of *Majestic's* quarterdeck. Eric repeated his message.

Nothing happened. Eric wasn't sure if they thought *Duke* was bluffing. He put the speaking trumpet down and turned to the captain. "I think we need to prove that we are serious."

"One ball, Mr. Laredo, just one shot. I don't want to damage the ship beyond repair, nor sink it."

Eric saw Suffern standing half out of the aft companionway and called out to him, "Fire the number one gun into the hull and reload." Suffern bent down and gave commands. The 9-pounder chewed *Majestic's* bulwark, just aft of bowsprit. for a long while there was no response.

Eric was about to order the number two gun to fire when the Union Jack flying from the stern fluttered down. A seaman gathered it before it reached the quarterdeck. On the deck, men released sheets from the racks of belaying pins and *Majestic* slowed noticeably.

Captain Glenn issued a stream of orders to slacken sails and get both cutters ready to launch. Glenn sent Eric and Grant, along with a 24-man prize crew, over to *Majestic*. When Eric climbed over the bulwark, he fully expected to be greeted by a volley of pistol and musket fire. Instead, the man from the quarterdeck was waiting for him. "I am Nelson Brant, captain of His Majesty's Merchant Ship *Majestic*."

From the papers Brant showed, *Majestic* was carrying bales of Scottish wool, bolts of cloth, and finished wool blankets. She was headed for Copenhagen, and Lloyd's of London had insured the cargo for £8,000 sterling.

By the time Eric was back on board *Duke* and had described *Majestic* and its cargo, Suffern and his prize crew had the merchant ship's sails set. Soon both ships were running with the wind, headed so' east toward Amsterdam.

On board H.M.S. Deer, *November 1775*

For a lad born and bred on the coast of England, the climate of the south Atlantic was extraordinary. There was not a cloud in the sky, and the temperature was in the seventies. Telltales, the thin strips of cloth affixed to the top of the masts and on the rigging, indicated that *Deer* was being pushed by a steady wind as it knifed through the green-blue water. At seven knots, the frigate swiftly passed north of Caicos Island.

The night before, the crew had enjoyed a vivid red sunset. Captain Tillerson had murmured, "Red sky at night, sailor's delight." According to sailor lore, the following day's weather would be good. Conversely, "Red sky in the morning, sailor take warning," forecasted storms. Smythe, who had never heard either expression, had filed the phrase in his memory.

When Smythe assumed the forenoon watch, Lieutenant Roote informed him that *Deer's* lookouts had spotted a ship at sunrise and they were following it. Smythe could just discern the stacked trapezoids of sails on the horizon.

"Well, Mr. Smythe, we hope to catch that fellow before sunset. I want you on the quarterdeck when we do."

Smythe turned to face his captain, who had walked up behind. "Splendid, sir. I think we're gaining on him."

"We are. And now that young Mr. Rathburn is ready to return to duty, after this watch I'd like you to take him below to familiarize him with our magazines. If we get into any action, I'd like an officer down there."

In other words, Tillerson didn't want any members of the gun crews hiding on the orlop deck. The Royal Navy was struggling to find enough men with needed skills; having midshipman Rathburn in the magazine would ensure a steady flow of powder cartridges to the cannons.

Like most Royal Navy frigates, *Deer's* magazine was really two compartments located just aft of the foremast. It rested on a raised platform mounted on the bottom of the hull. Plaster covered the planking, and all the iron fittings were covered with putty. The largest room had casks with two types of gunpowder lashed to racks. Coarse powder was used to fill the cartridges for the cannon. Fine gunpowder went into paper cartridges for pistols and muskets, as well as the flasks used to fill the cannon touch holes.

Forward of the storage room was a smaller compartment known as the filling room. It had a workbench where powder cartridges were assembled, with racks for 150 filled cartridges, enough for roughly five broadsides. The rooms had clear glass panels along the top that allowed light to filter down from the hatches on the main deck.

On the gun deck, there were racks for cannon balls between the guns, but due its weight most of the iron shot was stored in the hold, just aft of the pump well, forward of the mainmast and as close to the ship's center of gravity as possible. Five hundred cannon balls, 50 canvas bags of canister, and 50 of chain shot were stored in racks to keep them from rolling around and affecting *Deer's* stability and steering. During battle, ship's boys, sure-footed and strong of hand, ran back and forth to bring necessary supplies up to the gun deck.

"Aye, aye, sir."

"And have the surgeon show Mr. Rathburn all the new tools he got from your father's company," the captain added.

Tillerson was referring to the contract Smythe's firm had won from the Royal Navy to supply all its ships with a standardized set of steel surgical instruments.

Arriving in England in 1608, Joakim Schmeitz had anglicized his last name to Smythe and founded Smythe & Sons to make the high quality surgical instruments he designed to supplement his income as a surgeon. In the early 1700s, Darren's grandfather had added an apothecary, based on drugs he imported and medicines he made.

During the Seven Years' War, Darren's uncle had been a surgeon on a ship of the line. He'd become friends with the Surgeon General of the Royal Navy. It took his uncle took five years to convince the Royal Navy that it would benefit from a standardized set of surgical instruments and medicines on every ship. Before he died, he'd helped fill the first commissions.

After the forenoon watch finished its turnover, *Deer* was only a mile behind the other ship, and its name, *Duchess*, could be discerned through a spyglass. It flew a red flag with a horizontal blue stripe in the center filled with white five pointed stars. In the upper left corner, Darren saw a crescent and a tree.

Captain Tillerson sent for *Deer's* officers, the Marine lieutenant, three midshipmen, his first and second lieutenants, and the ship's master.

"I don't recognize the flag *Duchess* is flying," Tillerson announced. "It could be a neutral merchantman or a rebel privateer. She has eight gun ports on each side. The captain is a skillful seaman who has managed to force us to either tack or stay on his leeward side. But we have a size and slight speed advantage, so we will continue on our present course and finish this exercise before dark. We will beat to quarters at two bells. I want the guns loaded and run out. We will deploy our Marines on the deck with muskets loaded. We are not going to slow down to lower our boats to tow them behind. Mr. Crenshaw, I know Mr. Smythe is the senior midshipman and is responsible for signals, but I think communicating with this ship will be good experience for you. Therefore, I want Mr. Smythe on the gun deck assisting Mr. Gladden. Lieutenant Roote and I will be on the quarterdeck. In my absence, if we have to board, I want Mr. Gladden and Mr. Smythe to lead the charge."

Tillerson looked at each of his officers, then continued.

"Here is how I see the action going forward. We will come alongside *Duchess* 200 feet from its port side. I will request them to stop so we may examine their papers and inspect the ship for contraband. If they fire on us, we will fire until they strike their colors."

Of the officers, only *Deer*'s captain, Master Hyde, and Lieutenant Roote had been in combat. Gladden had just been promoted to lieutenant in Portsmouth, and none of the three midshipmen had seen any action. The last time *Deer* had fired its guns had been as a salute to a departing admiral while they were loading supplies in Port Royal. Tillerson had fired his training allotment of powder and iron shot on the way from Great Britain to the Caribbean, expecting to resupply in port. But at Port Royal, he'd been told there wasn't enough to spare for practice.

Smythe took one last look at *Duchess,* now only a half a mile ahead, then followed Mr. Gladden below. One ship's boy was sprinkling the red-painted gun deck with sand to give the barefooted gun crews traction if the deck got slippery with water or blood. Gladden, taking his station at the forward end of the gun deck, gave the command, "Port side, cast loose and provide. Load with solid shot." Eight young boys, the powder monkeys, swarmed forward with cartridges and cannon balls, and the gun crews readied for action.

Light filtering in through the gun ports, fore and aft companion ways, and gratings in the main deck cast an odd pattern of shifting shadows. Some parts of the deck were well lit, others were dimly illuminated by the yellow light of a lantern. Smythe and Gladden counted twelve glowing tips of slow match held up as a signal that the port gun captains were ready to fire.

A grinning Rathburn stuck his head out of the forward companionway that led to the magazine. "We're ready down here for the fun to begin."

On the quarterdeck, as soon as *Deer's* bow was amidships of *Duchess,* Midshipman Crenshaw raised the speaking trumpet to his mouth. *"Duchess,* this is His Majesty's Ship *Deer.* Heave to. I repeat, heave to. We wish to board and inspect your papers and cargo."

A man, dressed in blue but not like an officer, came to the aft corner of his quarterdeck and cupped his ear. Crenshaw repeated his request. The man stuck out his arms and raised his shoulders as if to say, "I don't understand.

Deer's bow was almost alongside that of *Duchess.* Crenshaw changed the message. "We do not recognize your flag. What country?"

The man on *Duchess'* quarterdeck held up a finger and went over to the man at the wheel of his ship. They had a short conversation and the man came back to its quarterdeck, now even with *Deer's.*

Crenshaw scowled with frustration. He bellowed out, "*Duchess,* show us your true colors and heave to."

The man nodded and went to the fantail and yanked on a rope. As he did, gun ports on *Duchess* popped open and eight 9-pounder cannons belched flame, one right after another. From the rigging, the flag of the Continental Navy, with a British ensign in the upper left corner and horizontal red, white and blue stripes, now streamed in the breeze.

On the quarterdeck of *Deer,* Tillerson saw the gun ports popping open and yelled, "Get down!" It was too late. Chain shot carried the wheel away and Hyde fell to the deck headless, blood gushing from the stump of his neck. Swivel guns on *Duchess'* quarterdeck, double loaded with canister, swept *Deer's* quarterdeck.

Two balls caved in Crenshaw's chest. Another hit Tillerson in the head and a third took off Lieutenant Roote's left arm at the elbow. A seaman ran up to him and tied a tourniquet around what remained.

Duchess's cannon were double loaded with chain shot, and the result was *Deer's* rigging was ripped apart. Sheets, stays, halyards and braces on every mast were severed. The main and fore mast's port side shrouds fell to the deck; main and foremast stays parted with a twang everyone on deck could hear. Sails on its fore and main masts luffed. *Deer* lurched and slowed as the foremast snapped just above the foretop. It slowly fell forward into the sea on the port side, taking the upper section of the mainmast with it.

Hearing the gunfire, Smythe and Gladden yelled almost simultaneously, "Fire as you bear!"

One by one her 12-pounders fired, but *Deer* was slowing and slewing noticeably to the left, a result of the sea anchor made from the foremast's spars, canvass and rope. *Duchess* was pulling ahead. Chunks of wood flew off *Duchess'* bulwarks and holes appeared in her hull, but the American ship didn't slow down.

Duchess passed in front of the slowing *Deer* and tacked to cross 200 feet in front of *Deer*. One by one, its gunners fired well-aimed rounds of chain shot, aimed at *Deer's* rigging and masts, not its hull.

On the gun deck, Smythe had the bow chasers loaded and run out. Each got off a shot before *Duchess* sailed out of range. Suddenly, it was quiet except for the moaning of wounded men and the strange creaking of the ship. *Deer* was wallowing as if it were drunk, and as Darren ran aft, he yelled to Gladden, "We're out of control. I'm going to the quarterdeck and see what is going on."

When Smythe emerged on the main deck, he was astonished by the carnage. Unwounded men were hacking at lines, trying to keep what was left of the mainmast from being dragged down by the debris in the water.

On the quarterdeck, there were only three living souls—the boatswain or bosun, Roote, who was weak from loss of blood, and the assistant quartermaster, who had been hit in the leg. "Lieutenant Smythe," he said, "we have no helm, but we can steer the ship from below."

Smythe turned to the ship's bosun, Bart Sherbourne. "Mr. Sherbourne, secure from quarters, and ask Mr. Gladden and Mr. Rathburn to meet me on the quarterdeck. Rig the block and tackle so we can steer using the rudder bar, and luff all the sails until we figure out how to save what's left of the mainmast."

The bosun knuckled his forehead and disappeared down the companionway to the gun deck. Smythe could hear the rumbling sound of gun carriages being rolled back into their stowed position and secured. The gun ports banged closed. Smythe next saw to it that the wounded Roote was escorted below. Suddenly, there was a loud crack. Smythe turned in time to watch the middle section of the mainmast fall and land partly in the water and partly on the deck. Sailors leapt forward to cut away the rigging so it wouldn't drag the rest of the mainmast down.

Brandon Gladden came onto the quarterdeck. Smythe saw him and saluted. "Sir, Lieutenant Roote has been wounded and is taken to the surgeon. The captain, master, and Midshipman Crenshaw are dead. Sir, you are in command."

"That means you are the first lieutenant."

Smythe nodded grimly. "Aye, that I am." Smythe gave a summary of the commands he'd given and what he thought necessary to get *Deer* underway again. He had a sinking feeling that Gladden, while a nice enough man and a good officer, wasn't the brightest lamp on the street. He had to be careful not to give the impression he was usurping authority. If he did, the consequences could be fatal, literally.

"Carry on with your plan to get the ship repaired. I will go to the captain's cabin and plot a course to take us to one of our bases."

Smythe put his hand on his forehead. "Aye, aye, sir."

Smythe went down the forward orlop platform. Lieutenant Roote was sitting at one end, his back against the bulkhead and his head resting on a ship's rib. Smythe forced himself not to wrinkle his nose at the stench, compounded of poor ventilation, smoke from lanterns and candles, and the smells of wounded men. "Surgeon Gaines, what's the butcher's bill?"

"Including the captain and other officers, two dozen dead and 20 wounded, four of whom probably won't make it." The surgeon looked up from bandaging a sailor's bleeding ribcage. "The American ship ambushed us, didn't it?"

Smythe nodded. "That it did. They shot out our rigging, brought down our masts, and got away."

When he emerged from the companionway to the main deck, the ship's carpenter, Alvin Henry, was waiting for him. Henry knew his way around Royal Navy ships because he'd gone from powder monkey to carpenter's mate to ship's carpenter. Early on, Smythe had spotted Henry as a fount of useful information, none of which had been included in the Naval Academy tutelage.

"Sir, it'll take us another hour or so to have the mainmast rigging repaired, then we can rig a mainsail. We have enough logs to add a section to both the main and foremasts, so we can hang a jib and staysail. We've rigged block and tackle to a tiller attached to the rudder, so we can steer. Commands from the quarterdeck will have to be relayed below. It will be a mite clumsy, but should work."

"My recommendation to Mr. Gladden will be to leave this area as soon as we can. I don't want *Duchess* to come back and pick us off. Let me know when we are ready to sail."

"Aye, aye, sir."

On the quarterdeck, Smythe walked up to Gladden. "Sir, Mr. Henry says he can raise a new foremast while underway for a nearby base. We have 20 wounded and two-dozen dead. We should bury our dead as soon as we are ready to sail."

"Good plan, Mr. Smythe."

"Thank you, sir. We have three unwounded officers: Mr. Rathburn, you and I. If we add the bosun that's four, which means we can stand six on and eighteen off. I can adjust the watch bill so that you don't have to stand a night watch."

Gladden turned around suddenly and Smythe could see fear in his eyes. "I don't think I am cut out for command. When I walked onto the deck, I froze. I didn't know what to do. In the captain's cabin, I couldn't remember how to plot a course. When we get to one of our bases, I am resigning my commission. I will let you run the ship as the First Lieutenant. Just don't embarrass me."

"Sir, are you sure that is what you want?"

"Yes. I have been considering this for some time. I used to worry that I would never make commander, and now I realize I do not even wish to be captain. it is time for me to leave the Navy. I'll find something to do here in the Caribbean. At least I will be alive." His face worked for a moment, then he added, "And it's much warmer here than at home."

* * *

They made slow but steady headway, and true to his word Captain Gladden let Darren Smythe manage all the details of commanding a ship—in Gladden's name. Right after breakfast, the surgeon reported that two more members of the crew had succumbed to their wounds. That made 26 crew members whose deaths could be attributed to *Duchess'* ambush. Darren's conclusion was that *Duchess* had used an effective variation of French tactics. If he ever became a captain, he would do the same thing, because once the enemy can't sail, he is at your mercy.

Darren was looking at the clouds, wondering if it would turn into a squall line, when he heard a loud crack. He turned, dreading what he might see. Sure enough, the repaired upper section of the foremast had broken under the strain of sail. Slowly it fell to the starboard side, as the men on deck skipped and scampered out of the way. Getting to Port Royal would now take longer.

When Darren returned to the quarterdeck after seeing to repairs, he felt a freshening wind, and Drew Rathburn pointed to coming rain. Gusty winds from the nor' west were going to make it hard for *Deer* to maintain a west by so' west course. The two midshipmen stood side by side, swaying slightly with the movement of the ship.

Drew said, "I don't think this is a hurricane, but I do have some experience hanging on to spars, so in the event *Deer* should go down, stay near me."

Darren chuckled. "Its my job not to let that happen. Call the watch. We're going to alter course to run so' east with the wind. Let us hope this passes over before it drives us aground on Santo Domingo."

On board Frigate Alfred, Philadelphia, *November 1775*

The sun's light was pale and watery compared to the southern brightness Jaco was used to in his home town of Charleston, and the bitter cold was made worse by a westerly wind and pervasive dampness. The wind offered one benefit: it made it easy for *Alfred* to move away from the pier and down the Delaware River.

The shrouds were cold to the touch. By the time Jaco reached the foot ropes on the mainmast, his fingers were stiff. The cold from the wooden spar, pulled close to his body by his left arm, caused him to shiver as he sidestepped along the ratline. He struggled to untie a stiff, cold gasket that kept the mainsail furled.

"Here Mr. Jacinto, let me give you a hand." The speaker was a topman whose last name was Landry. "It is good to see you up here." Left unsaid were the words *unlike the other midshipman.* Landry struggled with the cold, knotted rope. Finally, it came free.

Jaco looked between the horizon and the yard, trying not to look down at the deck 50 feet below. His stomach was queasy and he felt light-headed. He'd discovered his fear of heights when he'd crossed to Europe, working on one of the ships carrying cargos for his father's company. Jaco had thought the feeling would go away, but it hadn't. Each time he went up the shroud, it was a battle against a feeling he didn't like or understand. Once the stiff, cold canvas topsail dropped down, Jaco gladly descended the shrouds to oversee seamen sheeting home the mainmast's topsail.

The other midshipman, James Lodge, came from a wealthy and influential Boston family, and he made sure all the officers knew it. Furthermore, it was obvious Lodge could do no wrong in Saltonstall's eye. When Reasoner invited him to participate in the daily gun drills, 17-year-old Lodge airily declined. A captaincy was in his future, he said; he would leave gunnery to his lieutenants and the details of furling and unfurling sails to his future bosun mates.

He treated Jacinto with disdain. It was a given that Southerners were not the equals of someone from Massachusetts or Rhode Island. After all, Jacinto wasn't a Cabot, a Lodge or an Adams.

One day while they were loading food, water and beer, Lodge sarcastically referred to Jacinto as the 'Spaniard Midshipman'. Rather than be offended by the comment or Saltonstall's preferential treatment of Lodge, Jaco decided no matter what task he was given, he would do it to the best of his ability without complaining.

Alfred passed the S-turn where the Delaware River widens into Delaware Bay. Saltonstall tacked *Alfred* back and forth across the bay to gauge how the ship, now several tons heavier than originally designed, handled. His order to set the topgallants sent Jaco back up the yards. Two tacks later, Saltonstall had the crew set all six staysails—the fore and fore top, the main and main topgallant, the mizzen and mizzen top. Once they were sheeted home, he let *Alfred* run on a port tack for several miles before wearing the ship to starboard and re-crossing the bay.

Besides learning how the bluff-bowed ship sailed, Saltonstall was also training his crew, most of whom had never been to sea. The crew was divided into port and starboard watches with a team for each mast. Jaco was assigned the port watch, and Lodge the starboard.

On the second tack, the seamen under Lodge were so slow getting the yards around that *Alfred* almost came to a stop. The next tack was nearly as bad. Lodge's team had to be corrected several times before they got the foremast's sails trimmed to the captain's satisfaction.

As *Alfred* turned through the wind on the fourth tack, Jaco's group brought the yards around smartly in sequence, fore, main and mizzen, keeping each mast's yards in line. The sequence of the commands, the names and purpose of all the lines, braces and sheets were second nature to Jaco. From the quarterdeck, Lieutenant Jones bellowed in his Scottish accent, "Wealle duuune, Mister Haycinto, weeall duuune!"

Gregory Struthers, *Alfred's* Second Lieutenant, stood behind Midshipman Lodge to coach him through the commands for the next tack. Lodge was slow giving the commands and allowed the main staysail to foul the starboard main topmast stays. As a result, the yards didn't come around, and again *Alfred* almost came to a stop.

Saltonstall, red of face, started to yell, but seeing it was his protégé, he stopped. He ordered the quartermaster to ease off the helm and let *Alfred* fall off the wind in preparation to try tacking again.

Lieutenant Jones was not nearly so reserved. "Damn you, Lodge! How many times will it take for you to get this right? Even with Lieutenant Struthers help, you bollixed it up. You could bloody well demast us before we fight a bloody British frigate."

Lieutenant Struthers swapped two bosun mates working for Jacinto to work the starboard tack. Even so, the next tack was not much better, and Struthers again had to intercede to keep Lodge from damaging the ship.

Jones was livid. He leaned over the quarterdeck railing and demanded, "Mr. Lodge, what kind of bloody idiot are you? You've managed to cock-up every tack. You need to get on with it, or I'll personally toss you off this bloody ship. I don't care who your bloody parents are!"

Tack number five was sloppy, but not bad enough to prevent the ship from turning through the wind. It took four more tacks before Lodge got the timing and sequencing of the needed commands to keep the yards stacked and get the stay sails through the rigging without fouling on a halyard, brace or shroud.

Now, with *Alfred* steady on a so' west by west course, a quartermaster mate tossed the small triangle of wood over the stern to estimate the frigate's speed. For practice, each quartermaster mate went through the process, and all confirmed *Alfred* was making eight knots.

Approximately a half-mile off the Delaware coast, *Alfred* tacked again. Once steady on a nor' nor' easterly course, Saltonstall ordered the helmsman to ease up the helm so he could see how close to the wind the square-rigged *Alfred* could sail. About 60 degrees off the wind line, the jib and fore staysails started to luff.

When it was Gregory Struthers turn to maneuver the ship, his commands came out in a soft but forceful voice. The youngest of three boys, he'd left New York at 14 to be a midshipman on a merchant ship. Now 22, he had joined the Continental Navy as a second lieutenant. Struthers' experience in ship handling showed. When he made corrections, he used humor to make his point. It was an example Jaco took to heart.

At the end of their watch, the two midshipmen made for their quarters, where at least it was warmer than the open deck. Jaco was reflecting that it was much colder work to stand and give orders than to haul the ropes. James Lodge's face was an interesting mix of red and pale: part shame, part fury, and part chill. He was not used to having his actions criticized or corrected. Jaco wondered if he could forestall whatever aristocratic outburst was imminent. The merchant ship captains he'd worked for had drummed into his head that if the seamen respect you for your knowledge, they'll happily work for you. If they don't trust you, then you'll have both performance and discipline problems. "Struthers is a true gentleman," he ventured, "and a fine instructor. He got even the newest hands to pull together. We're fortunate to have him as second lieutenant."

Lodge gave him a withering look, as if to say, "What would *you* know about how real gentlemen behave?"

Jaco decided that silence was, perhaps, the best outcome he could hope for.

The next day, *Alfred* tacked back and forth between the Jersey and Delaware shores. Saltonstall stayed alone in his cabin, except to watch Jones or Struthers supervise the tacks. If he knew about the tension between Lodge and the other officers, he didn't show it. Before accepting this command he'd been the captain of a Boston-based merchant ship. He knew the Lodge family was extremely powerful and influential, in Boston and beyond.

* * *

Both Struthers and Jones noticed the difference between Jacinto and Lodge. When not on duty, the South Carolinian was all over the ship, asking questions and learning as he helped the seamen under his command. Lodge always tried to stand near or next to Saltonstall.

This morning, Saltonstall stood at the aft end of the captain's cabin with his hands clasped behind his backs to address his officers. "Gentlemen, we are going to continue this course until we close on the New Jersey side of the bay. We will then tack, furl the topsails and topgallants, and commence gunnery practice. The starboard battery will shoot at the sand cliffs, then we will reverse course and exercise the port battery. I am interested in both rate of fire and accuracy."

Once they were dismissed, Reasoner headed down to the gun deck, while Jaco studied the target area, a mile long and 30 feet above the water. As a target, the sand banks were *perfecto!*

Struthers was ordered to remain on deck along with Jones and Saltonstall, to judge the gunnery. Normally, the Second Lieutenant was in charge of the gun deck, but for this exercise, Jaco and Gunner Reasoner would be the officers supervising the gun crews.

Walking to the forward end of the gun deck, Jacinto yelled out, "Starboard battery, cast loose and provide. Remember, gentlemen, on the first round, we don't have to sponge out."

The rumbling of the carriage trucks on the wooden deck resounded along the starboard gundeck.

"Load cartridge."

When the gun captains stood back, Jaco yelled, "Load ball."

The time it took for ten iron balls to roll down the barrels of cast iron cannon was one indication of how coordinated the crews were. The metallic sounds of 10 cast iron balls rolling down cast iron gun barrels was almost in unison.

"Run out."

Wooden wheels on the wooden deck made a hollow rumbling sound as the cannon were pulled forward so their barrels stuck out of the gun ports. Despite having witnessed the proofing, Jaco wondered if any of the cannons would fail.

"Gentleman, target is the sand cliff. Load and run out, but do not fire until I give the command. I will walk down before the first round and check the gunner's aim. After the initial broadside, I want to fire two more within three minutes. After that, we will fire at will until the order to cease fire is given. Gun captains, do you understand?"

All 10 gun captains chanted, "Aye, aye, sir."

Lieutenant Struthers came down the ladder. "Mr. Jacinto, you have permission to fire when ready."

Jaco saluted and took two steps toward the mainmast. "Fire."

All 10 guns fired within two seconds. Jaco chanted the commands. "Sponge!" He watched to make sure that, as the sponge was rammed home, the gun captain pressed his hand on the touchhole to make sure no air entered the gun barrel. This prevented any powder bag fragments from continuing to burn. Five seconds later, "Load cartridge." Another five-second interval. "Load ball." On the same count, "Ram round."

"Run out." When the last gun carriage stopped moving, he yelled, "Fire!"

The carriages jumped back and he repeated the command sequence, "Sponge.... Load cartridge.... Load ball.... Ram round.... Run out.... Fire!"

Now that the first three broadsides were fired, the crews fired at will as fast as they could load. Pungent white smoke filled the gun deck, making it hard to see. Jaco's eyes watered, and there was an acrid taste in his mouth. The temperature rose markedly; despite the gun ports being open, sweat streaked the black powder grime on his gunners' faces.

The crews fired three more rounds before Lodge stuck his head down below the main deck and yelled, "Cease fire. Mr. Jacinto, the captain wants you on the quarterdeck."

As Jaco was climbing the ladder, Struthers met him and said quietly, "That was good, fast shooting. Every ball hit the cliff."

Jaco nodded, stepped back down on the deck and passed on what Struthers had said. He added, "Lads, your shooting was *perfecto,* I mean perfect!" Then he turned and climbed into the fresh and much colder air of the quarterdeck.

"Captain, Midshipman Jacinto reporting."

"Mr. Jacinto, how many broadsides did we fire?"

"Three, sir. Then I had the crews fire at will."

"Were they aimed shots?"

"Yes, sir."

"Do you know that your gun crews got off three broadsides in less than four minutes?"

"Yes sir. We have been training to a goal of a shot every minute. We're not quite there yet." Over the captain's shoulder, he saw Lieutenants Jones and Struthers grinning.

"Well, in about ten minutes we'll exercise the port battery and see if they are as good as the starboard side."

"They are, sir."

"I hope so." Saltonstall looked over the deck and ordered, "Stand by to come about." Jaco returned to the gun deck.

The second pass was as good as the first, and after *Alfred* anchored, Saltonstall ordered a double ration of rum for the gun crews. The next two days were a repetition of the first; on the third day, the ship headed back to Philadelphia to prepare to go to sea.

Two weeks later, after meeting with Commodore Esek Hopkins, Saltonstall returned to the ship and summoned his officers to the captain's cabin. James Lodge wormed his way through the officers crowded around the table to stand next to Saltonstall at the stern windows. At the forward end, Jaco squeezed himself into a corner, where it was warmer. The officers fell respectfully silent. With a note of pride in his voice, Saltonstall announced that Commodore Hopkins had chosen *Alfred* to be the flagship of a squadron of five vessels, to consist of the frigates *Alfred* and *Columbus,* the brigs *Andrea Doria* and *Cabot,* and the sloop *Providence.*

Port Royal, Jamaica, November 1775

Smythe's voice was calm as he gave the command, "Let go the port anchor." The anchor hawser, flaked out on the main deck in neat rows, played out and was tied to two different bitts. Once it was secure, Smythe ordered the starboard anchor released.

The only emotion Darren felt was relief. The aftermath of the battle with *Duchess* was finally over. For 16 days, he'd been the de-facto captain of *H.M.S. Deer,* wishing someone would come on board and tell him what to do next. Gladden was no help. His answer to every query was, "Do what you think best."

Darren watched a small cutter with a single sail approach. The officer sitting in the bow grabbed hold of *Deer's* ladder and looked up. If he was surprised by the youthfulness of the officer in charge, he made no show of it. His manner and his speech were curt.

"I am Lieutenant Horatio Winthrop, assigned to Admiral Lord Howe's staff. I would like permission to come aboard." Winthrop's tone made it sound more like an order than asking permission. Darren leaned over the gunwale. "Permission granted."

Winthrop ascended with the ease one accustomed to boarding ships and came over the side. He was wearing the uniform of a Navy Lieutenant—blue coat, gold buttons and white breeches—and sweating in the heat. His highly polished shoes had shiny brass buckles. Smythe was barefoot, wearing a white shirt, open at the collar, and white breeches. There was nothing to distinguish him from an ordinary seaman.

"I wish to speak with the captain."

"You are, Lieutenant."

Winthrop's face-hardened and he looked around at the crew standing casually on the deck. "And who are you?"

Darren swept his hand down across his mid-section and bowed ceremoniously. He was enjoying Winthrop's discomfort. "Midshipman Darren Smythe, at your service. This is acting first lieutenant, Midshipman Drew Rathburn."

Winthrop looked at Darren and then Drew, and demanded, "Where are the *commissioned* officers?"

Darren met his gaze and replied, "Dead or incapacitated. Captain Tillerson and our master, Mr. Hyde, were killed when the rebel privateer *Duchess* ambushed us. A canister ball took off our First Lieutenant's left arm at the elbow and he came down with a fever that raged for two weeks. He's now recuperating on the quarterdeck. Our Second Lieutenant, Mr. Ian Gladden, is indisposed. That leaves me, the senior midshipman, in command."

Darren saw the subtle shift in demeanor as Winthrop realized that the young man he was speaking to was indeed the acting captain of *H.M.S. Deer.* Winthrop gestured at stump of the main and foremasts. "I see. Well then, I must inform you that Admiral Lord Howe will hold a board of inquiry into the events that caused *Deer* to lose two masts. It will take place tomorrow at nine a.m. sharp, on the West Indies Squadron's flagship, *H.M.S. Barfleur."*

"I will be there."

"Good. And, Smythe, *do* wear something appropriate. You look like a bloody pirate."

Smythe grinned. "Aye, I will. And, please inform Admiral Lord Howe that Mr. Rathburn will come with me to take questions on the loss of *H.M.S. Temptress."*

Winthrop's head snapped back. "*Temptress.* What happened to her?"

Darren moved his hand in indication that Drew should answer.

"We capsized in a hurricane about a month ago. There were only four survivors."

It was clear that Winthrop was suffering from information overload. He had been sent to *Deer* to deliver a simple message; now he had a double load of bad news to report.

* * *

A squall line blew through with strong winds, causing *Deer* to swing thirty degrees, left and right. Darren walked toward the bow to see if the ship had dragged its anchor. He looked over the port side at two other ships that were farther in the harbor. The relative bearing and distance hadn't appeared to change.

"Mr. Smythe, we're secure as a ruddy rock."

Smythe recognized Bosun Mate Hammersby's heavy Scottish accent. "Good. I wouldn't want *Deer* to start drifting around the anchorage. It would make the other captains unhappy." The young midshipman continued to look at the shoreline.

"Mr. Smythe, may I speak freely?"

"Of course, Mr. Hammersby."

"I've been in the King's navy now for over ten years, and that was as fine a piece of seamanship bring *Deer* here that many captains I've served under could never do."

"I just did what was needed."

"Well, sir, many of us on the berthing deck think that one day you'll be the captain of a three-decker."

Smythe laughed softly. "I'm a long way from being a captain of anything. Tell me, why did you join the Royal Navy?"

Hammersby rubbed his chin with the back of his hand. "My mother died giving birth to a young lass that was her sixth child. Two of my brothers died before we was 12. We never had any money nor enough to eat, so I signed on when I was sixteen and never looked back. The Royal Navy feeds and pays me. My prize money was more than my father earned in his life, and it still feeds my brothers and sisters. The officers may talk all they like about God and King and Country, but I serve my family."

* * *

The next day, Smythe crossed over in the cutter and was directed to the aft end of *Barfleur's* upper gun deck, where a chair in the shade was provided, along with a pot of tea. He was scheduled to be the third person to appear before the hearing. His journal, as well as the ship's log he'd kept after the battle, rested on his lap.

Lieutenant Roote came out, walking slowly, still weak from the effects of fever. Darren stood to greet his shipmate. "I'm to wait ashore for the next packet to take me to England. A board will determine whether or not I am fit to remain in His Majesty's Navy. I told them I didn't remember much after I was wounded. Gladden is in there right now."

A bell rang, signifying that 30 minutes had passed, and shortly thereafter Gladden came down the passageway, looking glum. "His Lordship did not approve of my actions. He said he has three choices: release me here in Port Royal, or send me back to England and let the Admiralty decide what to do with me, or hold a court martial here in Port Royal, which means I could go back to England as a prisoner. I have been ordered to gather my things and bring them to *Barfleur* to wait."

"I'm sure there's no fault to find in your actions, Mr. Gladden. Come, have a dish of tea to warm your spirit." Darren offered the pot of tea.

A man clearing his throat interrupted the conversation. It was Winthrop. "Mr. Smythe, the board will see you now."

Admiral Lord Stephen Howe's cabin was three times the size of the one for *Deer's* captain. Darren entered to find Admiral Lord Howe, the Fourth Earl of Marlowe, seated at a polished oak table flanked by two captains. The table was set between two 32-pound carronades, painted black.

Five feet from the table, there was a single chair. The admiral waved. "Mr. Smythe, please sit. From what I understand from Lieutenants Roote and Gladden, you have much to tell us."

Darren put his journal and log on the polished deck next to his chair. As he bent down, he noticed Winthrop sitting at a small table off to the side, with paper, a bottle of ink, and several quill pens.

Admiral Lord Howe spoke in a formal voice. "For the record, Mr. Smythe, please tell Mr. Winthrop your full name and billet on *Deer*."

Darren complied.

"Mr. Smythe, you have been asked to appear before the board of inquiry into how *H.M.S. Deer* came to be severely damaged by a rebel privateer, during which encounter the captain and members of the crew were killed. Both Lieutenants Gladden and Roote told this board that you served as acting captain after Captain Tillerson was killed and Lieutenant Roote was wounded, and brought the ship back to Port Royal. Is that correct?"

"Yes, sir, I did, after Lieutenant Gladden told me to take command in his name."

"Yes. We would like you to describe what happened from the moment Captain Tillerson ordered *Deer* to chase down the rebel privateer *Duchess*." Admiral Lord Howe nodded to the captains on either side of him. "We may interrupt from time to time to ask questions. You may begin."

Darren started with the initial chase of the mystery ship, and the rescue of the survivors from *Temptress*. He noticed that his description of *Duchess's* actions caught them by surprise. He explained how the privateer's broadside of chain shot had caused two masts to fall so there was no way *Deer* could pursue the privateer.

"Mr. Smythe, what can you tell the board about *Duchess* in terms of its size and number of guns?"

"Sir, it was about 100 feet long and carried sixteen 9-pounders, plus swivel guns on the bow, quarterdeck and masthead."

"Where did the fight occur?"

"According to the morning sighting, *Deer* was 140 miles due east of Crooked Island and 60 north of Caicos Island."

"Why did you sail to Port Royal? Nassau was much closer."

"Sir, Mr. Gladden and I discussed it, and we didn't think we could navigate the narrow channels with shortened and weakened masts. We thought it would take 10 days to sail the 490 nautical miles, but it took 16. We had to work our way into the wind and were lucky to make three knots. Twice we had to stop to make repairs. We also stopped several times to bury our dead."

The questions came one right after another. How many men died? Who conducted the burial service? What repairs were made? Who did the navigation? Darren answered confidently. After a pause, Admiral Lord Howe tone changed from one of an admiral to one of a father.

"Smythe, how old are you?"

"Seventeen, sir."

"How long have you been in the Royal Navy?"

"Sir, five years if you include the three years at the Royal Navy Academy, and two years on *Deer*."

"Where are you from?"

"Gosport, sir."

"Are you the first of your family to be in the King's Navy?"

"Nay, sir. I had an uncle who was a surgeon in the Navy during the Seven Years War, sir."

Admiral Lord Howe looked at the two other captains. Their body language suggested they viewed Smythe favourably.

"Mr. Smythe, I must say, this is a remarkable achievement for a midshipman."

"Thank you, sir."

"You may go back to *Deer*. We have some decisions to make about the ship and its crew. Dismissed.

* * *

The breeze blowing through the open windows of *Deer's* captain's cabin was not the only thing the ship's three officers—Roote, Rathburn and Smythe—found refreshing. They were enjoying something none of them had ever had before: fresh squeezed mango juice.

Lieutenant Roote put down his glass of the sweet, syrupy, orange-colored liquid. "I think a little rum in this would be wonderful." His sea chest was packed and he was waiting for a boat to take him ashore.

They were discussing the board of inquiry when a knock on the door sounded. It was the boatswain's mate from the deck watch. "Mr. Smythe, Lieutenant Winthrop wants to speak with you. He says it is urgent."

Darren followed the man to the hatch in the gunwale that swung open to let visitors step onto the deck from the ladder. Winthrop was sitting in the bow of the small cutter he'd used yesterday. Without waiting on formalities, called out, "Mr. Smythe, Admiral Lord Howe would like to speak with you forthwith. I am to bring you over to *Barfleur*."

"I'll get my coat, shoes and hat and be right down."

This time, Winthrop led Smythe directly into the admiral's cabin. Howe's post-captain, Jonathan Bourneville, was the only other man in the room, and both senior officers were standing. For the first time Darren saw how portly the admiral was.

"Mr. Smythe, the board was impressed with the leadership and skill you exhibited by bringing *Deer* to Port Royal. I am holding a lieutenant's examination on Monday, November 27th, and would like you to sit for it."

"Sir, thank you very much, but I have not had time to prepare."

Bourneville was tall enough that he had to stoop slightly so he would not hit his head on the overhead beams. "Mr. Smythe, Lord Howe and I are of the opinion you will pass. You've already demonstrated more skill than we ask of our junior lieutenants. However, I understand your reluctance, so here is his lordship's proposal. Sit for the examination. If you pass, you are a lieutenant. If you fail, there will be no record of your appearance. Are you game?"

"Sir, thank you for your confidence in me. I will sit for the exam."

"Good," Lord Howe said with a sigh of satisfaction. "Lieutenant Winthrop has the details."

On his way back to *Deer*, Smythe considered the enormity of what he just agreed to. In a lieutenant's exam, a midshipman was grilled for two to three hours on tactics, navigation, etiquette, history of England and the Royal Navy, gunnery, ship handling, The Articles of War and anything else the captains wanted to ask. Only one in three midshipmen passed the first time. Most midshipmen got a second chance—but rarely a third.

Rathbun received orders to report to *H.M.S. Barfleur* as its senior midshipman. Smythe spent every waking hour of the weekend holed up on the captain's cabin on *Deer* with Lieutenant Roote, who peppered him with questions he remembered from his lieutenant's e exam.

On Monday, Smythe was ferried to the admiral's ship in the cutter. *Barfleur's* new midshipman was waiting to wish Darren good luck when he stepped onto the main deck. Darren in turn congratulated Rathburn on his own good fortune, and asked his friend if the midshipmen's quarters were more accommodating on a three-decker. "Oh yes, the gun room is larger than *Deer's* captain's cabin, but then there are six of us," Rathburn replied with a grin.

As the most junior of the three midshipmen appearing for the exam, Smythe was last. When he was summoned, Darren drew a deep breath to help himself relax, and remembered his experience aboard *Deer* and his training at the Academy. It was as if those younger Darrens were at his side, ready with their knowledge to help him.

Most of the questions began with, "As a lieutenant in such and such a situation, what would you do?" Some started with, "if you were the captain of the ship, what actions would you take?" Many questions required him to decide whether to use diplomacy or force. No sooner had he answered one query then another followed. There was no logical grouping, and his mind had to shift rapidly between ship organization and handling, navigation, gunnery, and history.

There was a pause in the stream of questions before Bourneville asked about proper punishment for a sailor convicted under the Articles of War. The correct answer was that the offender be flogged. Smythe remembered the churning in his stomach as he forced himself not to retch when he witnessed the flogging of Truckee. Afterwards, Tillerson had confided in his officers that he hated flogging, but the Articles of War were specific and clear.

Smythe gave the copybook answer, then hesitated. The hawk-faced Captain MacIntosh, who sat next to Bourneville, sensed the midshipman had something more to say. "Mr. Smythe, is there something you wish to add?"

"Sir, this may cause the board to vote against me, but I would avoid ordering a man to be flogged unless I had no other choice. As the captain, I do not want to rule by fear. I want the crew to respect me for my ability to lead and my skills as a naval officer. I want them to have confidence that in any action, whether it is in a fight with an enemy ship, an accident at sea or sailing into a storm, I will make the right decision for the ship and its crew. If I have their respect, I believe that rarely, if ever, will I have to have a man flogged."

Smythe sat back, feeling as if he were balanced on the edge of a knife blade.

A silence hung over the room that seemed to go on forever.

Captain Bourneville looked left and right. "Do any of you gentleman have any further questions for Mr. Smythe?"

Heads shook.

Bourneville nodded. "Very well, since there are no more questions, Mr. Smythe, you are dismissed. Please join your fellow midshipmen on the main deck, where refreshments should be waiting. We will send for you when we have finished our deliberations."

The two other midshipmen were a year and two years older than Darren. This was their first board as well, and they had been preparing with the lieutenants from their respective ships for the past week.

Smythe thought he had been doing well until he made his last comment; in retrospect, he worried it may have sunk his candidacy. He did not speak of that fear with his fellow midshipmen. When they found out he was from *Deer* they asked him about the fight with *Duchess*. It almost felt like a second exam.

The three candidates and *Barfleur's* six midshipmen were discussing exam questions when Lieutenant Winthrop materialized. "Gentlemen, the board is ready for you; one at a time in the order you appeared. Those of you who passed will be brought back into the Admiral's cabin for a brief celebration."

The second midshipman was grinning when he returned. The first man, the oldest of the three, was already on a boat taking him back to his ship. Then it was Smythe's turn to be ushered into the Admiral's cabin.

The chair he'd sat on was gone. Smythe stood before the board, Admiral Lord Howe was sitting in the center of the row of captains. It was the admiral who spoke. "Smythe, please tell the board your age. The truth, man."

"I turn seventeen in December, sir."

"Ah." The heavy-set man stood up, came around the table and held out his hand. "Allow me to be the first to congratulate you, Lieutenant Smythe. You are, I believe, one of the youngest lieutenant in the Royal Navy."

"Thank you, sir."

Bourneville was the next to congratulate him. "I had no doubt you would pass, And your passionate statement at the end removed all doubt about your fitness for promotion. Well done, young man, well done."

Chapter 3

Passing in the Night

On board H.M.S. Jodpur, *December 1775*

The day after Darren Smythe was promoted, *H.M.S. Jodpur,* a 32-gun *Richmond* class frigate, arrived in Port Royal. It had left Portsmouth a month prior, carrying dispatches and orders for the West Indies Squadron. On the way over, the ship's second lieutenant had fallen down a wet companionway and smashed his head. He died four days later. *Jodpur's* third lieutenant became its second, and Smythe was ordered to the frigate as its new third lieutenant.

While he was waiting on the quay for the boat to take him to *Jodpur,* a stranger in a captain's uniform walked up. "You must be Lieutenant Darren Smythe. I'm Captain Horrocks."

Smythe's hand disappeared in the man's large hand as they shook. Horrocks was much broader at the shoulder than Smythe, but about the same height. "Yes, sir, I am Lieutenant Smythe."

"Glad to have you on *Jodpur.* Admiral Lord Howe was most impressed with you."

"I'll try to live up to what you've heard."

"We're going hunting, and if we are lucky enough to catch us a prize, I'll need someone to sail it to either Halifax, Bermuda or here. I hear you're an experienced navigator."

"Thank you, sir. I do my best."

"Don't be modest, Smythe. There are many captains who couldn't navigate their way out of a whorehouse even if the whores showed them the door."

Smythe smiled. "I'll not be one of them, sir."

On board Frigate Alfred, *early December 1775*

Despite the bitter cold, a small crowd was on the wharf. Everyone, including the band, was bundled up in wools and furs an attempt to keep warm. The biting wind stung Jaco's cheeks, but he didn't care. He was part of the row of officers in front of the crew, assembled in neat rows on the main deck and facing aft. In a short speech, John Adams, the Chairman of the Marine Committee announced that the five-ship squadron let by Commodore Esek Hopkins in the *Frigate Alfred* would sail down the Delaware and off to war!

With a drum roll from the band, Lieutenant Jones hauled on the halyard to raise the Grand Union Flag for the first time on a Continental Navy ship. The flag whipped smartly in the brisk wind; the Union Jack in the upper left corner and the horizontal red and white stripes were visible to everyone. It was a sight Jaco would never forget.

On the command, "Ready to make sail," Jaco climbed the shroud to the mainmast's topsail yard. He wasn't sure which was worse, the wind or the queasiness in his stomach from being 75 feet off the deck as he untied the gaskets and let the sails drop. it was a huge relief to return to the deck.

Saltonstall ordered the lines to be cast off. Jaco's port side team pulled to bring the yards around so that the sails would fill when they were sheeted home. With the wind billowing out the main and topsails, *Alfred* moved slowly down the Delaware River, followed by *Columbus, Andrea Doria, Cabot* and *Providence.* Jaco heard a series of clunks and looked over the gunwale in time to see a large chunk of ice banging its way down the port side.

Late in the afternoon, Saltonstall ordered the squadron to anchor inshore of Reedy Island, a flat piece of sand on the west side of the Delaware River.

Jaco stopped on the ladder leading to the quarterdeck when he heard Jones contend that as long as the ice was broken, the ships could push through it. Once in the Atlantic, ice wouldn't be a factor.

The discussion got heated. Both Saltonstall and Hopkins insisted on waiting for the ice to melt, which the commodore believed it would take only for a few days. Despite Jones' warning that a delay would compromise their mission, Hopkins' caution won the day.

All five ships anchored. That night, the shallow areas of the bay froze and ice imprisoned the squadron. All the captains could do was wait until the ice melted, and watch as their crews consumed provisions.

Alfred and the other ships burned through their loads of coal, and more had to be delivered in burlap bags from the Delaware shore. It was dirty work, and the sailors had to use freezing cold water from the bay to clean off the coal dust.

The ship's stove provided heat for the berthing deck, which was the warmest place on the ship. There the men huddled, some of them busying themselves with scrimshaw work, woodcarving, or teaching the ship's boys how to tie knots. At night, with those not on watch asleep in their hammocks, it looked liked rows and rows of giant sausages hanging horizontally from the beams producing a symphony of snores, grunts and farts. There was not much room and to pass through; one had to bob and weave around the hammocks and sometimes push them aside.

The commissioned officers' quarters were warmed by cannon balls heated until they were red hot, then placed in iron pails that were hung from the overhead. Every four hours, one of the officers took the pail to the galley and exchanged cold cannon balls for warm ones.

After two months of ice-bound tedium, Hopkins summoned all the captains and senior officers to *Alfred* for a conference. As usual, Midshipman Lodge found a spot on Saltonstall's right side. Commodore Hopkins was on Saltonstall's left, with the other ship's captains arrayed around the table. The rest of the officers squeezed in where they could. Jaco stood back in the corner where it was warm.

Hopkins spoke. "Gentlemen, the Army is desperately short of gunpowder. The Royal Navy stores hundreds of barrels in Nassau, along with spare muskets and cannon. Our reports are that Forts Nassau and Montague are lightly defended, so we will land on the far side of the island and take them from behind. If this damnable ice ever breaks up, we will leave in time to land by March 1st."

Hopkins rolled out a chart of Nassau, and Saltonstall secured the corners with a brace of pistols and two large hunting knives. Hopkins pointed to where he wanted to land and the route the force would take to the two forts guarding the harbor and the city.

Jaco looked over at Lieutenant Jones, who looked less than pleased with the plan, but held his tongue.

Two weeks later there was a thaw, and the ships set forth.

On board Privateer Duke, *February 1776*

One hundred miles south of the British base at Bermuda and directly east of Charleston, *Duke* wallowed in the warm Atlantic. The night before, a squall line had battered the ship with heavy rain and shifting winds. After a particularly strong gust, the crew had heard a distinct crack of wood breaking.

In daylight, it was obvious where the sound had originated. The upper two thirds of the mizzenmast swayed drunkenly back and forth. Captain Glenn sent volunteers up to cut the sails loose. Thankfully, none of the men fell overboard or onto the deck. The mainsail draped itself over the gunwale, but the mizzen's topsail was caught by an errant wind and dropped into the sea. It took 10 men to haul the wet canvas back on board.

The ship's carpenter recommended that the mizzenmast be lowered to the deck. Once a block was rigged on the main mast and a rope lashed to the main sail, two men cut the mizzenmast middle section in two. It was then maneuvered so it rested athwart ship on the gunwales between the stump of the mizzen and the mainmast.

The damaged mast was stripped of usable components before the rest was dumped over the side. To keep sailing, Captain Glenn ordered *Duke's* royals and topgallants set on the main and foremasts, along with the jib and forestaysail. "Mr. Laredo," he said to his First Lieutenant, if we are lucky, we will make our planned rendezvous with *Prince* for our run into Charleston. Yet I fear we are now fair game for any British frigate that spots us."

On board H.M.S. Jodpur, February 1776

Horrocks stared out the stern windows at *Jodpur's* wake. Open on his desk were sailing orders and the ship's log. *Jodpur's* mission was to intercept and capture rebel merchant ships bringing supplies from the Caribbean, and sink any privateers he should encounter. Where he patrolled to accomplish this mission was up to him.

He'd sailed *Jodpur* to a point east of Charleston and Savannah, the two largest rebel ports in the south. The weather off North Carolina was raw and stormy, and the shores were especially treacherous. They hadn't seen another ship in three weeks. By going south, *Jodpur* would be in warmer weather. and he hoped they might intercept a colonial ship heading to Charleston or Savannah, or north to Philadelphia, New York or Boston.

Unlike other captains, Horrocks didn't believe he needed a servant or someone to look after his clothes or cook his food. He preferred to eat what was prepared for his sailors and dine with his officers rather than eat alone. Once a week he ate supper with his sailors on the berthing deck. He would get his rations from the cooks, just as the seamen, did and encouraged the sailors to crowd around. Horrocks would ask and take questions. It was, he explained to Smythe, one day on the quarterdeck, the best way to take the pulse of his men, who in turn could get the measure of their captain.

To break the boredom, Horrocks held gun drills in the afternoons, although to conserve ammunition none of the guns were fired. Not only did the port and starboard watches compete to see which side could be ready for action faster, gun crews were paired off to see which one could complete the reload drill faster. Winning crews earned an extra ration of rum, which, unlike ammunition, was not in short supply.

Smythe was officer of the watch. From where he stood, halfway between the ship's wheel and the windward railing on the quarterdeck, *Jodpur's* bowsprit rose four feet above the horizon as it climbed up a swell, then pointed down on the far side. He checked the trim of each sail, starting with the topgallant, then the top, finishing with the main on each mast. When the wind shifted, blowing from the nor' west, Horrocks ordered his lieutenant to wear the ship around to so' west by south.

"Aye, aye, sir." Smythe turned to Bosun Hunting. "Bosun, call the watch."

Gerald Hunting had been in the Royal Navy for 11 years. He always wore a hat because he was bald as a billiard ball. He touched the back of his hand to his forehead. "Aye, aye, sir." He put his metal pipe to his mouth and the shrill, high-pitched notes could be heard all over the ship. The port watch was ready to handle the sails; the starboard watch was asleep in their hammocks.

The time it took the sailors to reach their stations allowed Smythe to visualize and plan the maneuver. "Master Shilling, stand by to wear ship starboard to new course of so' by so' west."

"Aye, Mr. Smythe. Starboard, so' by so' west it is, sir."

Smythe cupped his hands around his mouth so the bosun mates could hear him clearly.

"Stand by wear ship.

"Master Shilling, up helm."

Slowly, *Jodpur's* bow started to respond to its rudder. "Bosun Hunting, loose all the braces." Smythe glanced at the deck to make sure the men had the braces in their hands. "Starboard hands on the braces, top, main and topgallants, all haul, lads. Put your backs into it!"

Darren saw some irregularities in how the sails were handled, but rather than issue a stream of corrections, he let the bosun mates do their work. They knew how the yards should be aligned on each mast. *Jodpur* heeled to port and accelerating as the bosun mates trimmed the sails.

"Deck there! Sails ho! Two ships, two points to starboard."

The call from the masthead sent Smythe racing to the starboard rail, Captain Horrocks pacing behind. Through a spyglass, Smythe made out two smudges of white just above the horizon.

The hands were called to wear the ship. Now the wind, instead of coming over the starboard quarter, came over the starboard beam. The yards and sails were almost lined up with the centerline of the ship, and Smythe felt *Jodhpur* accelerate. He ordered the bosun to record the speed and was pleased to have his estimate of nine knots confirmed.

Soon *Jodpur* was gaining on what looked like a brig and a sloop.

"Let's see what these two fellows are about, Mr. Smythe. If they are Colonials, they will run. If they are ours, they will maintain course or slow up."

"They could be privateers, sir."

"Aye, that they may be. The bigger ship has an odd rig. Perhaps it is missing a mast and is the sloop's prize. If that is the case, we shall see some action."

Captain Horrocks gave his young lieutenant a considering look. "How would you fight a privateer?"

"Sir, I would do what the Americans did to *Deer*. Our first broadside should be chain shot to disable."

"You do realize that high command back at the Admiralty would have apoplexy if they heard what you just said. They want us to put our ships alongside the enemy and pound them into submission with rapid fire into their hulls."

"I know that, sir. But to get to that point in a fight, one must be able to maneuver. *Duchess's* captain never gave us the chance to fire a proper broadside at his ship. After dropping our foremast and spraying the quarterdeck with canister, *Duchess* could have continued to rake us fore and aft until we hauled down our flag. For some reason, the captain of *Duchess* didn't want to fight, he wanted to escape."

Horrocks was intrigued. Very few newly minted lieutenants responded so readily to questions, or with such originality of thought and assurance. "How would you fight two ships, assuming they are rebels?"

"Sir, I would close to 400 yards from the larger ship. At that range chain shot is inaccurate and the distance prevents them from spraying our ship with canister from swivel guns while we fire our broadside. As far as the smaller sloop goes, it presents a danger only if we are trading broadsides with its larger mate and it rakes our bow or stern, so I would keep the bow chasers ready. But I don't think the sloop will get close because our 12-pounders would rip it apart."

"Would you attempt to board the larger rebel ship?"

Smythe shook his head. "No sir. Not until they haul down their colors."

"If we pound them, the ship may not survive and we don't get a prize."

"I understand, sir. What I am suggesting will minimize casualties on *Jodpur,* for I would rather sink the rebel ship than allow it to do to *Jodpur* what *Duchess* did to *Deer.*"

"Point taken. Very well. Until we are ready to open fire, I'll want you on the quarterdeck, not on the gun deck."

"Yes sir."

"Good, go take a break. I'll send word when we get within a mile."

On board Privateer Duke

Both Captain Glenn and Lieutenant Laredo studied the onrushing British frigate with grim faces. Without a mizzenmast, *Duke* had lost its speed advantage. It was clear *Duke* could not get away. Unless *Prince,* with its eight 6-pounders, could rake the British ship's stern and force it to break off the action, *Duke* would be forced to surrender; it couldn't survive trading broadsides with a Royal Navy frigate.

Glenn turned to his second in command. "Eric, I fear we are doomed, but we are not going to make it easy for the British buggers. We want to sail closer to the wind and force him to tack. If that happens, we may be able to escape into the night."

"Aye, Captain. And I'll clear the ship for action."

"Do that. I'll signal *Prince* to wait until the last minute before running for Charleston."

On board H.M.S. Jodpur

It was easy to tell it was mealtime. The smell of salt pork boiling in a cast iron kettle filled the ship. Crew members sniffed appreciatively. Horrocks also authorized the cooks to dip ship's biscuits in rum before serving them to the crew.

The officers were eating in the gunroom, the usual banter replaced by unspoken tension. Smythe guessed the others were wondering if, when the sun came up next day, they would be alive, or lying mangled on the orlop deck, or dead.

There was a knock on the gunroom door, and a mate stuck his head in. "Mr. Smythe, captain's compliments, sir. He'd like you to come to the quarterdeck."

Smythe dumped the remaining boiled peas into the trash and wiped his dish before putting it in the rack alongside the bowl he used for oatmeal in the morning. He paused at the foot of the companionway and glanced up at thickening clouds. Rain was in the offing, and once it got dark, the Americans could change course and disappear into the blackness.

Jodpur had another problem. With the ship heeled 10 degrees to port, its starboard guns would have to be fully depressed to fire at the smaller ships, which made aiming and firing difficult. Meanwhile, *Jodpur*'s copper would be partially exposed, making her vulnerable to hits below the waterline. On the other side, the port guns were pointed at the water. If the sloop came alongside, the elevation wheels on *Jodpur*'s guns might not be enough to compensate. Reefing *Jodpur*'s royals would reduce the heel but slow the frigate, and that might let the ships get away, if they were indeed privateers.

When he reached his captain's side, Horrocks handed Darren his spyglass. "Take a look."

Through the glass, he saw a familiar flag—red and white stripes with a red and yellow snake. On the ship's stern, he read the letters D U K E.

"Look familiar, Mr. Smythe?"

Darren saw two men at the aft end of its quarterdeck looking at *Jodpur* through spyglasses, and he wondered what they were thinking. "Yes, sir. It is the same flag flown by *Duchess*. The ships look to be of the same design and is probably from the same yard."

"This is not a time to be subtle. When we beat to quarters, take command of the gun deck and run out the two bow chasers. On my command, fire a shot off *Duke's* bow as a signal for him to stop. We'll fire two warning shots. If they don't shorten sail, on my command, fire into *Duke's* stern."

"Aye, aye, sir."

In the 10 minutes it took to clear for action, sailors scattered sand from buckets hanging on the beams on the gun. Powder monkeys went down to the magazine to get powder canisters. Buckets for the sponges were dropped into the sea and then hauled aboard by the gun crews, while the gun captains went to the ships stove to light their slow match.

Smythe peered through the open bow chaser gunport, wondering if the sound of *Jodpur's* drummer could be heard on the rebel ships. He estimated the range as half a mile, a long way even for a long nine, but a fair distance for a warning shot. He stepped back and addressed the gun captains. "Bow chasers only. Load ball and run out."

The metallic sound of an iron ball rolling down a cast iron barrel gave Darren the chills. It heralded the beginning of battle. The hollow rumbling sound of wooden wheels on wooden decks followed as the guns were run out.

Smythe watched with a practiced eye as the gun crews went through the drill. After each gun captain finished aiming, he stepped back so Smythe could sight along the black barrel.

"Mr. Smythe, the captain says fire two balls when ready."

Smythe recognized the high-pitched voice of the senior midshipman, 17 year-old Alan Hearns. *Jodpur* was his second ship. Four years ago, Hearns had walked into the Admiralty Office in Whitehall in London and said he wanted to be a midshipman. At the time, the Navy was desperate for volunteers. He didn't tell the officer who interviewed him was that he was an orphan; he'd spent his last coins on a bath, a meal and decent clothes.

Hearns was a fast learner, and Smythe was confident that when the time came he would pass the lieutenant's exam.

Turning to the gun captain for the port bow chaser, Smythe said, "Do you think we can reach *Duke?*"

"Aye, sir, this black beauty will put a ball alongside or up its arse."

"Splendid! Then fire."

The assistant gun captain blew on his slow match before he put the glowing end on the small rise of gunpowder at the top of the touchhole. As *Jodpur's* bow rose there was a flash, and the long 9-pounder gun, its barrel two feet longer than the standard nines, jumped back. Both Smythe and the gun captain peered through the gunport. They saw a splash off the starboard bow of *Duke.*

Smythe walked behind the starboard bow chaser and nodded. *Jodpur's* bow rose, and before it started down, the slow match was dropped to the touchhole and the cannon fired. A second waterspout rose on *Duke's* starboard side. Through the starboard gunport, Smythe saw that neither *Duke* nor the sloop made any attempt to shorten sail.

Smythe turned to Midshipman Hearns, standing a few paces behind him. "Mr. Hearns, ask the captain if I may fire at will at *Duke.*"

Hearns disappeared. Smythe, confident he would get permission, sent several powder monkeys, who had just dropped off powder canisters, to bring more balls.

Through the gunport, Smythe saw a row of signal flags run up a halyard on *Duke's* starboard side. They didn't resemble any sequence used by the Royal Navy. Shortly afterward, the sloop's crew shook out another jib. If it chose to run, there was no way *Jodpur* was going to catch it.

Hearn's voice brought him back to the task at hand. "Mr. Smythe, the captain says you may fire at will at *Duke,* and use whatever shot you think will slow it down."

"Mr. Hearns, supervise the port gun. We will fire balls into the stern until we get within range to aim chain shot at their rigging."

Smythe checked the aiming of the gunner of the starboard gun, already loaded. A nod, a flash as the slow match touched the fine grain powder, then a loud blast and the cannon jumped back against its tackle. Wind pushed acrid white smoke back into Smythe's face and down *Jodpur's* gun deck. He didn't see a splash from the ball. He hoped it had hit the privateer. The port gun bellowed and more smoke blew back into the gun deck. Again, no splash.

"Sir, I think we hit the bloody rebel!" Hearn's voice cracked with excitement.

"Gun crews, load, aim and fire as fast as you can. Do not wait for my command!"

The next ball entered the captain's cabin of *Duke,* and Smythe saw the flash of glass shattering. The one after that sent a chunk of wood flying off the stern. The gun in front of him barked, and more glass and wood flew. Smythe assumed the cannon balls had gone down the deck of the rebel ship, and tried to imagine the carnage they were wreaking.

The next cannon fired. More white smoke blew back into his face, momentarily blinding him, and his ears rang. Behind him, a pall of smoke obscured the gun deck.

Smythe saw *Duke* stagger. Before he could figure out why, there was a series of large orange flashes, one right after the other. Seconds later, the concussion rocked *Jodpur*. *Duke's* masts poked through the top of a billowing cloud of smoke, wavered and sagged before they toppled into the sea.

When the wind pushed the smoke away, there was nothing other than sticks of wood floating on the Atlantic. Smythe yelled, "Cease fire, cease fire!"

He stuck his head out of the gunport for a better view. He could feel the bow-chaser's heat. All that was left of *Duke* was the bowsprit pointing to the sky. *Jodpur* slowed suddenly, and the thudding of feet on the main deck told him that Captain Horrocks had ordered the crew to slacken sail and get a boat ready to pick up survivors.

Smythe ran up the forward companionway. Already, the 15-foot cutter was being swung over the side. The battle had become a rescue.

The junior midshipman assigned to search the debris was a 14-year-old from Dublin named Sean O'Hare. His carrot-red hair was a beacon as he took his place at the aft end of the boat and directed the crew forward. The six rowers maneuvered the cutter through the flotsam that had been *Duke*.

Jodpur rocked easily in the three-foot waves, 100 yards from the wreckage. Four men were pulled from the water and brought back. Two of them were burned. On a second trip through the wreckage, O'Hare found two more survivors. Until it grew too dark to direct the rowers, O'Hare plied the wreckage-strewn waves. Two more survivors, both too injured to do more than cling to spars, and six bodies were recovered.

Once the cutter had been swung onto the deck, Captain Horrocks ordered the ship to set sail on a southerly course to a station 15 miles off Charleston.

Solemn-faced sailors laid the six bodies on sections of canvas and watched the sailmaker prepare them for burial.

The two burned men were down on the orlop deck under the care of the ship's surgeon, and the six uninjured sailors were sitting under guard against the bulwark. Horrocks ordered a tot of rum for each man.

O'Hare ran to the starboard head by the bowsprit and vomited. Darren followed and put his arm across the back of the sobbing, retching midshipman. There was nothing Smythe could say that would wipe from O'Hare's' mind the horror of what he'd seen. It would likely haunt him until he died.

The young man turned to his lieutenant. "All through the wreckage, there were bloody torsos with no heads, bodies with no arms or legs,. The sharks were already starting to feed on them! We pulled out the bodies of the men who were whole—"

O'Hare dry heaved; there was nothing left in his stomach. Darren pulled the midshipman around to look at him. Vomit was still on O'Hare's chin. "Sean, the men on *Duke* knew the risks when they signed on board. Look at it this way, they died for a cause they believed in, just like every man on *Jodpur* and in the Royal Navy. There is no better way to die."

The young midshipman's eyes widened, and he nodded slowly.

"Go below, clean up, and have a glass of port. It will settle you. Over time, what you saw will fade from memory. You cannot let it prevent you from doing your duty, whatever that duty is."

O'Hare nodded again. "Thank you, sir." He wiped his mouth self-consciously and headed below. Not long after, Smythe was summoned to the captain's quarters.

When Smythe entered, he saw a stranger seated at the captain's table. Captain Horrocks was standing by the aft window.

"Lieutenant Smythe, allow me to introduce to you Lieutenant Eric Laredo, late of the rebel privateer *Duke*. He is the sole surviving officer. I thought you would find it interesting to hear what he has to say. Mr. Laredo...."

Laredo, whose dark hair still damp with sea water, wore a white linen shirt that clung to his skin. If he'd had a coat, either it had blown off or he'd discarded it in the water. Smythe thought the man looked more like a Spaniard than an Englishman.

"*Duke* was carrying two tons of gunpowder," he said. "Both our powder and shot magazines were full to capacity, as was the hold where we normally store food. We carried only enough food for the time it would take us to sail from Amsterdam to Charleston. We rendezvoused with the sloop *Prince*, who told us which ports were not blockaded."

Laredo took a sip from the glass of Madeira Horrocks had poured for him. "We were carrying as much sail as we could and lost our mizzenmast a few days ago. That's why you caught us."

"Lieutenant Laredo, how did the powder explode?"

"Several of your early cannon balls broke open the powder kegs in the aft hold. I think one of your cannon balls hit a metal barrel stave, and the sparks set off the powder. It was not one explosion, but a series that ripped the bottom out of the ship. I saw the fire come up through the companion way just before I was blown into the water."

Neither Captain Horrocks nor Lieutenant Smythe said anything. Laredo took another sip of wine. "What becomes of us now?" he asked.

"We will take you to Bermuda as prisoners of war."

"You are not going to hang us?"

Captain Horrocks answered immediately. "No. You are not pirates. We will treat your injured sailors as if they were our own. Unfortunately, your men will be confined to the orlop deck except for meals and time on deck, weather and operations permitting. We will find space for you with our officers as long as I have your parole, your word that you will not try to disrupt *Jodpur's* routine. And I hope you will join the officers' mess in my cabin for meals."

"You have my word, and thank you, sir. You are most kind."

Horrocks sighed. "I would hope that your navy would do the same if the circumstances were reversed."

"We would, sir."

Smythe was eager to ask the question that had been on his mind since he read the name *Duke* on the back of Laredo's ship. "Lieutenant, does *Duke* have a sister ship?"

"Aye, she does. *Duchess.* I heard that it got into a scrap with a Royal Navy frigate and got away."

"Where is *Duchess* home ported?"

"Savannah." It was a deliberate lie. A Charleston based consortium led by the Laredos owned both *Duke* and *Duchess.*

"The frigate was *Deer,* and I was on it during that fight." Smythe tried to be matter of fact, but it was hard to keep his emotions in check. He thought he saw Laredo's eyes soften. It suddenly occurred to Smythe that, in different times and circumstances, he would probably like Eric Laredo; but not today, because he was the enemy.

Nassau, British Crown Colony of the Bahamas, March 1776

Alfred and the small squadron anchored in Abaco Cay on March 1st. Two schooners converted into warships—*Wasp* and *Hornet*—were already there waiting for Hopkins along with two prizes they had taken. Commodore Hopkins summoned all the ship's captains to go over his plan for taking the two British Army forts. Jaco was included because he was part of the assault force.

The previous day, Hopkins' initial foray had failed. The guns at Fort Nassau had fired on the task force, and Hopkins ordered the entire fleet to retreat to Abaco. He didn't leave any of his squadron to watch the harbor.

The Commodore's new plan was for the Marines and sailors to land on the eastern end of the island, take Fort Montague first, then the city, and finally Fort Nassau.

The sun was just beginning to peek over the horizon as *Alfred's* boats were lowered into the water to ferry its part of the landing force ashore. Jaco was waiting to board his boat when Captain Samuel Nicholas, the senior Marine, said, "This is the first landing for our Marines. I hope it is not the last!"

Each Marine and sailor carried a musket with 25 rounds and a cutlass. Jaco had two pistols, a cutlass, and two weapons he'd inherited from his grandfather: a long hunting knife with a 12-inch blade, and his grandfather's tomahawk.

As they rowed towards the shore across dark water, the rhythmic creaking of the oars against the wooden posts was hypnotic. Jaco had to shake himself to stay alert. At last the bow crunched softly against the strand. Jaco stepped over the gunwale into warm, ankle-deep water.

Captain Nicholas formed the sailors and Marines into a skirmish line 50 yards from the water along a three-foot rise in the sand. Once Commodore Hopkins and the rest of the sailors and Marines arrived, the 200-man force-marched toward the town of Nassau.

Three cannon shots from Fort Montague boomed out and Hopkins stopped the column. Nicholas formed the men into two rows facing the city, ready to repel an attack by the British Army garrison.

When a British army lieutenant came from the town under a flag of truce, Hopkins ordered Nicholas to have his men lower their muskets. Hopkins told the lieutenant, whose name was Burke, that the forts, and the town to deliver had 24 hours to surrender or be attacked, The lieutenant readily agreed to the temporary truce and said he would convey the message to the governor-general.

At dawn on March 2nd, Hopkins ordered the march toward Nassau resumed. Just outside the city, the governor-general of the Bahamas surrendered the island without a fight.

However, when the Marines marched into the forts, they found nearly all of the powder they'd come for was gone. The British had used the delay to load powder onto *H.M.S. St. John* and *Mississippi Packet,* and both ships were already at sea headed for the British base at St. Augustine, Florida. The remaining munitions—several casks of gunpowder, several hundred muskets, a dozen cannon and thousands of musket balls—went into *Alfred's* hold.

After two weeks in Nassau, refitting and provisioning the ships, the squadron sailed for Boston on March 17th.

On board H.M.S. Jodpur, *Bermuda, early April 1776*
H.M.S. *Jodpur* anchored in translucent blue waters. This was spring as Darren had never seen or smelled or felt spring before. He very much wished he could join the sailors when several of them jumped into the water to swim. But business came first, and a long boat was approaching from shore.

Captain Horrocks was requested come to the base's headquarters immediately. Horrocks sent back a note, saying that he had six American prisoners, one of whom was a lieutenant. Later, a boat came alongside *Jodhpur* to fetch the captain and the American prisoners. Smythe made a point of saying goodbye to Lieutenant Laredo. They shook hands, and Smythe wished him good luck before Laredo climbed down the ladder with *Duke's* other survivors.

When Horrocks returned, he passed the word for all his officers to join him in his cabin. Smythe was the first to enter and he found Horrocks poring over a chart. When all three lieutenants, two midshipmen, a Royal Marine captain, and the ship's master were gathered, Horrocks cleared his throat.

"Gentlemen, we've been ordered to sail to Halifax. Once there, we will escort an unnamed number of supply ships to Boston and report to Admiral Graves. So as soon as we've finished taking on supplies, *Jodpur* will depart and proceed with all due haste. We are expected in Halifax by April twentieth and Boston by the end of April. Once we join Admiral Graves, we will find out what he expects us to do. Mr. Blackwell, when do you think we will be finished loading?"

Jodpur had left England without a purser or a gunner, because none were available. They were fortunate to have a doctor. The ship should have had 220 sailors and Marines on board when it left Portsmouth, but its muster sheet showed a crew of only 200. The under-manning was not a major problem yet, but a concern if they took prizes.

Smythe was assigned as the gunner, and Lieutenant Blackwell filled the role of purser. As such, Blackwell was responsible for ordering needed stores and supervising their loading. Nigel Blackwell was a hawk-faced man who kept to himself. Now he looked at his captain. "Sir, we'll need at least ten days. We're out of nearly everything."

"Why ten?"

"Sir, it will take four days just to clean and refill our beer and water casks. Then the sailmaker needs more cloth and yards. If you remember, we left England without a full complement of spare rope, spars and logs to replace masts. We also need to replenish the powder and shot we expended in training and in the battle with *Duke*. With all hands turning to, I am confident we could get everything inspected, loaded and stored in ten days. May I suggest you ask the port captain to give us priority on the supplies we need and the lighters to bring them out to *Jodpur?*"

"Lieutenant Blackwell, we have to be on station with Admiral Graves by the end of the month. We must beat windward all the way to Halifax, and I estimate it will take us ten days to get there. As a practical matter, today is gone. If we are underway by the thirteenth, we get to Halifax on the twenty-third. It does not give us room for delays. I will talk to the admiral and the port captain. Meanwhile, figure out how to get *Jodpur* loaded in seven days."

Blackwell looked grim as he nodded. "Aye, aye, sir. I will do my best."

Horrocks looked at Blackwell coldly and his tone was hard. "We weigh anchor on the morning of April 11th. Do I make myself clear?"

"Yes, sir."

Chapter 4

First Battle

On board the Frigate Alfred, *April 1776,*

A bland vista greeted Jaco when he came on deck in the morning: light gray clouds over a gray-blue Atlantic, broken only by the dirty white sails of the four other ships of the squadron as they followed the flagship in an inverted V formation.

Jaco stood by the starboard bulwark looking east, hoping the sun would come out. The temperature had dropped noticeably. Instead of a warm spring day, it was cold and raw. He was about to go below to get his coat when he heard the lookout's hail, "Sail ho! British schooner, three points aft of the port beam." Based on the ship's estimated position, Jaco calculated that *Alfred* was 100 miles south of Cape Cod, between the Royal Navy schooner and the safety of a British-held port.

On the quarterdeck, Hopkins ordered Midshipman Lodge to signal *Cabot* to engage. Sending *Cabot* was a logical move, since it was closest to the schooner. Hopkins didn't follow this order with another signal for any other ships in the squadron to support the 14-gun brig or prevent the unknown ship from escaping. Instead, Hopkins ordered Lodge to signal, "Make all sail."

Jaco climbed the ratlines to the mainmast's first section. He paused just below the lookout platform, trying to quell the fear that made his stomach turn and his arms weak. He took a deep breath and forced his dislike of heights to the back of his mind. Once he was on the platform, a lookout offered him a spyglass. Through it Jaco saw a large Royal Navy ensign flying from the schooner's stern.

The bosun piped the duty watch onto the deck. The first topman coming up the mainmast shrouds yelled, "Cap'n wants the royals and topgallants set."

Not looking down, Jaco swung his leg onto the shroud and climbed. Before stepping out on topgallant yardarm, he had to pause again to gather his resolve.

The royals would be loosed first, which meant he had to go up the last shroud, only one step wide to the smallest spar. He hugged the mast with his left arm and looked down as he stepped onto the footrope. The heel of the frigate put him 100 feet above and well out over the water. He swallowed hard.

One of the young seamen, Abner Jeffords, spoke softly, "Mr. Jacinto, you don't have to go out on the footrope." Jeffords could have added the words, "if you are afraid," but didn't.

"If you have to go out, so do I." *Even though it scares the hell out of me.*

"Yes, sir. Let us get by you so the three of us can free the gaskets on this side. There will be enough of us on the topgallants yard for you to go down and find out how the cap'n wants the sails set."

Jaco kept his left arm wrapped around the spar while he pulled one of the gaskets that held the starboard side of the furled royal; between the three of them, the sail came free.

The shift in weight nearly dragged Jaco from his perch. His stomach lurched as he clutched the spar tighter, and he gasped. To cover the sound, he said through very white lips, "Hopefully, *Cabot* will take the schooner as a prize."

"Aye, sir. But we won't get a shilling if it does. *Alfred* needs to take its own."

Jaco answered slowly, "A prize taken by *Alfred* would be good for all of us and our cause."

As the topmen dropped the royals, Jaco descended. The moment his foot touched *Alfred's* deck, the knot in his stomach and the light-headedness disappeared. He arrived just in time to supervise the port watch haul on the braces. The yards were neatly stacked, and his men sheeted home the sails on the port side. On the starboard side, Lodge was pushing men into position while sheets waved in the wind.

Jeffrey Swain, *Alfred's* master, called out, "Stand by to come about, lads. We need to do this smartly. We don't want the Royal Navy to think we are a bunch of ruddy landlubbers." He leaned over the quarterdeck railing to assure himself that the men by the masts were ready, "Loose the foremast and the fore staysail and the jib!" He turned to the helmsman, "Helm a lee. New course so' west."

Alfred's bow began to turn to port through the wind. Jaco watched Lodge's men and the triangular fore staysail and the jib. Done right, Lodge should have ordered his men to release the starboard sheet to the jib, and once it started luffing, his men on the port side could haul it through and then do the same with the forestaysail. Lodge was late with his command to release on the jib's starboard sheet, and it fouled with the staysail.

Jaco raced forward and tapped the seaman at the back of the line holding the jib sheet. "Let it out," he ordered. The sail billowed. "Haul, port lads, haul. Do it now and we can get it through."

The forestaysail fluttered in the wind, no longer fouled. *Perfecto!*

Jaco let Lodge give the order his men to tie the sheet, and Jaco returned to his station.

Schilling boomed out. "All haul. Let's get those braces around smartly. I don't want another bollixed maneuver."

Jaco looked up. All four yardarms—main, top, topgallant and royal—were moving in unison. When they were in position, he commanded, "Tie off the braces, lads, and sheet home the sails." Then he looked to the other side. So far, Master Swain hadn't said anything. Jaco crossed to the starboard side, where Lodge was staring blankly at his sailors, and started issuing commands. Quickly, the sheets and braces on the starboard side were tied.

Alfred heeled as it picked up speed from the added push. Jaco was walking aft when Lieutenant Struthers came to his side. "Everyone on the quarterdeck, even Captain Saltonstall, saw what you did to help Mr. Lodge. Well done, Jacinto."

There was the dull report of cannons being fired. Smoke obscured *Cabot's* side as she fired a broadside at the two-masted schooner. Smoke erupted from the side of the smaller British ship as the British captain maintained his honor by firing back, before he hauled down his flag and luffed his sails.

Captain Saltonstall ordered *Alfred* to come about to west by nor'. Lieutenant Jones bellowed from the quarterdeck, "Mr. Lodge, let's not have another cock-up like the last one."

The men under Midshipman Lodge's command pulled on the one-inch diameter hemp rope and the foremast's yards creaked around. Their movements, even after two months at sea, were still uncoordinated. Seeing Lodge was still having problems, Jaco again crossed the deck. He made sure the ropes were all off their belaying pins and the men were lined up properly. "Let's go, men, all four yards on all three masts together, now haul!" The four yards came around as if they were one piece.

Once *Alfred* was a few hundred yards from the British schooner, Saltonstall ordered Master Swain to let the sails luff. *Alfred* gently pitched and rolled in the three-foot seas, while Captain Saltonstall and Commodore Hopkins watched *Cabot* transfer a prize crew to the schooner they now knew as *H.M.S. Hawk.*

Jaco wondered how many men were left on the *Cabot.* When the five ships of the squadron had left Philadelphia, instead of a full complement of 220 officers and men, *Alfred* had only 190. He'd overheard Hopkins tell Saltonstall that, after putting prize crews on the ships they'd captured in the Bahamas, the squadron was undermanned by over 20 percent.

The under-manning reduced each of *Alfred's* gun crews by one man. Jacinto wondered how it would affect their ability to fire broadside after broadside when cannon balls were going in both directions.

* * *

Commodore Hopkins sent *Hawk* to New London, Connecticut, which he believed was not blockaded. With favorable winds, *Hawk* could slip between Block Island and Long Island during the night and be there by late morning.

By the time *Hawk* disappeared over the horizon, it was past noon. Hopkins had the squadron reform into a V headed north. Not long after, everyone on the main and quarterdeck heard, "Sail ho, three points off the larboard bow."

The words send Midshipman Jacinto, now the officer on watch, to the railing with a spyglass. He could barely make out the ship, so he cupped his hands around his mouth and yelled to the maintop, "What do you make of it?"

"It's a brig of some kind."

Alerted by a messenger, Commodore Hopkins and Captain Saltonstall came onto to the quarterdeck. Midshipman Lodge quickly crossed to the foot of the ladder leading to the quarterdeck and asked Jaco for permission to come up. Jaco didn't want him on the quarterdeck, but rather than make a scene and be overruled by the ship's captain, he nodded approval, then returned to the railing.

Saltonstall and Swain both strode over to stand beside Jaco, who pointed in the direction of the ship and addressed his captain. "Sir, it's a brig with a full set of sails, headed in our direction."

Saltonstall looked through his spyglass, then handed it to the ship's master. "Master Swain, what do you make of her?"

Swain had been a lieutenant in the Royal Navy during the Seven Years War, put on half pay when that war ended. Money from two prizes had paid for a small farm west of Philadelphia. When war broke out, he'd offered his services to the new navy. He'd reached an agreement with the Marine Committee that, since there weren't enough ships to offer him a captaincy, he would serve as the master on *Alfred,* and when there were more frigates available, he would captain one. As a matter of fact, he had more experience of war and sailing than most of the navy's captains.

"Sir, by the make of its rigging, I'd say she's Royal Navy. My guess is either gun brig or an armed merchantman."

Hopkins had strolled over in time to hear this. Now he said, "Let's find out. Mr. Jacinto, signal to the others—Follow *Alfred.*"

Saltonstall faced Jaco. "Mr. Jacinto, you have the watch until we beat to quarters."

"Aye, aye, sir. Sir, may I make a suggestion?"

Saltonstall looked at the young midshipman who, several times in the past, had spoken his mind. He glanced at Hopkins, then nodded permission.

"Sir, on our present course, we'll pass behind the British ship. I suggest that we alter course to retain the weather gauge. That will let us cross her bow, which forces her to fight the whole squadron."

The Bostonian's lips pursed. The young midshipman had analyzed the situation correctly, and he hadn't. Their present course and speed would take the frigate well aft of the British ship and force the squadron to come about, taking hours to run the brig down. He turned to Master Swain. "Alter course to west by nor 'west. Mr. Jacinto, signal the other ships to let them know of our course change."

"Aye, aye, sir."

Two hours later, the captain of the bomb brig *H.M.S. Bolton* hauled down its colors. Lieutenant Struthers found the brig loaded with powder for the British Army based in New York. The prize crew, captained by an officer from *Columbus,* came from all five ships.

Hopkins was in an expansive mood, because *Bolton's* cargo partially made up for the failed Nassau raid. He invited the ships' officers to dine with him in Saltonstall's cabin. After a meal of salted beef, wine and biscuits, Hopkins told the officers they were participating in a historic cruise. For the first time, the Continental Navy had operated as a squadron, landed Marines on enemy territory, seized a town and captured prizes at sea. There would be prize money for all, and it was time to make for Providence, Rhode Island or New London, Connecticut. There the crews would be paid off and the ships re-fitted, repaired, re-armed, and re-supplied as necessary for their next voyage.

After several glasses of port, Jaco quietly left the other officers and climbed into his hammock. *All we did was overwhelm smaller ships. Saltonstall thinks like a businessman, not a Naval officer. His majesty's navy can afford to lose sloops, schooners and brigs. We need to take a frigate to prove that we are a force to be reckoned with.*

The ship's bell, mounted on a stanchion just above where the midshipmen slept, rang twice, paused, rang twice again, paused, rang two times, paused and rang once, signaling to the crew that it was seven bells, or three hours and thirty minutes into the eight p.m. to midnight watch. In layman's time, it was 11:30 p.m. Jaco closed his eyes. He had the forenoon watch and had to be on deck at 7:30 a.m. for the turnover.

* * *

After breakfast the next day, Jaco stood facing the wind so the fresh breeze cooled his face. He felt a little groggy and wrote it off to having had too much wine the night before. Overhead, there were patches of bright blue between the puffy white clouds. Hopkins dispatched the 12-gun sloop *Providence* to scout ahead. Once it left the formation, the squadron shifted from the inverted V to a diamond, with the 28-gun *Columbus* trailing the 30-gun *Alfred* by a mile. The 14-gun brigs slid into position on either side, *Andrea Doria* on the port and *Cabot* starboard, a mile apart.

Jacinto walked to the windward side of the quarterdeck and scanned the horizon to the west and north. Seeing nothing, he crossed to the leeward side and slowly scanned the sea. Nothing. But as he was headed toward the windward corner he heard the hail, "Sail ho! Three points forward of the port beam."

Jaco stopped and called up, "What type ship?"

One of the two seamen in the maintop called back. "By the looks of her sails, I'd bet a ration of rum she is a British frigate, showing royals, topgallants and mains. She is heading towards us."

Jaco wondered if it was a fifth-rate ship with 40-plus guns, or a sixth-rater with 20 to 30. *We'll find out soon enough.*

Jacinto turned to Abner Jeffords, standing next to the helmsman. "I forgot to congratulate you on becoming a quartermaster mate. Well done, Jeffords."

"Thank you, sir."

"Well then, please pay my respects to the captain and commodore and ask them to come to the quarterdeck."

The young seaman put the back of his hand to his forehead. "Aye, aye, sir."

The ship was in view, headed directly toward the squadron, when Jaco heard a familiar deep voice. "What do you make of her?"

Turning to face his Commodore, Jaco saw Saltonstall and Hopkins. Mr. Jones was studying the unknown British ship through a spyglass. Behind Jones, Lodge stared blankly at the horizon.

"Sir, the lookouts think it is a British frigate. We don't know if it is a fifth or sixth rater. Either way, if we are clever about our business, our four ships can overpower her."

Saltonstall tried to keep the sarcasm out of his voice. "And, young Mr. Jacinto, pray tell how would you do that?"

"The ship is headed towards us and may take us for a Royal Navy convoy."

"Interesting theory. Go on, Mr. Jacinto."

"I would not change our sails or our formation until he is within signaling distance. Then I would spread our formation so we are in a line with *Cabot* and *Andrea Doria,* with *Alfred* and *Columbus* in the center. This limits the Britisher's ability to escape. No matter which direction it turns, we can box him in. *Columbus* and *Alfred* can pound him from both sides, while *Cabot* and *Andrea Doria* rake his bow and stern."

"So you would try to trap him?"

"Yes, sir, I would."

Hopkins didn't say anything for a few seconds. "Have you been talking to Lieutenant Jones?"

"No, sir. But as part of our midshipman training, we discuss tactics with Mr. Jones."

"I see." Hopkins beckoned Captain Saltonstall, and they walked to the aft railing to confer. Midshipman Lodge started to follow, but was waved away. He came over to Jacinto, who handed him a spyglass. By now, the British frigate's gun ports was clearly visible. "That, Mr. Lodge, is a Royal Navy frigate in a hurry."

When the two senior officers came forward, Hopkins looked at the on-rushing frigate, then at the senior midshipman. "Mr. Lodge, signal the other ships. 'Spread out in a line. Brigs on the wings.' Once they acknowledge, signal '*Alfred* and *Columbus* engage first. Brigs when able.' Can you remember that, Mr. Lodge?"

The 17 year-old Bostonian nodded vigorously. "Yes, sir."

"Good. Mr. Jacinto, once the second signal has been acknowledged, clear the ship for action. Then Mr. Jones and I will assume the watch."

Jaco put the back of his hand to his forehead as a salute. "Aye, aye, sir."

Hopkins turned away. Jaco saw Lodge fumbling with the signal flags and turning pages of the signal book. "Jim, do you want some help?"

Lodge nodded, and Jaco handed him the flags in sequence. They went up the halyard, and both midshipmen watched until each ship send up the flag that signaled, "Message received and understood." Then Jaco walked over to the ship's bosun, who was standing with his pipe in hand. "Bosun Penway, beat to quarters, if you please."

The staccato from the snare drum sent the crew scurrying around the ship. Most found their way onto the main deck to take a look at the British frigate before going down the fore and aft companionways to the gun deck.

Jaco was halfway down the aft companionway when he heard Commodore Hopkins say loudly, "Let's show them who we are. Break out the colors."

Gunner Reasoner put his hand on Jaco's shoulder and said in a soft voice that was almost a whisper, "Jaco, you'll do fine. Just concentrate on the job at hand, and what will be, will be."

Reasoner headed to the ship's magazine, where the young boys were readying for battle. Jaco was sure the Royal Navy captain believed it was his duty to fight despite the odds, and teach the upstart Continental Navy a lesson. He wondered if the British captain would have some tricks up his sleeve to even the odds.

As Jaco started to run to his position at the forward end of the of the gun deck, Lieutenant Struthers grabbed him by the arm. "Walk, Jaco, walk. It shows the men under your command that you have a sense of purpose and are not afraid."

Jacinto's post was just aft of the foremast. Lodge came three steps down the companionway and called out, "Captain says load and run out. Do not fire until ordered."

Struthers, just forward of the mizzenmast, spoke for the gun deck. "Does the captain want us to fire ball or chain shot?"

The midshipman gave Struthers a puzzled look, then disappeared. It was as if he had forgotten part of the order. A few seconds later, his head came back in view. "Ball, aim at the hull."

Struthers walked a few paces to the middle of the gun deck and spoke in a loud, calm, and commanding voice. "Lads, you heard Mr. Lodge, we're shooting solid shot. Make ready!"

Jaco repeated the order, thinking, *This is not how we trained. We have 9-pounders and they may have 12s. We practiced aiming at the rigging with chain shot to cripple the enemy. Why are we changing tactics?*

One of the young powder monkeys, a boy of 11, almost ran into Jaco as he headed down to the magazine. Jaco set his back against the foremast.

Once the canvas cartridge bags with thin wood disks at each end were delivered, Struthers gave the next command, which Jaco repeated. "Load powder."

He waited until the men came back to attention on the sides of their respective guns before commanding, "Load shot and prime." At each gun, the gun captain used a large pin to prick a hole in the powder canister, then poured fine powder into the touchhole.

Jaco walked down middle of the gun deck, speaking loud enough so that every sailor could hear him. "This first round is ball. If you can, aim at the gun ports. If it goes where it is supposed to, we take out some of the enemy's guns. Once we close with the enemy, fire at will. Remember the drill. In practice, you fired and reloaded in less than a minute. Now is when you will show the Royal Navy how good you are."

Struthers gave an approving nod as Jaco took his position with his back to the foremast. The black painted 9-pounders, ten on each side, glistened in the light coming through the open gun ports.

Jaco peered through the forward-most gunport. The Royal Navy frigate was 200 yards ahead and would pass along *Alfred's* starboard side about the same distance away. The fifteen cannon he could seen meant they were about to face a ship with a heavier broadside. Looking aft, he saw *Columbus* lagging slightly behind, poised to pass on the enemy ship's other side.

He wasn't sure what Captain Saltonstall had in mind, but as Jaco looked at the other ship, he guessed that *Alfred's* captain hoped to cripple the enemy ship, then come back around and run her down. *But why ball? We should be using chain shot to take out the enemy ship's rigging and slow it down.*

Lodge stuck his head down so he could be heard on the gun deck. The loudest sound was the rushing of the water by the hull. "Captain says fire as you bear."

The command didn't need an acknowledgement. Jaco walked behind the breech of the number one cannon on the starboard side. Through the open gunport, he saw red-coated Royal Marines in the shrouds and blue-coated officers on the quarterdeck.

Struthers said, "Mr. Jacinto, you have the honor of firing the first shot."

"Aye, sir. Thank you." The gun captain handed him the wand with the glowing slow match. Jaco blew on it and the end glowed bright orange.

But the delay in orders had proved fatal. As Jaco sighted does the barrel, the Royal Navy frigate fired. He saw a flash of flame and a puff of smoke, and heard a thunderclap. *Alfred* shook as the 12-pound iron ball hammered into the hull just forward of where he was standing.

The number one gun captain had aimed the gun's elevation to hit the forward-most cannon on the Royal Navy ship. With an intent expression on his face, he gauged *Alfred's* movement. "Now, Mr. Jacinto."

Jaco touched the glowing slow match to the touchhole. The gun barked, the carriage leapt back, and smoke poured back into the gun deck. One after the other, the 10 guns on *Alfred's* starboard fired. At the same time, Jaco could feel *Alfred* taking hits in the hull below him. How badly the ship was being damaged wasn't his concern at this moment, however; he had to make sure their guns kept firing.

He saw a blue-jacketed shape run past him, but didn't turn to see where he was going. Jaco was more interested in the movement of the powder monkeys, who kept the guns fed with powder and shot.

The two forward-most guns were being run out when there was a flash and explosion on the gun deck. Jaco heard splinters whiz past. When the smoke cleared, he saw the starboard number five gun carriage was on its side. He yelled to the gun captains, "Keep firing!" and ran aft.

Sprawled around the damaged cannon were half a dozen bleeding and maimed men. He ordered a gun crew on the port side to get the wounded men below.

The crews on the number six and seven starboard guns were staring at the carnage, and Jaco ordered loudly. "What are you looking at? Reload and fire!"

Jaco lost count of how many guns fired while he directed the shifting of the number five cannon barrel from off a sailor. Men from the port side lifted the carriage high enough for others to pull the man out. He had been silent before, whether from stoicism or shock, but he screamed in pain when he was moved, and it was obvious from his bloody pants that both legs were crushed.

Jaco looked out a gun port. The British ship was out of sight, and *Alfred* was wallowing as if it were adrift. He could hear sails snapping as they luffed.

He wondered where Lieutenant Struthers was, and look around the gun deck. The smoke was ebbing out of the gun ports and up the companionways, revealing the damage. Two starboard side guns were out of action, leaving eight. Jaco found Struthers sitting with his back to the mizzenmast, holding his thigh closed where a large splinter had ripped it open. He'd managed to wrap a strip of cloth around his upper thigh to slow the bleeding.

"Give a hand here," Jaco ordered. "Get Mr. Struthers to the surgeon."

Four seamen picked Struthers up in a seating position and headed toward the companionway leading to the orlop deck, where the ship's surgeon and his assistant had set up shop. With only lanterns for illumination and poor ventilation, it was a dark, dank place.

Jaco walked the gun deck, making sure each gun that was still serviceable was loaded, then ascended to the main deck to see why the ship had turned into the wind. Now he could see the British ship, half a mile behind *Alfred,* exchanging fire with *Columbus.* Both *Andrea Doria* and *Columbus* were trying to maneuver so they could rake the enemy ship.

Spotting Lieutenant Jones, Jaco asked, "Sir, why are we not chasing the enemy?" Commodore Hopkins and Captain Saltonstall were staring at the *Columbus,* whose hull was enveloped in gun smoke.

"A ball carried away our steering ropes. Do you know where Mr. Lodge is?"

"No, sir."

"What about Lieutenant Struthers?"

"He took a splinter in the leg and was taken to the surgeon."

"Turn the gun deck over to Mr. Reasoner. We're not going to be able to fire at anyone. After you do that, supervise the carpenter while he rigs a way to steer the ship from below, then report back."

Jaco took in the scene around him—the luffing sails, and gaps in the upper bulwarks where British cannonballs had torn through the wood. Both boats had gaping holes in the planking, and two of the 6-pounders were in pieces, with the barrels laying at odd angles. "Aye, aye, sir."

Below, Jaco found the small space at the aft end of the berthing deck where Leo Gaskins, the ship's carpenter, a man in his fifties, was re-threading ropes through the blocks and tackles that controlled the rudder bar. A gaping hole in the side that Jaco could easily fit through provided ample light. He wondered where the ball was, since there was no hole on the far side.

Seeing the midshipman, Gaskins called out, "We'll have the ropess ready in 10 minutess or thereabouts. The ball took out the ropess from the wheel to the rudder tiller bar, but didn't damage the bar itself, nor the rudder post."

He handed Jaco a rope and pointed to a block over his head. "Make yourself useful, ssir. Pull thiss through that tackle."

Jaco did as he asked. He fed the rope through a pulley, and Gaskins knotted it.

Gaskins grinned, revealing two missing teeth. When he talked, some of the words came out with a hissing sound. "Mr. Jacinto, pay my respectss to the captain and tell him we can ssteer the ship. When we get back to port, we'll do a proper ssplicing. Now get out of here, and let me and my matess patch that hole!"

"*Perfecto*, Mr. Gaskins." Jaco went back up to the quarterdeck to let Saltonstall know he could now steer the ship. He was glad to breathe fresh air untainted by gun smoke or reeking of the dank interior of the ship. In the distance, he saw one ship standing by itself and two others off to the side.

Behind him, he heard Hopkins order the quartermaster to signal, "Break off the action."

Lieutenant Jones strode over to the commodore and Captain Saltonstall. "Beggin' the commodore's pardon, but sir, we can rejoin the action and take *Glasgow*."

It was the first time Jaco had heard the name of the enemy ship.

"We're damaged, *Cabot* is damaged. We need to save our ships to fight another day."

"Commodore, it is not often we will get a chance to capture a British frigate. We outnumber it four to one. We *need* to take *Glasgow*."

Hopkins went rigid. His face was livid as he answered, "Goddamn you, Lieutenant! I have had enough of your insolence. Just because you were a captain once doesn't mean you know what to do on this ship or with this squadron. Count yourself fortunate I have not had you court-martialed for insubordination. When this cruise is over, I will make sure you never command an American ship ever again."

"I doubt you'll do that, Commodore. We need experienced captains like me, captains who know how to fight. You made a hash of the Nassau raid, and now this."

"Damn your impertinence! Go below before I have you put in irons for insubordination!"

"With all due respect, sir, I am not insubordinate. I want to close on the enemy and capture their ships. That is what *Alfred* and this squadron *is supposed* to do. We may die in the process, but we must demonstrate that we can defeat the British in a naval battle."

With that, Jones turned on his heel and departed. Master Swain looked up at the sails, trying not to be noticed. Seeing Jaco, he said, "I think the rudder is out of rig. Go below, find Mr. Gaskins and pass the word that we need to adjust the lines to make the rudder match the wheel. When you come, back, ask for captain's permission to clear all the guns by firing. Or do you prefer to unload them?"

"If the cartridges are pricked, firing would be safer."

On the gun deck, he went from gun to gun to find out how many were loaded on the starboard side. They all were.

Rather than put the wad-screw, a device that looked like a coiled spring, down each barrel to grab first the ball and then the powder cartridge, Jaco ordered to fire the cannons. This way, there was no risk of sparks setting off the powder charge. killing or maiming the men of the gun crews.

Chapter 5

Privateer or Not

New London, CT, April 1776

There were no bands or dignitaries to greet the squadron when they sailed up Connecticut's Thames River. There was only the steady, light wind and an empty harbor. *Cabot* was the first to tie up, followed by *Alfred, Columbus, Andrea Doria* and *Providence.*

Once *Alfred* was tied to the pier, Lieutenant Struthers and the rest of the wounded were carried off and taken by wagon to a hospital near the center of New London. Then Saltonstall mustered the remaining crew onto the main deck. Lieutenant Jones, Gunner Reasoner, Master Swain and Midshipmen Lodge and Jacinto stood in a row on the quarterdeck, two paces behind Captain Saltonstall and Commodore Hopkins.

Alfred's captain called Lieutenant Jones forward, then spoke in a voice pitched to carry so that every man aboard would hear him.

"Lieutenant John Paul Jones, Commodore Hopkins and I have decided to relieve you of your duties as an officer in the Continental Navy based on your insubordinate behavior during the action against *H.M.S. Glasgow.* As part of your punishment, you will forfeit all back pay and prize money. You are to leave with your possessions immediately. Do not stop to say good-bye to any member of the crew."

Jaco could see Jones's cheeks tighten and his lips compress as he struggled to control his anger. He saw disbelief on most of the upturned faces of the crew. Jones was a hard taskmaster, but fair and well liked.

Lieutenant Jones pivoted smartly and went below to get his sea chest. Minutes later, Jaco saw Jones leave the ship, put his sea chest on a cart and walk down the dock.

* * *

The day after Jones left *Alfred,* Jaco walked to the hospital to visit Struthers. the pungent smell of gangrene from infected wounds greeted him at the door. Struthers and the others were lying on beds in a large room, some awake, some fast asleep. Between the terrible smells and the bleak look on the faces of men who realized they would never be whole or sound again, Jaco felt worse in the hospital than he had during his worst bouts of fear on the masts of *Alfred.* His stomach twisted and he feared he might be sick.

Struthers was in a foul mood; he had just been told that removing his leg was the only way the surgeons believed they could save his life. After listening to Struthers rage, and speaking what words of comfort he could muster, Jaco was glad to escape.

It was raining as Jaco walked back to *Alfred.* He checked at every inn in the small town, hoping to find Lieutenant Jones, but without success. The lowering sky matched his mood. Not only had *Alfred* lost a fine lieutenant in Jones, there was only a 50-50 chance that Struthers would survive the amputation and the fever that followed.

He entered the midshipmen's compartment and noticed that Lodge's sea chest was gone. Jaco was not really surprised. After three months at sea, Lodge still could not use the reflecting octant to fix the ship's latitude, and he struggled with basic seamanship tasks.

Jaco asked Abner Jeffords, who was on watch on the main deck, if he knew where Lodge might be. "Well, Mr. Jacinto, to my way of thinking, Mr. Lodge will not be coming back. And if I may say so, sir, good riddance."

Jaco's head snapped back as if he had been shot. He had not anticipated such a blunt statement. "Jeffords, I would be careful to whom you say such things."

"Aye, sir. But Mr. Lodge had no business being aboard a ship, save as a passenger. And, sir, while I am spouting off, most of the crew think Mr. Jones should not have been relieved, and all on account of he didn't see eye to eye with Captain Saltonstall and Commodore Hopkins. Sir, I would sail with Lieutenant Jones again, but going to sea with the other two gives me fair pause."

Jaco wondered how many of the other officers shared this view. Master Swain would often roll his eyes when Saltonstall gave orders, and over a glass of port in the gun room he'd so much as said a competent commodore would have taken *Glasgow*.

At the evening muster, Captain Saltonstall informed the crew that as soon as the ships were repaired, they would go back to sea. Prize money would be paid out once the prize ships and their cargos were auctioned.

It was just after nine p.m. when Bosun David Penway found Jaco in *Alfred's* gunroom, writing a letter to his father. "Sir, I just got word that the schedule of the lieutenant's board has changed. They want you to appear tomorrow at 11 a.m. at the Yankee Tavern."

"Tomorrow? I wasn't supposed to appear until next Tuesday."

"It's to be held tomorrow. Sir, Gunner Reasoner and Master Swain, my mates and me, think you'll do fine. Good luck."

Jaco thanked the bosun, but he was angry. Swain and Reasoner had told him that midshipmen in the Royal Navy were usually given a week or more to study, and they were coached by other lieutenants. He had a leaden feeling in the pit of his stomach that Commodore Hopkins had changed the time because he wanted Jaco to fail. *He knew I respected Lieutenant Jones. He doesn't want another officer who makes recommendations that run counter to his opinions.* The prospect of staying on the *Alfred* was suddenly much less to his liking. He decided to ask his father's advice.

* * *

The next morning, on the way to the Yankee Tavern, Jaco stopped by a fast sloop that was transporting passengers and mail to Philadelphia. The mail courier added his letter to the mail pouch, and told Jaco that his father would likely receive the letter in four days.

With time to spare, Jaco walked the four blocks to the three-story building that was the Yankee Tavern. Along the way, he rehearsed potential questions and answers. To help him prepare for the board, Reasoner and Swain had plied him with likely questions long into the night, but since this was the first board of its kind in the Continental Navy, neither knew what Jaco should expect.

The front door to the Yankee Tavern was propped open with a large stone. He could smell a mix of wood and candle smoke, cooked bacon, stale ale and beer, along with unwashed bodies. He stopped for a moment to let his eyes adjust from the bright April sun to the dark interior of the inn.

Seeing Jaco in his blue uniform coat, white breeches and black shoes with a square buckle, the tavern proprietor pointed to the stairway. "Second floor, third room on the right." Jaco chuckled; his uniform and age made plain the reason for his being at the inn's front door.

The room on the second floor of the Yankee Tavern was occupied by three strangers who sat behind a long table and eyeballed Jaco like a pack of wolves about to pounce on a deer. On his side of the table was an empty wooden chair, looking forlorn and outnumbered. Jaco spoke into the silence. "Good morning, sirs. I am Midshipman Jaco Jacinto."

"Please sit down, Mr. Jacinto," said the man in the middle. "I am Captain Barr, the board's senior officer. Sitting on my right is Captain Hazelton, and to my left is Captain Williston. Are you ready to sit for the lieutenant's exam?"

"Aye, sir, I am." *No, I'm not! But I told Swain and Reasoner I'd do my best.*

For the next two hours, Jaco was grilled on gunnery, sailing, which sheet went to which sail, halyards, signaling, dropping and weighing anchor, navigation, the difference between tacking and wearing the ship. He tried to make his answers short and to the point, bordering on terse. Finally, there was a pause. Jaco sat erect in the chair, waiting for the next question.

Captain Barr stroked his face, then looked at the other members of the board. The captains nodded slightly. "Mr. Jacinto, as you may be aware, the Continental Navy expects to expand rapidly. Not only do we need competent officers"— *Did he just say competent, or was that my imagination?* —"we need officers with initiative and daring, as well as a sense of responsibility. There are many dangers at sea, even in times of peace. The wind does not care who one's father is, nor do waves have any regard for one's wealth. Captains Hazelton and Williston and myself are in agreement, that we may in all good conscience place upon your shoulders the triumvirate burden of obedience, cooperation, and command that befits a lieutenant in our young navy. You are experienced, that is clear from your replies, and I detect in your voice and manner the bearing of of a man whom others will obey with a will. Mr. Jacinto, I will be blunt. The question I ask myself at the end of any interview is this: Would I entrust a son of mine on a ship on where this man served? And if the answer is no, I have to think long and hard before I approve his advancement. Having no such qualms, may I be the first to address you as *Lieutenant* Jacinto."

As Captain Barr had spoken, Jaco had felt his spirits lift in a mixture of astonishment and relief. Perhaps there was hope for the new navy after all, with men like these at the helm. "Thank you, sir. I will do my best not to disappoint you."

Barr took up a quill pen, and there was the scratching sound of its point across the paper as he wrote his name at the top and signed two copies. After blotting each page, he slid them first to Williston, then to Hazelton for their signatures. When they were done, one copy of his commission was given to Jaco.

"Lieutenant, before you go, we would like to ask questions about your time on *Alfred*."

Should I tell them Hopkins is an ass and Saltonstall is not much better? Or that they ran off the best officer on the ship, and I'm not the only one who knows it, not by long shot?

Captain Barr' continued. "We understand Mr. Jones frequently disagreed with the decisions made Captain Saltonstall and Commodore Hopkins. Is this true?"

"Yes, sir, it is."

"Did you personally witness any instances? Please answer our questions candidly. I assure you that you will not be punished for your answers."

Jaco forced himself not to squirm. These men had just put him in a very difficult position, and they knew it. He also realized this might his one opportunity to speak on behalf, not only of Lieutenant Jones, but the other junior officers and the crew. "Yes, sir, I did. Mr. Jones often disagreed with the strategy and tactics chosen by Commodore Hopkins and Captain Saltonstall. It was probably why he was relieved and ordered off the ship without his pay or prize money."

Captain Hazelton, a heavy-set man who wheezed, inquired sharply, "Did you say Mr. Jones was relieved?" He leaned forward intently, and Jacinto pitied the poor chair supporting Hazelton's weight. He wondered how the captain got up and down a companionway on a ship.

"Yes, sir."

"When?"

"At muster on the morning after we arrived, sir."

"Do you know Lieutenant Jones's whereabouts?"

"No, sir."

"Do you know the subject of their disagreements?"

During the lieutenant's board, there had been pauses between Hazelton's questions, but now they came rapidly.

Jaco asked, "Before I answer in detail, may I ask what is going to happen to Lieutenant Jones?"

Captain Hazelton seemed to condense into something that a cannonball would not dislodge as he rejoined, "Why?"

"Because I think Lieutenant Jones was the best officer on the *Alfred*. If Commodore Hopkins and Captain Saltonstall had followed Mr. Jones's suggestions, the squadron would have taken *H.M.S. Glasgow*."

Captain Barr's head jerked noticeably. "Mr. Jacinto, that is a very strong statement about the judgment of two senior officers. Explain yourself."

Jaco looked at each of the captains before answering. "Sirs, may I remind you that you asked for my candid opinion." Jaco took a deep breath and forged on. "As I stated before, this was not my first time at sea. At twelve, I started sailing as a midshipman on cargo ships to the Mediterranean and Europe. From what I can tell, Captain Saltonstall and Commodore Hopkins are excellent merchant seamen, but they are not Naval officers. They view everything as if it were a business transaction, with risk analysis and a primary concern for the survivability of the ship. But we're a Navy, not a business. Both Commodore Hopkins and Captain Saltonstall ignored Lieutenant Jones's recommendations, which were sensible and in keeping with our orders. Our job was to take Royal Navy ships, and that comes with a price that I do not think either man is willing to pay."

Barr looked at his fellow officers, then at Jaco. "Would you be so kind as to give us an example?

"Sirs, I can give you three. First, as we sailed from harbor..." Jaco described the months spent frozen in the ice, then what happened at Nassau, and how the British were allowed to spirit the powder away. Finally, he described the debacle with *Glasgow*.

"Commodore Hopkins and Captain Saltonstall did not make effective used of the squadron. They ordered ships to attack singly, instead of surrounding *Glasgow*. Then they delayed our orders to fire, which gave the Royal Navy ship the advantage of firing first. Furthermore, we had practiced using chain shot to damage an opponent's rigging to make it more difficult for enemy ships to maneuver. Mr. Jones believes this is a more effective way to fight than aiming for hulls, because our ships are converted merchantmen and don't have the stout sides of a warship. But we were ordered to fire directly into the hull of the *Glasgow*. If we had fired into *Glasgow's* rigging, there is a good chance we would have crippled her and taken a great prize: a 30-gun frigate. Instead, *Cabot, Columbus* and *Alfred* were damaged, and *Glasgow* escaped."

"Will you swear to what you just said?"

"Yes, sir."

Captain Williston had not said a word since asking Jaco several pointed questions about navigation; now he spoke. "Mr. Jacinto, would you serve under Lieutenant Jones again?"

Jaco didn't hesitate. "Yes, sir, I would."

Williston nodded an acknowledgement. "Given the choice, would you prefer Captain Saltonstall or Lieutenant Jones to be your captain?"

"Mr. Jones. Without a doubt. And sir, I am confident many of the officers and crew would say the same."

Captain Barr drummed his fingers and once again seemed to hold a silent conversation with the other captains, a conversations of glances. Then he asked suddenly, "Mr. Jacinto, do you know where Midshipman Lodge was during the fight with the *Glasgow*?"

Jaco looked at the floor, trying to decide whether to tell the truth or simply say he didn't know. Lodge was gone, and he didn't want to accuse a man of cowardice. Instead, he asked, "Sir, may I ask why I am being asked this question?"

Barr nodded slightly. "Mr. Jacinto, there are discrepancies in the reports about his performance. One, signed by Captain Saltonstall, says that Midshipman Lodge performed his duties in an exemplary manner. Others are... not so kind. Do you know where he was supposed to be?"

"Mr. Lodge's station was to supervise the firing of the swivel guns and 6-pounders on the quarterdeck, and to raise any signals the Commodore wanted."

"Was he there?"

Jaco took a breath and hesitated. Captain Barr offered, "Mr. Jacinto, the truth, whatever it may be, will not cast doubt on your actions. So again I ask you, *where was Midshipman Lodge during the battle?*"

"Sir, I saw him run the length of the gun deck and then go down the companionway to the orlop deck right after the firing started. I did not see him again until we finished fixing the steering."

"Thank you, Mr. Jacinto. Your candid comments about the decisions and actions of Commodore Hopkins, Captain Saltonstall, and Midshipman Lodge support what Lieutenant Struthers, Master Swain and Gunner Reasoner reported. The ship's surgeon saw Mr. Lodge wedged against a rib near the entrance to the ship's stores."

"What is going to happen to Mr. Lodge?"

"We are recommending that he not be offered any further employment by the navy. However, his family has many powerful friends, and we do not know what the Marine Committee may decide. Thank you, Mr. Jacinto. That will be all."

* * *

Saltonstall was his usual dour self when he returned to the ship after a few days leave in Boston. His mood did not improve when Jaco displayed his Lieutenant's commission. Saltonstall looked surprised before he offered cool congratulations.

At noon, Captain Saltonstall mustered the crew. They crowded around the mizzenmast to hear what he had to say.

"Men of the *Alfred*. I have the sad duty to tell you that the crew is being paid off. At two bells of the afternoon watch, the paymaster will give you your pay and prize money. At that time, you will leave the ship with your sea chests. In a few months, *Alfred* will go to sea with a new crew after the Marine Committee finds the money to repair her. I wish each of you the best of luck, and when our Navy again needs you, I trust you shall return. May God bless you. That is all."

Jaco was stunned. Just moments before, he was a Lieutenant on the frigate *Alfred*. Now he no longer had a ship on which to serve.

Jacinto waited until all the seamen were paid before he approached the paymaster. The man counted out silver and gold coins, which Jacinto put in a pouch. Now he had to decide what to do.

* * *

Jaco bought a horse and traded his sea chest for a set of brown leather saddlebags and duffel bag which he lashed to the to the back of the saddle. They were enough for all his possessions, the most important of which was his diary.

The old British cavalry saddle had pistol holsters on each side, and a loop through which he could slide his sword. With his transportation secure, Jaco stopped say good-bye to Lieutenant Struthers. Jaco was both relieved and pleased that he had survived the surgery.

"Jaco, lad, where are you off to? The paymaster came by this morning to pay me off."

"To Philadelphia, to see my father. What will you do?"

"I don't know. What *can* a one-legged man do? I cannot even work on a fishing boat."

"Why don't you come to Philadelphia when you can travel and work for my father?"

"It will be weeks before I will be strong enough to leave."

"Come when you are ready."

"I'll think about it."

Jaco held out an envelope. "Take this letter. It is an introduction to my father and his brother, who will offer you a job. You have skills and experience, and I have told them about you."

"A job in Philadelphia?"

"No, Charleston. It is not a bad place. The weather is much nicer than New York, and there are many pretty girls."

"I don't want to be a burden on anyone," Struthers said slowly, painfully. "What woman would want me?"

"Many, because you a very good man. Trust me."

Struthers fell silent, twisting his hands over the sheet of the bed. At last he said, "How do I find you?"

"Contact my father; he will know where I am. He bought a house in Philadelphia and the address is in the letter."

The two men hugged, and Jaco walked out of the hospital with tears in his eyes. He wasn't sure if it was for joy that his friend was going to live, or that it might be the last time he would see Gregory Struthers, who taught him so much.

As Jaco walked out the door, Struthers thought to himself, *I may just do that.*

On board H.M.S. Jodpur, *April 11, 1776*

The Royal Navy frigate weighed anchor at first light. Casks containing beer, wine, rum, salt beef and pork were stashed in the hold, along with a fresh supply of powder and cannon balls. On the deck were 22 casks containing oats, flour, hardtack, flour and rice. They were lashed against the port and starboard bulwarks and would be stowed once the ship was headed toward Halifax.

To get the casks below, they were rolled into a rope net, lifted off the deck, then down a hatch. If a cask split, any of the food that spilled out had to be, by Royal Navy rules, swept up and dumped over the side.

In the dim light of the hold, Sean O'Hare's red hair appeared dark red. The junior midshipman was helping manhandle the casks into their assigned position. It was sweaty, dirty work in a space that smelled of bilge water, spoiled food, rat feces and other decaying matter.

By noon, *Jodpur* was under full sail, headed due north toward Halifax. As a treat, now that the casks were stored, the crew got a mid-day meal of fresh eggs and bacon.

On the road to Dobbs Ferry, NY, *April 1776*

Jaco rode to New Haven, enjoying the roadside sights and scents of spring. His uniform, however, was not well suited to the saddle, so before locating an inn for the night, he purchased two tan shirts and two pairs of brown trousers. He folded his uniform coat and cream-colored breeches and put them into his saddlebags.

The April days were bright and approaching what he considered a passable temperature. But the nights were cold, so he was glad of the warmth of an inn's fireplace and a steaming bowl chowder with fresh baked bread.

On his second day on the road, Jaco, continued down the Connecticut coast to a small town on the water called Norwalk. After an uneventful night in a room he was lucky to have to himself, he set out for Dobbs Ferry, north of British-controlled New York, a place where he could pay for a ride across the Hudson River.

Not knowing who was a Loyalist and who was a rebel, Jaco decided to travel alone. He was more worried about British patrols looking for deserters, spies, and Continental Army units than he was of highwaymen. For the average citizen, being searched wasn't a problem, but with a uniform and a commission letter in his saddlebags, being stopped by the British Army would lead to being sent to one of the British prison hulks in New York harbor, where, he had heard, men were dying of disease and starvation every day.

Jaco rested in the shade of oak trees at the edge of a broad meadow to eat a lunch of crusty bread, cheese and jerky, while the horse grazed. With his hunger appeased, he remounted and continued on the road until he saw British Army Dragoons at a roadblock. He immediately guided his horse into the woods, but it was too late. The Dragoons had already spotted him, and four men mounted their horses and galloped after Jaco.

He rode a good half-mile into the woods before he dismounted. From the concealment of a stand of maple and white birch trees, Jaco watched the red-coated British cavalryman pick their way through the forest 100 feet away. He waited until he was sure the cavalrymen were out of sight and out of hearing, then remounted and eased the horse west through the woods toward the Hudson River, hoping to intercept the road on the far side of the roadblock.

He was picking his way through the trees when a man stepped in front of him with a musket aimed at his heart. The man's long hair was uncombed and turning gray. "Stop and get down," he ordered. "And don't touch that sword."

The horse snorted as Jaco leaned forward, his hands on the saddle horn. "Who are you?" He could see rust on the musket's barrel.

"The man who is going to take your money. I'll kill you if I have to. Some people will pay good money for that sword." There was a pause. "Bart, see what is in his saddle bags."

Turning around, Jaco saw another unkempt figure emerge from behind a tree. He let the horse step toward the man with the musket. Time slowed down as Jaco remembered what his father had taught him. *If you cannot avoid hand to hand combat, be ruthless and give no quarter. You must fight to win, because there is no other way. Start with a plan, because if you do not have one you have already lost.*

Ten feet away from the man with the musket, Jaco stopped and swung his left leg out of the stirrups to get down. The movement allowed him to use the horse to shield himself from the musket. It also hid the hand sliding his tomahawk out of his belt.

Holding the reins of his horse in his left hand, he waited until Bart reached for the saddlebag straps. In one swift movement, Jaco swung the tomahawk at Bart's head. The thin blade dug into Bart's neck with a sickening, sucking sound, and his sudden movement caused the horse to move into the man with the musket. Bart tried to scream, but all that came out was a gurgling sound as he choked on his own blood.

With his right hand free, Jaco pulled a pistol from the saddle holster while the man with the musket was forced backward. The thief started to come around the horse's head. Jaco ducked under the horse and eased the hammer back. He held the reins in his left hand as tightly as could and pulled the trigger. The gunshot caused the horse to whinny and rise up on its hind legs, but it didn't bolt. The 55-caliber ball shattered the man's breastbone and the musket flew out of his hands as he fell onto his back.

Jaco soothed the horse, then looped the reins around a tree branch. He picked up the musket, broke the stock over his knee, and tossed into the woods. Next, he retrieved his tomahawk. Grimly, he wiped it as clean as he could on Bart's dirty clothes.

Then he knelt next to the grey-haired man, whose breathing was labored. "How many more of you are there out here?" Jaco demanded.

The man shook his head weakly. He didn't have the strength or breath left to talk.

"I'm sorry, but I was not going to let you rob me."

The man nodded slightly; his last breath exited his lungs and his eyes glazed over. Jaco crossed the dead man's hands across his chest. Still kneeling, the South Carolinian looked at the sky. "God, forgive me," he murmured, and said a prayer for the dead.

Jaco reloaded his pistol before he got back on his horse and headed into the afternoon sun. Later, he came across a small stream. He let the horse have a long drink while he washed the dried blood off his tomahawk, hands and face.

Eventually, he reached the road. It was dark when he rode into the small town of Dobbs Ferry, and too late to cross the river. The two-story Ferry Tavern had a bed to spare, so

Jaco stabled his horse and stayed the night. Tomorrow, he would pay the shilling for a ferry ride across the Hudson.

* * *

Right after breakfast, Jaco collected his horse and got in line for the ferry. The flat-bottomed boat had a large lateen sail and blade keels that the boatman lowered on the leeward side to keep the boat tracking on his desired course. It took two tacks and over an hour to sail the mile to the west side of the river.

Jaco didn't know much about the Hudson, its currents, or the winds in the area. He was just a passenger as he stood patiently next to his horse, keeping the animal calm. He was one of four men with horses, and the farther the ferry sailed into the Hudson, the more nervous the animals became. When they docked on the west side, just north of the New Jersey border, he wasn't sure whether he or the horse was more relieved to be on land.

The ferryman pointed to the road to Morristown, warning that British patrols were about. Fortunately, throughout the day Jaco saw no soldiers, only an occasional farmer working his fields.

In Morristown, he stopped at a tavern for lunch before getting back on the road to Trenton. The hilly terrain changed from heavily wooded hills to flatter farmland and well-maintained fields of corn and wheat. Just as was done in South Carolina, cattle were kept in corals near the farmhouses.

Jaco enjoyed riding alone. When he saw a farmer close to the road, he asked about British soldiers. None had been seen, which he took for a good sign. It took him eleven hours to reach Trenton. The inns were full, so Josh found a stable that let him sleep in the hayloft for just the price of stabling his horse for the night.

After a much shorter ferry ride across the Delaware River, Philadelphia and his father—someone with whom he could talk openly—was just a few hours away.

The weather turned foul. A cold wind blew, and lowering clouds darkened the sky as far as he could see in every direction. It began to rain heavily, and the downpour made the road a muddy mess. The reins grew cold and slick in Jaco's hands.

A blast of thunder caused his horse to rear up in fear and nearly dump him into the mud. It was so loud and there was so much lightning that he stopped and sheltered under a broad tree. He tied the horse to a branch and shivered as he waited for the storm to move past. It wasn't any drier, but the leaves kept him from being pelted by the rain.

When the rain stopped, Jaco did his best to dry off the saddle with his damp handkerchief, then climbed back on the horse, debating what was worse—riding out a storm on land or on a ship. At sea, thunderstorms brought gusty winds from unpredictable directions, they ripped sails and tore yards off masts. One minute the wind would be over the port side, and the next the wind shifted to come over the bow. On a ship, the best course of action was to shorten sail until the storm passed. He decided thunderstorms at sea were worse. At least on land he couldn't drown.

Jaco was cold and soaking wet when he arrived at his father's house. Two other horses were tied to the railing, indicating company was present. Jaco placed the pistols and tomahawk into one of the brown leather saddlebags, then cradled the connecting strap in the crook of his left arm as he untied the duffel at the back of the saddle.

He rapped on the door with the hilt of his sword. Not hearing a voice, Jaco rapped three more times, this time a little harder.

"Who is there?"

"Lieutenant Jaco Jacinto!"

The metal bolt was drawn back and the iron latch released so that the door swung open. Javier Jacinto stood in the doorway, arms held out wide. "Come in, my son, come in."

Jaco lowered what he was carrying to the floor and hugged his father. When they broke apart, Javier's shirt was damp at the front. The older man put his hands on his son's shoulders. "Let me look at you." He beamed, then said, "I will get you some dry clothes. Are you hungry?"

"Yes, it was a long ride on short rations."

His father ruffled Jaco's damp hair, then stumped upstairs. "It is so good to see you!!!"

A few minutes later, Javier came back with clothes draped over his arms. "Take off your boots and change here. We will dry your wet clothes in the kitchen where I have a fire going. I also have bread, smoked meat and cheese. I am so proud of what you have done, and I want to hear more than what you wrote in your letters."

Jaco peeled off his wet clothes, toweled off, and changed into dry clothing. His father took the pistols, sword and tomahawk to another room, then took charge of the wet garments. When he returned, Javier waved towards a door. "Come, come."

They walked past the kitchen, where Jaco saw his clothes draped over the table and chairs, to the parlor room where a fire crackled in an immense, marble-topped fireplace at the far end. Four men stood up as they entered.

Javier waved in the direction of his guests. "Gentlemen, this is my youngest son, Lieutenant Jaco Jacinto of the Continental Navy."

Javier indicated a stocky man with graying hair. "John Langdon is a shipbuilder from New Hampshire." Jaco shook hands with Langdon, and turned to the next man.

"John Hewes from Pennsylvania is now the deputy chairman of the Marine Committee. He is determined to make sure that naval officers are picked for their ability."

Jaco nodded. "It is a pleasure to meet you, sir."

The Pennsylvanian had a soft voice, but Jaco sensed there was steel backing the softness. "Your father let me read your account of the squadron's voyage. Allow me to congratulate you on your well-deserved promotion. Captains Barr and Williston were most impressed."

"Thank you for your kind words, sir."

Javier put his hand on his son's shoulder to signal Jaco to face the next man. "This is Bertrand Houston. He is a merchant from Rhode Island who has a similar business to ours, as well as similar interest in ensuring that the Navy is properly funded."

"It is a pleasure to meet you, sir."

"No, Jaco, the pleasure is mine."

Jaco stared at the last man standing patiently off to one side, grinning. Javier said, "And I believe you already know Lieutenant Jones."

"Lieutenant, I offer my congratulations. Your promotion was well deserved. *Alfred* had the best gun crews in the squadron."

Both men hugged tightly for a few seconds before breaking apart. Jaco was the first to speak. "I was worried about what happened to you, sir. What ship is yours now?"

"Ah! That is the very topic we were discussing when you barged in and bloody well stopped the discussion!"

* * *

After his father's guests departed, Javier handed a refilled glass of red wine to his son and pointed to a chair. It was a signal he wanted to talk. Being the son, Jaco waited for his father to speak first.

"I have some bad news. *Duke* never made it back to Charleston. We don't know what happened."

Jaco's stomach contracted and his eyes swam. This hurt. Eric Laredo was his best friend. The two of them had often talked about being officers on the same ship, but now that would never happen. Eric was gone.

"How are the Laredos taking his loss?"

"Not well. They understand he sacrificed his life for the cause of freedom, and it has made them even more determined to kick the British out. Eric's brother is an officer in the South Carolina militia, and we think that Charleston may soon be attacked by the British."

Jaco nodded. "How is *mamá*?

"She is well, and proud of you. After I read your letters, I send a summary that she reads to your sister Shoshana and your brothers Saul and Isaac."

"With you here in Philadelphia, how is the family business?"

"The war is causing problems for the bank that Gento and I started. Many of our neighbors are unable to pay their loans. We make accommodations so they can stay in business or keep their farms. Englishmen still like Carolinian hides, tobacco and indigo, so our cargo ships dock in Belgium and the cargo is transferred to a British flagged ship. We may be at war with the king's army and navy, but we are not at war with fellow merchants."

Unlike many landowners in Charleston, the Jacintos did not grow indigo or tobacco, nor did they keep servants. It was against Jewish law to own slaves. Their ancestors had been enslaved in Egypt and elsewhere in Africa, and what was wrong to suffer was wrong to impose.

Javier took a sip from his glass of wine. "The Royal Governor of South Carolina and the Loyalists want us to foreclose on any loan given to someone supporting our cause that cannot make their payments. My brother Gento told them to go to hell. The British cannot revoke our bank charter as long as it is solvent. We will be fine. For others it is a struggle, and we are helping out as best we can."

His father had more gray hair than Jaco remembered. For the first time in his memory, his father looked old and tired.

Javier took a deep breath and looked at his son. "I need to ask you a question, and we on the committee need to know the answer."

"*Papá,* I'll do my best to answer."

"Tell me about Lieutenant Jones."

"In what way?"

"How is he as a leader and captain? Would you serve under him again?"

"Gladly, *Papá.* Lieutenant Jones is aggressive and knows what he is doing. He can be abrasive and arrogant at times, but he is fair. I told the lieutenant examination board that if Lieutenant Jones had led the raid in Nassau, we would have captured all their powder and munitions, and we would have taken the *Glasgow.* Does that answer help?"

"Yes it does, Jaco. Many members of Congress are going to help fund new ships. We don't want to make a mistake about who captains them. Lieutenant Jones will be *Sloop Providence's* next captain. It was a compromise we made on the committee. Stephen Hopkins, who is Commodore Hopkins' brother, and John Adams from Massachusetts insisted that we see what Jones can do before we give him a larger command. Do you want to go with Captain Jones?"

"I do, *papá.*"

Javier Jacinto looked down at the floor, then into his glass of wine. He was about to send his youngest son back to sea, possibly to his death. As a father, he didn't want Jaco to risk his life in a naval battle. As a member of the Marine

Committee of the Continental Congress, he wanted the best men on the few ships the cause could afford. That meant his son had to go.

"Jaco, I will make the necessary arrangements for you to be his second lieutenant. Once your assignment is approved by Mr. Hewes, you will return to New London to help Jones supervise *Providence's* fitting out. We want her at sea as soon as the yard can get it ready."

Jaco moved so he was kneeling in front of his father. He took both his father's hand in his. "Thank you, Father, I won't let you down."

"I know you won't. But you have a choice. I have an unopened letter that I was told contains a very lucrative offer from a consortium for a commission as the second lieutenant on a privateer operating out of Charleston, named *Duchess*. It is the sister ship to the *Duke*. You need to give them an answer."

"I would rather sail with Lieutenant Jones. I will send them a letter declining right away."

"Then that's that." Javier abruptly stood up. "I almost forgot. I have a letter for you from an admirer."

The elder Jacinto left the room and returned a few minutes later, holding a letter with a wax seal and the letters R E L in fancy script. "This is for you."

Jaco was wondering who R E L was as he tugged on the paper flap. The letter's handwriting was neat and precise, and a four-inch lock of jet-black hair bound by a red ribbon fell into his hand as he unfolded the paper.

Jaco,
By the time you read this, you may already know that my brother Eric perished at sea doing what both of you loved, and that is sailing. I do not know how he died, only

that he is gone, and I am sure you will miss him as much as I do.

The Loyalists here in Charleston are trying to make us believe that the British will win this war, but I am sure that people like Eric, our parents, brothers, and you will prevail. We will win our independence.

Your father has kept us informed about your exploits, and we are all very proud of you. Promise me that you will avenge Eric's death and help us win so he will not have died in vain. Enclosed is a lock of my hair as a good luck token.

Godspeed, and come back safe to Charleston so we can meet again.

Reyna

He sat for a few minutes, absorbing the power and passion of Reyna Esther Laredo's words. Her hair had an intoxicating scent.

"*Papá*, when you were in Charleston this past winter, did you see Reyna?"

The elder Jacinto grinned broadly. "I did, and she asked me if I would ask you to write to her. She is no longer the little girl whose pigtails you pulled and in whose hair you rubbed handfuls of mud. Reyna is now a strikingly beautiful young woman who cares deeply for her family and friends."

Jaco smiled as he remembered the mud battle. *Maybe she's forgiven me. I've always liked Reyna because she has spunk and always fought back.*

Charleston, late April 1776

Behind the Laredo's house was a swing framed by a large trellis, on which honeysuckle plants thrived. The vines now ran along the top, and anyone sitting on the swing enjoyed the fragrance of the trumpet-shaped blossoms.

Reyna Laredo spent mornings sitting on the swing, reading medical textbooks. She wanted to be a doctor and was one of three women taking biology classes at the College of Charleston. Philadelphia and New York had medical schools, but did not admit women. Even if they did, her parents would not let her go alone at age 16. Instead, she studied chemistry, anatomy and biology at the college and assisted a local doctor—Brannan MacKenzie, a graduate of the University of Edinburgh's medical school—four afternoons a week.

Just after lunch, Reyna answered a knock on the door. A young man who said he was a sailor from the *Sloop Cutlass* handed her a letter sealed with a blob of dark blue wax. She took the mysterious letter, returned to the trellised back yard, and settled herself in the swing. She broke the wax seal, opened the letter, and began to read,

Reyna,

I want to thank you for your kind letter and words of encouragement. Your lock of hair is with me on board my new ship, *Sloop Providence,* on which I am the Second Lieutenant.

Like you, I am saddened by Eric's loss. When I come home to Charleston after this war, I will miss his cheerful countenance. He was my best friend, but knowing he died fighting for our independence makes a difficult loss easier to bear.

When you receive this letter, I will be at sea. What our orders will be, I do not know. How long we will be gone is also unknown, but I suspect it will be for *several months. My father will keep you informed until I return.*

Please write, and I hope this letter finds you well. The next time I am in Charleston, I <u>will</u> come calling — without any mud!!!

Jaco

Reyna laughed aloud at Jaco's last sentence. Then she read the letter again and clutched it to her chest. *Godspeed, Jaco Jacinto, and come safely home.*

CHAPTER 6

A FAST SHIP IN HARM'S WAY

On board Sloop Providence, *June 1776*

Lieutenant Jaco Jacinto reported to the *Providence* when it docked in Philadelphia. The sloop had been sent to the seat of the rebel government to pick up 100 soldiers who'd volunteered to join the Continental Navy. None, however, would be assigned to *Providence.*

Back in New London, *Providence* was hauled up on shore, its bottom cleaned, and several planks replaced and re-caulked to fix leaks. Both Lieutenant Jones and Lieutenant Jacinto were working 16 hours or more a day. Provisions not only had to be procured, they had to be transported, and the crew had to be recruited and trained.

Lieutenant John Paul Jones' approach to recruiting was mercenary. He reduced the captain's prize money percentage from one quarter to one eighth because he believed that contributing to the cause of independence wasn't enough inducement to most men to risk their lives. He felt the prospect of more prize money would entice men to join the Navy.

On the flyer shown to recruits and signed by the members of the Marine Committee, it listed how the money would be paid out in British pounds:

Continental Congress	1/8
Captain	1/8
Navy and Marine commissioned officers	1/8
Warrant officers—bosun, carpenter, gunner, sailmaker	1/8
Midshipmen and mates	1/8
Crew	3/8

To a prospective recruit, dividing up three eighths of the prize money would make a huge payday. Jones' novel approach worked. When *Providence* set sail, it had a full crew of 54. In addition to the names of 20 sailors and 20 Marines on its muster sheet, the captain's log showed listed its commissioned officers and warrants to be:

- John Paul Jones—Lieutenant and captain
- Benjamin James—First Lieutenant
- Jaco Jacinto—Second Lieutenant
- John Bentley—Lieutenant of Marines
- Swain, Geoffrey—Quartermaster
- Hastings, Dwight—Bosun
- Gaskins, Leo—Carpenter
- Hitchcock, Levi—Sailmaker
-

To Jaco's delight, Abner Jeffords was quartermaster mate.

With the sloop back in the water, First Lieutenant Benjamin James took the lead in ship and sail handling drills, while Second Lieutenant Jacinto trained the men on how to handle the sloop's twelve 6-pounders and fourteen swivel guns. Barrels of salt beef and pork, peas and dried fruit, cheese, hardtack, beer, water, rolls of sailcloth, coils of rope, logs to repair spars and booms, powder and shot were brought aboard and stored under the watchful eyes of Bosun Hastings and Carpenter Gaskins.

Early on the morning of June 13th, *Providence* sailed down the Thames River, named after the river in London by the town's founders, and into Long Island Sound. *Providence* had originally been built as a small cargo ship named *Lark* before it had been modified into a fast, lightly armed ship for prize taking and raiding. It had a single mast and a sail plan that was a mixture of a traditional fore-and-aft rigged gaff main and topsail, with a square-rigged topgallant and royal. The lookout platform was 50 feet above the water, and the top of the mast extended 20 feet higher. The sloop's first sailing orders were to escort a collier to Philadelphia.

Charleston, Friday, June 1776

Right after the war began, the South Carolina General Assembly realized that Charleston was vulnerable and ordered defenses built to prevent the Royal Navy from entering the harbor. Construction of the fort on the southern end of Sullivan's Island began in March 1776. It had parapets with sand between two rows of palmetto logs, and cannon platforms 20 feet above the beach.

The redoubt, named Fort Sullivan, was situated so its guns could fire on any ships trying to enter the harbor, but it wasn't completed when the British fleet carrying troops evacuated from Boston anchored in Breach Inlet across from the north end of Sullivan.

On June 7th, British General Sir Henry Clinton sent an emissary to Charleston demanding the city to surrender. Not only did Colonel William Moultrie reject the terms, he built another fort on the north end of Sullivan's Island, manned by 780 men and two cannon.

General Clinton realized that his troops could not wade across Breach Inlet, so Royal Navy Admiral Sir Peter Parker decided to force the harbor. Two 50-gun ships of the line were among the nine that anchored off Sullivan Island to support an assault on Fort Sullivan, which was defended by four hundred and thirty-five men from the 2nd South Carolina Infantry Regiment and a battery of the 4th South Carolina Artillery.

Reyna Laredo was one of several women who accompanied Dr. MacKenzie to the fort to care for the wounded. The women were quartered in a small wooden building at the rear of the fort set up as a hospital. The South Carolinians planned to evacuate the wounded to Charleston at night.

When Reyna heard drums beating, she ran to where her older brother Amos, a company commander in the 2nd South Carolina, stood facing the harbor. Theoretically a non-combatant, Reyna had her 62-inch rifled musket in her right hand, and wrapped around her left were the leather straps of a powder horn and a pouch containing 20 paper cartridges.

Only 5' 1", Reyna had to stand on her toes to see over the parapet. Smoke billowed from the side of one of the Royal Navy ships, 600 yards away. The faint crack of a cannon sounded a second later and an iron ball sent up a geyser of dirt at the base of the fort's wall.

Amos Laredo said firmly, "This is no place for a 16 year-old girl. You need to go back to the hospital to help treat our wounded."

Reyna looked up at her brother. She shook her head causing the ponytail of her long, jet-black hair to swing back and forth. "No! I can shoot better than most of the men here, and if the dammed British get close they are going to have to deal with one very mad and dangerous woman."

Amos, 21 and nearly six feet tall, knew how feisty his baby sister could be. "Please, Reyna, this is man's work. I do not want to have to tell our mother you were maimed, or worse, killed. We have already lost Eric."

"She knows I am here to avenge Eric's death."

"Then go to the infirmary. I fear you will soon be needed there, and you know as much as Dr. MacKenzie and the other doctors do about medicine."

"No, damn it. I am staying here!" She glared up at him.

Rather than argue with his strong-willed sister, Amos smiled. He couldn't help it; her musket was as tall as she was. Besides, he'd seen her drop a running turkey at 100 yards and kill a deer at 300. "Come join my company, then."

A ripple of cannon fire indicated the Royal Navy's barrage had begun in earnest. Through the smoke that obscured most of the masts of the ships, Reyna could see orange flashes as the guns fired. Their iron balls threw up geysers of sand in front of the wooden platforms where the South Carolinian's cannon were mounted. Some thwacked into the soft palmetto logs, but none of the balls damaged the fort.

The South Carolinians return fire was slow, deliberate and well aimed. Fires next to the gun positions were turning cast iron balls red-hot before the ball was rammed into the barrel. Steam hissed out of the barrel when hot iron met a damp wad. Through spyglasses, the gun crew captains saw fire parties frantically dousing fires on the British ships, so the South Carolinians knew their 'hot shot' rounds were working.

The artillery duel between the fort and the ships ended at dark. When Reyna accompanied her brother to his position the next morning, all but three of the Royal Navy ships were gone. Two of the remaining ships were trying to pull a third off a sandbar. By noon, they gave up and set the abandoned ship on fire.

RAIDER OF THE SCOTTISH COAST

On board H.M.S. Jodpur, *July 1776*

Jodpur was ordered to patrol duty, with instructions to seize or sink rebel ships, and to impress able seamen as it patrolled off between Nantucket Island and Montauk Point. Smythe unrolled one of J.F.W. DesBarre's charts of the east coast of North America. It showed extraordinary detail. Using the tip of his forefinger, Darren traced a line from the southern tip of Nantucket Island to Montauk Point on the eastern end of Long Island on the linen-backed chart. Using a pair of dividers, he calculated the distance as only 56 miles.

"Sir," he said, "given that a visual horizon on a clear day is 30 miles, when *Jodpur* is at either end, only 20 miles of the gap between the two points of is out of sight, because we will not sail closer than three miles to either coast. Our patrol line is 50 miles, or 10 hours at five knots. If *Jodpur* makes five knots as it tacks back and forth along this line, there is never a gap of more than two hours that our lookouts can't see. So, if rebel ship tried to slip through near the coast opposite where we were, we would still spot them before we were halfway back."

"I like this course of action, Smythe. Tonight at dinner, you'll explain this to the rest of the officers."

"Splendid, sir."

Given how the winds varied from the so' west to nor' west, sailing Darren's patrol line was easy. *Jodpur* sailed a course east nor'east to three miles from Nantucket, came about and sailed west so' west until the ship was three miles from Montauk Point. They'd been on station for days in the heat of the summer, and as Smythe read the level of the red fluid in the thermometer, screwed to a stanchion next the wheel, he was thinking that even *Jodpur* was sweating. The liquid was at the 92° Fahrenheit line. Pitch oozed from seams on the main deck, its oily smell pungent throughout the ship. To keep the hot main deck from burning the bottom of sailors' feet, Captain Horrocks had the men splash seawater on it every hour.

Even with her main, top and topgallants set, *Jodpur* was barely making enough speed to hold a course, so there was no wind to cool the ship and its crew. Horrocks ordered the gun ports and all the hatches to be opened to provide some ventilation, but it scarcely helped. The berthing deck was stifling, so the crew slept on the gun deck, which wasn't much cooler, but at least it was better ventilated.

Jodpur had not seen a ship worth pursuing since the doldrums started. Horrocks allowed those who wanted to go shirtless to do so. However, if they beat to quarters, he insisted the officers be properly dressed. Soon, Smythe reflected, *Jodpur* would be relieved and sail to cooler Halifax, where they could stand on solid ground for the first time in months and get out of this damned heat.

To the west, Smythe saw a brewing line of thunderstorm and hoped it would bring an end to the heat and lack of wind. As the storm approached, Horrocks had the crew furl all but the mainsails and jib and head east into the Atlantic, so his ship wouldn't be forced aground.

The rain was a welcome relief from the heat, and the wind brought another gift. As the frigate emerged from a rain shower, *Jodpur's* lookouts spotted a rebel merchantman less than two miles away, headed so' west by west. Smythe was writing in his journal in his small cabin when Tillerson ordered the watch to tack *Jodpur* toward Cape Cod so it could run the unknown ship down. Smythe felt the ship change direction, corked his ink bottle, and came out onto the main deck.

On the quarterdeck, Lieutenant Griffin was barking out orders, sequencing the hauling of the yards and, once they were in position, the trimming of the sails. Grinning ear to ear, he waved to Smythe, an invitation to join him on the quarterdeck. When Smythe came over, Griffin handed his fellow officer a spyglass. "Let's hope this rebel ship doesn't blow up like the *Duke!*" he said cheerfully.

The name on the stern was *Betsey Anne,* but the ship flew no flag. Tillerson ordered the Marine drummer to beat to quarters. The captain took over the watch and ordered Blackwell and Smythe to have the gun crews run out, but not load; he didn't see any gun ports on ship, which looked to be a merchantman.

The faster *Jodpur* easily ran *Betsey Anne* down. Faced with a row of 13 twelve-pounders pointed at his ship, the captain surrendered *Betsey Anne* and its cargo of Spanish sherry and spices.

Horrocks impressed 20 of the merchantman's crew before putting a prize crew aboard under Nigel Blackwell, with orders to sail *Betsey Anne* to Halifax, then find the first packet ship coming back to the fleet off Boston so the prize crew could return to *Jodpur.*

Two weeks later, *Jodpur's* lookouts spotted an approaching sloop. Figuring that no rebel sloop-of-war would approach his frigate, Horrocks maintained course; the sloop gave the proper recognition signal, and both ships hove too. Blackwell and the *Jodpur's* seamen came on board with word that *Betsey Anne* and its cargo were worth £15,000.

In his diary, Darren created a table marked '*Betsey Anne* prize money' and used the formula taught at the Royal Navy Academy to calculate his portion, assuming he survived.

Below the table Darren wrote £375 ad circled it. Since his annual salary was £ 40, *Betsy Anne* would bring him a splendid payday.

Blackwell also brought a sealed packet. As he did before, Horrocks opened the orders in front of all his officers while they drank port. *Jodpur* was to remain on station until July

	Share	Share in Percent	Share of Total	# of Participants	Individual Share
Admiral	1/8	12.50%	£1,875.00	1	£1,875.00
Ship's captain	1/4	25.00%	£3,750.00	1	£3,750.00
Lieutenants, Surgeon, Royal Marine captain, Master	1/8	12.50%	£1,875.00	5	£375.00
Warrant officers: RM offcers, Bo'sun Carpenter, Quartermaster	1/8	12.50%	£1,875.00	5	£375.00
Midshipman, mates, RM sergeants	1/8	12.50%	£1,875.00	12	£156.25
remainder of the crew	1/4	25.00%	£3,750.00	195	£19.23
		100%	£15,000.0(	218	

10th when it would be relieved so it could return to Halifax to re-provision and perform any needed maintenance.

Halifax, Nova Scotia, July, 1776,
H.M.S. *Cerberus* relieved *Jodpur,* and under freshening winds the ship flew through the water, averaging seven knots for the trip north.

Two days out of Halifax, the ship's carpenter, Edwin Morgan, reported to Captain Horrocks that *Jodpur* had two serious leaks in the forward hold. He'd repaired them, but recommended that the shipyard have a look because some of the wood was, as he said, "awfully bloody soft." When asked what he meant by soft, he replied, "Rotten is a better word."

On the next tack, everyone on deck heard a loud crack. Anyone who'd ever heard a large tree branch break knew the sound. The unusual swaying of the upper section of the foremast told Horrocks the source of the noise. Immediately, he ordered the topgallants loosed and the jib and fore staysail lowered to reduce the strain on the mast. As long as the rigging held the broken section in place, *Jodpur* could continue on its current course. His fear was that the broken mast would fall and bring the mainmast down with it.

Morgan, along with his mates, went up the rigging to lash a splint to the upper section of the foremast. It would, Morgan said, hold until they got to port. Horrocks decided not to test it, and only allowed the main sail flown on the foremast.

On the day before they sailed into Halifax, Horrocks laid out his expectations for the crew's behavior while in port. He wanted them to enjoy their time ashore, but he would deal harshly with any who deserted, or got involved drunken brawls, or who harmed a local resident. The crew knew *harshly* mean flogging.

Just past the seaward tip of McNab's Island at the entrance to Halifax harbor, a sailboat from the naval base came alongside. A Royal Navy lieutenant by the name of Handley clambered up the side, followed by a Canadian who introduced himself as Emile Beaulieu, the harbor pilot who would guide *Jodpur* to a berth at a pier. Handley, the Halifax Naval Dockyard's Master Shipwright, looked as if he hadn't missed a meal in years. Smythe wondered if he had ever been to sea.

Handley asked Horrocks what was wrong with his foremast, and if his ship needed any additional repairs.

"Aye, we do. My carpenter thinks he found rotten wood in our forward hold."

Handley's eyebrows went up. "I'm what is called a marine engineer, and my job is to make sure your ship is fit for duty. So I'll give *Jodpur* a thorough look over. Unless we find more problems, we can have you back at sea in a jiffy." Smythe thought that if Handley were going to inspect the ship himself, he would have a hard time fitting into some of the cramped spaces in *Jodpur's* hold.

As soon as the gangway was laid down, Horrocks sent Blackwell ashore to deliver their victualing order, to find fresh meat, fruit and vegetables for the crew, and to inform the naval base officers' mess that all of *H.M.S. Jodpur's* officers were dining ashore tonight. Until Handley finished his inspection, there was little for the crew to do.

* * *

Smythe admitted to himself that his initial assessment of Lieutenant Handley was wrong. Over the next three 14-hour days, the chunky engineer personally inspected every nook and corner of *Jodpur,* occasionally poking a sharp thin spike into the frigate's timbers to test the wood for rot. Handley made notes as he went, by the light of a lantern held aloft by a dockyard worker.

Captain Horrocks assigned Smythe to follow the marine engineer. At first, Darren didn't like the idea of crawling through *Jodpur's* dirty, smelly bilges, but he quickly realized that if he ever again commanded a damaged ship, what he learned from Handley would be invaluable.

Today Handley was in the empty forward hold that normally held water casks. As they worked their way along the port side, Handley told Smythe that his father owned a shipyard and he had earned an engineering degree from the University of London before joining the Royal Navy. After a year on a frigate as a lieutenant, and another on a three-decker ship of the line, he'd been sent to Halifax to supervise repairs.

Another poke into the foremast, a foot above where it was stepped, and Handley grunted. A third poke was followed by two words: "Not good."

"What's not good?" Smythe asked.

"The base of the foremast is rotten, and so is its step. Both will have to be replaced. I've already found wood rot in in six places on the port side in this hold, and two on the starboard side just above the water line. If they were hit by cannon balls, *Jodpur* would likely sink. Those planks will have to be replaced. This is not new rot; it should be repaired in England in a proper graving dock. We can do it here, but not as easily."

Handley stood up. With only his breeches and linen shirt on, it was evident that Handley was stocky and well-muscled, not overweight. "I want to take another look at the base of the main and mizzen masts. In my report to the Admiralty, I will note that the yard that overhauled her did shoddy work. What the Controller of the Navy will do is unknown, given the Navy's need for ships. But when *Jodpur* leaves my yard, she will be right, you can count on that."

On July 21st, *Jodpur* was pulled to a dock closer to the shore. Its cannons, gunpowder and shot were hoisted onto the pier and moved into a warehouse. Its water and beer casks were flushed before they were moved into the storeroom. The few remaining casks of biscuit, salt beef and pork went to another warehouse. The crew shifted to a barracks ship moored to a nearby pier.

With the ship empty, dockworkers used ropes to pull *Jodpur* over so it was 45 degrees from the horizontal. Posts with flat planks every 10 feet kept *Jodpur* from rolling onto its side. Handley found several of *Jodpur's* copper plates were loose, either because they were improperly fitted or the wood to which they were attached was rotten. It all had to be fixed before *Jodpur* could go back to sea.

On *board* Sloop Providence, *late August 1776*

Before *Providence* could go to sea, the Marine Committee had to agree on its officers and its mission.

In a series of meetings at Independence Hall, John Hewes insisted, "Performance counts, and Lieutenant Jones has demonstrated the élan the committee expects of Continental Navy captains." Over the objections of John Adams and Stephen Hopkins, the Marine Committee promoted Lieutenant Jones to Captain.

Providence was tasked to "capture prizes and disrupt English shipping" and left Philadelphia on August 21st. Once into the Atlantic, Jones cruised off the New Jersey coast, drilling his crew. On the 24th, lookouts spotted an easy prize, the unarmed brig *H.M.S. Britannia* and sent it to Philadelphia.

Jones kept the sloop running close-hauled, heading nor' east by north. *Providence's* bow rose and fell as the sloop knifed through the water off the New Jersey coast.

The call "Sail ho! Two points off the starboard bow" from the maintop caught everyone on the quarterdeck by surprise. Less than a mile away, a Royal Navy frigate was upwind and closing as it emerged from a fog bank less than a mile from *Providence*.

"Bloody hell!" Jones blurted, as he studied the larger, more heavily armed ship. "The bugger's lookouts must have been above the fog and they must have been tracking us."

Over the wind rushing through their sails, Jaco could hear the drummer on the British frigate beating to quarters. Through his spyglass, he saw red-coated Marines climbing the ratlines so they could rain musket fire down on the sloop's deck. Clearly, the captain of the British ship was preparing for a fight, and it wouldn't take many 12-pound cannon balls to turn *Providence* into matchsticks. Everyone on deck could already see the black noses of the British ship's guns sticking out on both sides.

Jones turned to his officers. "I want all the Marines to get below and have only sailors on deck. We have the advantage because we can tack quicker and sail closer to the wind. We're going to force the British frigate to maneuver so that by the time he comes around to deliver a broadside we'll be out of range." Then he bellowed, "Break out the colors so that the Royal Navy knows who is about to out sail them."

Grinning, Abner Jeffords, quartermaster's mate, tugged on a line tied to a cleat at the aft end of the quarterdeck. The large Continental Navy flag with the British Union Jack in the upper left corner and white and red horizontal bars snapped smartly as it streamed out from its stay.

A puff of smoke billowed from the frigate's bow chaser, followed by a dull boom. A spout of water erupted 300 feet from *Providence*. A second puff was followed by another boom and the screech of a 9-pound cannon ball passing overhead.

Captain Jones yelled, "Stand by to come about. On my command."

Jaco ran down the deck to make sure the sheet handlers for the jib did their work well.

"Mr. Swain, hard a lee. Come about smartly to nor 'west by north."

Swain spun the wheel. As *Providence* turned, it slowed. "Let go starboard sheets."

The four men holding the jib and staysail sheets on the starboard side let go of their lines and ran over to the port bulwark to help their compatriots pull in the lines. Behind Captain Jones, two men slackened the boom vang slightly and let it swing from the starboard side of the wheel to the port side.

By the time the sheets were dogged down and the wind filled the sails, Swain had *Providence* steady on its new course. The British frigate captain's plan to hammer the rebel sloop with a broadside had flown into the wind as *Providence* headed nor' west by north and out of range. Through a glass, Jaco read the name *Solebay* on the stern of the frigate.

The wind carried the shouted commands of the frigate's captain as he tried to wear *Solebay* from running with the wind to a starboard tack to bring his guns to bear. Jaco could see the shoulders and heads of sailors pulling on braces as *Solebay's* captain tacked his ship.

With *Providence* sailing 30 degrees off the wind line, the square-rigged Royal Navy frigate couldn't match its course. *Providence* sailed away.

* * *

The weather stayed warm as the sloop headed nor' by nor'east following the trade winds. After the close-call with *H.M.S. Solebay*, *Providence's* officers gathered around the small table in the captain's cabin. In front of them was a French *Dépôt des Cartes et Plans de la Marine* chart, dated July 1766, depicting the coast from Cape Cod to Nova Scotia.

"Gentlemen, many merchantmen coming out of the Caribbean and headed to Great Britain will come this way to take advantage of the winds blowing generally from the west. If we take any prizes, they will be sent to Philadelphia, Newport or New London. If those ports are blockaded, make for Norfolk in Virginia."

Navy Lieutenants Benjamin James and Jaco Jacinto, the Marine Lieutenant John Bentley, and Midshipmen Hedley Garrison and Jack Shelton nodded in understanding.

"Our problem is manpower. We can only spare a few men for each prize. So where are we going to find more sailors?" Jones tapped a small town on the northern end of Nova Scotia, just south of Cape Breton Island on the chart. "Right here, Canso, Nova Scotia. This is where we are going. Many of the Canadians living there are poor, and the promise of prize money may cause some to join us."

The officers studied the map. Jaco picked up the dividers, spread them to measure one degree of longitude, which corresponded to 60 miles. He then walked them along a course from *Providence's* position to Cape Breton Island. It was 450 miles, or, with favorable winds, three and a half days away at an average of five knots over the bottom of the Atlantic.

Captain Jones rolled up the chart and put putting it in the rack against the aft bulkhead of the cabin. He filled each officer's glass from a bottle of Portuguese Madeira.

Holding up his glass, Jones said, "Gentlemen, to our success."

Each man repeated the word "Success" and looked to their captain.

"Each of you was handpicked to be on *Providence*. If you do well, you will be promoted and, in time, be captains of your own ships. Mr. Hewes charged me to train naval officers capable of outwitting our enemy, the Royal Navy. As I see it, four words define what makes a great naval officer— leadership, seamanship, tactics, and courage."

Perfecto! Jaco took a sip of his wine, anticipating an interesting lesson from an officer he admired for his élan and ship-handling skills.

Jones gestured with the hand not holding his glass of madeira. "The Navy is different from the army. At sea, the crew is alone and must depend on every sailor to succeed. There's no place to hide, no place to run. We can't send a messenger back to an admiral asking for advice or reinforcements, because he is weeks if not months away. Once we leave port, we have to deal with whatever challenges come our way." Every junior officer's eyes were on *Providence's* captain.

"*Leadership* is all about respect and motivating men. Effective captains earn the respect of the men they command by respecting each sailor's skills and listening when they offer suggestions. Often, your men will give you a morsel you can use. Effective leaders make tough decisions that are in the best interest of their ship and its crew. Over time, they will see the results. If your men respect your skill as a sailor, your knowledge of tactics, and your judgment and courage to make difficult decisions, even though you are not always right, they will follow you through the gates of hell to deal with the devil himself." Jones looked at each of his officers. Shelton and Garrison had just turned 16, Jacinto was 17. Bentley and James were the oldest at 20.

"Next is *seamanship*. The ships we take to sea are fragile. Misjudge the weather and you can be de-masted, or worse. Your sailors must believe you know how to handle a ship in any conditions. Yes, you can take counsel from your master, quartermaster and bosun, many of whom will have more years at sea than you, but in the end, it is your skill as a sailor that matters." Jones took a sip of his wine, then put the glass down on the table.

"*Tactics* and seamanship go hand in hand. Tactics are much more than gaining the weather gauge. They involve planning your maneuvers to give your ship the advantage or negate those of your enemy. Your tactics must be based on the skills of the sailors and marines under your command, as well as the weapons you have. Proper tactics and seamanship can often overcome bigger and better armed ships.

"Last on my list is *courage,* and it is part of leadership. Going into an action, if you are not afraid, then you do not understand the nature of a battle. We are all afraid, but you cannot show your fear. Fear is contagious and saps the fighting strength of a ship. A good captain doesn't believe he is going to win a battle with an enemy ship, he *knows* how he will do it because he has thought out his plan and keeps refining as the engagement develops. If your leadership is built on mutual respect, your men will have confidence that you will not waste their lives. Yes, they may die or be maimed, but they will willingly take that chance because they have faith in you as a leader; in your ability to handle the ship; and the tactics you will use to carry the day. If you demonstrate courage as a leader, your men will follow you to their last breath."

* * *

Dawn revealed a low, gray overcast. The sloop's main and quarterdecks were wet from the humidity, and water dripped from the rigging. On the western horizon, Jaco saw rain coming and wondered how long before it reached *Providence*.

Halfway through the forenoon watch, the lookouts spotted a brig flying its studdingsails along with its main and mizzen staysails. Through a spyglass, Jaco saw the extra spars that extended the brig's yards; it didn't look like the brig could add any more canvass. Either the ship was in a hurry or its lookout had spotted the sloop first and was fleeing.

Captain Jones came over and looked through a spyglass. "Mr. Jacinto, how would you catch this prize?"

"Sir, I'd tack around and come to nor 'west by north to intercept. Then I would lay out our main staysail and see how fast *Providence* will go close-hauled."

"Mr. Jacinto, do it. Time is, as they say, awasting."

Jaco turned to Bosun Penway. "Call all hands to make sail. We need to get the main staysail up as fast as possible."

With the sailors in position, Jaco gave the order to stand-by to come about. Then, "Mr. Swain, easy on the helm. Hard a-lee, come port to nor 'west by north, if you please."

"Port to nor 'west by north it is. A good heading it will be."

Swain turned the wheel and *Providence* groaned as the bow started to come into the wind.

"Release the port jib sheets."

As soon as the tacks of each sail passed in front of the mast, Jaco called out, "Haul in the jib the starboard sheets."

With the triangular jib in position, Jaco ordered the sheets on the main sail released so the boom could swing to the leeward side. The blocks on the boom vang clattered as the boom swung over the quarterdeck to the starboard side.

"Haul in the mainsail sheets."

The hemp rope on the boom vang hissed as the sailors pulled the rope hand over hand. Jaco wanted the boom about five degrees downwind of the centerline; when it was, he turned to the bosun. "Secure the sheets."

Next, "Hoist the fore staysail."

The head of the sail, which was laid out on the starboard side, was already attached to a halyard. As it was hoisted, men held the starboard sheets so it would not foul the rigging or the jib.

Everyone on board could felt *Providence* surge forward. With the ship on its new course, Jaco decided its gaff topsail on the main mast could be used.

"Hands to the main top. Release the gaff-topsail and get ready to haul."

Jaco watched as the six men released the lines that held the sail in place. he was glad he did not have to be one of them. When it was free, he looked at the sailors on the main deck. "Lads, haul the gaff topsail halyards."

The gaff-topsail filled the wedge between the boom at the top of he mainsail and the mast. The two lookouts moved to the front of the platform to get out of the way.

"One more time, haul." The topsail was now almost in line with the keel of *Providence*. It was up as far as it would go.

The mainmast groaned as the wind pressure increased. Jaco examined the rigging to make sure that it wasn't applying so much tension that would cause the mainmast to snap.

"Weaaall duunne, Lieutenant. Now catch us a prize, lad."

An hour later, Jaco could read the name *Favourite* through a spyglass. Now that *Providence* was close to the British ship, Jones came back on the quarterdeck. "Mr. Jacinto, it is time we show our colors and that we mean business. Have the Marine drummer beat to quarters, then tell me the next steps in your plan."

The snare drum started its staccato beat. Those not on watch, or already on deck watching the brig, came up from the berthing deck. Green-coated Marines climbed up the rigging. Sailors in the maintop took the canvas covers off the two swivel guns mounted on the crow's nest.

"Sir, as we approach from their starboard rear quarter, I will ask them to heave to. Since we do not have any bow chasers, if they need some encouragement to strike their colors, I plan to fall off, pass astern and fire into the captain's cabin. Our 6-pound balls won't do much damage, but it will show them we mean business."

"If they don't haul down their flag, then what?"

"*Providence* is a handier ship. We come around, catch back up and fire chain shot into her rigging from her stern. We may have to tack back and forth several times until she surrenders. I'd like to avoid having to take her by boarding or exchanging broadsides. I think my plan will cause *Favourite* to haul down her colors."

"Very well, Mr. Jacinto. Let's see if it works. You are relieved to take up your position on the main deck with the cannon, now that Mr. James is on the quarterdeck."

"Aye, aye, sir." Jaco climbed down from *Providence's* tiny quarterdeck to the center of the main deck. "Starboard battery, load ball and run out. Port battery, stand by."

The wooden wheels rumbled over the seams of the planking of the main deck. Jaco watched the gun crews ram home a cartridge, then a wad, before shoving a cannon ball the size of a grapefruit down the barrel. Jack Shelton looked up for the next order. "Mr. Shelton, if we need to fire a second broadside, we will use chain shot aimed at *Favourite's* rigging." Shelton waved.

Providence was about 100 yards from the *Favourite* when Jaco heard the distinctive Scotch accent of his captain calling across the water. "*Favourite,* this is the Continental Navy Sloop *Providence.* Please heave to immediately."

"Rebel, take yourself and your sloop straight to hell. Do you think your piddling popguns can stand up to ours?"

"Bloody hell," Jones muttered. "The stupid bastard wants a fight." He stalked over to the forward railing. "Mr. Jacinto, fire on my command, and then fire as you bear according to your plan."

"Aye, aye, sir." Jaco turned to the gun captains. "Aim at the captain's cabin. I want the balls to go through the windows. Port battery, load chain shot and stand by, when we tack to come back, it will be your turn, aiming at the rigging."

Each gun captain held up his stick with a section of glowing hemp in acknowledgement.

Jones raised the trumpet again. "*Favourite,* I intend to fire until you surrender. There is no need to get any of your crew hurt if you strike now."

"Rebel, you'll have to pay in blood to take my ship."

Captain Jones shook his head. "Bloody dumb bastard. The blood is going to be his." Then he turned to the master. "Mr. Swain, fall off to port so we can teach the captain of *Favourite* a lesson in seamanship and manners."

Leaning over the rail, Jones said, "Mr. Jacinto, you may fire as your guns bear. Apparently, we need to encourage the British captain to haul down his flag."

Jaco walked up to the forward-most cannon on the starboard side. "On my command, fire." He looked down the gun barrel, checking the elevation. *Favorite* was less than 100 yards away, and still *Favourite* had not opened its gun ports. The Union Jack streamed in the breeze.

Twenty yards, and the bowsprit of *Providence* was well past the port side of the stern. For a second, he debated whether or not he should have the forward swivel gun aim at the quartermaster standing by the wheel of the *Favourite.*

Staring at the men on the Royal Navy ship, he remembered another of Captain Jones' points about fighting at sea. Jones had said, "We will fight like the devil and give no quarter until our enemy asks for it. Then, we will treat our enemy with honor as if they were our shipmates. There is no reason to kill or maim them except during a battle."

Jaco looked up at the mast. "Maintop swivel guns and Marines, hold your fire."

The forward-most cannon was just passing the outboard window of the captain's cabin. Jaco shouted, "Number one port gun one, fire! Port cannon two through six, fire as you bear."

The gun captain touched the glowing hemp to the touch hole and the little 6-pounder barked. *Providence* didn't have anything that would roar. The glass on one of the windows of the captain's cabin shattered.

Gun two barked. White smoke blew back and aft. Jaco strode down the deck, standing behind each cannon as it fired. Looking into the captain's cabin, he could see the main deck. Someone had left the door open, or it was blown down. Gun four fired. Splinters flew above the gunwales and the ball hammered into the rack of belaying pins and coiled rope at the base of the brig's mizzen mast.

Gun six fired and the sloop sailed clear of the cloud of gun smoke. The frames around the windows to the captain's cabin were shattered and all the glass was gone.

Behind him, he heard Captain Jones order, "Mr. Swain, stand by to come about to port." Jones went to the railing at the forward end of the quarterdeck. "Mr. Jacinto, we are about to come about. Have your men lend a hand to handle the sails, then return to your guns."

On the second pass behind the stern, *Favourite's* port main mast shroud flew apart as chain shot cut it five feet above the deck. *Favourite's* jib and foresail collapsed to its deck as halyards parted.

Captain Jones commanded, "Stand by to come about. This time we are going to come along side."

The tack brought *Providence* on a parallel course to the brig, now 50 yards ahead on their port side. Jones yelled to have the main and top gaff sails slackened as the sloop drew even. Then he picked up the trumpet. "*Favourite,* are you ready to heave to?"

"Go fuck yourself, Rebel!" Only now did *Favourite's* captain start issuing commands to ready a broadside. Now that they were coming along side *Favourite*, the difference in size of the two ships was even more apparent. *Providence* was much smaller.

Jones looked up. "Marines and swivel guns, do your work."

The swivel guns on the masthead fired first. Chunks of wood erupted from the deck and railing. A hole appeared in the ratlines for the mizzenmast; the boom for the studdingsail on the starboard side snapped and plummeted to the water. Stays snapped and fluttered in the wind. A sailor on the *Favourite* hacked away at the lines to the sail that was acting as a sea anchor. It took him three whacks at a thick hemp rope before it gave way.

Jaco saw two of the gun ports facing *Providence* open. He yelled at the swivel guns on the bow and the crews on the quarterdeck. "Sweep the quarterdeck! Let's put an end to this nonsense!"

The captain of the bow swivel gun grinned as he fired. Chunks of wood flew off *Favourite's* quarterdeck railings, and one man went down.

Jaco knew their guns were outmatched. He was also puzzled by *Favourite's* slow and partial armament, but he wasn't about to waste the opportunity *Favourite's* arrogant captain had provided. Their best chance was to bring down so much sail that *Favourite's* gun crews were blinded before they were ready to fire. "Main battery, keep firing chain shot at the rigging."

The swivel guns on the main and quarterdeck were useless because they had to fire up at the *Favourite*. Up in the maintop, one lookout rammed home the powder charge, a wad, and loaded a canvas bag of 25 half-inch diameter balls. The other lookout poured powder into the touchhole and pivoted the weapon to aim at *Favourite's* quarterdeck. The cannon barked, and the quartermaster at *Favourite* wheel and the man next to him went down in a cloud of red mist. Two other men on the quarterdeck fell.

While the swivel gun was being reloaded, a figure ran to the stay holding the flag and swung his cutlass to hack the line in two. The Union Jack fluttered to the quarterdeck.

"Cease fire, cease fire!" Captain Jones moved to the starboard railing. "Do you surrender?"

A man called back, "Yes. Yes, we do."

Jones turned to Swain. "Ease us in a bit closer." To the man on the *Favourite,* he yelled. "Luff your sails and heave to."

The brig's sails flapped in the breeze and *Providence's* boom banged noisily, no longer sheeted home. Jones yelled, "Stand-by to receive a boarding party. Any resistance will be dealt with harshly." Then he summoned his lieutenants.

"Mr. Jacinto, you take ten Marines onto the *Favourite.* Lock up the crew and do not tolerate any nonsense. If the captain and the master are still alive, bring them to me. Mr. James, prepare a prize crew."

CHAPTER 7

NOVA SCOTIA

On board H.M.S. Favourite, *September 1776*

Low, scudding clouds dumping rain reduced visibility to less than a mile. The cool dampness penetrated the small captain's cabin, and acting captain Benjamin James wondered how it would affect the barrels of sugar in the hold. But, at the moment, that wasn't his concern. Getting to a friendly port so they could be sold at auction was.

The mystery of why *Favourite* hadn't use its 9-pounders had been solved as soon as they boarded. Barrels of sugar blocked access to its magazine because the owners had expected the brig's speed would keep it safe. For his crew to get to the ship's powder, they'd had to cut lashings to barrels and then move them out of the way to clear a passageway. By the time *Providence* came alongside, it was too late.

Light winds had made repairing the rigging easy. Nothing was done to repair the gouges in the ship's deck. It would fall to the new owners to fix those, along with the glass in the captain's cabin, and the splintered walls of the berthing area.

Since they'd parted company with *Providence,* the sea had been empty. James' plan was simple: slip into Long Island Sound by sailing between the southern tip of Cape Cod and Nantucket, and hug the coast. Once past Martha's Vineyard, *Favourite* would run for Newport and safety.

It was a small prize crew, and there was always a chance that the British crew would try to retake their ship, despite James' assurances that they would not be treated as prisoners. When they reached Newport, they would be given the choice of joining the Continental Army or Navy, or being taken to the nearest occupied city and released.

The prize money for *Favourite* would be substantial. According to papers in the captain's cabin, Lloyds of London had insured the sugar for £12,000 pounds, and the ship, James estimated, was worth about £3,500. He just had to get the ship to a friendly port.

Now, closer to the coast, *Favourite* was in and out of thick fog. Benjamin James felt as if he was was sailing blind. The good news was that patrolling British frigates had the same problem. Not being able to see sun or stars for two days, James relied on speed, time and course to estimate his position and the entrance to Nantucket Sound.

He was off by 15 miles. In the open ocean, it wasn't much of an error. But the land on the starboard side was the south side of Nantucket Island, not the south shore of Cape Cod.

The lookout yelled, "Sail ho, three points off port bow!"

"What kind of ship?"

"Looks like a British frigate."

James saw three masts and sails looming out of the mist less than half a mile away. There was no time to get *Favourite's* surviving officer to run up the recognition signals, even if James did trust him. James debated whether or not he could bluff his way past.

Any hope that the British frigate would ignore them evaporated when he saw a puff of smoke from its starboard bow chaser. The cannon ball skipped over the water 50 feet past the bow on the starboard side. Before he could give the order to slacken sail, he saw a second puff of smoke. This cannon ball shrieked by the ship and splashed aft. They had the range, were upwind, and there was no way *Favourite* could outrun the frigate. James felt as if he had failed his captain and shipmates.

Halifax, early September 1776

Jodpur now had a new foremast; when they'd lifted the old one out of the ship, they'd found rot halfway up the mast and in the upper section. New sections of copper plate gleamed in the fall sun, and a 15-foot long section of the starboard side of the hull had been re-planked and re-sheathed. Inside the hull, buttresses were bolted in place to reinforce four cracked ribs. With the heavy work done, *Jodpur's* crew helped paint the new planks and the railings.

To get *Jodpur* afloat, a team of men and horses pulled the 19-year-old frigate upright and into the water. Next it was towed along the dock to where it could be re-supplied and re-armed. After the ballast was placed in the hold, the next items to be hoisted aboard were the cannon.

Each 560-pound carriage was lifted off the dock and lowered through a hatch in the main deck to the gun deck. Then, the 2,450-pound cannon was hoisted off the dock, over the bulwark and lowered on its carriage. Formed iron straps were bolted down over the carriage's trunnions before 12 sailors used blocks and tackle and muscle power to haul the cannon across the slightly humped deck and into position, where the ropes and pulleys used to be run it out were attached.

Reloading *Jodpur's* main battery of thirty-two 12-pounders took two full days. Getting the smaller 6-pounders onto her forecastle and quarterdeck took another half a day.

With the heavy work of loading the cannon done, casks of food, water, beef, beer, rum, gunpowder, and ammunition, along with rolls of canvas, spare spars and logs from which a mast could be constructed, were next. Lieutenant Blackwell inspected every item brought to the ship before he allowed it to be loaded. Once it was aboard and properly tied down, he checked it off his list.

In the hold, Smythe supervised the placement of the round shot in racks, and canvas bags of canister and chain shot just forward of the mainmast. Coarse powder came in 100 pound barrels for the cannon cartridges. Smaller, 50-pound kegs of fine gunpowder for muskets, and pistols and the flasks the gunners used to fill the touch holes were lashed in racks in the magazine and lashed down. Last to come aboard were the ready set of 150 powder cartridges.

The crew now brought their sea chests and hammocks from the barracks ship back onto *Jodpur*. When it was stocked, Horrocks would take *Jodpur* to sea for a week of sea trials, and if there were no additional repairs needed, he would receive his sailing orders.

On board Sloop Providence, *early September 1776*

To the west, the sky was a deep red with the sun framed by clouds as it descended toward the horizon. Jaco turned from the bulwark amidships and headed toward his captain's cabin to have the conversation he had been putting off for a month. It could no longer wait.

The Marine sentry posted outside Captain Jones' door came to attention with the butt of his musket and attached bayonet by his right foot. His white breeches, black boots and dark green coat were immaculate. How the Marines maintained their uniforms the way they did while at sea always amazed Jaco.

After entering and gently closing the door behind him, Jaco walked up to his captain's desk. Captain Jones was writing in *Providence's* log and looked up. "What can I do for you, Mr. Jacinto?"

"Its personal, sir."

"Out with it, lad."

Jaco cleared his throat. His stomach was turning. "Sir, I believe you know I am Jewish. Rosh Hashanah, our second holiest day of the year, begins tomorrow; and our holiest day, Yom Kippur, begins on the night of September 22nd and continues until sunset on the 23rd."

Captain Jones put his quill pen back on the cloth on his desk and nodded as if to say, *Go on.*

"I would like to switch watches so that I have some time off the 14th and the 22nd. If needed, I will stand double watches. And if on either day we have a scrap or are at Canso, I will do my duty."

"You know, in my native Scotland, the Anglicans still don't like Scotsmen because most of us are Catholic. It's bloody awful, because they call us Papists and accuse us of being loyal to the Pope even though we swore allegiance to the British crown. So I do understand. Very well, with whom will you be switching?"

"On the 14th, Master Swain said he will take my second dog watch and I am assuming his first watch. Both Midshipmen Garrison and Shelton said they would swap watches as needed on the 22nd."

Captain Jones smiled. "You have my approval to change watches." He paused, then continued. "You do know there are several senior officers in our Navy who do not like Jews."

"Yes, sir. I do, and my father knows who they are."

"Aye. I will let you deal with them. What is important is what you do as a Naval Officer. Nothing else matters. As you know, I have my detractors on the Marine Committee. Commodore Hopkins thinks I am arrogant ass. I think he is an incompetent moron who shouldn't command anything larger than a small long boat. And, because I am not one of their fellow New Englanders, Adams and the Hopkins brothers will do what they can to destroy my reputation.

Nevertheless, I am here. The lesson, Mr. Jacinto, is this. Results count if they are done with honor. Everything else is bloody claptrap."

* * *

From the quarterdeck, Jacinto watched the bowsprit rise up and down in the longer swells of the North Atlantic. The water that blew back from the waves was noticeably colder, and so was the temperature. The wind added a chill to the air. Everyone on *Providence* sensed that winter along the eastern seaboard was not far away. The corkscrew motion of the ship made it difficult for the lookouts to maintain their balance and to scan the horizon. Their solution was to lash themselves to the railing.

Earlier in the day, Captain Jones had notified the officers of his intention to rescue their countrymen from the coal mines near Canso, where, as prisoners, they were being used as forced labor. Since the region was also thick with fishing and sailing vessels, he held out hopes that they might seize more prize ships as well. "And if we can set our countrymen free, we should have the manpower to crew the prizes we take."

When he finished outlining his plan, Captain Jones told his officers to think about how they could make the plan better. Tomorrow, they would discuss their suggestions.

Jaco's mind was half on the upcoming raid and half on his duties as officer of the watch when he heard the "Sail ho" call. The unknown ship whose sails were barely visible over the horizon was sailing in the same direction as *Providence*.

Jaco tried to determine whether it was a large merchantman or a frigate that would try to make their sloop its prey.

"Mr. Jacinto, what do you make of it?" Captain Jones had come alongside for a look.

"Sir, it is too soon to tell. We're in part of the world where we can assume that most ships are British. I would pass out of gun range but close enough to get a good look. If it is a frigate, we change course and run. If it is a merchantman, we decide if we can take her."

Captain Jones steadied himself on the railing for a better look at the unknown ship. "I make it to be a frigate. We're too far away for him to identify us, so let's play along. Maintain your course. I like your plan to pass closer to see her true colors. Carry on, Mr. Jacinto. Let me know when we are closer." He turned to go.

That sounded a bit casual to Jaco. "Closer, sir? How far away is that?"

"You're the officer of the watch and second in command of *Providence*," Jones called over his shoulder, "you figure it out. Just don't cause me to lose my ship."

Jaco stared at the on-coming ship and ran scenarios through his mind. If it was a warship, he would recommend that the fore and main staysails be set and fall off to a course of west by nor' to open the distance. In this wind and on a beam reach, *Providence* could make 12 knots, much faster than a frigate that, on a good day, might make nine or 10. In two hours it would be dark, and they could alter course.

If it were a merchantman, he would recommend tacking to come up behind the ship's starboard side and demand that it surrender. If the captain refused, he would let *Providence* fall off the wind, pass astern and do what she had done to *Favourite*.

"Deck there, she's a frigate!"

A black hull with a yellow band and 15 black squares was now clearly visible.

"Bosun, pay my respects to the captain and ask him to come to the quarterdeck. Tell him our mystery vessel is a 30-gun frigate."

Soon all the officers and most of the crew were on the port side, looking at the on-rushing frigate. "Sooo, Mr. Jacinto, how do you plan to get away?" said a familiar voice in a Scottish accent.

"Sir, I would add both staysails and maintain course. That captain will be planning for a broadside exchange. He's running with the wind, so he can easily wear his ship three points to either port or starboard. If he goes port, we sail close-hauled, west nor 'west. If the frigate goes starboard, we sail nor' east by north. Either way, we time our course change to stay out of the range of his broadside. By the time the frigate tacks around to chase us, we should have a good head start and can disappear into the night. Once we are sure we are clear, we alter course to head back to Canso."

Jones nodded in approval. "Would you fly the topsail?"

"No, sir. If we add the topsail, we won't be able to sail as close to the wind as we would need."

With the strong wind, *Providence* surged ahead. The bow of the onrushing frigate loomed larger as the distance closed. If neither ship changed course, they would collide. Because *Providence* was downwind, they heard the Royal Marine drummer beat to quarters. One after another, the black snouts of her cannon poked out of her sides like rows of lethal dowels. Clearly, the British captain was taking no chances.

Jaco stood next to the Jeffords so he didn't have to shout to be heard. "Quartermaster, come one point to starboard. It will give us more distance from the frigate."

Captain Jones leaned over and whispered in Jaco's ear. "You are supposed to let me make those decisions, Lieutenant. I want a mile between us and that frigate."

"Sir, when we are just over a mile from the tip of his bowsprit, I plan to fall off to port to a course of west by nor 'west. By the time he comes around, we'll be well past him."

Captain Jones tucked the spyglass under his arm and picked up a speaking trumpet. He wanted to make sure that the men on the deck heard him, because the increased ship's speed and the wind through the rigging was noticeably louder. "You tell me when."

Jaco's eye measured the distance; it was too soon. Captain Jones was depending on his judgment of how *Providence* would respond to the helm. There was no room for error. If he waited too long, the frigate's broadside would smash the sloop to bits. Too soon and the frigate would be able to adjust its course and get off a broadside.

"Captain, I would say now is a good time to change course."

Jones handed Jaco the speaking trumpet. "Agreed."

Jaco put the trumpet to his mouth. Stand by to come about." Turning the man the wheel, "Quartermaster, turn smartly port to a course of west by nor'."

As soon as the bow began to move, Jaco called out, "Release the starboard jib and staysail sheets. Get ready to haul on the port sheets. We need to be smart about it, lads."

The bow of *Providence* was passing north when the bow chasers on the British frigate boomed. Plumes of water erupted short of where the sloop would have been had it not changed course.

Providence was pulling away when the frigate turned about 15 degrees. One after another, its cannons fired in an attempt to disable *Providence*.

The waterspouts and spray from skipping cannon balls would have drawn a crowd if they were along a beach and if they weren't so deadly. Two thumped loudly against *Providence's* hull. But that was all. The increasing distance meant they were safe. And now they could read the name of their opponent—*H.M.S. Orpheus*. The British frigate tacked to the west, but was unable to sail the same course as *Providence.*

Captain Jones informed Midshipman Shelton to take in the staysails an hour after sunset. There was no need, Jones said, to risk de-masting the ship. Once the sails were in the sail locker, he was to alter course to nor' by west.

* * *

A day and a half after the encounter with *H.M.S. Orpheus,* a dark shoreline slowly revealed itself to be a rocky coast backed by tall pines trees that came almost to the water. In the still morning air, a smell of pine mixed with the burnt wood odor from kitchen fires wafting out from the harbor.

The town of Canso, founded in 1604 by the British, didn't have a harbor or piers in the conventional sense. It was an anchorage protected by islands to the north and east. Small boats were pulled up on the gently sloping rocky beach. A French attack during the Seven Years War had prompted the British Army to expand its fort on the south side of Grassy Island across from the town.

Jaco felt his excitement build as *Providence* slipped down the channel unchallenged by the lookouts in the fort and glided to a stop opposite the small fishing village. Yes, it was September 22nd and Yom Kippur, but doing his part in defeating the British was the most important thing in his life. Today, religion needed to ride in the back of the buggy.

The sloop dropped its anchor near two anchored fishing schooners larger than *Providence.* Closer inshore, dozens of smaller boats were tied to log buoys.

As soon as Jones was sure the anchor would hold on the rocky bottom, both of *Providence's* 15-foot cutters, with eight men apiece, and its 20-foot long boat with 16 sailors and Marines and Captain Jones, were lowered to the water.

One cutter and the long boat crunched softly on the rocks of the sloping beach. Captain Jones was the first to step onto Canadian soil. Both boats were hauled up on stones smoothed by centuries of wave action. It was extremely quiet as the 24 men created a defensive position amongst the overturned boats on the shoreline.

In the second cutter, Jaco headed to the largest schooner and looped a line over a cleat before climbing aboard. Armed with a pistol in one hand, a sword in the other and his tomahawk in his belt, Jaco was ready for a fight as he crept around the two-masted schooner. Satisfied it was unoccupied, he waved aboard the prize crew of Midshipman Shelton and five sailors, and they began raising the sails.

Before he pushed off in the cutter, Jaco handed Shelton an octant, the book with the necessary tables to estimate the ship's position, and a chart covering Nova Scotia to New York. "Good luck my, friend. Remember, wait south of the harbor, and we'll transfer some food from *Providence* after the raid. Good luck."

Shelton grinned. "A little help from God will be nice too."

"Well, I hope the Almighty inscribes me in the book of life, even if I am conducting a raid on Yom Kippur."

The load on the cutter for the next trip was different. Unlit torches, a tub with a coil of slow match with a glowing tip, and several axes were its cargo. A seaman in the middle of the cutter held the sloop against the side of the second schooner while Jaco climbed aboard, followed by four men. On the unoccupied schooner, they splintered wood and ripped canvas, heaped them them in piles in the deck and hold. One man found a barrel of pitch and spread it along the deck. When they were done, a sailor in the cutter blew on the slow match until it glowed brightly and lit a torch handed to Jacinto.

While Shelton's schooner sailed into the Atlantic, four more ships were set on fire. Where *Providence* was anchored, in the soft light of the dawn, the burning ships made the harbor look like the entrance to hell.

While Jaco was burning boats, Captain Jones stood in front of his line of Marines, who were standing at parade rest. The butts of their muskets were next to their right feet, their left hands held at the small of their backs. Jones faced a crowd of men and women who looked from Jones to the burning ships. Jones spoke loudly so everyone could hear. "Where are the captured American sailors?"

A man stepped forward. "I am Roger Rafferty, mayor of Canso. There are no rebel sailors here. They are all at Glace Bay, on the north side of Cape Breton island."

This was unwelcome news. Not only did it mean they were unable to rescue prisoners, it meant they were desperately short-handed for manning prize crews. But Captain Jones had one more card to play.

"We are at war with Britain, so we have burned or captured the ships that are the greatest threat. Most of your smaller fishing boats are intact, so you can fish and eat. But I also invite able-bodied men to join my crew. Each man who joins and swears allegiance to our cause will get a full share of prize money for any captured ships from this point on, paid in British pounds."

Jones slowly waved aloft several pieces of paper, then handed them to Rafferty and stepped back. "Mayor Rafferty has the prize money formula. Any who want to join us, go stand by the boat that just arrived. I will wait five minutes."

The crowd broke up into knots of families. Most older men looked dour, and several women looked frantic. But five minutes later, 14 young men had hugged their fathers and mothers and worked their way to the front.

Captain Jones called in a loud voice, "Lieutenant Jacinto, take these men out to their new home. Mayor Rafferty, citizens of Canso, I believe our business here is finished. We shall now depart forthwith."

Captain Jones and the Marines retreated, leaving the crowd on the beach. No one moved toward them as they boarded the boats and pushed off.

Once the newcomers were added to the ship's muster, their first task was to operate the capstan and haul the anchor on board. With its sails filled, *Providence* left Canso just after eight in the morning. Several miles out to sea, they could still see the funeral pyres of the burning ships.

Royal Navy Dockyard, Halifax, September 1776

Halifax had been the official headquarters for the North American Station since 1759. When *Jodpur* returned from its proving run, the harbor was full of ships and the town of Halifax was crowded with Loyalists evacuated from Boston.

Captain Robert Dennis ran the base as the Resident Commissioner of the Navy, Halifax. He had accepted the posting rather than be invalided out of the Royal Navy after the Seven Years War. Dennis had been injured when his 80-gun ship-of-the-line had defeated a 44-gun French frigate and a 70-gun third-rater at the same time. Normally, a post-captain who had commanded a three-decker could look forward to an appointment as an admiral. In Dennis' case, due to his injuries, such an appointment would never come. However, with the money from French warship prizes he was well off. He had purchased a large tract of land outside Halifax, where he lived in an English style manor house he'd had built.

A messenger bearing a sealed note came aboard *Jodpur* at 7:20 a.m., when Horrocks was enjoying a breakfast of bacon and eggs, a luxury of being in port. The note was from

Captain Dennis, summoning Horrocks to the base's headquarters at 9 a.m.

Horrocks pulled on his royal blue coat and hat, and stopped momentarily at the watch station. He told Midshipman Hearns to inform First Lieutenant Griffin that he was in command of *Jodpur* until he returned.

From where *Jodpur* was tied up to the pier, it was a nine-minute walk to the three-story stone building overlooking the harbor that was the base's headquarters. The air was a crisp 29 degrees. By walking briskly, he didn't feel the cold. He was surprised to find Lieutenant Handley waiting outside the port captain's office. The door opened, and the port-captain's secretary ushered them in.

Captain Dennis came around his desk, walking with some difficulty and using a cane, and the two captains shook hands. "Captain Horrocks, may I offer you some tea? Handley?"

"Captain Dennis, tea would be refreshing."

Handley waited for Horrocks to answer before he spoke. "For me as well, sir."

Dennis sent for tea, then seated himself. "Captain Horrocks, thank you for coming on such short notice. I am glad to make your acquaintance, having heard good things of you as a captain."

Horrocks took this greeting as a good sign that he wasn't about to be called onto the carpet for anything his sailors had done. *But why is Handley here?*

Captain Dennis waited until the tea was served. He spooned in some raw Jamaican sugar into his cup and stirred. "Captain Horrocks, I would like to share with you the full contents of Lieutenant Handley's report that will go to the Admiralty. It is most alarming."

Horrocks inclined his head. "Is there something wrong with my ship? I thought all the needed repairs were made."

Dennis nodded to Handley, who spoke. "Sir, the honest answer is I am not sure. Is it seaworthy as I can make it? Yes. What bothers me is not what I saw and what we repaired, but we didn't see and fix. In Captain Dennis's cover letter to my report, he suggested the Admiralty consider having *Jodpur* sail back to England where it can be put in a proper graving dock, so we can take off all her copper sheathing get a proper look."

"Why?" Horrocks demanded.

"Sir, we could only inspect half the bottom, and I fear that if we pulled off all her copper, we'd find more rotten planks. And I have concerns about the masts. If there is rot in the wood, the ship could lose a mast in battle, or during a storm. I know the Navy needs frigates, but we can't send ships to sea that are not fully seaworthy."

Speechless, Horrocks turned to Captain Dennis.

"This report will go on the fast packet sloop leaving tomorrow. If history is a guide, the Admiralty will send a ship to relieve *Jodpur*. I suspect your replacement will get here in two or three months. In the meantime, I suggest you sail *Jodpur* cautiously."

"Sir, *Jodpur* is a warship. If I take your word as meaning that *Jodpur* will not be able to take punishment from a rebel ship, nor take a full spread of canvas, what good is it?"

"Our report did not cast any doubt on your abilities as a captain, nor on its crew. You have an excellent record and your crew has been extraordinarily well behaved while here in Halifax. That is a credit to your leadership. I will be sending a note to the Admiralty commending you and your crew. It should help get you a larger command." Captain Dennis stirred his tea and chose his words carefully.

"Lieutenant Handley's report, which has my strong endorsement, is an indictment of the poor work by one of our shipyards. Unfortunately, this is not the first time we have seen this problem. I hope the Admiralty will take our report into consideration when it awards future contracts. In the meantime, Captain Horrocks, you are caught in a dilemma for which I cannot provide any advice. It is your ship, and you must decide how to execute your orders."

Horrocks nodded. *What if its bulwarks cave in when hit by rebel cannon balls? My men will die unnecessarily. What if we spring a leak and the pumps can't keep up?* "Sir, do you have my sailing orders?"

"I do, and I was going to give them to you when you were ready to depart. When do you think that will be?"

"In less than a week."

"Come see me when you are ready. Your orders from Lord Howe arrived yesterday on the packet sloop."

He extended his hand, and Captain Horrocks shook it firmly. "Thank you, sir."

CHAPTER 8

LIEUTENANT SQUADRON COMMANDER

Off Cape Breton Island, September 1776

After leaving Canso, Jones took *Providence* well out of sight of land to rendezvous with Midshipman Shelton on the captured schooner *Acadia*. Jones transferred two more men for the prize crew, along with casks of food, beer and water. Shelton's orders were to wait out of sight of land, 20 miles due east of Canso. Further prizes would sail out of Petit de Grat, rendezvous with *Acadia,* and wait for *Providence.*

Before sunrise of the 24th, *Providence* glided to a stop off the small fishing village of Petit-de-Grat, just 10 miles as the crow flies north of Canso. When the anchor splashed into the water, there were eight large schooners anchored between Cape Breton Island and the much smaller Petit de Grat Island. Before the French ceded Canada to the British at the end of the Seven Years War, Cape Breton Island was part of an area known as Acadia. Those who lived there were known as Acadians.

Providence's cutters swung over the side, followed quickly by its long boat. With 12 men crowded on board, Jaco steered one cutter for the schooners.

Ashore, the Marines formed a line behind Captain Jones, just as they had at Canso. A crowd gathered, and again Jones offered shares of prize money to any who wished to join him. Twenty-two men did.

Jones withdrew to *Providence* to swear in the 22 new sailors and enter them onto the ship's muster sheet. While Jones was at work, Jaco ferried prize crews to the schooners. Each crew had a quartermaster's mate or bosun's mate as its captain, four sailors from *Providence,* and four Acadians. This left *Providence* with none of its original sailors except for Master Swain and Midshipman Garrison. With 26 Marines aboard, it was a risk Jones was willing to take.

As Jaco started to climb back on *Providence,* Captain Jones was standing at the gunwale, holding rolled up charts and a spyglass. He had a box at his feet. "Mr. Jacinto, where are you going?"

Confused, Jaco stood with his head and shoulders above the main deck and said nothing.

"Mr. Jacinto, you are going to take command of the largest schooner, *Granite.* Mr. Shelton on *Acadia* will be your second in command. Once you get it underway, *Acadia* and the schooners we just took, *Alexander, Brilliant, Cape Breton, Defence, Kingston Packet, Lancer,* and *Success* will join on *Granite,* which will be the flagship of the flotilla. Then you will follow *Providence.* If we become separated, lead them to any port you feel will be safe. I suggest Newport. Good luck, and Godspeed."

On the way to *Granite,* Jaco stopped at each one of the schooners to tell the acting captains, all of whom had captained fishing vessels before they joined the Continental Navy, of their orders and how he wanted to communicate. *Granite* would be his first command as a Naval officer.

After helping his mixed Acadian and American 10-man crew raise the anchor with the capstan, Jaco hauled on the halyard to raise the mainmast's lateen-rigged sail. *Granite* started to move. With the mainsail on the mizzenmast ready, Jaco spoke in a firm and loud voice, "Haul away."

Jaco directed three Canadians to grab the sheets that controlled the booms at the bottom of both masts' mainsails. As they pulled them in and were aligned and *Granite* accelerated. *Perfecto!*

Abner Jeffords, fourth and most-junior quartermaster's mate from *Providence,* already had the jib laid out on the deck. He hooked the head of the triangular sail to the halyard while an Acadian looped a rope through the clew of the sail. As each iron shackle was slid onto the forward stay, the bolt was screwed in. When they were all attached, the sail was raised.

Jaco took the wheel to get a feel for how *Granite* sailed. His schooner was the fifth boat out of Petit de Grat, and the others slowed to let *Granite* take the lead. As Jaco looked at each schooner, he was scared. These men were depending on his skill as a leader, as a navigator, and as a seaman to get them safely to port.

Granite plowed easily through the long Atlantic swells at the head of a ragged V, with the ships spaced a quarter mile apart. On the left, *Brilliant, Lancer, Defence* and *Acadia* sailed in echelon. To his right, *Alexander, Cape Breton, Kingston Packet* and *Success* were strung out. From behind the wheel, Jaco could see the hull of *Providence* headed east by so'.

Based on the chart in the cabin, the course would keep them about 100 miles off the coast of Nova Scotia. When they reached Cape Cod, he assumed Captain Jones would lead them in a sprint to either Newport or New London.

His anxiety went up several notches when he saw dark clouds forming to the so' west. They meant rain and heavy winds, and a long, wet and cold night.

With Jeffords at the wheel, Jaco went into the schooner's small cabin, looking for a large piece of red cloth. Finding it, he came out on desk and tied a rope around each of the two corners. It was his signal to the others to "Do as *Granite does.*"

Looking at the darkening sky, he said, "Jeffords, let's slacken sail to let the others close up."

Fear knotted Jaco's stomach. Already, they'd lost sight of *Providence.* As the commander, he no longer had anyone to confide in, or consult. He was more afraid of failing to bring the fleet back as prizes than he was of sinking and dying. He looked at the sky and muttered, "God, help me get through this!"

The other schooners approached until they were wallowing, with their sails flapping and the booms banging. Using the speaking trumpet he found on *Granite,* Jaco called out his plan to sail so 'west by south on a starboard beam reach and stay three miles off the coast. Once the storm passed, they would head back out to sea.

By the time each ship fell off and pulled in its sails, strong wind buffeted the schooners. Jaco ordered both main sails furled to less than half their size.

In the heavy wind, the waves picked up and spray added cold salt water to the cold, heavy rain. The staccato hammering from the large, wind-driven raindrops on the deck was distinct from the waves bashing the hull or the wind howling through the rigging, trying to rip the sails from the mast.

Jaco sent his crew into the small cabin so they could stay dry, as he stood at the wheel and kept the schooner running close hauled. Twice during the night, strong gusts rolled *Granite* 20 degrees, but the sturdy schooner righted itself each time.

As the lightening sky in the east hinted at dawn, the wind calmed and the rain stopped almost as fast as it had started. First light revealed an empty sea.

Jaco felt sick. *Granite* had survived; but where were the others?

Exhausted, he turned the wheel over to Jeffords. Through his spyglass, he could see the coastline and trees with orange, red and yellow leaves. Scanning the horizon, he spotted what might be a schooner wallowing in the sea closer in-shore. None of its sails were up.

It could be a fishing boat, or it could be one of mine.

He called his small crew to raise the main sails on both masts and the jib. With its sails sheeted home, *Granite* sluiced through the water on a westerly heading. Occasionally, its bow sent sheets of cold spray over the forward hatch.

Jaco studied the ship with his spyglass. They weren't fishing, they were trying to haul a boom on board.

The first man he recognized through the spyglass was quartermaster mate Graham Henderson. Jaco didn't know him well, but did know he was from a small town in New Jersey. He was *Brilliant's* captain. Seeing *Granite,* the men on *Brilliant* stopped what they were doing.

Jaco put the trumpet to his mouth. "Are you in danger of sinking?"

Henderson came to the railing near the wheel and cupped his hands over his mouth. "Yes, we're taking on water. The wind ripped the sails off, and we were trying to get one back on board."

Damn, damn, damn. Time is of the essence, and the men are more important than the schooner. Jaco raised the trumpet. "Get all your food and water on deck. We'll throw you a line."

Henderson nodded.

Jaco turned to his crew, gathered along the starboard gunwale. "Can anyone throw a line to *Brilliant*?"

One of the *Acadians* raised his hand. Jaco felt a twinge of regret that he didn't know the man's name.

"If *Granite* has a monkey fist on board, I can do it. Or I can make one, if there is rope."

"I apologize, but I don't remember your name."

"I am Henri Dupuis."

The man's accent suggested he was of French descent, so Jaco decided to try his rusty French. *"Êtes vous un Huguenot?"*

Jaco knew Huguenots were French Protestants who came to Canada to avoid persecution by Catholic French kings. Many came to the territory known as Acadia—eastern Quebec, Nova Scotia, Newfoundland and Maine. The New World gave the Huguenots and French Jews a place to live where they could practice their religion openly, rather than in secret. Defeated by the British in the Seven Years War, France gave up its rights to Canada. Now British citizens, Huguenots kept the right to practice their religion, become government officials, and vote. Nonetheless, old animosities died hard, and many Acadians did not like their new masters and didn't want to be ruled by kings.

"Oui, je suis, mon capitaine. My ancestors came from France, but now I call myself an Acadian, as do the men who joined you."

Dupuis headed toward the forecastle and untied the rope that held the hatch to the compartment where sailing supplies were stored. He came out holding in one hand a ball of tightly wound twine that had a tail with a small loop—a monkey fist. In the other, he had a coil of rope an eighth of an inch in diameter. *"Mon capitaine,"* Dupuis said, "this will do."

Barrels and crates now lined the deck of *Brilliant*. Jaco called over, *"Brilliant,* stand by to take a line." Five men lined *Brilliant's* railing as the Canadian twirled the monkey fist over his head. The circle began to get larger and larger, and Dupuis looked behind him to make sure the ball of twine didn't wrap itself around a stay or halyard. He let it go in the direction of *Brilliant*.

The ball sailed in an arc and crossed the gap between the two schooners. On *Granite*, the smaller line was square knotted to a line about half an inch thick. Two men on *Brilliant* pulled it in and secured it to a belaying pin in one of the racks. Its 10-foot long cutter was quickly loaded and four men boarded it.

Hand over hand they pulled themselves over to *Granite*. When the first man came aboard, Jaco asked him, "How fast is *Brilliant* sinking?"

The man replied, "It has taken on enough water so it will be hard to sail. Hours maybe."

"Tell Henderson to set *Brilliant* afire before we abandon it."

When everyone else was aboard *Granite*, Henderson smashed a lantern in the hold of *Brilliant* and used a torch to set the small cabin afire. Another torch went into the sail locker. The canvas sails quickly flared into flickering tongues of yellow fire.

Henderson climbed into the cutter and used an axe to cut the line tying him to the schooner. By the time he was pulled aboard *Granite*, *Brilliant* was on fire from bow to stern.

"Jeffords, I have the wheel. Find a place to stow that cutter. We may need it later." *Granite* sailed away from the blazing *Brilliant*.

Thankfully, none of the men from *Brilliant* were injured. They were, however, wet, tired and hungry. Jaco sent Jeffords off see what could be arranged to feed everyone.

Now with two quartermasters on board, Jaco had three people to share time at the wheel. He was looking at the sea, but not seeing it. His mind was focused on the four words Captain Jones said made all Navy captains successful.

Leadership. Take care of your men, respect their abilities and treat them fairly, and they will follow you through the gates of hell. No matter how scared you are, you must show your men that you are confident.

Seamanship. Know your ship and how it sails. *Granite* was a simple lateen rigged schooner. It was easy to sail, but still needed a crew.

Tactics. Know what your ship can do. He'd already found it was seaworthy in a storm, but didn't want to test its limits again.

Courage. It is not about risking your life, but making the right choices. Make choices that put your ship and crew's well-being first. If you do that, you won't have to worry about success. Your men will bring it to you.

When they'd boarded *Granite,* they'd found a small cask of rum. Jaco ordered a tot for every man. He took a large swig from the cup offered by Jeffords, and enjoyed the fiery sweet taste as the alcohol worked it way down to his stomach.

They were sailing in smoother water about a mile from the shore when the lookout called out, "Deck there, I see a schooner wrecked on the beach, two points on the 'larboard bow."

It took some searching before Jaco spotted the hull on the rocks. After studying the stern of the ship with his spyglass, he saw it was *Acadia.*

Jaco turned to the men on the deck, "Mr. Dupuis, would you please join me by the wheel?"

The French Canadian finished the knot he was tying that secured the *Brilliant's* cutter on top of *Granite's.*

"*Mon capitaine,* what do you need?"

"How well do you or the other Acadians know these waters?"

"Very well. We fish them every day."

"How much water do we have beneath our keel?"

"Out here, hundreds of feet. You can sail within 100 yards from the shore and be safe. Inside 50 yards, there are large rocks that come up close to the surface."

"Mr. Dupuis, are there any currents or fast moving water close inshore?"

"No, *mon capitaine*. Only what the tide and wind cause."

"Here's what I plan to do." Jaco explained his plan to the Acadian, who offered suggestions based on his knowledge of the region. It called for some tricky sailing, but the crew successfully brought Granite to within an eighth of a mile north of the *Acadia*. Jaco ordered all sails slackened. The jib flapped in the light breeze and the booms attached to the mizzen and main masts were swung over the port side so the sails would be totally luffed.

The only sound other than the creaking of the rigging and masts was the water lapping the hull. "Mr. Henderson, launch our boat and row it to the *Acadia*. Bring injured men back first, then the rest of the crew. When that's done, strip it of supplies and set it on fire."

Henderson brought back two injured men, who were gently lifted onto the *Granite*. Jaco leaned over the railing. "Mr. Henderson, how many more men?"

"Four, sir, that's all that's left. They lost four in the storm."

"Make sure Mr. Shelton brings his octant, chart and anything else he thinks as valuable and helpful to navigate."

A nod and an "Aye, aye, sir," preceded Henderson pushing off from *Granite*.

The quiet on the deck gave Jaco a chance to talk to the injured sailors. Both had broken bones, and one was bleeding from the mouth, which suggested he had internal injuries. Without a surgeon, there was nothing Jaco could do for them other than make them as comfortable as possible in the four small bunks in *Granite's* cabin.

Fires leaped up from *Acadia's* rigging. Jaco watched Jack Shelton push *Acadia's* cutter into the cold water before leaping on board.

The cutter dripped water over the deck as it was swung into place. Midshipman Shelton, now the second officer on board, counted noses to make sure his five survivors were on board before he walked aft.

Holding out his arms, the two friends enjoyed a manly hug. "Once we get underway, you can tell me what happened." Turning to Jeffords, Jaco directed his helmsman to move out about a mile off the coast. With any luck, they might find more of the schooners.

On board Sloop Providence, *September 1776*

Providence was running so' by so 'west, pitching up and down in six foot swells at night. Cold spray chilled everyone on the quarterdeck. To get out of the storm, Captain Jones had headed so 'east toward the warmer waters of a current Benjamin Franklin called the Gulph Stream.

While Franklin had been the Royal Mail Commissioner for North America in 1768, he had drawn a chart based on information from his merchant ship friend, Captain Tim Folger. Neither the Royal Navy nor the Royal Mail hd been interested in his chart which showed how the current paralleled the eastern seaboard of North America before bending east toward Iceland and Ireland. And so, very few naval officers knew of the current. Jones was one of the few who did.

When dawn broke, Jones wasn't surprised that none of the schooners were in sight. Being caught in a fall storm of that ferocity was dammed bad luck. He suspected that by now, whatever ships the Royal Navy had in Halifax had sortied with orders to find him. Hoping to find to one or more of the schooners, he ordered Master Swain to reverse course. It was September 27th, 1776.

Halifax, September 28, 1776

With *Jodpur* tied to a pier at the naval base, Horrocks allowed half the crew to go ashore. Horrocks was writing in his log when he heard the hollow sound of horseshoes clomping on the wood of the pier. Looking through *Jodpur*'s cabin window, he saw Captain Dennis lower himself from a carriage.

Horrocks pulled his coat off a peg and had the gold buttons fastened by the time the bosun of the watch rapped on the door. Horrocks opened the latch and Captain Dennis lumbered in. "Sorry, Horrocks, for the intrusion. How soon can you put to sea?"

"We're nearly ready. We should finish loading munitions tomorrow. Why?"

"A rebel ship raided Canso and Petit de Chat. They burned or took the largest fishing schooners as prizes."

"Do we know what ship did this?"

"Yes. According to a local who arrived first thing this morning, it is the rebel sloop *Providence,* captained by a man named John Paul Jones. He had the audacity to offer the Canadians prize money if they joined his crew!"

"When did this happen?"

"The mornings of September 22nd and 24th."

Horrocks picked out a chart and rolled it out on the wardroom table. "Where is Canso?"

Captain Dennis pointed at the two villages, and Horrocks marked out the distance.

"The rebel has three choices. One, he can go north. Two, he can head east into the Atlantic, or three he can head south. East is unlikely because it gets him nothing. There is a chance he will go north and conduct more raids, but if he has many prizes in tow, so to speak, his most likely course of action is to go south and run for home. With the port's help, I can be underway as soon as everyone is back on board."

Captain Dennis held out his hand to shake Horrocks'. "I have already sent patrols into Halifax to bring back your men who are in town. Good luck, Horrocks. I will have official sailing orders delivered within the hour. Sail as soon as you are ready."

* * *

The wind blew from the nor' west by north, letting *Jodpur* leave Halifax running with the wind under its mainsails. Once past McNab's Island, Horrocks ordered the top sails and topgallants released. The rigging and the masts creaked as they took on the pressure from the wind-filled canvas. Horrocks couldn't help wondering if one would break under the strain.

As the sun set, Smythe watched the crew reef the topgallants. Horrocks wanted to sail under just the main and top sails until first light. *Jodpur* had one sound and two repaired masts, and Darren still wondered if one would fail. His sea legs were back, instinctively absorbing the corkscrew movement of the frigate caused by the ship going through the waves at an angle.

At six bells on his watch, Smythe had the quartermaster's mate toss the white-painted wooden triangle over the stern and let the twine play out. Next to him, another sailor turn over the hourglass that timed 28 seconds. In the log, Smythe noted *Jodpur* was making five knots.

After dinner, it was time for the traditional Wednesday toast. The officers all grinned while the decanter of port was passed around the table. On Wednesdays, after toasting the king and his Navy, wardrooms on Royal Navy ships around the world raised their glasses to honor themselves, saying, "Ourselves, because nobody else is likely to bother."

Monday's toast was to "Our ships at sea." On Tuesdays, the officers raised their glass to "Our men." On Thursday, they would toast "To this bloody war, may it bring us all faster promotions." When Friday came, they would drink to "A willing foe and always having sea room." Weekends brought special toasts. Saturdays were dedicated to "Wives and sweethearts, may they never meet." On Sundays, the officers remembered "Absent friends who we lost."

Once the toast was finished, Horrocks his officers cleared the table so a DesBarres chart of Nova Scotia to Cape Cod could be rolled out. It was held down by pistols at each corner.

"Our primary mission is to either take or sink the rebel sloop *Providence*. If we can find the schooners, we are to bring them back to their rightful owners. This is not a fool's errand, because selling the prizes would help the rebels fund their dammed revolution."

Horrocks looked around the table. "As you know, we only have provisions for two weeks, and half our allowed amount of powder and shot. Practice firing is out of the question. However, we will drill the gun crews every day so they do not think this is a pleasure cruise."

The captain waited while Blackwell refilled each officer's glass with port, then continued. "We will sail so' west by south until we get to a point about 100 miles south of Clark's Harbour, at the tip of Nova Scotia. Then we will head west by south to a point 50 miles from Boston. That should take us about a week. If we do not find *Providence* or any of the schooners, we will return to Halifax and re-provision. Remind all the lookouts to be extra sharp. A sloop is hard to see, and schooners even harder. Mr. Smythe, you will be the navigator for this voyage. Assuming we run out from under these clouds, take a sighting to fix our position so we know precisely where we are."

"Aye, aye, Captain."

"One last thing. Taking *Providence* will not be easy. The ship is much faster than we are, even though we have a clean bottom. I will not risk having a mast come down because we are using too much sail. No royals, stun sails or staysails between the masts. If we are so fortunate as to find *Providence*, we will have to outsmart Captain Jones and get close enough to use the heavier shot and take advantage of the longer range of our guns." He regarded the search for *Providence* as a training cruise rather than a hunt, for *Jodpur's* chances of finding, much less catching, the rebel sloop were slim indeed.

On *board prize schooner* Granite, *early October* 1776

Granite was cutting through the water at eight knots with the wind coming over her starboard rear quarter. In the cabin, Jaco was working through the math of calculating *Granite's* position. A half-eaten stale biscuit dipped in rum and molasses lay on a wooden plate next to the chart. Shooting the sun from the pitching, rolling deck of *Granite* was much harder than from *Providence*. Because Jaco doubted the accuracy of his first fix, he'd done it three more times, an hour apart. The result was an odd shaped quadrangle that put *Granite* 55 miles so' east of Halifax.

He took another bite as he debated what route to take back to New London. Heading west by so' west would take *Granite* straight to Cape Cod and pass close to the southeastern tip of Nova Scotia. There, he could head west into Boston, or they could stay farther out to sea before running into the mouth of Long Island Sound, where they could go to Newport or New London. Boston was closest, but according to Dupuis, that route meant the greatest chance of running into the Royal Navy.

Newport was 200 miles, and New London 225 further than Boston. Walking off the distance to Boston with a pair of dividers, Jaco estimated that with favorable nor' west winds, Boston was three days away at six knots. New London or Newport would take five. They had food and water for six days without cutting rations.

Decision time. Where would he go? Before he could decide, he heard the call, "Sail ho, dead ahead."

Jaco placed the dividers he had been tapping absentmindedly on the table, and stuffed the rest of the biscuit into his mouth. Swiftly, he made his way to the wheel and called up, "What type ship?"

"Don't know, sir. I just saw it for a few seconds."

His stomach churned, and it was not from the difficulty of digesting the rum-soaked biscuit. *Out here, it could be any ship—merchantman, another fishing schooner,* Providence, *or a Royal Navy frigate.* But it was also possible that he'd just found another of the prize schooners.

When he'd been a midshipman on *Alfred,* Master Swain had explained that, from the deck of a warship, a small ship on the horizon could be seen from three to four miles away. A sharp lookout with a spyglass 50 feet above the water could spot a sail at 12 miles. At almost 80 feet, common on most frigates, the detection distance was about 15 miles, and on a ship of the line, where lookouts stationed were 150 feet above the water, they could see the sails of another ship at 20 miles. Swain also said the bigger the ship, the farther away it could be seen. The bigger ship with the taller masts had an advantage in that its lookouts could see farther. On the other, bigger ships could be spotted at longer distances by a smaller ship.

So, which am I?

Twelve miles meant at least an hour and a half on their present tack. He would wait until he could see the ship's hull before he decided what to do.

To pass the time, Jaco walked up and down the deck, looking at how the lines were secured and coiled. Back aft of the wheel, he stared at the ocean, willing the lookout to make a call that would help him make a decision. The waiting, as Captain Jones often said, was the worst part. At least when you are in action, you know what to do.

"It is lonely out here, is it not?" The French accented voice of Henri Dupuis caused Jaco to turn around. Jaco was not sure whether he was referring to a ship at sea or the loneliness of command.

"Deck, ahoy... I see three ships, two points on the port bow. They're schooners by their rigging."

"Are you sure there are three?"

"Aye, Captain. Jenkins and I have been watched for five minutes to make sure. It's three schooners, by God."

"Well done! Keep a sharp eye and call out if they bend on more sails. Jeffords, keep our course true. Mr. Shelton, please join Mr. Dupuis and me at the aft end."

The *Granite* didn't have a quarterdeck per se. It did have a small raised platform housing the wheel and the binnacle just aft of the mizzenmast. Aft of this was an open area Jaco appropriated as his quarterdeck.

"Gentlemen," he said, "what do you make of this development?"

Shelton answered first. "Jaco, I mean Lieutenant Jacinto, this is the course Captain Jones suggested we take to get home. They could be our prizes."

"Mr. Dupuis, are Acadian and British fishing schooners ever out this far?"

"It depends. This time of year, we go out into the warm current where the fishing is good. It could be fishermen from southern Nova Scotia."

"What about merchantman?"

"The British don't use small schooners to carry cargo across the Atlantic, and they use fast, small, three-masted square-rigged sloops as packets."

"So, it is unlikely they are Royal Navy schooners."

"*Oui*, but they could be shepherded by a Royal Navy sloop. During the Seven Years War, the British used their sloops to capture our schooners if they thought we were feeding the French Army."

"Mr. Shelton?"

"Sir, God willing, they are ours. However, I would be careful not to get to close until we know."

Jaco looked in the direction of the schooners, whose hulls were not yet visible from the deck of the *Granite*. "Mr. Dupuis, you know what *Alexander, Cape Breton, Defence, Kingston Packet, Lancer* and *Success* look like. If you please, go up on the maintop and take a look."

"Deck there, I now see four ships, all schooners."

"*Oui, mon capitaine.*" Dupuis headed toward the shrouds that let him climb up to the tiny platform above where the gaff's throat, which looks like a large, two-pronged fork, wraps around the mainmast.

"Mr. Shelton, did you save the flag we gave you for *Acadia?*"

"I did."

"If you will, please get it."

"Aye, aye, sir."

Dupuis climbed up the rigging and steadied himself on the small platform by looping his arm around the mast. The lookout handed Dupuis a spyglass. He scrutinized the schooners, handed the glass back to the lookout, and turned aft. "Deck, two of the ships are *Alexander* and *Cape Breton* headed roughly so' east."

The French-Canadian started back down the rigging as Shelton brought over a carefully folded flag.

"Mr. Shelton, hoist the flag, and then make ready to bend on as much sail as we can."

"But, sir, what if the Acadians took over the ships?"

"Mr. Shelton, if they retook the schooners with the intent of going back to Petit de Grat, they would be going no' nor' west, not so' east."

But where was *Providence*?

On board Granite, *October 1776*

Once *Granite* joined with *Alexander, Cape Breton, Defence* and *Success,* they rafted together so Jaco could outline his plan to get back to a port where the prizes could be sold. No one had seen *Lancer* since soon after the storm started. Of the eight captured schooners, five had survived the storm. Jaco said if they slipped through the British blockade with five ships, it was still a major victory.

Twice on the way south, they spotted the topsails of a square-rigged ship. Each time, the schooners added sail and slipped eastward and away. The convoy arrived off the mouth of Narragansett Bay around several hours before sunrise. *Granite* led them in a line a quarter mile apart as they tacked back and forth across the entrance until first light, so they could see the shoreline and avoid the notorious rocks along the deep but narrow channel.

Granite led the four schooners into Narragansett Bay with its Continental Navy ensign flying from its maintop. One by one, the schooners dropped anchor with enough room to swing with the tide.

Jaco spotted a cutter headed toward *Granite,* carrying an officer and four soldiers with muskets. On the pier, one cannon was pointed at *Granite* and a second at *Success.*

The coxswain luffed his sail and guided the cutter to the ladder that led to *Granite's* deck. When the officer came on board, every man on *Granite* was standing in a row between the masts. Jaco wore his blue Navy uniform coat and saluted. "Lieutenant Jacinto arriving with five captured prizes."

"I am Horatio Randolph, Newport's port captain. On what warship were you an officer?"

"*Sloop Providence* under Captain John Paul Jones, sir. We seized these schooners in Canso and Petit de Grat, Nova Scotia on September 22nd and 24th."

"And where is *Providence?*"

"I do not know, sir. We were separated by a storm. My orders were to bring the schooners to either New London or Newport to be sold as prizes."

"Very well, then. Would you and one of your officers come with me to my office?"

"Aye, aye, sir." Jaco turned to Midshipman Shelton. "Mr. Shelton, you are in command. Mr. Dupuis, shall we follow Captain Randolph?"

* * *

It was later in the week, and from the house where he was billeted on Corne Street, it was a short walk to Touro Street. Jaco crossed the road and opened the door to a beige, two-story building. The usher at the door to the sanctuary walked up to Jaco. "Sir, I think you are in the wrong place."

In his soft South Carolina accent, Jaco responded, "No, sir. I am Jaco Jacinto from Charleston, South Carolina, and my family is a member of synagogue Kahal Beth Kadosh Elohim. I came to pray and reflect."

"Are you Sephardic?"

"Aye, that I am. My family came from Spain via the Netherlands toward the end of the Inquisition."

The usher looked Jaco up and down. Jaco's oft mended clothes were a testament to the time he had been at sea. The tears had been stitched by a sailmaker, and while they would never rip apart, it was not the work of a tailor or seamstress.

"Are you in the Navy?"

"Yes, I am."

"Please join us. Many of our men are off fighting the British." The man guided him to the sanctuary of the Touro Synagogue, which had been completed in 1763. The wood paneling reminded him of Beth Elohim, built around the same time. Off came his naval officer's hat and on went a soft cap, knitted by his mother.

Jaco remained in his seat after the service was over, enjoying the quiet and serenity. He was at peace with his decision to join the rebellion.

Francis Salvador had been the first from their congregation to die in battle against the Tories and their Cherokee Indian allies on August 1st, 1776. By now, other members besides Eric and Francis would have been killed. He didn't want to be one of them, but if he needed to die to win, then he would.

* * *

A block from the naval base headquarters, each of the captured schooners were pulled to a pier and inspected, and notices went out to Boston and New York. The sturdy ships would be sold at an auction in three weeks.

Using his log and diary, Jaco wrote his report of *Providence's* and *Granite's* cruises. Official statements from the schooner crews were signed, or, if the man could not write, he made his mark over his name before they were added to his official report.

A cannon went off, followed by a second, and then more in a rapid sequence. To Jaco, it sounded like a broadside. Afraid the port was under attack by the Royal Navy, Jaco and other sailors ran outside, only to see *Providence* emerging from a cloud of gun smoke, flying signal flags from its mainmast yard and its halyards.

A larger ship followed *Providence* with the Royal Navy Ensign hanging upside down on its aft halyard. From the smokestack between the fore and mainmast, Jaco could tell it was a whaler, probably from Nantucket.

Providence tacked and headed toward an empty pier. Jaco and Midshipman Shelton and the schooner crews lined up on either side of the gangway.

Captain Jones was the first off *Providence*. After shaking hands with Captain Randolph, Jones put both hands on Jaco's shoulder. "It is good to see you. And I see you got most of the boats home. Well done, Lieutenant. When we have time, you must tell me how it went."

The Scotsman went down the row and shook each man's hand. For the Acadians, he asked for their name and then reassured the sailor that they would get their share of prize money.

With Randolph at his side, Jones faced the crowd. "Fellow citizens, this is only the beginning, and we will prevail at sea and on land. We just need more ships and men and we will beat the bloody British!"

On board H.M.S. Barfleur, *early October 1776*

Jodpur's long boat was dwarfed by the three-decker *Barfleur*. It was not the first time Horrocks had been on a 90-gun, first-rate ship of the line. He'd served on one as a midshipman until he'd been promoted to lieutenant. Serving on a frigate, he'd distinguished himself by leading the boarding party that captured a 44-gun French ship. As a reward, the captain had assigned him to bring the French ship back to Portsmouth. When the Seven Years War ended, Horrocks was a commander and the "captain" of an 18-gun sloop-of-war sailing back and forth between Portsmouth,

Bermuda, and Halifax, with detours to the Caribbean. It kept him out of England and off half-pay. When war broke out in North America, Horrocks was promoted to captain and given *Jodpur*. Horrocks could continue as a frigate captain until age, death, injury or illness ended his career. Or he might be selected for a bigger ship, probably a third-rater with 64 guns.

As the son of a merchant, Horrocks didn't have the connections many of his fellow captains had. He had to make himself noticed by his accomplishments. It was the only route to a larger ship and promotion to admiral.

Now *Jodpur's* captain sat in the canvas seat and held onto the ropes of the bosun's chair as he was hoisted up the side of the side of *Barfleur*. On the deck, he straightened his blue coat and stood at attention while the bosun piped "general call." *Barfleur's* bell rang three times before the officer on watch spoke through a trumpet, "*His Majesty's Ship, Jodpur*, arriving."

Horrocks doffed his hat and treaded the red carpet of welcome with six seamen at attention on each side. At the end, the chief of staff for Vice Admiral of the Fleet, Richard Howe, the First Earl of Howe, held out his hand. "Welcome to *Barfleur*, Captain Horrocks, I am Captain Samuel Pritchard."

Below on the long boat, Lieutenant Darren Smythe waited until the ceremony on deck was finished so he could climb the ladder. When he arrived on the *Barfleur's* main deck, the ship's fourth lieutenant was waiting to escort him to the officers' mess. Smythe was offered a drink. *Barfleur's* officers assumed he was making a social call while his captain met with the Admiral. Smythe wasn't. He was there to gather intelligence about rebel ship movements. He posed several polite questions to *Barfleur's* First Lieutenant. The officer excused himself and came back a few minutes later with a chart of the coast between Boston and the entrance to the Delaware River.

In the Admiral's cabin one deck below, Horrocks took a seat in front of Vice Admiral Howe. *Barfleur's* captain, a lean man by the name of Grant, sat on Howe's left. Pritchard, the chief of staff and a post-captain, sat on the admiral's right. Pritchard's demeanor suggested that he was confident that as soon as there was a vacancy, Lord Howe would see to it that he became a rear admiral.

"Captain Horrocks, we weren't expecting *Jodpur* for another month. What brings you to us so early?"

Horrocks explained his mission, concluding with, "Captain Jones and the captured schooners have disappeared."

Pritchard cleared his throat an an affected manner. "Horrocks, the rebel ships have not fared well. We are capturing their small frigates almost as fast as they make 'em. If they think that capturing fishing schooners will discomfit us, they are grasping at straws."

"Sir, more and more of their frigates are putting to sea, and soon, I fear, we may be chasing them all the way to England. Captain Jones has operated with impunity near our main base in North America. I say the best way to defeat them is to burn their shipyards. If the rebels cannot replace the ships we capture, soon they will no longer have a navy."

Pritchard glared at him. "That is a very... bold proposal. However, when the rebels lose, we shall want those yards to build ships for the Royal Navy. North America has all the timber we need. Are you saying we have the wrong strategy, and that a Royal Navy frigate cannot defeat this Captain Jones in his sloop?"

One false word and Horrocks' future promotion was gone. "No, sir, I am not. I am merely suggesting that any captain of a Royal Navy frigate who meets Jones must keep his wits about him." Horrocks stopped short of saying "or he will lose his ship."

Pritchard tone bordered on sarcastic when he spoke. "And, Captain Horrocks, you know his how?"

"While in Halifax, I spoke with two captains who were out-sailed by *Providence*. And I talked with a captain of one of our merchantman who served under Jones when he was the captain of a British merchant ship. He said Jones is a very, very capable and resourceful man."

"Jones..." Grant said in a thoughtful voice. "Welsh, is he?"

"No, sir. Scottish."

Vice Admiral Lord Howe clasped his hands on his desk. He smiled as he spoke in a condescending tone. "Then, we must put this Scottish Captain Jones out of business."

After some tea, Howe asked what mission Horrocks wanted for *Jodpur*. Horrocks decided not tell Howe there was a letter on its way to the Admiralty recommending *Jodpur* be recalled to England and thoroughly overhauled. "To hunt off Florida and in the Caribbean, sir. I am most familiar with those waters. *Jodpur* could also escort our merchants ships coming north."

Pritchard's tone didn't hide his sarcasm. "So, Captain Horrocks, you prefer warm water to going after Captain Jones?"

"Just the opposite, Captain Pritchard. I would relish the opportunity to catch this rebel, if I were lucky enough to meet him at sea. However, one ship by itself is not enough. If we want to catch him, a squadron of frigates acting in concert is needed to hunt him down. If we do not, I fear he will continue to embarrass the Royal Navy."

Pritchard sat back as if he were shot. This was not an answer he expected from Horrocks. Reports about Horrocks said he was very, very good and ran a very happy ship that could fight. They did not say he was not afraid to speak out.

The admiral saved his chief-of-staff from answering. "That is an interesting answer, Captain Horrocks. Who knows, when you return, you may get your wish."

As the boat rowed back to *Jodpur*, Horrocks was silent until they were back on the deck of the frigate. "Mr. Smythe, a word in my cabin, and then we will call the others."

Horrocks closed the door behind them and motioned Smythe to join him facing aft. It was Horrocks signal that he didn't want the conversation to be overheard through the thin walls separating his cabin from the main deck.

"So, Smythe, what did you learn?"

"I probably earned a bad report from *Barfleur's* number one. He was very reluctant to show me anything. When he showed me the rebel ship movements and the disposition of our ships, it was obvious that we are waiting to catch the rebels as they come out, rather than getting in close and preventing them from sailing. I do not think they take the rebel navy seriously."

Horrocks sighed. "I agree. They certainly underestimate this Captain Jones. Their attitude will not change until one of our frigates is captured. Then our seniors will pay attention. Unfortunately, that captain will pay with his career."

"Captain, I am counting on it not being us."

Horrocks motioned to the door. "It will not be. Now we need to let the others know about the fruits of our visit to his Lordship's flagship."

CHAPTER 9

BACK AT IT WITH ALFRED

Halifax, October 1776

Fearing that an unsound mast might break, Horrocks never had more than the mains, tops and topgallants set during the return to Halifax. He hid his worry from his officers by flying different sail combinations as a way to test their furling and reefing skills.

Horrocks was in his cabin, writing the report on each officer's performance he was required to send to the Admiralty for use in promotions. He heard the bosun's whistle, the ship's bell ring four times, and the officer on watch announce, "Naval Dockyard Halifax, arriving." He was applying the wax seal to the report when Midshipman Sean O'Hare rapped on the door and, in as manly a voice as a 15-year old could muster, announced, "Captain Dennis is here to see you, sir."

Horrocks crossed his cabin to get his uniform coat. "Mr. O'Hare, please send him in."

Captain Dennis lumbered in, using his cane by his right hip for support. He pulled a chair out from the table where Horrocks and his officers ate their evening meal and sat down heavily.

"Sorry to bother you. Horrocks, but I wanted to talk to you as soon as you arrived."

"Sir, it is always a pleasure to speak with the port captain, for with his help, *Jodpur* will quickly return to the sea to do its job."

Captain Dennis chuckled at Horrocks' facetious and slightly sarcastic tone, "I gather you did not find the rebel Captain Jones."

"We did not. All we found was an empty sea until we met up with Lord Howe and his fleet."

"How did that go?"

Horrocks held up a decanter of port. Captain Dennis nodded, and the frigate captain fetched two glasses from a shelf with a wood bar to keep them from falling out. He filled them, then handed one to Captain Dennis, who held his up. "To the King and to our service."

The two officers touched glasses and sipped the burgundy-colored liquid.

Horrocks held up his glass. "Friends we have lost."

The glasses clinked when they touched, and Horrocks took a large swallow before speaking. "Let us say we have different opinions on how to defeat the rebel navy. I think we should burn their shipyards. Captain Pritchard didn't take kindly to my suggestion that any Royal Navy captain better know what he is about if he meets up with Jones."

"Pritchard is an ass. I don't know why Lord Howe keeps him around, other than his brother is a member of parliament and on the committee that oversees funding the Navy."

"I didn't know that."

"Some day they will make Pritchard an admiral, and if we are lucky, he will die between his appointment and his posting. I am not sure if Pritchard is more dangerous to us at sea or in the Admiralty."

Horrocks couldn't help smiling at Dennis' castigation of one of his own.

Captain Dennis got to the point. "Captain, my letter with its recommendation to send *Jodpur* back to England should have arrived at the Admiralty by now. I give them a week to pen an answer, which should arrive on a sloop around October 25th. Rather than give you an order that could get us both in trouble, there will be a delay in the arrival of *Jodpur's* supplies. In fact, it may be November 1st or later before *Jodpur* is fully provisioned and ready to sail. And, if I get the response I am expecting, you will be going to England to get another ship, not joining Lord Howe."

Horrocks nodded. "I understand, sir. But what will happen to my crew?"

"Most likely, your officers and crew will be assigned to other ships."

Horrocks said nothing for a long while. This was not the outcome he wanted, but it was the reality at hand. He slid the envelope he'd just sealed across the table. "Sir, this has my evaluation of my officers. All of them should move up, and young Mr. Smythe should be given a ship sooner than later. At the very least, he has earned a first lieutenant's posting on a frigate. I've been around many junior officers, but he is the best I've seen. The men look to him as much as they look to me."

"All of this is in this envelope?"

"Aye, 'tis, along with some additional details."

"I find it commendable that you ask about your officers and men before you want to know what will happen to you."

"That will, I presume, take care of itself."

"In my report, I recommended that you be given at least a third rater. You've earned it, and my recommendations carries a fair amount of weight with my friends on the Admiralty Board who make such decisions."

Horrocks nodded. "Thank you, sir. I would be delighted if I were given a third-rater to command, but I would also be happy with another frigate."

"Ahh, yes. Frigates are where my heart will always be. They are the soul of the Royal Navy."

Newport, October 1776

Captain Randolph informed Jaco that *Alfred* was being fitted out in Providence, but could not tell him when the work would be finished. From the vagueness and evasiveness of Randolph's answers, Jaco figured the Navy didn't have enough money to get *Alfred* ready to go to sea.

In a letter to his father, he offered to contribute half his prize money to help pay to refit *Alfred*. In another letter, he asked if his father could get him a command of a sloop or a small frigate. Finished with his Navy related business, he penned another note.

Reyna,

We just pulled into Newport, Rhode Island. It was an eventful voyage and we captured nine prizes, but three were lost in a storm off Canada. My share of the prize money should be more than £900. I know it is a nice sum but I am not in the Navy to get rich. I am serving because I want independence from the British. I don't know when Providence goes back to sea, or if I will be on it. My father will know what ship I am on, so keep sending your letters to him.

If I am given enough leave, I will come to Charleston to see you. This time of year, the weather in Charleston is much better than here in Newport, where it is cold, gray and rainy. I look forward to seeing you.

Jaco

Every day, he mustered with the crews of the schooners at 7:30 a.m. on the pier. At last, on Tuesday, October 22nd, he was instructed to report to Captain Randolph's office at 9:30 a.m.

In Randolph's anteroom, he was joined by Captain Jones and a Captain Bergstrom, and they exchanged greetings. Just before 9:30 another officer arrived, Captain Hoysted Hacker, a merchant captain born and raised in Providence, Rhode Island. Jaco began to feel hopeful that assignments would be coming their way, but then the inner door opened, and there stood Esek Hopkins. Jaco's heart sank. *Not him again!* He entered the room with a growing sense of trepidation and glanced at Captain Jones, hoping for some indication of where this meeting was going.

The captains took chairs and Jaco stood against a wall. Captain Hacker jerked a thumb at the young lieutenant. "Why is he here?"

Commodore Hopkins smiled as if he were a fox about to eat a chicken and replied, "Because his father is a senior member on the Marine Committee and has helped fund the adventure on which we are about to embark."

"So besides having a wealthy family, how is he as an officer?"

Captain Jones answered. "I'll vouch for his skills, Captain Hacker. Lieutenant Jacinto will do more than pass muster."

Hacker grunted and eyed Jaco sourly. "He'd better." He turned back to face Captain Randolph and Commodore Hopkins.

"Gentlemen," Hopkins said, "Captain Jones brings us intelligence that 300 of our sailors are being forced to work in a coal mine near Louisbourg, Nova Scotia. You are going to retake our men, and, if you find any Royal Navy ships along the way, you are to capture or sink them. Captain Jones, carry on."

The Scotsman addressed the other captains. "As I know the waters, I shall lead with *Alfred*. Captain Hacker, you are to have command of *Providence,* with Lieutenant Jacinto as your First Lieutenant. Captain Bergstrom, you will command the brig *Hampton*. The commodore has your officer assignments. We meet tomorrow at ten. Bring your officers; we will go over the plan and my expectations. Captain Randolph has committed to have our ships ready to leave on November 11th."

Unbeknownst to Captain John Paul Jones and Lieutenant Jaco Jacinto, before they left Newport, Commodore Hopkins had a private meeting with Captain Hacker. Over several glasses of brandy, Esek Hopkins warned the merchant captain that Jacinto was a disciple of Captain Jones, and like his mentor the lad was an ambitious, insubordinate hothead. The two men glumly commiserated over the Marine Committee's refusal to beach Jones.

Halifax, early November 1776

In keeping with Dennis' strategy, supplies were slowly meted out to *Jodpur*. Since there was plenty of food and ammunition in the warehouses, Horrocks had to restrain Blackwell from lambasting the supply officer.

From the main deck, Smythe supervised the crew hoisting rope baskets of 12-pound cannon balls from the pier, up over the bulwark and down to where the powder monkeys stacked them in racks mounted to the hull. Horrocks, meanwhile, watched the captain of a sloop-of-war handily bring his ship to the pier. As soon as the gangway was in place, a blue-coated officer saluted the flag at the stern of the ship and headed toward the port captain's offices, carrying a large leather bag. Assuming the letter Captain Dennis expected was in in the mail satchel, Horrocks' would soon know the fate of *Jodpur* and his crew.

With nothing else to do, Captain Horrocks went below. A gleeful Lieutenant Blackwell was waiting at his cabin door. "Sir, I have the pleasure to inform you that by the end of the day, *Jodpur* will be fully provisioned and ready to go to sea. I will have the full inventory ready for you to sign sometime early in the first watch."

"Well done, Lieutenant. I will let Captain Dennis know, and hopefully we will be out of here before winter sets in."

"By any civilized standards, Captain, this *is* winter. I brought on an extra load of coal for the oven, and I ordered the cook to keep the oven hot to keep the berthing deck warm. We have new iron pails, so all we have to do is heat up cannon balls in the stove and hang them in the officers' quarters. If that doesn't work, I fear we shall all be sleeping in the berthing area."

Horrocks laughed. "Right you are, Mr. Blackwell. Just make sure your sums agree with what we really have on board before I sign off. That will keep the victual boffins back in London happy."

"Trust me, sir, they always match."

As he watched his second lieutenant depart, Horrocks mused, *That is precisely why I recommended that you be transferred to a victualing billet. You're a good officer but only a middling seaman, and you belong in a supply position for the Royal Navy. Your talents would be wasted if you were assigned to a ship, even though any ship would be fortunate indeed to have you as purser.*

An hour after the sloop docked, a messenger from the base commander arrived, bearing two envelopes. He insisted that he personally give them Jodpur's captain and wait for a response.

Horrocks set aside the letter with the Admiralty seal and opened the one from the port captain with a small dagger he had taken years ago from a dead French sailor.

Captain Horrocks,

Over the past few months, it has been my pleasure to make your acquaintance and become a friend. Again, I want to congratulate you on the exemplary behavior of your crew as they have billeted in port; I have communicated that to the Admiralty.

I am afraid, you may not like your orders, but they are what they are. H.M.S. Jodpur will become a winter project for my master shipwright, Lieutenant Handley.

It would give me great pleasure if you would again honor me for dinner at my home on Wednesday evening. I will have a carriage call for you at 6:30 p.m. Please convey your wishes to my messenger.

Respectfully,

Captain Robert Dennis
Royal Navy

Horrocks looked at the messenger, who was probably was all of 16. "Please give my respects to Captain Dennis and inform him that it will be my pleasure to dine with him."

With the messenger gone, Horrocks stared at the second letter resting on the polished wood top of the table. He decided he needed a drink before he read it, and filled a glass of port almost to the top. After two fortifying swallows, he slit open the envelope. Inside, a single sheet of paper was written in the fine, precise hand of someone to whom official correspondences are dictated.

Captain Horrocks,

The Admiralty has concluded that _Jodpur's_ hull is not sound. Rather than risking further damage, _Jodpur_ will be careened and all its plating removed so its hull can be examined and repaired in Halifax. You and your crew will provide whatever assistance Halifax needs to pull Jodpur out of the water. At such time, you are relieved of your command and are to return to Portsmouth. Immediately upon your arrival, you will report to the Admiralty for further assignment as a captain of a third rate ship-of-the-line.

Jodpur's professionals, to wit, its sailmaker, carpenter, caulker, rope maker and their mates will assist the Halifax yard until such time the ship is repaired and will then join its new crew. The others will be distributed amongst the North American Squadron as replacements. Inform the following to return to England immediately via packet:

Lieutenant Andrew Griffin to report to the Admiralty Board for further assignment as a commander of a sloop-of-war.

Lieutenant Nigel Blackwell to report to the Victualing Board for assignment.

Lieutenant Darren Smythe shall remain to assist you as needed and then return to England for further assignment on a frigate as a First Lieutenant.

As soon as you receive these orders, report to Captain Dennis to make the necessary arrangements for Jodpur's repairs and transportation of the above mentioned officers.

John Montague

First Lord of the Admiralty

Fourth Earl of Sandwich

Horrocks was exasperated. *Jodpur* would have to be unloaded *again!* And if the necessary repairs were deemed uneconomical, *Jodpur* would be ripped apart. The thought of his ship being broken up made him sick to his stomach, but, he had to admit, the risk of a rotted plank failing in the freezing cold water someplace between Canada and England was worse. So were rotted timbers giving way to rebel cannon balls and forcing him to surrender. Either thought was terrifying.

He laid out enough glasses for his officers and opened another bottle of port. It was time to tell them and the crew what the Admiralty has decided.

On board Sloop Providence, *November 1776*
The voyage didn't start well. Coming out of Narragansett Bay, the brig *Hampton* hit a rock. The hole was large enough so that it couldn't continue, and its crew was distributed amongst the other two ships.

Alfred and *Providence* sailed nor' east into the Atlantic to avoid Royal Navy ships blockading Boston. On the fourth day out, lookouts on both ships spotted *H.M.S. Active.* The brig carried eighteen 9-pounders, but when she was boxed in by *Alfred* and *Providence,* its captain decided discretion was the better part of valor and surrendered his ship, which was loaded with muskets and gunpowder for the British Army. A prize crew was drawn from both Continental Navy ships, and *Active* was sent to Boston.

Captain Jones then ordered *Providence* to scout 20 miles ahead of *Alfred* and return back just before dark.

Despite their northerly latitude of 42 degrees, the weather was pleasant, with daytime highs in the 50s thanks to Ben Franklin's Gulph Stream. A steady breeze pushed the ships under high thin clouds that filtered out the bright fall sun. Two bongs of the sloop's bell followed by a pause and two more bongs informed Jaco that two hours of his forenoon watch had passed and two more remained. Behind him, Quartermaster Jeffords held two spokes of weather helm as *Providence* splashed through three-foot seas under its square top sail, mainsail, jib and fore staysail in a 12-knot sprint to get to 20 miles in front of *Alfred.* Once in position, *Providence* slowed and tacked back and forth across Captain Jones' planned route to Glace Bay on the north side of Cape Breton Island. Each tack was two hours long and covered about 12 miles. Captain Jones' orders to Hacker were to take any prizes it came across. If, however, *Providence* spotted a British squadron of warships, Hacker was to lead them away from *Alfred* and rejoin the following day.

Jaco had asked what their orders were if they came across a Royal Navy sloop used to carry orders and messages. Hacker had glared at him and said that he interpreted the the order to mean he was to avoid *all* warships.

Back at the forward upwind corner of the quarterdeck, a position he favored while on watch, Jaco stared at the sea. He was scanning the horizon when he heard Henri Dupuis, up on the lookout platform, call out, "Sail ho! One point off the port beam."

Hacker had offered Dupuis a commission as his second lieutenant. Jaco liked Dupuis, but he wondered if it had been a foolish decision to make him an officer so soon after his change in allegiance. But there was no question the man was a competent watch stander and knew the waters around Nova Scotia. As *Providence* rose on a wave, Jaco spotted topsails on three masts.

Once the captain had used the spyglass to verify there was only the one ship in view, he told his first lieutenant, "I think it is a merchant ship. I suggest you think about when you want to clear for action."

Jaco called up to the lookout, "Mr. Dupuis, please find our midshipmen and Mr. Swain and have them join me."

Dupuis descended and disappeared down the forward companionway. Moments later, all four men climbed onto the quarterdeck.

Jaco handed the spyglass to the most experienced seaman. "Master Swain, what do you make of her?"

"Merchantman, heavily loaded and probably lightly armed. She is not a frigate, and she has every sail out that she can hang."

Swain handed the spyglass back to Jaco, who handed it to Dupuis. "Henri?"

The French Canadian studied the ship through the glass. "I agree with Master Swain."

"The captain is allowing us to approach. Unless it alters course, my intent is to pass down its port side out of gun range. Then we can tack to get behind and run her down. If it is an armed merchantman, we cross her stern close enough to rake her. We go back and forth until the ship surrenders. I want to avoid a battle in which we exchange broadsides."

Swain was the first to speak. "With all those sails out, her captain is going to make it as hard as possible to run her down from behind."

"Understood, but we sail several knots faster. My fear is that she is going to run us to a Royal Navy frigate. If that happens, we break off and escape." Jaco glanced in the direction of the merchantman. "Mr. Swain, at six bells order the ship cleared for action."

Dupuis waited until the others left the quarterdeck, then said with a grin, "Every prize we take makes us richer. This looks like a fat one."

Jaco shook his head. "Prizes only count if we bring them to port, and first we have work to do to get our popguns ready for action."

They were about four miles from the ship when Jaco heard a faint drumming sound from over the water. He focused his spyglass on the black hull. Suddenly, four of the black squares popped open and the ends of gun barrels, probably 9-pounders, emerged.

Jaco turned to the bosun mate. "Let's show him our colors, since he doesn't think we're British. Then pay my respects to the captain and ask him to join me on the quarterdeck."

A little later, Hacker coughed slightly to announce his presence. "Mr. Jacinto, what have we got?"

Sir, an armed merchantman riding low in the water, carrying twelve guns that look like 9-pounders. Based on the sails she is carrying, she is hoping we come alongside to do battle, believing her bigger cannons will carry the day. She's playing porcupine by showing us her bristles. I'd like to load chain shot and execute the plan I suggested."

"Very well. Continue."

Jaco put the back of his right hand to his forehead. "Aye, aye, sir." He turned to the bosun, who already had his pipe in hand. "Sound all hands and beat to quarters."

Word had already spread that they were about to take on a British ship, so the Marine drummer was already at his post next to the aft companionway. He waited until the bosun finished piping before starting the steady, staccato rattling noise of the snare drum that sent men scurrying around *Providence*. As the Marines mustered on both sides of the ship, Jaco yelled out. "Marines, hold fast. We have some tacking to do, so form up."

Lieutenant Bentley waved a hand in acknowledgement, and his 26 green-coated Marines, 13 on each side, moved aft and out of the way of the sailors who would be handling the lines. Lieutenant Jacinto turned to Hacker. "Captain, we're ready for action. When we tack to get astern of this merchantman, I recommend letting out our mainsail, jib and fore staysails to keep us in position astern longer. Done right, we should get off two shots from every gun before the Britisher gets out of range. Then we can accelerate and come about to do it again."

Hacker looked at his young lieutenant, thinking, *You're a bloodthirsty bastard, just like Captain Jones.* He could all too vividly imagine cannon balls crashing into a merchant ship similar to the ones he used to command.

"Do you still want to use chain shot?"

"Yes sir, I do. Chain shot take out stays and shrouds without damaging the hull or the cargo, and may bring down a mast. The swivel guns on the masthead, bow and stern will sweep the quarterdeck. Against a merchantman, the combination should get the captain to haul down his colors."

While Jaco didn't like the idea of causing casualties, he also realized blood and guts all over the deck might cause a captain to surrender sooner.

"Very well, let's start with chain-shot, Mr. Jacinto."

"Aye, aye, sir." Jaco walked to the forward edge of the quarterdeck. "Port battery, load chain-shot. Mr. Dupuis, we will be close; make sure each shot is aimed true."

Jaco saw a puff of smoke from the merchantman's forward gunport. A row of three geysers erupted from the water off *Providence's* port quarter as the ball skipped.

"Captain, they're taking ranging shots. We're at the extreme end of their range. I recommend that we maintain our current course."

Before Hacker could answer, two guns on the port side erupted in flashes of flame and clouds of smoke. The first geyser was 50 yards from the bow of *Providence*. It was followed by a dull thump as a ball hit the sloop's hull after skipping three times and losing most of its energy .

Guns three through six on the British ship thundered. Jaco heard the screech of a cannon ball passing overhead. He spun around and saw a geyser 200 feet aft of *Providence*. Two more balls skipped several times before hitting *Providence's* hull.

Hacker glared at his first lieutenant. "Mr. Jacinto, I fear they have our range. Mr. Swain, wear off a half a point to starboard!"

Providence's quarterdeck was now even with the merchantman's. "Captain, I suggest we come about to the port and cross the merchantman's stern."

Jaco saw Hacker tightly gripping the rail. The man was scared. *So am I, but letting them shoot at us while we do nothing is not going to improve our situation.* The next command was needed, but Hacker didn't move; he just stared at the British ship. Jaco went to the forward edge of the quarterdeck and yelled, "All hands, man the sheets. Stand by to come about."

Turning to the ship's master, he commanded. "Bring us smartly port to nor' nor' west. We may have to adjust afterwards. On my command, I want the sheets released for the mainsail and the jibs. Mr. Swain, you are going to have to keep our broadside perpendicular to our British friend's stern."

"Aye, aye, Mr. Jacinto."

"Ready about, release the starboard jib and foresail sheets."

"Helm a lee, let's get around quickly, Mr. Swain."

The bow of *Providence* swung toward the wind line. "Release the main sail sheets and braces for the top sail."

Jaco waited until the sloop accelerated and the bow of the sloop was almost perpendicular to the merchantman's course. Overhead, the mainsail boom creaked and rattled. "Hold on to the sheets, men. Steady, steady. I will let you know when to let it luff."

Gold letters on the stern of the British ship spelled *Mellish*. No stern chasers poked out of the captain's cabin, but several men on the quarterdeck were looking down at the much smaller sloop, now less than 50 yards behind. *Providence* was starting to cross *Mellish's* stern when the merchantman began to turn, trying to avoid a broadside fired directly into its stern.

Jaco turned to Master Swain. "Turn with him to keep square on his stern. *Mellish* will have soon have problems if the captain keeps wearing the ship."

Patience, Jaco, patience. Soon, you will be in position. Anticipate how fast the ship will slow!

At the right moment, Jaco yelled out. "Release the mainsail, jib and foresail sheets." Abruptly, *Providence* slowed as if she had grounded on a sandbar. Jaco turned to his captain. "Your orders, sir?"

"You give the orders, Mr. Jacinto. You seem to know more about this than I."

Is the captain being sarcastic and making fun of me, or saying what he really thinks? Emotions and fear had to be put aside. Jaco yelled, "Port battery fire as you bear!" *Providence* wasn't perfectly square to the stern of *Mellish,* but it was good enough.

The forwardmost 6-pounder fired, followed by one of the swivel guns on the masthead. Smoke billowed out from the second and the third 6-pounders. *Providence* was barely moving, so by the time the sixth 6-pounder fired, the gun deck was thick with smoke. Jaco could barely discern the outlines of the men's heads. The steady barks of the 6-pounders and the increase in smoke meant the gun crews were firing their second shots. *Mellish's* lower starboard mizzenmast shroud suddenly collapsed, leaving the top 15 feet swinging in the wind. Then the merchantman's studding sails gave way and the mainsails started flapping, no longer tied down. *Mellish* slowed abruptly.

Jaco bellowed, "Cease fire, cease fire!"

Jaco issued fresh commands, and the sloop accelerated. *Providence's* bow pitched down from the additional thrust from the sails. Jaco turned to Captain Hacker, who waved his hand and nodded. "Mr. Swain, we are going to come about again to port run with the wind so we can catch our prey. I want to approach from *Mellish's* starboard rear quarter, again luff up behind, and pound her again. We're going to have to eyeball the course."

"Aye, aye, Mr. Jacinto."

Leadership—The men are following my lead. Seamanship—we're doing what we have to do to gain the advantage. Tactics—we're crippling Mellish. Courage—I'm doing what is right, even though Hacker may try to have me court-martialed for taking over.

Jaco went to the forward railing of the quarterdeck. "Mr. Dupuis, solid shot this time from the starboard battery, aimed at the captain's cabin." After an acknowledgement from the Second Lieutenant, he cupped his hands around his mouth. "Marines on the maintop, I want you to shoot at anyone on the quarterdeck with the swivel gun."

Looking at *Mellish,* Jaco decided they had gone past its wake far enough. "Stand by to come about to port on my command." On the deck in front of him, Lieutenant Dupuis had men ready to handle the sheets of for the jib and fore stay sail. "Helm a-lee. Smartly, Mr. Swain, smartly."

Swain spun the wheel to the left, and as *Providence's* bow turned through the wind, Jaco called out commands until they were almost in position to fire on the stern of the slow-moving *Mellish.*

Jaco handed the trumpet to Captain Hacker. "Sir, will you ask them to surrender?"

Hacker nodded vigorously and raised the speaking trumpet. "*Mellish,* are you ready to haul down your flag?"

A man on the merchant's deck yelled back, "Go fuck yourself! It will be a cold day in hell before I surrender to rebel jackanapes!"

It was all Jaco needed to hear. "Swivel guns, fire." He saw the blood spray out of the man's body as he staggered back from the impact of 53-caliber musket balls. Jaco didn't see the man who released the halyard, only the Union Jack fluttering down.

Chapter 10

End of a Crew

Halifax, mid-November 1776

The wind whipped the Royal Navy's ensign behind Captain Horrocks as he stood at the forward end of *Jodpur's* quarterdeck. Arrayed in front of him were the 190 seamen of its crew. Behind Horrocks, Lieutenant Smythe stood next to Master Schilling and Lieutenants Blackwell and Griffin in a line with the ship's surgeon, carpenter, bosun and two midshipmen.

Jodpur had been stripped of its guns and most of its rigging. The ship's spars and upper parts of the masts lay on the pier. Its sails, 12-pounders and their carriages were returned to the nearby warehouse.

The frigate was ready to be pulled across the harbor and up onto the rocky shores of Georges Island. *Jodpur* was "dead." Horrocks knew it, and so did the crew. It was time to say good-bye. If it was ever repaired and returned to sea, the new crew would bring *Jodpur* back to life. Horrocks looked at the upturned faces and failed to keep the emotion out of his voice.

"Sailors of *Jodpur,* over the past two years, it has been my honor to be your captain. You have done everything the Navy and I have asked of you. Because of you, *Jodpur* was a highly respected member of the fleet. After today, I will no longer be *Jodpur's* captain, nor will you be its crew. Some of you will remain with *Jodpur* while it is being repaired. The rest will return to the barracks ship and be assigned elsewhere in the King's Navy. I expect you will serve your new captains as well as you served me. I wish you all good luck, Godspeed, fair winds and following seas, and hope that someday we all return to England."

Horrocks paused; his voice had cracked during the last sentence. "Join me on the gun deck so we may share a tot of rum together and toast our king, our country, and our navy."

Someone in the pack of sailors yelled out, "Three cheers for Captain Horrocks!"

"Hurrah! Hurrah! Hurrah!"

Horrocks turned to his officers and shook their hands.

Out of the wind and cold air, a tub of rum was ready on the gun deck, and wooden cups with *H.M.S. Jodpur* branded on the side. One by one, sailors filed by and Horrocks filled the cups. He shook each man's hand as he handed over a triple ration of rum.

With all the men standing on the empty gun deck, Horrocks stood by the mainmast. "To England."

"To England." Each man raised his cup to his lips.

"To King George."

The assembled group responded, "The King."

Horrocks raised his cup. "To our Navy."

"The Royal Navy."

A sailor stepped forward and turned to face his fellow seamen. "Empty your cups in a toast to Cap'n Horrocks."

"Captain Horrocks!"

On board Sloop Providence, *November 1776*

When Henri Dupuis climbed aboard *Mellish* to officially take possession, he found its rigging was in tatters, and the mizzen and main masts were on the verge of toppling. The wheel had spokes shot away. Both the captain and its master were dead, leaving a terrified lieutenant and a midshipman in charge. Eleven of *Mellish's* seamen had been killed and 14 wounded, many of whom Dupuis doubted would make it to port. The merchant ship's surgeon came on deck, acknowledged *Mellish* had been captured, and returned to his bloody orlop deck.

The eight sailors who'd rowed *Providence's* long boat to *Mellish* held the unwounded officers and sailors at gunpoint, while Dupuis followed the lieutenant on a tour of the ship to determine what repairs were needed. Their last stop were the holds to make sure that *Mellish* was not taking on water. It turned out that *Mellish* was carrying winter clothing, muskets, musket balls, powder and cartridges for the British Army based in New York.

Leo Gaskins, *Providence's* carpenter, and his mate were ferried to *Mellish,* and alongside their British counterparts they began to repair the ship's rigging enough to make the ship sailable.

Hacker wanted both ships underway immediately. When he heard Dupuis' shouted report that the ship couldn't carry much sail, Hacker didn't believe him and had himself rowed over to *Mellish* to make his own determination.

In the captain's shot up quarters, Hacker made an important discovery: *Mellish* was a payroll ship. A locked strongbox was carefully stored; a key, found on the person of the dead captain, opened it, revealing stacks of paper currency. Captain Hacker, an avid look on his face, counted it out and found the tally was £25,000. Dupuis, at the sight of this, whistled long and low.

Alfred arrived just before dark, and Captain Jones took Captain Hacker's report. Hacker stayed on *Mellish*, insisting it was his prize. For most of the uneasy night, Hacker paced back and forth on *Mellish's* quarterdeck. The big merchantman would bring at least £5,000 at auction, which meant his one-quarter captain's share for the ship alone would be over £1,400. They would get nothing for the cargo, however, for that would be taken directly by the Continental Congress for Washington's army.

Several times Hacker asked if the carpenters couldn't work in the dark, and each time he was told no. Work on re-rigging *Mellish's* mainmast would resume at first light after more rope and additional supplies were brought over from *Alfred*.

Throughout the night, the three ships sailed slowly so' east away from Cape Breton Island. In the morning, Hacker shouted at the men to work faster, and asked Dupuis how much longer repairs would take. Not liking the answer, he asked Gaskins the same question, and got the same answer: "Sseveral more hours, sssir. And you might be wanting uss to clear the captain'sss cabin of all that broken glassss, ssir."

Dupuis's suggestion that Captain Hacker return to the comfort of his command on *Providence* won him an icy stare and a terse, "No, I need to be here." Translation: *I want to make sure the ship gets back to port so I collect my prize money.*

The Acadian started to say that his interference was slowing the men down as they made repairs, but decided to hold his tongue.

* * *

Later in the day, *Alfred's* lookouts spotted a small vessel five miles to the west. Using a speaking trumpet, Captain Jones ordered *Providence to* investigate.

Hacker ran to the side of the ship where the cutter was tied and started yelling for a crew to row him to the sloop. Captain Jones bellowed back, "Captain Hacker, Mr. Jacinto is more than capable of taking that ship, whatever it is. You focus on getting *Mellish* ready to sail. If she sinks, everyone on the squadron will lose their share of the prize money. You don't want that to happen!"

The Bostonian scowled and gripped the railing so hard his knuckles whitened. If the wood had been soft, his grip would have crushed it. Work stopped momentarily, as those on board *Mellish* watched his reaction. Hacker felt their animosity and snapped at Gaskins, "What are you looking at? Get this ship fixed, and be damned quick about it!"

Jaco also witnessed his captain's discomfiture, but he was too exhilarated to care. Under his command, *Providence* accelerated towards what proved to be a two-masted scow, well down in the water. He grinned and, in a low voice, said to Geoffrey Swain, "I don't think they will fight us."

"Not much they can do," Geoffrey remarked. "She's a working vessel." He sniffed. "And by the smell, all they can throw at us is fish."

Jaco ordered the decks cleared for action and the gun ports opened. Then he invited Master Swain to take command of the approach. He hoped this time there would be no need for battle, for the memory of *Mellish*'s bloody quarterdeck still bothered him.

Mr. Swain studied the slow moving scow; he estimated it was doing at best four knots, while *Providence* was easily making ten, even though she would lose some speed as she came around. He didn't want to get ahead and give its captain a chance to do something dumb, like ramming *Providence.*

"Wearing the ship, now Mr. Jacinto." With its sails almost perpendicular to the wind, Swain turned the wheel to the port and the sloop responded quickly. As the bow passed through the wind line, he called out, "Release the starboard sheets for the jib and foresail."

With the two sails flapping in the wind, he yelled, "Lower both jibs."

The two sails slid down their stays to the deck. Jaco noticed that a bosun mate was already directing his sailors to bunch the canvas so they could be quickly raised when needed. He made a mental note to commend the mate in his report.

Under Swain's direction, *Providence* came neatly alongside the scow, named *Kitty.*

"Well done, Mr. Swain. Well done." Jaco spoke loud enough to be heard by everyone on the quarterdeck. Then he walked deliberately to the forward starboard corner and raised the speaking trumpet. "Captain of *Kitty*, this is the Continental Navy sloop *Providence.* Lower your flag and heave to, or we will sink you."

The man at the wheel of the *Kitty* waved. Its flag came down, followed by both mainsails. Jaco blew out a breath of relief.

Providence rolled gently in the swells, 100 feet on *Kitty's* leeward side. Now Jaco could identify its cargo of fish oil by the distinctive odor of dead fish.

"Mr. Garrison!"

The 16 year-old midshipman turned and faced aft. "Yes, sir?"

"Take Quartermaster Jeffords, six sailors and four Marines and go claim our prize. We will escort you back to our small but growing squadron."

Unfortunately, when *Providence* and *Kitty* rejoined *Alfred* and *Mellish,* repairs were still underway, and dark, lowering clouds on the western horizon threatened bad weather. As soon as the carpenters pronounced *Mellish* seaworthy, Captain Hacker returned to *Providence* and immediately retired to his cabin.

Through the night, high winds and cold, pelting rain battered *Providence,* and eight-foot swells made the deck feel like a teeter-totter. When Jaco came on watch at 4:00 a.m., he couldn't see the lanterns of the other three ships, and he feared for his friends on *Mellish* and *Kitty.* A merchantman was fairly stable, but a flat-bottomed scow, even though it could carry more cargo than a keeled ship of the same size, was at high risk in a heavy sea.

As the sun came up, he was relieved to see all four ships were still in a ragged diamond, with *Alfred* in the lead, *Mellish* to starboard, *Providence* to port, and *Kitty* bringing up the rear. *Mellish's* repaired rigging had held. *Kitty* was wallowing, but keeping up.

"Mr. Yassinto, a word, sssir." It was the old carpenter, Leo Gaskins whose missing front teeth caused him to hiss as he spoke.

"Yes, Mr. Gaskins?"

"Ssir, we sssprung a leak lasst night in the forward hold. I fixssed it, but we ought to start the pumps to clear the bilges sso I can sssee what other damage we have. That sstorm worked the hull pretty hard."

Before Jaco could answer, the quartermaster's mate came up. "Sir, *Alfred* is signaling for all ships to close up for orders. Should I acknowledge?"

"Yes, please do." Then he turned and called out, "Bosun!"

The second bosun mate, a young man nearly Jaco's age, came forward. "Mr. Joyner, pay my respects to the captain, and ask him to come to the quarterdeck."

"Aye, aye, sir."

Gaskins had walked over to the forward railing by the ladder to the quarterdeck. Jaco joined him. His voice was soft and quiet as he asked, "Gaskins, how bad is the leak?"

"Ssir, it would have quickly flooded the forward hold. The truth iss, *Providence* hassn't had a proper refit ssince it was built as the *Lark*. They sstrengthened the main deck to handle gunss, added more timber to the sssides and bulwarkss and built a magazine, but that was about it."

"Gaskins, start the pumps. Use our prisoners to work them, and ask Lieutenant Bentley to have two Marines supervise them. As soon as I inform the captain, I want to inspect the leaks."

"Aye, aye, ssir."

"Mr. Jacinto, what's all the commotion about?"

Jaco turned to see Captain Hacker wearing his uniform coat, standing his hands clasped behind his back, and rocking back and forth on the balls of his feet.

"Sir, Captain Jones has signaled that all ships close up on *Alfred* for orders. And Mr. Gaskins has informed me that *Providence* has a major leak in the forward hold serious enough to warrant the pumps."

"I was told of this last night. It isn't serious. All ships take on water during a storm." Hacker's tone was dismissive.

Jaco swallowed; his throat had gone suddenly dry. "Sir, I authorized Mr. Gaskins to pump the bilge out so he and I can inspect our hull."

Hacker rocked on his toes some more. "So, Mr. Jacinto, based on *all* your years of sailing, you think a little water in the bilge is a *problem*?" The sarcasm was heavy.

Jaco was scared, but he kept his tone even and matter-of-fact. Gaskins wouldn't have sought him out if he had not though the leak was serious. "Captain, we won't know if we are taking water until we pump the bilges. If we have a serious leak, we need to find and fix it."

"Mr. Jacinto, if crawling around our bilges looking for a small leak will make you happy, so be it. Permission granted —after your watch."

Hacker disappeared down the companionway, saying only to call him when *Providence* was within shouting distance of *Alfred*. Soon the sucking sound of the pumps pulling water out of the bilges provided a rhythmic counter to the hissing of the wind through the rigging and the slap of water rushing past the hull.

Jaco turned over his watch to Mr. Swain. With Dupuis on *Mellish,* and Garrison on *Kitty,* there were only three qualified watch standers—Jaco, Jack Shelton, and Geoffrey Swain. They agreed to alternate every eight hours. Captain Hacker, when consulted, had refused to take a turn. Geoffrey Swain came onto the quarterdeck and examined the sky. Gray clouds were giving way to blue sky. "So, Mr. Jacinto, what's happened since I went to bed?"

Swain raised an eyebrow when Jaco explained that he was about to inspect the holds with Mr. Gaskins.

"Well, let me know what you find. *Providence* has had a history of leaks over the years, going back to her days as *Lark*. It may be time to pay the piper."

Jaco found Gaskins by the pump hose. The carpenter gestured him over.

"Ssir, we're pumping fresh sseawater, not sstale bilge water. That meansss a big leak." Jaco swiped the water and sniffed. It didn't have the dirty, putrid stench of a bilge. It smelled like the sea.

Jaco waved toward the forward hold in the manner of a gentleman inviting a guest to the parlour. "Shall we, Mr. Gaskins?"

The forward hold was dark, dank, and smelled like sewage. Gaskins hung the lantern on a hook screwed into a rib, and produced two long, fat candles from a pocket. He lit both, handed one to Jaco, then pointed to strands of hemp sticking out of fresh pitch. "Here iss where I caulked lasst night."

Jaco examined the planking. Droplets of water oozed into the sloop. He worked his way aft and found water flowing in from two seams on the starboard side. In the aft hold where casks of food, beer and water were kept, the water was a foot deep.

"Mr. Gaskins, was this much water here earlier this morning?"

The older man shook his head. "No, ssir."

"So it is getting worse?"

"Yess, and if I keep pushing more caulk into the sseams, we rissk popping them completely, or forcing plankss apart ssomewhere else. We need to get to port, ssir, as ssoon as posssible."

In the magazine, the water was half way up the rack of powder kegs. "Well, Mr. Gaskins, figure out what you need. I am going to fetch men to move the powder and cartridges to the berthing deck to keep them dry. We can't defend ourselves with wet powder."

When he came on deck, *Providence* was slowly coming up the starboard side of *Alfred*. Hacker was not on deck, so after seeing to the transfer of the powder and cartridges, Jaco went below and rapped on the captain's door. He was filthy and smelled like a bilge rat, but the captain needed to know the scope of the problem.

Hacker did not look pleased to see him, and upon seeing —and smelling— the state of his lieutenant's clothes, ordered Jaco to stand in the doorway. When Jaco described assigning men to move the powder, Hacker grew livid.

"You moved the powder without my permission! Who do you think you are, *Lieutenant*? *I* am the captain and master of the *Providence*, not you, you lousy Jew!"

"Sir, of course you are the captain, and you make all the decisions, sir. But, sir, the carpenter is the expert on leaks, and he recommends we return to port for repairs. Now, sir, may we discuss what needs to be done to keep *your* ship afloat so *you* can make a decision on what we should do?"

Hacker had risen to his feet and was about to say something more when a bosun's mate appeared behind Jaco and begged the captain's pardon for interrupting. "Sir," he said, "Captain Jones wants to speak to all the captains on board *Alfred*. Immediately."

On their way up to the quarterdeck, Gaskins pulled Jaco aside and murmured, "Ssir, I found another leak on the sstarboard sside, a bad one that I can't fix completely. We need the pumps working more than ever."

Jaco passed this latest information on to Captain Hacker, who refused to acknowledge his lieutenant. Once on *Alfred*'s quarterdeck, Hacker deliberately distanced himself as far from Jaco as he could. Of course, that might have been because no one with any sense of smell would want to be near him just now.

Captain Jones sniffed, frowned, and scowled when he identified the source of the stink. "Mr. Jacinto, what have you been doing? You're bloody filthy, and you smell like a bilge rat!"

"Inspecting the bilges, sir."

"Might I ask why the *Providence's* First Lieutenant is mucking around the bilges of his ship?"

"Yes, sir. *Providence* is taking on water from leaks in her forward and aft holds. Our carpenter recommends we head home. I passed this recommendation on to Captain Hacker. Sir, we could escort *Mellish* and *Kitty* to Newport."

"Captain Hacker, is *Providence* in danger of sinking?"

Hacker didn't say anything for a few seconds. His jaw worked and he gave his first lieutenant a cold look, then addressed Captain Jones. "As much as I dislike the idea, sir, I believe the best course of action is to escort our prizes home."

"Agreed. Good luck, then, and Godspeed. Get everyone home, so our men can collect their prize money."

Hacker touched his hat. Captain Jones gave additional instructions to the prize captains of *Mellish* and *Kitty* before he ordered *Alfred* to make sail. He still had a raid to execute.

* * *

Providence's crew worked the pumps for an hour during each four-hour watch. By the end of the day, it took two hours per watch to get the water out of the sloop.

In the evening, Hacker allowed *Mellish's* sole surviving officer and *Kitty's* captain, a French Acadian, to dine with his officers. The Acadian spoke little English, so Jaco acted as his interpreter because Henri Dupis was on *Mellish*. Each time Jaco translated, Captain Hacker glared at him and interrupted. It was not a pleasant evening, and several of *Providence's* officers looked uncomfortable.

Jaco was sure that Hacker saw his fluency in French as another reason to dislike him. He suspected if Hacker knew he also spoke Spanish, the animosity would increase.

The next day, Gaskins found another seam in the bow leaking. The three ships hove to for two hours while hemp and buckets of pitch were brought from *Mellish* to *Providence*. Gaskins' efforts slowed the leak, but could not seal it completely.

Day five brought them within sight of Cape Cod, and Hacker ordered the *Mellish* to furl its topsails to make it harder to spot. A gray sky and showers of rain reduced visibility and helped conceal the three-ship squadron. By now, *Providence* was taking on water almost as fast as it was pumped out. Hacker divided the Marines, the British and Acadian sailors into four-man teams, who worked a rotation of one-hour shifts. The effort was wearing everyone out.

Shortly after sunrise on the 19th of November, the three ships, led by *Providence,* entered Narragansett Bay. *Mellish* had the Royal Navy's ensign flying upside down to show it was captured as it dropped anchor in Newport's crowded harbor.

After hearing about *Providence's* leaks, Captain Randolph sent over men to operate the pumps. He also gave Captain Hacker written orders, authorizing the men of a shipyard in Providence, Rhode Island to pull the sloop out of the water to keep it from sinking.

Before Hacker departed for Providence, he handed Captain Randolph a written report, and the two men spent several hours in a meeting, discussing what had happened during the voyage. Once Hacker was gone, Captain Randolph spoke with Master Swain, then sent for Henri Dupuis and Jaco Jacinto and questioned them closely. Finally, he slid two pieces of paper across the table and asked, "Is this the correct prize list by crew members?"

Jaco looked at it. It was in his hand. "Sir, I believe this is the one I gave Captain Hacker. I made two copies and have mine with me. If you wish, we can compare them. May I ask why?"

"The two prizes will fetch large sums. As officers, you will fare very well. However, Master Swain's report differs significantly from what Captain Hacker told me."

"In what way, sir?"

"Captain Hacker asserts you deliberately left him on board *Mellish* despite his direct order that he be brought back to *Providence* in the cutter, so that you could capture *Kitty* and cheat him out of the captain's share of the prize money. What say you?"

"Sir, Captain Jones told Captain Hacker that I should go take *Kitty*. I took temporary command of *Providence* as ordered by Captain Jones, who is Captain Hacker's superior officer, and captured *Kitty*. When I returned, Captain Hacker resumed command."

"And did you know what was on *Mellish?*"

"Sir, are you asking about the cargo or the strong box?"

"The latter."

"Sir, it is my understanding that Lieutenant Dupuis, Captain Hacker and Midshipman Shelton counted the money before it was brought to the *Providence*. There was exactly £25,000 in paper notes destined for Howe's Army in New York. That payroll does explain why *Mellish*'s captain refused to surrender."

"Yes, well, Captain Hacker's report states there was £24,000, so there appears to be a discrepancy. Where was the strong box and key kept?"

"In Captain Hacker's cabin, sir."

"Oh." Captain Randolph pursed his lips, then spoke. "Lieutenant, say no more about this."

Both Dupuis and Jacinto said, "Aye, aye sir."

Captain Randolph fell silent and drummed his fingers on the table. Then he asked abruptly, "Would either of you serve under Hacker again?"

Jaco looked at Henri, sitting quietly next to him. The Acadian nodded as if to say, *You answer for both of us.* "Sir, given a choice, no. He could not make decisions during a critical time when we were about to take *Mellish*. I can't imagine what would happen if we were fighting a real battle."

"Ah. Just so you know, Captain Hacker doesn't like either one of you. His report is not very complimentary of his officers or midshipmen."

"May I ask what Hacker said, sir?"

"He said you were insubordinate, much too aggressive, and needed seasoning under an experienced captain such as himself. He also referred to you a greedy Jewish bastard. Did he ever say anything like that to your face?"

"Yes, sir. After we took *Kitty.*"

"You know you could have challenged him to a duel, or requested a court martial."

"Sir, I don't believe in dueling. Men die for things they say in the heat of the moment that, if they thought about it, they would never say. And what would a court martial accomplish? It is not worth the time when the Royal Navy is at our doorstep and our Army is struggling to win battles. We are fighting for our independence, and we need every man. Those who perform well should lead our army and captain our ships. Captain Jones often says we have many capable merchant ship captains, but to win this war, we need more Navy captains." *And I believe I am a Navy captain.*

Randolph took a sip from his cup of tea to hide a smile. Jones' influence was unmistakable. What he heard was a very mature answer from a 17-year-old lieutenant.

"I have a task for you. There is a small sloop at the end of the dock. I need you to take the the captains' reports and my summary report, which I will have ready for you, and sail a at first light tomorrow to the Marine Committee in Philadelphia. Sail as fast as you can while avoiding the Royal Navy. The sloop does not have a crew yet, so you are free to take men from *Providence.* I suspect you will need a dozen. All you will have is muskets, pistols, cutlasses, and your wits."

Jaco looked at Henri, who nodded slightly. "Henri and I will ask Jeffords to be the quartermaster; he is ready to move up from being a mate. That's three. Midshipmen Garrison and Shelton probably will want to come along, so I only need eight able seamen. I'll have the names for you this evening. What is the name of the sloop?"

"*Pounds Sterling*. Appropriate, no?"

Both young men chuckled.

"You're sailing orders will be delivered with the sealed dispatch bag. *Pounds Sterling* is already provisioned, so take the rest of the day to get familiar with the boat. Oh, and make sure you bring *Pounds Sterling* back intact. It is owned by one of Newport's wealthier residents."

CHAPTER II

MAKING OF A HERO

Halifax, November 1776

A storm had deposited eight inches of snow on the ground. The temperature warmed to a degree or two above freezing during the day, melting the top, then dropping into the teens at night and refreezing, creating a hard crust that crunched underfoot.

The officers' mess at the naval base was small, but warm. At both ends of the dining room crackling, roaring fires kept the temperature in the upper seventies and allowed members to doff their heavy woolen coats and dine without shivering. The upper three floors were quarters for the officers assigned to the base. Captain Horrocks, due his rank, was given a room to himself. Those under the rank of commander shared a room with at least one other officer.

It had been 10 days since Horrocks had watched as *Jodpur* was pulled onto Georges Island and tilted onto a frame that supported its port bulwark. Once it was secured in position, workers had removed its copper sheathing. Through his room's window, Horrocks could see *Jodpur,* and it saddened him. His frigate was on the surgeon's operating table, and neither he nor the surgeon knew its fate. Overhead, a canvas cover kept rain and snow off the ship, but even with fires in pits near the hull, it looked like a cold place to work.

Horrocks had nothing to do while waiting to go back to England, and he didn't like it. Ever since he'd joined the Royal Navy, there had always been something to do, and he was either taking or giving orders. Now he was beached and out of work, just like *Jodpur*.

His parents had died 19 years ago, when he was at sea as a newly minted lieutenant. He'd gone back to Brighton and found strangers living in the house where he'd been raised. It had taken him three days to find his older sister, asking former neighbors who remembered him. She had sold the house and moved down the coast to Eastbourne. She made him welcome, but he'd felt betrayed by the the loss of what had been home. He'd walked away and had not spoken to her since. From that day on, he wouldn't trust a woman and had never married. For better or worse, until death or mandatory retirement do us part, Horrocks was married to the Royal Navy.

As ships stopped in Halifax to resupply, more and more members of his crew departed, for most crews were short-handed and the captains were more than happy to take men on. Lieutenants Griffin and Blackwell were long gone. Lieutenant Smythe's assignment, helping the newly promoted Commander Handley repair *Jodpur*, was drawing to an end, and soon he, too, would leave for England.

Lunching with Captain Dennis was one of Horrocks' few pleasures. Dennis enjoyed having a peer with whom to dine, and they swapped stories of life at sea and life at harbor for hours on end. By habit and custom, they addressed each other by last names without ranks.

Today the sight of one more ship departing for England, with him not on it, severely strained Horrocks morale. "Do you mean to say," he asked Dennis when next they dined, "that there was no space aboard that last courier?" His tone was exasperated.

"Now, Horrocks, you know perfectly well that policy and protocol are clear: ship of the line captains are to be transported by no less than a fifth-rate frigate of thirty-two to forty-four guns. So far, none has called here on its way back to England. I could turn a blind eye and put you on a sixth-rater, justifying that it was the only ship available, but the Admiralty would raise an eyebrow if I put you on a sloop or a packet."

Jodpur's former captain didn't want pomp and circumstance; he wanted his next command. "I am happy to write a letter formally asking to be sent back to England on the first available ship. Right now, I am damned useless to the Navy, and it galls me. I apologize for my persistence."

"No apology needed. If I were beached I would feel the same way. Hmm, hmm. Weather this time of year plays the devil crossing the Atlantic. With bad winds, a three week voyage can turn into six. Several packets are overdue. When one arrives, I will see what we can arrange. In the meantime, compose that letter but do not date it, and leave it with my secretary."

Philadelphia, November 1776

Rather than anchoring in the Delaware River, *Pounds Sterling* was directed to a berth at the pier. It was a 12-rung climb up to the pier from the small sloop. Slung over Lieutenant Jacinto's shoulder was a messenger's leather pouch containing the reports of Captain Randolph, Captains Hacker and Jones, Master Swain and himself. He was also carrying letters to the Marine Committee and the Continental Congress. All of these needed to be delivered as quickly as possible.

A heavy woolen overcoat over his uniform jacket kept the cold north wind at bay, and heavy woolen socks kept his feet almost warm. Jaco's keen eyes were quick to notice the changes war had brought to Philadelphia. Philadelphians were much more serious looking, even somber, and weren't displaying the gaiety and optimism that had abounded when the war began.

He reached his destination and rapped on the door. An impeccably attired Negro servant opened it. "Who might you be?" the man asked, with an expression that suggested that the usual visitors to this house arrived in carriages, not on foot, muddy and disheveled.

"Lieutenant Jacinto of the Continental Navy. I have reports from *Sloop Providence* and information on lucrative prizes taken by our ships for Mr. Hewes and the Marine Committee, as well as other documents."

The servant brought him to a waiting room, and Jaco stood shivering by an empty fire place, wishing there were a fire in the cold grate. The door opened.

Jaco turned, and his face lit up with surprise and delight.

Standing in the doorway was his father, arms spread wide.

"Welcome back, my son."

Royal Navy Base, Halifax, mid-November 1776

Captain Horrocks walked down the pier and watched *Sorcerer,* a small sloop-of-war, glide past and tie up. "I hope that is my ride home," he murmured under his breath. Water slapped against the hull impatiently, as if saying, *What do you stop for? Come back to the open sea.* Seagulls cried overhead and swooped down to investigate, in search of a bit of food. Later that afternoon, Captain Dennis sent a message, asking Horrocks to come to his office.

When Horrocks arrived, the shipyard commander was melting red sealing wax onto two letters. Before the wax cooled, he pressed a seal into the soft material. "I hope I have good news, my friend," he said, looking up and smiling. "*Sorcerer* is headed to Lord Howe's flagship with some urgent messages for both the admiral and his brother, Lord William Howe, in New York. It is supposed to wait for their response, then return to England. I am sending a note to Admiral Howe, asking him to allow *Sorcerer* to stop here on the way back to take both Mr. Smythe and yourself back to England. Your long wait may soon be over."

Horrocks wished he could sail out directly with *Sorcerer* and the letters, but procedure and authority would have their way. He thanked Dennis, even as he chafed at the delay. He took his leave of the commander, resolving to go over his kit and make any repairs or additions befitting a captain of His Majesty's Royal Navy.

Philadelphia, late November 1776

Lieutenant Jacinto received a summons from the Marine Committee to the Carpenter Building on Chestnut Street, where the committee held its meetings. As he buttoned up his overcoat, Jaco pondered what his father had told him over supper the night before. Esek Hopkins was now responsible for building and equipping ships, while Hewes was handling personnel and the Navy's finances. Hewes, Jacinto had assured his son, was more determined than ever to base promotions on performance, not on relationships, patronage, wealth, age or or seniority. Jaco hoped that was true.

He made his way along cold, crowded streets until he came to the tall door of the entrance. One of Hewes' staff members ushered him to a small room on the second floor with a small writing desk and a chair beside a window. Jaco looked outside and shivered; a sleeting rain had begun to fall. Soon it was pelting the cobblestones in a swift staccato, making them shine. He watched the precipitation until he was called.

The committee questioned him about Captain Hacker's conduct and Captain Jones' commands, as well as his own actions. John Adams and Stephen Hopkins sat with their arms crossed over their chests and glowered at the young lieutenant. They were the ones who had insisted that Hacker, a Rhode Islander whose family had connections to Boston's elite, be given command of *Providence*. After an hour of answering questions, Jaco returned to the waiting room while the committee deliberated in private. Then he was sent for.

Hewes was businesslike. "Lieutenant Jacinto, the Marine Committee has decided to give you command of a fast ship to fulfill a very important mission." The chairman of the Marine Committee looked the young officer in the eyes. He saw determination and fierceness, to go along with the confidence the lieutenant exuded.

"Your ship's mission is to carry dispatches and correspondence back and forth to our delegates in France, headed by Benjamin Franklin. You are not, allow me to emphasize this, *not* to risk the ship, nor allow the dispatches to be captured by the British. Defend yourself as necessary, but do not go prize hunting. You are a messenger, not a wolf hunting for food."

Jaco nodded. "I understand completely, sir." Sometimes, information was more valuable than gold and iron.

Nevertheless, he recognized that this assignment was something of a punishment. It directly prevented him from engaging enemy ships in the manner Captain Jones and he preferred, and, incidentally, prevented him and his crew from capturing prizes. The voice of Captain John Paul Jones echoed in his mind, comfortingly: *As you know, I have my detractors on the Marine Committee. ... because I am not one of their fellow New Englanders, Adams and the Hopkins brothers will do what they can to destroy my reputation. Nevertheless, I am here. The lesson, Mr. Jacinto, is this. Results count if they are done with honor. Everything else is bloody claptrap.*

"Good. *Cutlass* is a brand new, well-built, two-masted schooner with ten 6-pounders and six swivel guns. It has a sturdy hull, but its real strength is speed. It was not designed to trade broadsides with British ships, no matter how small they are."

"Yes, sir. Where is the ship, and when do you want *Cutlass* to sail?

"It is here in Philadelphia fitting out and it needs a crew, and we wish you to leave as soon as it is ready."

"Sir, I will visit the ship this afternoon and report back."

Hewes was pleased by this prompt assumption of responsibility, and glanced under his eyebrows at Hoskins, who merely continued to glower. "Do you have any officers in mind?"

"Yes, sir. I would like Mr. Dupuis for my first lieutenant, as well as Mr. Shelton and others from the *Providence*. I can send Mr. Shelton to Newport this evening to bring back the men I want for the crew."

"Do so, and report when *Cutlass* is ready to depart." Hewes held out his hand, and Jaco took it.

"Yes, sir, I will. Again, thank you."

Jaco forced himself not to run as he hurried to the dock where Henri waited, along with the rest of the crew of *Pound Sterling*. *Cutlass* was 100 yards farther up the river, gleaming in her fresh black paint, gently straining against the ropes tying her to the dock as if eager to depart.

When Henri and Jaco walked up *Cutlass's* the gangway, the bosun who was acting as the officer of the day knuckled his forehead. "Been expecting you, Mr. Jacinto. The name's Bradley Preston, and if you'll have me, I'd like to be your bosun."

Bemused, Jaco asked, "And how long have you known I was going to be *Cutlass's* captain? I only just found out."

"A messenger arrived from the Marine Committee this morning. And sir, he gave us a pretty fair description of what you looked like, dark hair an' all."

"I see. Can you tell me what needs to be done and how long it will take?"

"I can, sir. Our carpenter's mate, Jake Gunderson, he's on his way with the last of the rigging. The sails are ready; we can start hanging them once he returns. The cannons haven't been delivered yet. Come, I'll show you around, sir. This be a fine ship!"

"Please do."

Jaco noticed that *Cutlass* had a wheel with the rudder post under the forward part of the captain's cabin. In case of an emergency, one could remove a section of the floor and gain access to the top of the rudder and tiller bar. The tour ended in the small captain's cabin that would also be the officers' wardroom. Jaco was asking Preston more questions about how *Cutlass* handled, and who the suppliers were. The major unknown was the status of the cannon. All Preston knew was the name of the foundry. It was the same one that had produced cannons for *Alfred*.

Gunderson arrived with the ropes, reported to his new captain. Introductions were made all around, Preston returned to his watch, and Gunderson to the task of rigging sails. Jaco cocked an eye at his friend.

"Henri?"

"They seem good enough."

"Agreed, but we need a crew. I'll find out about the cannon if you man our new ship. I will tell Mr. Hewes that our departure date depends on when the cannon are ready."

"*D'accord*. Who do you intend to steal from *Providence*?"

Jaco grinned. "Jeffords as quartermaster, Shelton and Garrison as midshipmen. The Marine Committee has authorized a crew of 26 sailors and six Marines. Right now, we have Shelton, Preston, Gunderson, you and me. You get get the rest, and I'll look into the cannon."

"*D'accord.* With your permission, Shelton and I will take *Pound Sterling* and be back with the crew in a week."

"*Perfecto!*"

* * *

That evening, at his father's house, Jaco found three letters waiting for him on the kitchen table. Jaco recognized Reyna's impeccable handwriting on all three. He poured a glass of wine, lit one of the spermaceti candles that burned with the brightest flame, and sat down to read. The first was a description of the British attempt to take Charleston. He could easily envision the feisty Reyna wanting to do her part in driving the British out of South Carolina. In her second letter, Reyna described how tension and division between Loyalists and Patriots was rising in Charleston. Rumors were flying that British agents were stirring up the Cherokees to turn them against the South Carolinians.

Letter three had been written in early October.

Jaco,

I hope this letter finds you well. Your father's letters tell us about your adventures. We Charlestonians—I in particular—are very proud of you.

The British did not take kindly to their defeat here in Charleston earlier this summer, and we fear they will return with a vengeance. And the open seas are theirs to command. The British captured four of my father's ships. Lloyds, by the order of the King, will no longer insure our ships, so everything is at risk when one sails from either side of the Atlantic.

It is very difficult here. The harbor that used to be full of ships is often empty. Many shopkeepers have shuttered their doors because they have little or nothing to sell. The owners are living off the charity of their neighbors, or working for others. Many of the men are gone because they joined the army.

Mordecai Sheftall was appointed Commissary General of Georgia and South Carolina. Abigail Minis, from the congregation in Savannah, and my grandmother, Miriam Bildesheim, whom you know, are helping to feed and equip the soldiers under General Moultrie, who are defending our city. Mrs. Minis is well into her seventies, yet still has all her faculties and inspires all of us. The Royal Governor of Georgia has put out a warrant to arrest her and my grandmother, but no one, not even the most fervent Loyalist, will apprehend either. The scarcities are affecting everyone, and Miriam sees to it that anyone who has lost much will at least have food to eat.

The university has suspended classes because professors and students are divided in their loyalties. Instead of focusing on biology, anatomy and medicine, classroom discussions were becoming heated and contentious over politics. It is sad that this war for our freedom is pitting friend against friend. I hope that when it all ends, we can put our differences aside and once again be neighborly South Carolinians and Charlestonians.

I am confident, despite the hardships we are enduring, that our cause is just and we will prevail. Come back soon, safe and sound. I wish to hear you tell about your exploits.

Reyna

Thoughtfully, Jaco put down this last letter. *I wonder if she is putting on a brave face and things are really worse than she describes?* He made a mental note to ask his father.

* * *

Hopewell Furnace foundry was a three hours by horseback from downtown Philadelphia, roughly three-quarters of the way to Reading, Pennsylvania. Jaco set out at first light. At first, Gustav Freiburg, the foundry manager, didn't recognize Jaco from his earlier visit with Gunner Reasoner. Once Freiburg understood that Jaco was here to see about equipping a new ship he was to command, Gustav led the way to his proofing range and showed Jaco the four finished 6-pounder cannon currently mounted on carriages.

Jaco asked how long it might take for ten cannon to be readied.

"We have three molds for 6-pounders," Gustav explained. "We plan to cast three next Monday and three more on Tuesday. They have to cool for at least two days before we bore them out, and we can bore two 6-pounders a day."

"Sir," Jaco said, "*Cutlass* has orders to sail at the end of next week, or as soon as she is fully equipped. It will take a day to get the the cannon to Philadelphia, and another to load them onboard. I need all 10 as soon as possible."

"Lieutenant, we are one of only two foundries making cannon for the Army and for the Navy, and we can only make them so fast. But I shall make your order my priority. You may watch us pour three this evening before you leave. Come back next Wednesday with wagons, and we can proof the remaining six. I'll cast extras, so that if some fail we shall still have enough. I already have the carriages built."

"Thank you." Jaco's respect for Freiburg increased. Here was a man who understood the differential calculous of *planned* and *actual* outcomes, and how to adjust for inevitable discrepancies.

"Good. Follow me, sir, and we shall proof the four we have. I will have my men load and fire them."

"Actually, I would like to load and fire."

Freiburg was a fairly astute judge of character; he sized up the young man before him making the unusual request. A foundry manager had no business letting fools anywhere near untried cannon. Jacinto's lean face was weathered, his hands hard and calloused. That told Freiburg he was accustomed to manual labor and not a dandy who stood back and gave orders he himself could not execute. Freiburg decided here was an opportunity to proof more than cannon; he would learn something of this officer's mettle. "As you wish, Lieutenant."

The proofing or testing range had an earthen berm 15 feet tall about 50 yards from a bricked surface; there were no targets. A cart behind the guns held 24 cartridges and 12 iron balls.

"Is there something we can use as a target?"

"We have some old barrel ends. No one has ever asked for targets."

"*Perfecto!* I want my gunners to hit what they aim at. Please get them, and a lantern."

"And why do you need the lantern?"

"I want to look down the gun barrels. If the bores are smooth and true, the cannons will be more accurate."

Freiburg nodded. "As you wish."

As Freiburg saw to the placing of the targets, Jaco inspected the cannon. The bores looked acceptably smooth, but he also wanted to check the centering. With one cannon after another, he inserted a rammer down the bore and adjusted the shaft so it looked as if it were centered in the barrel. Then he put a small wedge of wood under the shaft to keep it in place before getting behind the breech and looking down the barrel. His theory was that if the shaft was down the center of the barrel, the iron balls would go where they were aimed. It was a check he planned to perform with each of the ten guns they took on board *Cutlass*. The first two barrels seemed centered, as did the fourth, but he had doubts about the third.

Returning to the first cannon, he removed the rammer and pressed first one and then a second powder cartridge hard against the breech, rammed the wad home, and shoved the ball down the barrel. Jaco slid the rammer in three times to make sure the ball was seated. Then he put the rammer back in the rack. Freiburg, who was observing his actions, handed him a small flask with fine gunpowder and a long needle. Jaco shoved the prick down the touchhole twice, feeling the canvas give way, before pouring gunpowder into the touchhole. Next, he turned the vertical adjustment screw so that the gun barrel was aligned with the target's center. When he stood up, Freiburg handed him a glowing piece of hemp lashed to an iron rod.

The powder at the top of the touchhole flared, and the 6-pounder barked. The first wooden barrel lid disintegrated into a shower of splinters.

Grinning, Jaco took the sponge, dipped it into the water bucket next to the cannon, and shoved it down the barrel while Freiburg put his hand over the touchhole. He pulled the sponge out, then shoved it in a second time. Freiburg's eyebrow went up. Not every man cleaned a barrel twice between loads.

Freiburg handed Jaco two fresh powder cartridges. Cannon two fired right on target. The third cannon shot very high and to the left, both times Jaco tested it. "Mr. Freiburg," he said, "the bore is off center. We won't accept it. Please make sure the bores are properly aligned in the new guns that are cast. My gunners need to to hit what they aim at!"

The cannon-maker rubbed his jaw and didn't argue. At this range, he couldn't blame an out of round cannonball. He also knew the army would be glad enough of any cannons this young captain did not take, and a gun team that knew a cannon's faults could compensate for them.

The fourth cannon was fine.

Jaco used a steel scribe to write his initials and the date on the three cannons he accepted.

Royal Navy Base, Halifax, early December 1776
Captain Horrocks was taking his daily stroll along the waterfront when he spotted *H.M.S. Sorcerer* entering the harbor. Its mizzenmast was tilted at an odd angle and not carrying any sails. As the sloop passed, he studied how the crew had adjusted the mast's stays to keep it from falling over.

Repairing a mast pier side was a simple task and well within the base's capability. Unless *Sorcerer* had sustained damage he couldn't see, Horrocks was confident that the sloop would be fixed and underway in a few days, hopefully with him and young Mr. Smythe on board as passengers. It was high time he was headed back to England!

Five days later, *Sorcerer* put out to sea from Halifax, with both Captain Horrocks and Lieutenant Smythe aboard as supercargo.

* * *

The first three days were bitter cold. Gusty arctic winds buffeted the *Sorcerer,* and eight-foot seas forced the sloop's captain to shorten sail. But by the morning of the fourth day, the front had passed and the sloop pushed eastward, running with the westerly winds.

Cognizant of his seniority, Horrocks deliberately stayed out of the way of *Sorcerer's* captain, Lieutenant Stephen De Gray. In a concession to his rank, Horrocks was given the small stateroom normally occupied by the sloop's other lieutenant, who now slept in a hammock with Lieutenant Smythe at the aft end of the berthing deck.

Horrocks ate with the *Sorcerer's* officers and midshipmen in *Sorcerer's* small captain's cabin. It was an opportunity for the junior officers to get to know a senior captain who, at some point, might help their career. In discussions about fighting rebel ships, Horrocks deferred to Smythe because his own combat experience came from fighting Britain's traditional enemy, the French, not their current enemy, the colonials.

Sorcerer's officers still viewed the French as the real foe. The two countries had been rivals for centuries, dating back to 1066 when William the Conqueror invaded England. De Gray's forebears had come to England with the Norman conquerors in 1066, and stayed. More recently, the British had fought the French in The Nine Years war that ended in 1697. Five years later, England was again fighting France in the War of Spanish Succession, with the British aligned with the Holy Roman Empire and the Dutch against the French and Spanish. That conflict had lasted until 1714. Three decades later, France and Britain were again at each other's throats in the War of Austrian Succession that lasted from 1744 to 1748. After five years of tense peace, the Seven Years War began in 1756 and continued until 1763. To the officers who knew their country's history, it was only a matter of time before France took the rebels' side.

When Horrocks was on deck, De Gray would ask the captain's opinion before he executed a decision on handling his ship. Rather than give approval, Horrocks posed questions that helped the young officer evaluate his alternatives. He did not want De Gray to become dependent on him for advice.

De Gray readily accepted Smythe's offer to stand watch, because as it reduced the workload on *Sorcerer's* officers. This was his quartermaster's first round trip and he was, as De Gray said, still learning his trade.

Standing watches and teaching the midshipmen gave Smythe something to do that he enjoyed. Twice a day, the midshipmen would take sightings so they could compare their plots to his. After five days, he was gratified to see all three plotted positions formed a triangle about 10 miles a side—close sightings on the open sea. Today, they were 400 miles south of the southern tip of Greenland, averaging six knots. If all went well, in about a week he would walk through the front door of his parent's house for the first time in two years.

On board Schooner Cutlass, *December 1776*

As they left the Delaware River and entered Delaware Bay, *Cutlass* surged like a horse wanting to lead a stampeding herd. Jaco felt as if he were holding the schooner back.

He grinned at Henri Dupuis, standing next to him on the small quarterdeck. "Mr. Dupuis, if you will, when we pass Cape May I want to set all our sails and see what *Cutlass* can do. Our course will be nor' east by north with the wind over our port side."

The Acadian smiled as he answered. "*Mais oui, mon capitaine!*"

At first, Jaco and the officers were surprised by how fast *Cutlass* could sail. Watch after watch, the schooner averaged close to 10 knots. Then the blue skies and steady winds were replaced by a cold, thick fog and light, variable winds. The sails flapped and the booms rattled as *Cutlass* slowed to a crawl. They were, Jaco estimated, at 17° west longitude, 50° north latitude, several hundred miles west of Ireland. *Cutlass* was about to turn southeast to head for Brest. On the quarterdeck, Jaco looked at the rolling Atlantic swells. The lack of white caps on the gray water was more evidence that the wind had slackened. Worse, a damp fog was settling in.

"Henri, what do you make of the conditions?"

"I think, *mon capitaine,* our days of making 250 miles per a day are over. And if we should run into one of His Majesty's men-of-war, we will not be able to run away."

"A Royal Navy frigate would have the same slack winds."

"Ah, *mon ami,* but if we are unlucky and one finds us in this fog, their cannon balls will catch us before we are out of range!"

"Aye, I think we should fly our gaff topsails to catch whatever wind there is. Mr. Jeffords, call the watch to make sail."

Once the gaff topsails were trimmed and sheeted home, *Cutlass* responded ever so slightly. At best, the schooner was making two knots.

On a large man-of-war, lookouts could be posted on the topmost yard that often stuck out above the fog. *Cutlass*'s lookout platform was, at best, 50 feet above the water. Not only was their visibility limited, a larger ship would be able to spot *Cutlass* and maneuver to intercept them while *Cutlass*'s lookout was still blind.

They'd not seen another ship in days, but now they were approaching the Royal Navy's backyard. Jaco's stomach churned, and his gut warned him that His Majesty's frigates were out there. He wished for a God's eye view of the ocean so he knew where they were.

The dispatch box bolted to the port bulwark in his cabin contained three oilskin pouches with letters from the Continental Congress to Benjamin Franklin. Each pouch had two-cast iron bars in the bottom; if they were in danger of being captured, he was to toss them into the ocean.

The cold steel of the key on a leather thong against his chest was a constant reminder that he needed to get to France and avoid the Royal Navy at all costs. The metal never seemed to warm up. The key was only to be removed if he was dead.

"Mr. Dupuis, inform the watch to head so' east by south to give the southern coast of England a wide berth."

"Aye, *mon capitaine*. I think that is a wise decision."

On board H.M.S. Sorcerer, *west of Ireland*

Smythe walked up and down the main deck. Striding back and forth in the cool, damp air helped relieve the boredom of the voyage. However, as Horrocks said, monotony on a trip like this was good. Battling storms or well-armed privateers was not. Last night at dinner, De Gray had announced that with the rebel colonial ports blockaded, most of the rebels' frigates were boxed in. He postulated that, based on their current position, the danger from rebel privateers was over. Smythe disagreed, but had kept quiet.

"Mr. Smythe, a word, if you please."

Darren hastened to join *Sorcerer*'s commanding officer.

De Gray led the way aft, so there was little chance their words would be overheard. "Just after first light, our lookout spotted the top gaff sails of a schooner. I had a midshipman go to the royals' yard, and he too spotted it. I've made this trip dozens of times and I have never seen a schooner in these waters. What do you make of it?"

"It is probably a fishing schooner, fumbling about as we are in the fog."

"Rarely do Irish or French fishing schooners come this far west during the winter. The French don't use them for cargo, nor do we."

"So, Mr. De Gray, you think it may be a rebel ship?"

"In spite of what I said last night, I do."

"And if it is, you want to take it as a prize?"

De Gray nodded. "If we can without jeopardizing our mission."

Smythe understood the unstated question was, *Would Horrocks prefer that they continue to Portsmouth and not risk a fight?* Passing the schooner by was the safe route. But in the back of both officers' minds was the allure of prize money. In their profession, it was the path to fame and fortune.

The same day, on board Schooner Cutlass

Through the thinning fog, patches of blue sky appeared. The boom on the mizzenmast creaked as the mainsail absorbed a puff of wind. Up forward, the jib alternated between hanging slack and being filled by gentle gusts. On the mainmast, Leading Seaman Newton Lofton was sometimes in bright sunshine and then enveloped in fog.

To Jaco, it was eerily quiet. He couldn't get the thought out of his mind that he was being hunted.

As Lofton scanned the horizon, he glimpsed a dirty white sail that almost matched the color of the fog. He blinked and looked again. Through his glass, he could see royals on three masts.

Lofton handed his glass to the other lookout before looping his leg around the stay and sliding down to the deck. Rather than shouting, which in this weather could carry for miles, he waited until he was in speaking distance to report.

"Captain, we saw a small square rigger about a mile away, two points aft of our beam. I make it out to be a Royal Navy sloop. I've seen the like before."

Jaco came over to the railing. His worst fear was realized. "Are you sure of the distance, Lofton?"

"Hard to tell, Captain, with this fog. She's been going in and out like us, and I barely got a view of her tops."

Jaco decided to take a look.

Halfway up the rigging, lost in a swirl of grey-white fog, the fear of heights overtook him. He stopped to shake the lightheadedness away. This was a matter of life or death, and fear must not prevent him from getting a good look. He took some deep breaths, then forced himself to finish his climb.

The lookout on the platform, a seaman by the name of Colin Gentry, was expecting Lofton to return, not his captain to show up and select a spyglass from the rack. "Show me the sloop," Jaco rasped though a dry throat.

Gentry pointed in the general direction. "Captain, I've seen her tops now several times."

Suddenly, the sloop emerged from the fog bank. Through the glass, Jaco could see men setting her studding sails to get every ounce of push from the small wind. The Royal Navy sloop was trying to sneak up *Cutlass* from behind.

"Good work, Gentry. I'll send Lofton back up; keep a sharp lookout but don't yell. I don't want to make any noise they could hear. We're going to play possum."

The terrible urgency of the situation drove away Jaco's fear of heights like a wolf pack routing a jaguar. He descended swiftly, without so much as a tremor.

Back on the quarterdeck, he turned to Bosun Preston. "Please wake up Mr. Dupuis, and then I want the ship quietly cleared for action. No drums, whistles or shouting. I'll let you know when to load and run out."

On board H.M.S. Sorcerer

Sorcerer emerged into the clear as the wind strengthened. As the sloop-of-war surged forward, De Gray got a good look at the schooner through his spyglass. The five black squares on the white stripe along the schooner's hull screamed warship. When both ships were in the clear, he handed the brass tube to Smythe. "What do you make of her?"

"She's certainly a warship, and not one of ours."

"Do you think she has seen us?"

"At this distance I would assume so."

Captain Horrocks walked up to the two junior officers. "Have you identified the schooner?"

De Gray answered. "No, sir. We have not seen a flag. In these waters it could be from almost anywhere—Danish, Dutch, French, Spanish or Portuguese." He paused. "It might even be from the colonies."

Horrocks' impatience with officers who hesitated in their answers showed. He expected officers to have a course of action already thought through. "So, Mr. De Gray, what are your intentions?"

"Sir, with your permission, I plan to catch up to the schooner. If it is a rebel ship, I intend to capture it."

"Lieutenant, Mr. Smythe and I are passengers on your ship, and we are not privy to your sailing orders. If they allow you to seize prizes, then you certainly do not need my permission."

"Yes, sir, they do."

"Well then, what are we waiting for?"

On board Schooner Cutlass

The sound of beating drums carried across the water from the sloop as *Cutlass* re-entered the cold, damp fog. Grey tendrils of cloud seemed to hang on the stays and shrouds. Droplets of moisture dripped down the sides of the 6-pounders and made them shine.

"Mr. Dupuis," Jaco said quietly, "get all hands ready to come about. We're going to turn north to where I think the top of the fog is higher, sail for 30 minutes, then turn west and sail as close to the wind as we can for 30 minutes. Then, if we do not see our Royal Navy friend and the damned wind allows us, we resume a southerly course toward Brest."

"Sir, you are counting on winds strong enough to maneuver."

"I think we have enough if we do it precisely. Hopefully, as the sun burns off the fog the winds will freshen. Remember, a schooner is a lot handier than a square rigger, and if God sides with our cause, we will have more wind!"

Leadership. Don't show your fear, even though you know Dupuis may be right. If Cutlass *can't complete the tack, the Royal Navy sloop will catch us. My best chances is to use* Cutlass' *speed and ability to sail closer to the wind. A good captain knows how he is going to win, and today, winning is getting away and safely making it to Brest.*

"Mr. Jeffords, on my command, we will come about to dead north. Mr. Dupuis, we will do it quietly. No yelling. The men know what to do. No need to let our Royal Navy friends know what we are about."

Pitching his voice to carry to the main deck but not beyond, Jaco leaned over the forward railing of the quarterdeck. "Everyone, ready about." Then, "Mr. Jeffords, helm alee. Come port; our new course is dead north."

Surrounded by fog, Jaco couldn't see the wind line on the water. Instead, he let the telltales on the sails tell him when to issue the next command. Slowly, almost reluctantly, *Cutlass's* bow swung to port. "Release the jib and foremast sheet. Mr. Dupuis, release the sheets for the main and mizzen sails. Easy on the vangs, gentlemen, I don't want to make noise."

When the sails started to billow, he issued the next command. "Sheet all the sails to catch all the wind there is. Smartly now. We'll trim them later."

Cutlass responded and rolled slightly to starboard as the light wind filled the sails.

On board H.M.S. Sorcerer

For a few seconds, *Sorcerer* was bathed in sunlight just in time for De Gray to watch the stern of the schooner disappear into the fog. He called to the maintop, "Can you see the schooner?"

"Not through this bloody muck, not even from the royal's yard. Sorry, sir."

There was nothing more to say. De Gray decided to consult with the officer closest to him in age and temperament. Besides, Smythe had a quality many men lacked: imagination. He walked to the starboard railing where Darren Smythe stood, "Mr. Smythe, what would you do if you were the captain of a rebel schooner?"

Darren answered promptly. "Assuming it is a rebel ship, it depends on his orders. They will dictate whether or not the rebel captain should fight or run. If he wants to run, he will bend on all sails and keep going, particularly if he believes his ship is faster. Or he could tack in one direction or the other to get away. Or, if he is audacious, he might come back on us and cross our stern."

De Gray clenched and unclenched his hands as he considered Smythe's comments. He had assumed that a rebel ship would run at the sight of a Royal Navy warship. "We can't see what the other is doing. It would be by far the best course if we could get alongside each other. Then we would see who has the better ship and crew!"

Smythe took a deep breath. He was worried. De Gray was a competent officer, but he had been brought up in the tradition of trading broadsides. Rebels used different tactics to gain the advantage. Out-sailing their opponent was one. Ambush was another. Tearing up an enemy ship's rigging to make their opponent an easier victim was a third.

"Mr. De Gray, my advice to you is to expect the unexpected. Rebel ships are often captained by very good seamen, and they can be quite unconventional."

"Aye, you've said that several times," De Gray said dismissively. He walked over to the wheel and studied the binnacle for a few seconds. "Quartermaster, maintain our course."

On board Schooner Cutlass

A 30-minute hourglass was housed in the small binnacle and used to time watch periods, so the officer of the watch knew when to ring the bell. Jeffords had turned it over, and the grains of sand had drained through the narrow waist. "Captain," he said, "it's time. Thirty minutes have passed."

"Thank you, Mr. Jeffords, I want to sail to the west as close-hauled to the wind as possible. Once we are steady up on a course, start the glass again."

"Aye, aye, sir."

Jaco stared at the sea. *I hope we have traveled far enough.*

Three teams of men lined up on the each side of the main deck. The forward one handled the jib sheets. The middle group had the lines for boom and sails on the mainmast, and the men farthest aft handled the mizzenmast boom and its sails.

"Lieutenant Dupuis, on my command, stand by to come about."

"We are ready, *mon capitaine*."

"Release the jib sheets. Helm a lee, Mr. Jeffords. Again to port."

Cutlass' bow responded. "Release the main sail sheets." As *Cutlass* turned, "Release the mizzen sheets."

"Sir, we're steady west by so 'west."

Jaco looked at the flapping sails wondering if the wind had shifted or if he'd misgauged it. It was more southerly than he'd expected and would take him closer to the Royal Navy sloop. The safer choice was to wear off to the north, but it would make it easier for the Royal Navy sloop to cut across the angle. By turning west, he'd hoped to lure the Royal Navy ship to reverse course in an attempt to catch *Cutlass*. "Wear off to so' west by west." The sails filled a bit more. "Ease off another two points, Mr. Jeffords. We need the speed."

The sails filled and *Cutlass* regained momentum. Out of the corner of his eye, Jaco saw Jeffords turn over the hourglass. *Cutlass* was heading southwest, meaning his ship would pass closer to the Royal Navy sloop than he'd intended. *I misjudged the wind direction and may have turned too early. Damn, damn, damn. Stay confident, Jaco. If we stay in the fog, we may still slip by unseen. If not, we need to be prepared to fight.*

"Mr. Dupuis, get the gun crews ready. Load chain shot and run out both sides. Don't prick the cartridges or fill the touch holes; I don't want the powder to get damp. I am going to extend another 15 minutes on this course before we turn south."

Cutlass sailed into bright sunlight in time to see the Royal Navy sloop emerge from the fog bank, less than 200 yards ahead on its port bow, heading on a course to where *Cutlass* would have been had he not turned south. The sloop's stun sails, staysails, and topgallants were all out to get the maximum push from the wind coming over her stern. Jaco gauged that the Royal Navy sloop would have a hard time tacking.

"Mr. Garrison, show our colors. Mr. Dupuis, prime the cannon and run out. We're going to wear a few degrees to port so we cross her stern and see what damage we can do. Then we'll decide what to do next. Fire on my command."

On board H.M.S. Sorcerer,

Smythe and De Gray saw the bowsprit, then the mainmast of the unknown ship emerge from the fog seconds before the rest of the schooner sailed into bright sunlight. The lookout yelled, "Deck ahoy! The schooner is one point aft of our port beam. It's a rebel!"

De Gray, seeing the schooner angling to pass behind his ship, spoke loudly to make sure those around him heard him, in a tone he hoped didn't reveal his fear. "Quartermaster, come starboard immediately! Mr. Smythe, fire as you bear and keep firing until the guns no longer bear."

Sorcerer was in trouble, and De Gray knew it. With all its sails out in his bid to catch the rebel ship, *Sorcerer* couldn't maneuver easily. Turning to engage was his only hope, even if it brought his ship to a standstill. His voice was at a higher pitch as he yelled, "Bosun, drop the stun sails. Cut the ropes if you have to, but get them down NOW!"

The sloop's forwardmost 6-pounder on the port side barked, then there was a ripple as the guns fired one after another. The stunsails on the leeward side fluttered to the water. Unfortunately, the ones on the windward side blew inward and landed on the gun crews, who had to push them aside. One gun crew fired their gun through the canvas, and it flared into flames as it descended onto the main deck. They had just set their own ship on fire.

On board Schooner Cutlass

Puffs of smoke accompanied the bark of the Royal Navy sloop's guns. Two balls hammered *Cutlass's* hull. One shattered the bulwark and sent splinters flying like arrows, stabbing into men and wood alike. Two more punched holes in the sails as the ships started a dance in which Jaco maneuvered to get behind the enemy ship and his opponent steered to trade broadsides. Gunderson disappeared down the companionway to check the hull of the *Cutlass*.

"Mr. Shelton, fire at will. Mr. Jeffords, we are going to wear ship to port to pass astern to rake His Majesty's sloop. If I fall, Mr. Dupuis and the midshipmen know the plan, so you can carry on."

He looked up to the midshipman in the maintop. "Mr. Garrison, sweep the British ship's quarterdeck with the swivel guns as soon as we are in range. Mr. Preston, to do the same with the ones on the main deck."

As Jaco moved to get a better view of the British ship and gauge when to wear *Cutlass,* he saw the name *Sorcerer.* Acrid smoke rose from *Cutlass's* guns. All the port guns were firing as rapidly as they could be loaded, while the guns on the *Sorcerer* were silent because they no longer pointed at *Cutlass.* He saw flames flare up on the Royal Navy ship abeam the foremast, but did not know its cause or intensity.

On board H.M.S. Sorcerer

The sloop started to turn to the port so its guns could again bear on the rebel schooner. De Gray had to pull his yards around, which meant his crew had to haul on braces, not man guns. Chain shot whistled overhead, ripping up *Sorcerer's* rigging, making the task harder as lines parted. On the main deck, Smythe was helping the crew pull the burning canvas off the number three cannon on the port side when he heard a loud crack. A section of the mainmast, just above the topsail, slowly toppled to the port side. On its way down, stays popped as they parted.

Its slow descent let two gun crews get out of the way before the mast section landed on the deck with a loud thump. Its royals and topgallants began to feed the fire.

This was the third time Smythe had seen this tactic work. He hadn't liked it the first two times, and he didn't like it now. And bad as the fire was, the rebel schooner was the bigger danger, for its bow was coming up on *Sorcerer's* stern.

On board Schooner Cutlass

Henri Dupuis manned the first of two swivel guns on the bow. Each was loaded with a cloth bag containing 25 musket balls half an inch in diameter. Sighting down the barrel, he could see men wearing blue coats on the quarterdeck gazing over the water at the smaller *Cutlass*. British sailors at the aft corners of the quarterdeck were frantically loading their swivel guns. Dupuis was sure they were just as afraid as he would be in the same situation. He pushed the thought out of his mind and touched the slow match to the gun. He forced himself to not notice what happened to men struck by shot, prepared a second round, and fired again. Before he reloaded for a third shot he paused, then stopped. No one was standing on *Sorcerer's* quarterdeck.

On board H.M.S. Sorcerer

Smythe heard musket balls hammering into the sloop and clanging off cannons. Above him, chain shot whistled by on its way to rip *Sorcerer's* rigging apart. Gun crews were crouching next to their guns for protection. He vaulted up the steps just in time to see the rebel schooner slide aft and begin to turn so it could tack and re-cross *Sorcerer's* stern. Behind him, flames crackled as splintered wood caught fire.

Blood and body parts made the wood of the quarterdeck slick. De Gray's head was lying on its ear against the railing on the starboard side. The quartermaster had one arm missing and was face down next to the wheel. A midshipman lay on his back, blood seeping out of four holes in his chest. The crews of the swivel guns were prostrate on the deck, either dead or dying from musket balls that had ripped their bodies apart.

Frantic, Smythe searched for Captain Horrocks. What he saw took his breath away, and he struggled to keep from sobbing. The captain was crumpled near the wheel, a splinter the length of his arm protruding from one leg, dark blood flowing from three holes in his chest. Smythe dropped to his knees by Horrocks' side and tried to staunch the flow. Horrocks' bloody hand touched his arm. When he spoke, blood frothed on his lips.

"Smythe, I am done for. You were the best young lieutenant I ever met. Take my spyglass and sextant, and whatever else you want from my sea chest; and when you use them, remember me."

Horrocks hand fell away as the life went out of his body. Smythe howled in pain as he stood up and looked around. On the main deck, the ship's bosun was directing men, splashing water from buckets onto the fire that now included the bulwark, a rack of belaying pins and coiled rope.

It dawned on Smythe that he was now the senior commissioned officer left alive on the *Sorcerer*.

Seeing the rebel schooner coming around to rake the *Sorcerer*, he yelled out, "Bosun, gather all the men on the main deck by the mizzen mast. Make sure you go below and bring up any wounded and shirkers. We're done." Desperately, Smythe unwrapped the flag halyard and let the flag descend into his arms. He draped it over Horrocks' body and knelt down.

A voice through a speaking trumpet sounded. "Ahoy there, *Sorcerer*. Have you struck?"

Smythe stood up and waved. "Aye, we have."

"Heave to, and I will send sailors over to help with your wounded and fight the fire. Are your pumps working?"

Smythe shook his head numbly, then yelled, "No, they are in the fire."

Looking aft, he saw both ship's boats were burning furiously, and flames were climbing the rigging.

Smythe heard the rebel officer order all sheets released, and the schooner glided to a stop, sails flapping. Then the same voice said, "Mr. Dupuis, I will take Mr. Shelton and four sailors over to *Sorcerer*. Keep us alongside and downwind far enough so we are not in danger from the flames."

Another voice replied, *"Mais oui, mon capitaine."*

Damn, Smythe thought, *It seems the French have not waited for an official declaration of war to join the rebels.*

Smythe had the bosun count heads while he waited for the rebel officer to arrive. Twenty sailors and eight Marines were still standing; ten of them were wounded. All the rest were dead. He had just finished taking muster when a young man in a blue coat came over the rail. The dark-haired stranger had two pistols and a strange looking weapon in his belt, part hammer and part axe, and a sword still in its scabbard.

"Good morning, sir, I am Lieutenant Jaco Jacinto, captain of the Continental Navy's schooner *Cutlass*. May I ask who you are?"

Smythe took in the olive skin and coal-black eyes. He guessed they were the roughly the same age. "I am Lieutenant Darren Smythe, sole surviving officer. Captain Horrocks, who is lying on the quarterdeck, and I were passengers on the *Sorcerer*."

"Do you think you can get the fire out?"

"No. It has spread to the hammocks on the berthing deck. *Sorcerer* should be abandoned."

"In that case, let's get started. I do, however, need to search the captain's cabin for documents and charts, and we shall salvage what we can of gunpowder and cannon balls and food, if we are able."

"I have one request."

"And that is?"

"We bring our dead to your ship so they can be properly buried."

"Mr. Smythe, we'll take them first."

CHAPTER 12

MY ENEMY IS NOW MY FRIEND

On board Schooner Cutlass

Lieutenant Smythe, holding Captain Horrock's bequest, and Bosun Preston were the last to board the cutter. Pushed by the light wind, *Cutlass* was now a half mile from the burning *Sorcerer*. Smythe and the British sailors joined their American counterparts at the railing to watched the sloop's demise. Flames found the remains of *Sorcerer's* magazine, and the explosion sent chunks of wood and planking into the air. When wind pushed the smoke away, *Sorcerer* was in two parts and its masts were gone. The ship's rudder was briefly visible as the stern sank. The ship's bowsprit pointed to the heavens before it slid slowly beneath the surface, leaving smoldering pieces of wood floating on the Atlantic.

Jaco could not stop thinking that if he had not sailed west, they would have not have had to exchange broadsides with the British sloop. Or he could have avoided the flight entirely if he'd gone farther north before turning west. He felt a pang of guilt. On the other hand, if they hadn't sighted *Sorcerer* when they did, the ship sinking might have been *Cutlass*. He couldn't imagine what Smythe and the British sailors were thinking.

Jaco insisted that Lieutenant Smythe lead the burial service for the British sailors and Marines. Each body was wrapped in canvas with two cannon balls placed at the feet, then covered in turn by the Union Jack stained with Captain Horrocks' blood. The Royal Marines fired a blank volley in honor of each fallen comrade, and survivors from *Sorcerer* tilted the plank. Each body made a small splash and sank quickly.

To show their respect for fellow sailors, *Cutlass's* crew watched from the aft end of the ship. The masts, booms and rigging that normally groaned and creaked were silent as the schooner rocked gently on three-foot waves.

Jaco waited a respectful amount of time after the last man was buried before ordering his crew to pull in the booms so *Cutlass* could catch the wind.

Jaco walked to the bulwark where Darren Smythe stood, staring at the sea. The agreement they'd reached on the burning deck of the *Sorcerer* was that the Royal Navy crew would not be confined to *Cutlass'* small hold. Instead, they would bring their sea chests aboard and berth with his crew on the condition that they gave their word not to attempt to interfere with his running of *Cutlass*. It was an honor system called parole, and Smythe readily assented.

On berthing deck, the two officers watched the men of *Sorcerer* stow their gear. "Mr. Smythe, it will be very crowded down here and that may lead to some fights. I trust your senior men will kept your men in check."

"Aye, they should. But if they don't, you are free to flog any Royal Navy sailor who violates our agreement or the Articles of War."

Jacinto nodded his head toward the companionway as a signal for them to go up on deck. "Mr. Smythe, I don't believe in flogging unless there is no other option this side of hanging the man." He saw a flash of interest in Smythe's eyes and made a mental note to ask him about it later.

Preston approached and said, "Captain, *Cutlass* is making twelve knots." He was grinning, knowing a Royal Navy officer was hearing what he said. "Sir, if we pulled in our sails a bit more and flew both jibs, we might get to fourteen."

"Thank you, Mr. Preston, that is good news. Let's leave the sails set as they are for now."

Preston nodded to both officers and headed aft.

"Twelve knots is very fast."

Jaco watched Smythe study *Cutlass*'s sails. "Yes, Mr. Smythe, it is. I suspect that if I spent time tuning her rigging, we might reach fifteen. Until we ran into the fog and the winds died, we averaged close to ten knots crossing the Atlantic."

"Impressive."

Jaco paused while he decided whether or not to ask the next question. "So, Mr. Smythe, tell me about Captain Horrocks. What kind of man was he?"

Smythe told how he had served under two captains, Horrocks and Tillerson, both of whom were excellent sailors and outstanding leaders. Both had been promoted based on their abilities, not patronage or family wealth. As he listened, Jaco thought about how Captain Jones defined effective naval officers. In different terms, Smythe was describing the same concepts. When the Royal Navy lieutenant finished, Jaco asked, "Mr. Smythe, would you do us the honor of joining my wardroom for meals? We have much in common."

Smythe was taken aback, wondering what he had in common with this rebel commander; nevertheless, he answered politely. "It would be my honor and pleasure." He was even more surprised by what the young officer said next.

"Perfecto!"

* * *

The only items left on the table were two glasses, a decanter taken from *Sorcerer,* and two bottles of port. A brass plaque engraved with *H.M.S. Sorcerer* and the date of the ship's commission—July 5th, 1768—and the ship's bell, liberated from the Royal Navy sloop, now rested on a shelf in Jaco's cabin. *Cutlass's* other officers and midshipmen were either on watch or sleeping, leaving Jaco alone with Darren. Jaco was trying to remember, through a faintly inebriated haze, what he'd intended to ask his prisoner of war when Smythe anticipated him.

"Lieutenant Jacinto, you said earlier that you do not like flogging. I share that opinion and believe it is a barbaric way to punish a man."

"I agree. We as officers need to earn the men's respect and set expectations of how we wish them to behave so we do not have to apply the Articles of War, which don't give us many choices."

"I agree. The Articles of War force us to be heavy handed." Smythe took a drink from his glass and brushed back a curl of blond hair. "Lieutenant, may I ask you a question about tactics?"

"Of course. And when we are alone, you may call me by my first name, Jaco."

"Thank you. That is an unusual first name. What nationality is it?"

"Spanish. It is a derivative of Jacob. My mother wanted my name to be distinctive. Rather like Sean, which can be spelled several different ways."

Surprise registered in Smythe's eyes. Jaco noticed, and gestured for Darren Smythe to ask his question. But Darren did not ask about names or family; instead, he asked the question that had been uppermost in his mind ever since the battle between *Cutlass* and *Sorcerer*.

"Jaco, I have been on two ships that have fought your navy. Each time, your gunners aimed at our rigging with chain shot and used swivel guns to kill our officers. Are those standard practices for the reb—for your navy?"

"The answer is, it depends on the captain. Some, like me, want to disrupt an enemy or prize ship's ability to maneuver. In especially dangerous situations, a commander may wish to put the burden of leadership on the ship's most junior officers. But we have officers who prefer the Royal Navy's traditional tactics." *I didn't want to say we aim to kill or maim senior officers, but I am sure Smythe understood.*

Jaco took a sip of wine. "What we did makes more sense than trading broadsides, which cause more casualties, damages the hulls, and adds a dangerous n element of luck to the battle. By that I mean a ball could damage a ship's rudder or set off a powder cartridge or something like that." He poured more port into Darren's glass. "Does that answer your question?"

Smythe's brain flashed back to sailing the rudderless *Deer* to Port Royal. "Yes, yes it does. The French use a similar tactic, but they don't often succeed because we have a better rate of fire when we are trading broadsides. Our Admiralty opines that rate of fire and the weight of the broadside will carry the day. So far, the tactic has worked against the Dutch, Spanish, and French, and even your ships when we can get alongside."

Jaco tipped his glass as if to say, *Now you know why we don't trade broadsides*, and changed the topic.

Later, Darren asked how Jaco's ancestors got to Charleston.

Jaco recounted the story, how after living in Spain since the 800s, the Jacintos left in 1492 to get away from the Inquisition. Jaco's grandfather had come to Charleston in 1708 from the Netherlands.

"And how long have the Smythe's been in England?"

Darren explained that his ancestors had left Germany during The Reformation to get away from priests who wanted his forebears to convert. They'd stopped in the

Netherlands, where Joakim Schmeitz practiced medicine, before landing in Portsmouth with a commission as a surgeon in the Royal Navy.

Now, with several glasses of port in each of them, Jaco asked the question he'd wanted to ask ever since the British lieutenant had come aboard. "Darren, what ships did *Jodpur* and *Deer* capture?"

"*Jodpur* was sent to find *Providence* after you raided Canso and Petit de Grat, but all we saw was ocean. Earlier, we nearly took a privateer, the *Duke,* but it exploded. One officer and six seamen were lucky to survive."

Jaco could barely contain his excitement. "Do you remember the name of the officer?"

"Yes, he dined with us as you and I have tonight. His name was Eric Laredo." Darren saw Jaco's face light up. "Do you know him?"

"Eric and I grew up together in Charleston. He was one of my best friends. Do you know where he was taken?"

"That I do not."

"I hope he survives the war." *Perhaps Eric was one of those Captain Jones went to rescue.*

Eventually, the conversation came around to the war in which they were both bit players. "Jaco, do you think you can win?"

"I do, because we're fighting for the same freedoms you enjoy. We're both Englishmen, but those of us living in America are treated as second-class citizens and are not represented in Parliament. Laws and taxes are imposed on us that you are not subject to."

Darren Smythe nodded. The rebel captain had a point. Fighting against their fellow Englishmen was stupid. He wondered how many other Royal Navy officers thought as he did.

Brest, France, December, 1776

Even though the *Cutlass* was in a neutral port, Jaco had Bosun Preston post two armed sailors on the pier at the end of the gangway and two more on the main deck. On the berthing deck, half of his Marines were armed with loaded muskets and on alert.

Trailed by Dupuis, Jaco hurried up the gangway. He'd just come from the British East India Company's office. Given the animosity between the two countries, he was surprised the firm had an agent in Brest.

He spotted Smythe standing near the bow with his blond hair blowing in the steady wind, and called out, "Lieutenant, gather your men and their possessions as fast as you can. You all have passage on a British East India merchantman called *Cardamon* leaving this evening for London. The French require us to provide an armed escort to *Cardamom* to make sure none of you slip into the country as spies!"

Darren laughed. "That sounds like the French!"

Jaco joined in the laughter. "I don't make the rules."

"Thank you. This is much better than rotting in a French prison waiting for the two governments to negotiate an exchange."

"Aye, Mr. Smythe, that it is. The British East India Company is paid handsomely to bring back Royal Navy sailors. The agent was *delighted* to book your crew's passage."

Smythe brushed back a curly strand of hair. "Aye, it is easy profit for them. Also they know we will help crew the ship, and defend it if need arises."

"Lieutenant Smythe, I wish you the best of luck and hope we meet again after this war is over. My family is easy to find in Charleston, where, by the way, there are many lovely, eligible young ladies."

"Lieutenant Jacinto, thank you. I too wish you the best of luck. If you are ever in England, please stop by my family's house in Gosport, which is near Portsmouth. I will leave word if I am not there that you are to be treated as an honored guest." The two men hugged.

As Jaco watched the Royal Navy sailors leave, he had mixed emotions. On one hand, he was happy because Smythe and he had become friends. On the other, he was afraid someday he would face Darren in combat, and killing a friend was not something he wanted to do.

Royal Navy Base, Portsmouth, December, 1776

Cardamom deposited Smythe and the crew of *Sorcerer* on a pier in Portsmouth where the sailors were taken to a barracks ship. Smythe was informed that he would be summoned to appear before a board of inquiry about the loss of *Sorcerer*. And indeed, two days later Smythe was summoned. Admiral Wycliff conducted the proceedings, seated between two senior post-captains at a table of highly polished oak. Smythe described the action in detail.

"Lieutenant Smythe, we are puzzled as to why Captain Horrocks did not wait for a frigate to bring him back. Can you enlighten us?"

Smythe nodded. "Yes, sir, I can. Captain Horrocks was eager to return so he could take command of his next ship. May I add, it was a privilege to serve under him."

"Ah." There was a long pause, and then Admiral Wycliff asked the hard question.

"Your report of the action against the rebel ship does not fault Lieutenant De Gray for his tactics or judgment. Why is that, seeing as how his decisions resulted in the loss of a ship?"

"Sir, Lieutenant De Gray performed with honor. Unfortunately he is dead, so he cannot explain his decisions. I do know he wanted to surprise the rebel ship and get off the first broadside. We lost sight of *Cutlass and* didn't know that the rebel captain had changed course until he emerged from the thick fog bank. What I think is informative, sir, are the tactics used by *Cutlass's* captain."

Captain King, a post-captain said, "How so?"

"He used the schooner's ability to sail in light winds and its maneuverability to get to our stern quarter. The rebels like to maneuver to rake, rather than trade broadsides. They train their gunners to hit our masts and rigging. I've been on two ships—*Deer* and *Sorcerer*—that were disabled by that tactic. If *Sorcerer* met *Cutlass* in the open ocean, the faster, more maneuverable rebel ship would have the advantage, even though it carried fewer guns."

Captain Hilton, sitting to Wycliff's right, demanded, "Lieutenant, are you suggesting that we change the way we build ships or the way we fight our enemies?"

"Neither, sir. I am saying that we should educate our captains so they are better prepared to win every fight. We should also consider training our gun crews to aim at the enemy's rigging."

"That's what the bloody French do, and it does not seem to work. In almost every battle in the Seven Years War, we took many more French ships than we lost. Why do you think it is effective for the rebels?"

"Perhaps, sir, because they emulate our rate of fire and our accuracy." *After all, most of them **are** us.*

Hilton looked at Wycliff, who tossed Smythe's written report onto the polished table. "Do you have anything else to add, Lieutenant?"

"I do, sir." Darren slid a sealed envelope across the table. "This is a letter from the captain of the *Cutlass*. You might find it informative reading."

Lips compressed, Hilton took the proffered envelope and opened the seal. He read the contents, then passed the page to the admiral, who scanned it and handed it to Captain

King. While this was going on, Smythe prepared to answer what he guessed would be the next question.

Rear Admiral Wycliff steepled his fingers and addressed Smythe. "Just why did this... Lieutenant Jacinto write this letter?"

"As a warning to the Royal Navy."

Captain Hilton snorted, and King looked as though he didn't know whether to be offended or impressed by the rebel's temerity.

"Lieutenant, that was very nice of him, but naïve to think a rebel lieutenant can influence the Royal Navy. You do realize that the Royal Navy has taken more rebel ships than it has lost? What qualifications does this young officer have to send us a warning?"

"Sir, he served under their Captain John Paul Jones on the *Sloop Providence* when it captured several ships considerably larger than itself. He participated in the raids at Nassau, Canso, and Petit de Grat in Nova Scotia, and as a midshipman, Lieutenant Jacinto brought five large schooners back to Narragansett Bay through our blockade. So, sir, I would say he is a very capable officer. It is only a matter of time before the rebels find him a larger ship, and I fear for Royal Navy captains who meet him in battle."

Wycliff grunted. "Noted. Do you have anything else to say?"

"No, sir, just a request."

"And that is?"

"My next assignment. I would like it to be a frigate."

The tone in the room changed in an instant. Wycliff smiled. "I am glad you asked, because that is what we were discussing before you came in. Your record, according to Captains Horrocks and Tillerson, is encouraging. We have three postings for first lieutenants on frigates being built. You should get your official orders after the first of the year."

"Thank you, sir."

"Keep up the good work, Smythe. Dismissed."

Smythe said thank you and departed. Once he was outside, he took in a huge breath of relief. He was not being cashiered out of the Navy. Being assigned as a First Lieutenant was another step of the ladder, and he could continue the life he had chosen.

On board Schooner Cutlass, *January 1778*

Cutlass left Brest on December 22nd. Weather and winds forced Jaco to tack back and forth along a so' so' west base course toward the Canary Islands before he reached the Trade Winds coming off the west coast of Africa. *Cutlass* then ran with the wind to a position south of Bermuda before turning north. Past Bermuda, the danger came from patrolling Royal Navy frigates. However, in any situation other than being surprised by a frigate looming out of the darkness or from the cover of fog and rain at close range, Jaco was confident that *Cutlass* could outrun any Royal Navy ship it encountered.

Cutlass was two days from entering Delaware Bay when Henri stopped by the captain's cabin. Jaco poured his second-in-command a glass of port. The two officers touched glasses, then Henri said, "*Mon capitaine*, I have bad news for you. There is no easy way to say this, but when we reach Philadelphia my commitment is up and I would like to collect my prize money and back pay. Then I will go back to Petit de Grat."

"Are you sure, Henri?"

"I am. This war was forced on me, and I chose to fight the British, whom I do not like. I am 25 and want to find a woman, have children and raise a family before I die. I cannot do this on a warship. I'm sorry, but I cannot put my life on hold any longer."

His friend's words were not a surprise. Jaco had always known that Henri was not a patriot. "Henri, I will miss you. In Philadelphia, I will talk to my father and make sure you are paid promptly. You'll probably have to go to New York to find a ship to take you to Halifax. If you ever need anything, please find either my father or me. I wish you the best." Left unsaid was the very real danger that Henri could be impressed into the Royal Navy. Were that to happen, they could end up on opposite sides in a naval battle.

Dupuis held up his glass and tilted it to his commanding officer. "*Merci, mon ami.*"

Gosport, January 1777

It was a cold and rainy morning. Inside the Smythe house, the smell of freshly cooked bacon still permeated the downstairs. Through the window, Darren could see the masts of the first-raters whose tops were hidden by the low clouds. The sight reminded him of how he used to run away from his lessons whenever he spied a ship coming into harbour.

Darren was stacking an armful of wood next to the fireplace when he saw, through the rain-streaked glass, two men approach the front door. One looked to be a midshipman carrying a leather pouch.

Smythe forced himself to wait until the young man, probably not more than 15 years old, rapped on the door. Taking a deep breath, he walked to the entrance, wondering what his future in the Royal Navy would be. He remembered his father opening this very door to Lieutenant Roote, four and a half years ago. For a moment, he wondered where Roote was, and what had happened to *Deer,* and if *Jodpur* would ever sail again. Then he opened the door.

"Please come in. The weather outside is only fit for sea creatures."

Both the midshipman and the sailor stepped inside. They were dripping wet. "May I get you gentlemen some tea?"

"Thank you, sir," said the midshipman, "but no. We have to be on our way. Are you Lieutenant Smythe?"

"I am." Smythe handed him a cloth to dry his hands. He noticed both the young officer and the sailor were each armed with a brace of pistols and a cutlass. The midshipman unlatched the leather bag whose strap went around his neck, and handed Smythe two envelopes sealed with wax. Then he excused himself and the two men departed.

In the sitting room, Smythe examined the seals. One was that of the Admiralty, and the other was from a rear admiral. Gently, he peeled back the flap of the one from the admiral.

Lieutenant Smythe,

You will soon receive your orders to a ship being built. The selection board strongly believes that the knowledge you gained working with Commander Handley will serve you in good stead as you supervise the construction of a new frigate.

The members of the board who heard your report on the demise of <u>H.M.S. Sorcerer</u> were impressed by your thoughtful answers even though they challenged Royal Navy doctrine and tactics. Continue to do well and you *will be promoted. Our Navy needs more men with your fire.*

David Wycliff

Rear Admiral of the Red

Smythe sat back in his chair. How far along was the ship? Where was it being built? What type of frigate was it, a fourth, fifth or sixth rater?

The second letter provided the answers.

Lieutenant Darren Smythe,

You have been assigned to <u>*H.M.S. Puritan*</u> *being built by Hillhouse Shipyard in Bristol. Scheduled completion date is June 30th, 1777.*

You are to report to the yard by the end of February 1777 and supervise the construction of the ship until its captain arrives. At such time, you will become the ship's first lieutenant and assist the captain in preparing <u>*H.M.S. Puritan*</u> *for sea and sailing as ordered.*

The Admiralty will pay reasonable expenses for quarters during construction, travel expenses and tolls.

First Naval Lord

Darren Smythe couldn't help smiling, and while he was not very religious he looked up, thinking, *Thank you, God.* Then he went to tell his parents.

On board Schooner Cutlass, *Philadelphia, January 1777*

Cold weather in Philadelphia and an ice-filled Delaware River kept *Cutlass* pier side. Even a three-day warm spell with 40-degree temperatures failed to melt all of the ice in the river. The news about the war was as bad as the weather. Washington had defeated the Hessians in Trenton in what was more of a raid than a campaign, but now the Continental Army was bivouacked in Valley Forge, 20 miles nor' west of Philadelphia, trying to survive the winter. Morale was bad and the army was short of everything except cold, snow, hunger and disease.

According to Jaco's father, the revolution was in crisis. The Continental Congress could not levy taxes, so it was dependent on loans from its citizens as well as France, Spain and The Netherlands. If it weren't for Hyam Salomon and Robert Morris and others raising money through donations and the sale of bonds, along with prize money from privateers, the war would be over due to a lack of money.

Jaco had to find another first lieutenant to replace Henri. Their parting left an empty feeling. He asked for Jack Shelton to be promoted and was pleasantly surprised when his request was granted.

The wait for his next set of dispatches to take to France gave him time to read and respond to Reyna's letters. The latest one asked whether he was planning to come to Charleston. Sadly, he responded, he didn't have leave, but would come as soon as he was given enough time off to make the trip. In the meantime, he had a job to do and hoped she would understand.

When the dispatches and letters arrived, his sailing orders were the same: sail to Brest, deliver the packets, wait for an answer from Benjamin Franklin, and return. *Cutlass* needed to get to France as soon as possible; he needed to balance sailing time versus risk of capture.

Warm woolen clothing, none of which was standardized, cloaked the erratically garbed crew as *Cutlass* made its way down the Delaware River. On both sides of the bow, Jaco stationed four men with long poles to push large chunks of ice away from the hull. Each thump against an ice floe made him nervous; he worried that the pounding might weaken the planking and the schooner would start leaking mere days out of Philadelphia.

The closer *Cutlass* got to the Atlantic, the less ice it encountered. Now, with Cape May and the Atlantic Ocean in sight, it was time to go!

"Bosun Preston, prepare to make more sail."

Bristol, England, February, 1777

Getting to Bristol was easier than Smythe expected. Smythe & Sons had deliveries to make to Bristol, Swindon and Gloucester, and used its own wagons and factory workers who, for extra pay, delivered surgical tools, medical supplies and medicines throughout England. The trip to Bristol took two days.

Smythe and the driver spent the night at an inn in North Wessex, before taking another toll road to Bristol. Darren was careful to get receipts for the government approved and posted tolls which were supposed to pay for the upkeep and improving the roads. From the number of ruts and bumps, he concluded that the money was going to the maintenance of the road's owner, not the road.

Hillhouse was near the mouth of the Avon River, where it emptied into the River Severn that flowed into the Bristol

Channel and the Irish Sea. There he found Commander Langdon, the Admiralty officer managing the contract to build for three *Active* class 32-gun frigates based on a design by Edward Hunt. Langdon had a leathery face and pudgy fingers. The commander had earned a degree in marine engineering and had asked for the job because he believed the Navy would always need new ships. By managing shipbuilding contracts, there was little risk of being put on half-pay, or worse, no pay. After glancing at Smythe's Admiralty letter, he asked if the newcomer wanted to see the ship.

"I would, sir."

Langdon headed out of the office. "Follow me, then." He led the young lieutenant past five ships nearing completion to one that was half a dozen ribs pegged to a keel. A few planks kept the ribs from falling over. A hand painted sign on a board leaning against the keel gave the ship's name.

"This, Lieutenant Smythe, is *H.M.S. Puritan.* According to the schedule, it will be launched on June 30th. With a little luck and the grace of God, Hillhouse may make that date. In a month or so, it will begin to look like a ship! When finished, *Puritan* will be a fifth rater with twenty-four 12-pounders, two 24-pound carronades in the fo'c'sle, and four more on the quarterdeck to give some extra weight to its broadsides."

Langdon looked at the young lieutenant and noted that he was listening carefully as well as eyeing the bare ribs of *Puritan.* "When she is fitted out, *Puritan* will be 125 feet long and have a beam of 35 feet, and displace just over 700 tonnes. Any questions, Mr. Smythe?"

"Not yet, sir. I am just trying to imagine what the ship will look like."

"Have you ever seen a ship being built?"

"No sir, I haven't." *But I've seen one taken apart.*

"I will show you where I keep the drawings. Can you read them?"

"Aye, I can. Our last ship, the *Jodpur,* had to be hauled out of the water and repaired in Halifax. I worked with a man by the name of Handley. Perhaps you know him?"

"Handley is a good man. He knows what he is about. I heard about *Jodpur.* There's no excuse for shoddy work by a yard. Someone should hang for it."

When they'd found out that rotten wood had been used on *Jodpur,* Horrocks had opined that the Admiralty ought to flog or hang the shipbuilder's manager and the Royal Navy officers who allowed it to happen. "Commander, *Jodpur's* captain felt the same way. What can I do to help?"

Langdon's gruff manner evaporated. Smiling, he said, "Come with me and I will show you where you can start."

They walked another half mile to a long shed with sides down to 10 feet off the ground. Langdon stopped and waved a hand. "Here is where they store and age the wood that goes into every ship. Now it comes mostly from Canada, Latvia and Norway. Before this bloody war, we were getting excellent quality oak from South Carolina, Georgia, New Hampshire and Maine, until our fellow citizens decided to rebel against their king. Most of what now arrives is a mixed lot. Some logs are acceptable, but many are not very good. Hillhouse dries the wood here before it is transferred to the sawmill to be cut into planking or masts. Your experience with *Jodpur* and Handley should make you an expert on poor wood."

Smythe nodded slowly and pushed a lock of blond hair off his forehead.

"You, Mr. Smythe, can help His Majesty's shipbuilding program a great deal by making sure that any log cut to go on one of His Majesty's Ships is properly aged, not rotten, and not heavily knotted. Green wood snaps when the yard tries to steam and bend it. Knots make it hard to work."

"Aye aye, sir. And I think I can figure out a way we can track what comes in and its condition."

"If you can, young man, you will have done your Navy, your country and your king a great service. However, you will also put yourself in danger of becoming shore bound like me!"

On board Schooner Cutlass, *February 1777*

The dispatches had been delivered, and Franklin's reports were safely locked away. *Cutlass was* under full sail as soon as it cleared Brest's harbor. The courier had stressed the importance of the messages the ship was carrying to Philadelphia, telling Jaco that the French would side with the colonists if Washington could win one more victory against the British Army. In one of the letters in the pouch, Franklin reiterated that Louis XVI would provide troops and a fleet to end the blockade of American cities if Washington could defeat the British on land. Until then, all the French would do was loan money and provide powder, weapons and shot.

Now, two days after leaving Brest and sailing so' so' west to get to the Trade Winds, *Cutlass* was loping along through the long swells of the Atlantic off the coast of Portugal under sunny skies. In his cabin, Jaco was finishing off a chunk of French cheese and a piece of bread when there was a sharp rap on the door. It was one of the quartermaster mates. "Sir, respects from Mr. Shelton. He would like you to join him on the quarterdeck."

As Jaco came out on the main deck, Shelton waved his hand to the starboard side. "Behold! We have found the Royal Navy."

Less than two miles away, two frigates were running with the wind, headed their way. Their bow waves were pushing white water along their sides, and with their bow chasers run out, they looked like dogs running with bones in their teeth.

Midshipman Garrison, who was looking at the ships through a spyglass, yelled out, "Sir, they are making some sort of signal. It makes no sense to me."

"Of course not, Mr. Garrison. They want to know if we are British and know their codes. Mr. Shelton, do you think we can outrun the Royal Navy?"

"I do, sir, and we won't need to ask God's help either."

"Good." Jaco looked at the British ships and began issuing orders. "Quartermaster, we'll sail close-hauled and diagonally across their bows. Stand by to come port to so' by east. Bosun Preston, get the hands ready to come about. And Mr. Shelton, don't you think it is time to show them our colors while we show them how nimble we are?"

"Aye, sir. I will find the largest flag we have so they don't have to consult their code books," Shelton replied cheerfully.

The British frigates were now only half a mile away. A puff of smoke from the ship on the right was their reply to seeing the Continental Navy flag defiantly displayed. Two cannonballs hit the water aft of the schooner. They were in now range, but the ships couldn't train their guns to track the fast moving schooner that was now heading so' east, 30 degrees off the wind line.

The frigate lagging slightly behind started to come about, its commander knowing he had just a few seconds to cripple the rebel schooner. Both of its bow chasers fired almost simultaneously. Their first shot was short, the second skipped past *Cutlass's* bow, sending up spurts of salt water. Jaco was sure that the captains were urging their gun crews to reload as fast as they could.

Two more shots rang out, and there was a pop overhead. The mainsail now had a hole. While it would only marginally affect their speed, it was too close to comfort. The nine-pound balls were dangerous enough; the heavier 12-pounders on the sides of the frigates could turn the *Cutlass* into matchsticks with one broadside.

Maybe I should have turned to a more southerly course. He remembered what Captain Jones had told him: Audacity and surprise can be effective. *Well, I am being audacious.*

There was another pop in the sail, a waterspout, and a crash. An iron ball smashed through one bulwark and carried away another section, just forward of the number three gun on the port side. But before the British could hit the schooner again, *Cutlass* was past and moving out of range, albeit in the wrong direction, i.e. so' east instead of so' west.

The men on the deck looked up, expectantly. Jaco forced himself to speak calmly, loudly enough for the crew to hear. "I believe we are done with the Royal Navy for today. We do, however, have some work for our carpenter."

Off to their port side, the two frigates had come around to pursue, but they could not sail as close to the wind as *Cutlass* could. Jaco kept the schooner headed so' by so' east until nightfall, before tacking to a so' west course for its run to Philadelphia.

Bristol, February 1777

Landlodger Trow, the public house on King Street where the Royal Navy billeted the officers, was in the heart of Bristol. The three lieutenants assigned to ships being built at Hillhouse shared a room. They took their meals in the inn's great room on the main floor where smoke was thick from candles, lanterns, and the great stone hearth used for cooking and heating.

The proprietor was fond of telling his new guests that Landlodger Trow was where Daniel Defoe met Alexander Selkirk, a Scottish seaman who became the inspiration for

Robinson Crusoe. He also warned that some of his guests claimed the four-story Tudor style building was haunted.

Each evening, the three lieutenants told stories about their adventures, the officers they'd served under, and speculated where their new frigates might be sent. Since the other two had spent their careers in the Mediterranean, when it came to fighting rebels, Smythe was the "expert," or as he said, "the one with some experience."

Lieutenant Ballantine surprised Smythe one night by questioning why the king was putting down a rebellion by British citizens who should, by English law, have the same rights of those born and raised in England. "The Royal Navy," he said, "should be helping the Army take French possessions in the Caribbean and India. What say you, Smythe? You have met the rebels. Am I wrong?"

Darren felt he had to be careful with his answer. For all he knew, Ballantine might write a letter quoting him to someone at the Admiralty and it could be career over; or worse, dangling from a yardarm in a hangman's noose.

Smythe chose his words. "The rebels seem to be determined to gain what they call their freedom at any cost. They claim they are not being treated as citizens; but then, neither are they behaving as proper English citizens. Some go so far as to attack their Loyalist neighbors and confiscate their properties. They have declared war on us. If our King's response means sinking ships crewed by our fellow citizens, so be it. You could say this rebellion is similar to a mutiny."

"Aye, and from what I hear, their ships are not well equipped nor well captained. When we come alongside, it is a short battle."

"Ballantine," Darren said seriously, "remove that thought from your mind. Their captains are every bit as good as ours, and they use effective tactics. If you expect them to fight like the French or the Spanish, you engage them at your peril."

The other lieutenant, an Irishman from Dublin who went by the name of Everleigh, tilted his glass toward Smythe. "That is so much shite. No navy or foreign ship can go toe to toe with us. Ballantine, you say this war is nonsense, but think, man. If these British colonials refuse to obey our king, what is to stop Ireland from declaring independence? If their experiment in self rule succeeds, *what need is there for kings*? If they can follow the Ten Commandments with neither king nor pope, they will accomplish a revolution more radical that King Harry's when he lifted the popish yoke from our necks." He paused to take a deep swallow of ale. Ballantine looked surprised, and even Smythe was struck by the argument. Everleigh, a true Irishman, had more to say.

"I tell you, there is no king in Christendom who wants this rebellion to succeed. The French are helping the rebels only because they want us to bleed. The one good this bloody war provides is opportunities for men like us to advance. If we are willing to risk our lives, and the lives of our crews, we may be fortunate enough to take prizes. But we may just as easily end up dead, drowned, maimed, or taken prisoner. In truth, fair trade and fair prices would be of more real good to us than a war. We'd not get rich, but we'd live longer to enjoy our wages."

He paused, then added thoughtfully, "And there'd be a sight less felling of trees in Ireland."

Chapter 13

Training and New Guns

Philadelphia, April 1777

Winter had finally given up its grip on the east coast. When *Cutlass* left for Brest in early March, snow had covered the streets of Philadelphia and the shores of Delaware Bay. On the way back, the schooner enjoyed steady trade winds and temperate weather. The only the sign of the war was the absence of merchant shipping.

No sooner had the wooden gangway banged into place than a Continental Army officer boarded the schooner. He bore a paper with stamps and signatures all over it, that authorized the bearer to receive the pouch of sealed communications and convey it to the Congress. He was followed by two older men.

"Jaco! Welcome back!"

Cutlass's captain turned toward the familiar voice. It was his beaming father, and standing next to him was fellow Marine Committee member, John Hewes. With the pouch on its way to Independence Hall, Jaco hugged his father and shook hands with Mr. Hewes.

Then Hewes said, "Lieutenant, may we have a word in private with you in your cabin?"

"Yes, sir." Jaco gestured to the gangway, and Hewes led the way.

Inside the tiny cabin, Jaco seated Mr. Hewes at the head of the table and asked, "Sir, may I offer you a glass of port, or a fine French brandy? It was recommended to me by Mr. Franklin himself."

"Hmm, I think a glass of port is more appropriate on a man-'o-war."

Jaco poured three glasses and handed them around. "Sirs, to our cause."

"Our cause." Hewes took a draught of the Portuguese wine and his eyebrows lifted in appreciation. He held the glass up in the light that came through the stern windows and admired the dark color.

"This is the last of the port we took from *Sorcerer*. As you see, it is quite good," Jaco explained.

"That it is. And so, to business. Lieutenant Jacinto, we are pulling you from courier duty. Not because you are performing poorly—on the contrary. What we have in mind is for you to supervise the construction of a new frigate and be its first captain."

Jaco was elated. This was more than he had dared hope for so soon, but he schooled his face to not show his excitement. "Sir, I am honored. What can you tell me about the ship?"

"It is based on the ship that Captain Jones just took to sea named *Ranger*. However, it is bigger, and we think you may have some ideas on how it should be armed."

"Where is it being built?"

"In Kittery, Maine, just across the bay from Portsmouth, New Hampshire."

Jaco considered what he knew of Maine and New Hampshire. "Is it likely the British will raid the shipyard? However much King George misses our taxes landing in his coffers, the dearth of colonial-built ships and wood for his Navy is a much greater loss."

"There is always that chance, but right now they are smarting from having been kicked out of New Jersey. That news is going to be sent back to France as soon as Mr. Shelton can get *Cutlass* re-provisioned and underway. If the French king is as good as his word, this will signal a turning point in the war that will make King George and his advisors wish he had agreed to our reasonable requests in the first place."

"Is there a cannon foundry nearby?"

"Yes, in Portsmouth on the other side of the river."

"And how soon do I have to be in Kittery?"

"When you are ready. They just laid the keel and started attaching the ribs."

"Then, sir, with the Committee's permission, I would like to spend some time with my father before I leave."

"That is understandable. I shall report to the Marine Committee that you have accepted, and I will document your promotion to captain."

Bristol, May 1777

With the help of a dozen workers, Lieutenant Smythe laid a row of fresh logs on a series of blocks, each log marked to the length it was to be cut. Beyond these marks, Smythe made Xs with a piece of chalk where he wanted test cuts made. Something about the heft of the wood made him suspect the logs were bad; he had already bored test holes with an auger, but the only way to be sure was to see cross sections. Under the watchful eyes of Langston and the Hillhouse yard manager Mr. Harkins, yard workers sawed where Smythe indicated. The center of the first log looked like sawdust. On the second, a few inches from the bark, the wood had turned soft and fibrous. Five more were tested where he marked, and all were unacceptable.

Harkins selected four more to test, saying, "They can't all be bad." It took ten yard workers to shift the heavy logs from the pile. Harkins himself drilled into the wood, and he almost fell over when the interior of the wood gave way. Cutting the log revealed a rotted core. Undeterred, he selected another log—with the same result.

Commander Langston waved his hand, spanning the storehouse. "It begins to look as though the whole lot may be bad. Cut them up under Mr. Smythe's supervision, then we will determine what you can salvage for trim and maybe planking. None of these can used as masts, spars, or ribs. No structural portion of any ship shall built of the wood in this yard."

"But, sir," Harkins protested, "it will take months to get new wood and age it."

Langston clasped his hands behind his back. "Then, Mr. Harkins, you should get cracking. Hillhouse is not going to build Royal Navy ships with rotted wood. So, if you want additional contracts, I suggest you find *proper* wood, and find it quickly." Langston turned on his heel and headed for his office.

Portsmouth, NH, May 1777

The shortest way to the foundry from the shipyard was a 20-minute sail across the Piscataqua River. Jaco and the ship's designer, James Hackett, were met by Elliot Simmons, the owner of the Portsmouth Foundry and Iron Works, who drove them in a wagon out to his range.

Under a shed, Simmons had a long 12-pounder mounted on a naval gun carriage. "As you can see, we replicated a gun deck here with the gun carriage on wood planking and a small wall simulating a bulwark of a ship. This gun is two feet longer than a normal 12-pounder; it is the third one we cast to that length. In our tests, the added barrel length gave the cannon much more power and a longer range."

Jaco gave the installation a quick once over. Five hundred yards away a cliff rose 100 feet above the range. Halfway between the cliff and the 12-pounder, Simmons had mounted stands with ten-foot wide sections of planking that Hackett had assembled and sent to the foundry. Large boulders were piled around the bases of the posts sunk several feet into the ground to keep them in place.

"I would like to examine those," Jaco said, pointing down range and turning first to Hackett, then Simmons.

"Of course."

As they walked toward the first wall, Hackett told the foundry owner, "I am just as interested in the results of this test as the Navy is. Joshua Humphreys, a ship builder like myself, and I have been exchanging ideas on designs that could reduce the damage a cannon ball does to the side of a ship. Today we are going to test some of those ideas."

"We are both trying new designs, then," replied Simmons. "This order for this new ship is my second for the Navy. The first was for the *Ranger*."

Jaco pushed and pulled on the posts. Satisfied they were solidly in the rocky ground, he nodded. "Well done, Mr. Simmons."

Meanwhile, Hackett prowled around the planking, peering at the joinings and rapping on the wood. "See, Captain," he said to Jaco, "this is the strongest, soundest wood you are like to find in any shipyard." Jaco stopped pulling at a post and ran his hands over the dense, smooth grain of the oak.

Simmons said, "Captain, shall we return and begin the test? The powder cartridges and priming flask are in the shed, the solid shot are on the cart next to the gun. My men are standing ready."

"Certainly, but if you don't mind, I would like to load and fire the cannon myself, to eliminate as many variables as possible." *Actually, I am doing what Gunner Reasoner taught me. You do the loading and firing so you are sure it is done the way you want it done.*

Jaco checked the blocks and tackle the workers would use to pull the 3,000-pound cannon mounted on a 600-pound carriage back into battery. He held the lantern so that he could see all the way down the barrel. Satisfied the bore was smooth, he picked up a charge and a wad held on the end by wax. It had been his idea to attach the wad to the cartridge, to remove a step from the loading process and shorten the reloading time. He'd forwarded his suggestion to Simmons via courier.

Jaco slid the cartridge into the bore and rammed it home twice to make sure it was seated. The ball went in next and was pushed home. Before he pricked the cartridge and filled the touchhole, he adjusted the elevation screw to aim the gun. "First ball at single, three-inch thick planking."

He touched the small pile of powder with the wand. It flared and, milliseconds later, the gun fired. Smoke billowed from the narrow mouth of the gun, temporarily blocking their view of the target 250 yards away. Once it cleared, Jaco examined the wooden wall through a spyglass.

"Hole is slightly to the left of center and high; it looks as though it went clean through. Let's fire a second ball."

With the help of four factory workers, Jaco hauled the gun back into battery, its four wooden wheels on the squares painted on the wood decking. This made sure the gun was in the same place for each shot. He set to cleaning the gun and loading it, then adjusted the aim slightly.

The next ball also went through the planking, this time in the center. Jaco looked at Simmons and Hackett. "Shall we examine the results?"

The three men strode to the planking. From the front, the hole made by the 12-pound ball was clean and rounded. In the back, shards of wood were blown out, some a foot long. The damage to the back of the three-inch thick planking was over four times the diameter of the hole.

"I think these results are most satisfactory," said Hackett. "Mr. Simmons, please have your people move the gun to shoot at the second set of planking at a range of 250 yards." This section was of double planking, composed of two layers of three-inch thick oak planks pegged tightly together.

Again, Jaco loaded the gun, carefully aimed, and ignited the cannon from the side so that he was well clear of the cannon's recoil. This time, the wood wall reverberated as the iron ball slammed against it—and bounced off. The sturdy wall shrugged off a second cannon ball as easily as it had the first. Through the spyglass, Jaco could see where the balls had struck, faint dents three feet apart, but there was no visible splintering, no penetration.

"Let's fire a third."

The third ball struck between the two dents. While Jaco was pleased with his accuracy, he knew that aiming on steady ground at a stationary target was a far cry from a naval exchange between ships that rocking on the waves and maneuvering for position.

Inspection showed that the three balls had caused significant splintering to the backside, but nowhere near as much as on the single plank wall.

The gun was then moved to fire at the third set of planking. Hackett explained, "This proves that double thick walls have merit. I am interested to find out if your idea, Captain Jacinto, of putting a two-inch layer of softer pine between the oak planks has any effect. It makes the design and construction much more difficult, but if it works, we will figure out a way to have it on your ship."

"Sir, actually, the idea is Mr. Humphreys. He told me about it when he was inspecting *Alfred* after he finished his modifications."

Jaco went through the gun drill, increasingly convinced that his idea of affixing the wad with wax to the end of the cartridge worked well. The gun boomed and smoke billowed out, followed by a loud smack. Through the spyglass, Jaco could not see a hole, only a puff of dirt forward of the wall and a cannon ball rolling away. He handed the glass to Hackett.

"Mr. Hackett, do you see where it hit?"

Hackett peered through the glass. "No, I don't."

"Let's try again."

The gun was reloaded and pulled back into position. This time, Jaco handed the glowing hemp to one of the foundry workers and stood well off to the side. The gun fired, and the loud smack of an iron ball hitting wood was heard. Again, there was no hole, no sign of so much as a dent.

Excited, Jaco said to the others, "Let's go check our wall."

Walking toward the wood, Jaco forced himself not to run, but he grinned when he saw one iron ball lying on the ground, and one that had broken into large chunks.

An inspection of the wall showed that, not only had neither ball penetrated the outer layer of planking, in the back, there was no damage at all!

"Mr. Hackett, I think we have something here. Let us shoot three more balls to test this wall's endurance."

These shots showed the same result, even though the wall was weakening from the impact. Jaco struggled to contain his excitement.

Hackett rubbed his chin, inspecting the wall closely. "Splinters cause most of the casualties during naval battles. Captain Jacinto, I think Mr. Humphreys just came up with a way to protect our crews. I will go back and figure out how we can install this without adding too much weight. Fortunately, pine is a light wood. There will be a construction delay, but if these results hold true, the lives of men are well worth the wait. I know which ship I'd want a son of mine serving on."

Jaco felt a soft breeze ruffle his head as he studied the sturdy wall. Humphrey's design worked. *Perfecto!*

Bristol, May 1777

A shipyard wasn't the cleanest place to work, but Smythe didn't care if his breeches and shirt got dirty. He paid a laundry woman to pick-up his clothes at Landlodger Trow and clean them every few days. Unlike the other lieutenants, Smythe helped wherever and whenever he could. Ofttimes, Commander Langston was at work in the shipyard himself, getting just as dirty. So when a yard worker delivered a message that Lieutenant Darren Smythe was to report immediately to Commander Langston, Smythe didn't change clothes. Pausing only to wipe his hands on a rag, he walked over to the Royal Navy office assigned to supervise their ship's construction. At the entrance, a carriage with two footmen was parked outside.

He walked into Langston's office, calling out, "Commander, you wanted to see me?"

A voice he'd never heard before answered. "Do you always barge into a senior officer's cabin without knocking or asking permission to enter?"

Smythe turned and saw a tall man wearing an impeccable blue uniform with the epaulets of a captain. The man's long hair was pulled back in a ponytail and he had bright blue eyes.

"No sir, but—"

"No buts, young man. Who are you and why are you here? My God, you look like you just crawled out of a pit."

Smythe put his hands by his side and his feet together as he'd been taught at the Royal Navy Academy. "Captain, I am Lieutenant Darren Smythe, First Lieutenant of the *H.M.S. Puritan*, which should be launched sometime in September if we get properly dried and cured wood."

The officer turned to Langston, who was tying rolled up drawings with a strip of blue ribbon. "I was told *Puritan* would be commissioned next month."

"Captain Davidson, Lieutenant Smythe here has been very helpful in overseeing the construction of your ship *Puritan*, as well as the others being built here at Hillhouse. He is the man who found the rotted wood intended for *Puritan*, so rather than build your ship with planks that would come apart when hit by rebel cannon balls, we stopped construction. The Third Sea Lord has been kept informed and knows about our problem, sir."

Smythe was sure he detected a hint of sarcasm directed at Captain Davidson. Langston didn't suffer arrogance gladly and had run off several impatient Royal Navy officers, telling them to come back after he informed them their ships were ready for sea. He'd also ordered Hillhouse to keep incompetent employees away from Royal Navy ships.

Davidson cleared his throat. "Mr. Smythe, why are you not in a proper uniform befitting the First Lieutenant of one of His Majesty's Ships?"

"Sir," Smythe said, speaking in a respectful yet confident tone. This was his future captain, and he hoped to make a good impression. "I supervise and perform many of the shipbuilding tasks to ensure they are carried out properly. It is a grimy, dirty business, but also educational. Such knowledge might come in handy if *Puritan* ever has a problem at sea."

Davidson pursed his lips and waved his hand. "I see. Well, then, carry on. However, once I find a suitable place to stay, you shall dine with me so I can learn more about your experience and background. And *do* clean up before we meet again. You look and smell like a hound that has had the worst of it during a fox run."

"Aye, aye, sir."

Philadelphia, May 1777

Seven men from the Marine Committee were gathered around a table in a room in Independence Hall, listening attentively to James Hackett and Jaco Jacinto explain Hackett's request for more money. He wished to install additional planking on what was known as the Kittery ship.

Jaco showed his sketches of the tests at the Portsmouth Foundry and Iron Works. The five men seemed impressed with the innovation that would protect crews and guns and enable a ship to engage Royal Navy ships at longer ranges. Hackett rolled out drawings that detailed how the three layers of planking would be incorporated in his design. The expense was modest compared to the cost of the ship. The Marine Committee asked for a few days before giving Hackett an answer.

John Adams was the first to speak after the younger Jacinto and Hackett left. "It is, I would say, a very good, albeit untested idea. But where are we to get the funds? We have not gotten anywhere near the money we requested from the colonies, not even from Massachusetts, I am sorry to say! Good as this design is, I'm afraid that we will have to tell Hackett no. But we will budget for the modification on the next ship."

Stephen Hopkins chimed in, echoing his fellow Bostonian. Hewes looked at John Langdon, who slowly nodded agreement with Adams. Silas Deane suggested they try to find the money, and was supported by Richard Henry Lee. Javier looked at his fellow committee members, then said, "If I can come up with the necessary funds, will the committee approve the additional planking?"

Lee and Deane heartily agreed, as did Hewes, which gave Javier enough votes. "So, gentleman, I move that we approve the modification to the Kittery ship on the condition that we find the money."

Deane quickly seconded the motion, and it carried. Hopkins eyed Javier Jacinto dourly. "Good luck finding the money. Massachusetts and Connecticut have contributed much to this war. Maybe you can find us some Carolinian money."

Javier didn't react to the jibe. Hopkins was still holding a grudge because Hewes had demoted his brother. Before he left the building, the elder Jacinto penned a note and asked a Congressional page to deliver it.

* * *

Jaco dashed back to his father's house. When he'd arrived from Kittery two days ago, he'd been warmly greeted by none other than his father's friend, Max Laredo. After asking how his wife and sons were, Jaco had inquired about Reyna. Laredo had laughed and said, "Why don't you ask her yourself?"

Hearing her cue, a smiling Reyna had walked into the parlor room, wearing a simple gray on gray busk. Her jet-black hair hung down below a white kerchief. Jaco guessed the garments had come from England or France.

The petite Reyna had curtsied and grinned as she spoke, trying to be both formal and facetious. "Captain Jacinto, it is my pleasure to meet you. I have read and heard *soooo* much about your exploits as a *naval* officer!!!"

Jaco had stared, his mouth open, too stunned at first to speak. Max had come to his rescue. Much of the evening was spent in recounting their experiences, hers on shore, his at sea, in shipyards and foundries.

Today, Reyna was in the sitting room reading a thick book on human anatomy. Seeing him, she stood up and twirled around. "What do you think?"

"Why are you dressed as a boy?"

"Because I have been going to lectures at the College of Philadelphia's School of Medicine. Women are not allowed, so I dress as a young man. It is ridiculous. I think anyone who has the brains should be able to go to a university or medical school, don't you?"

Jaco's traditional schooling had ended when he became a midshipman. Going to college had never entered his mind. He stammered, "I... I guess so."

Reyna closed the book and put it on the chair. "One way or another, I am going to become a doctor."

Jaco took off his uniform coat. "It is a lovely day. Why don't we take a ride along the Schuylkill River?"

"Shall I ride as a boy or a girl?"

"How about as a beautiful woman?"

Reyna pulled out the comb and hair pins that held her hair up. She shook her head, and her hair cascaded to below her shoulders. "But I am not going to ride sidesaddle." Translation: *I am going riding wearing pants!*

When they returned, Javier and Max were in the sitting room with a man Jaco recognized, but couldn't name. It was one of the men his father occasionally consulted. His father introduced the man as Haym Salomon, and announced that Mr. Hackett would also be joining them for dinner.

They shook hands, and Jaco, sensing that Reyna didn't want to be left out, said, "Mr. Salomon, please permit me to introduce Miss Reyna Laredo."

Reyna curtsied and daintily held out her hand, which Salomon took. "Miss Laredo, I am pleased to meet you. You are spectacularly beautiful." The man's accent suggested he was German, but he wasn't. Salomon had been born in Lissa,

Poland, which was now a part of Prussia. He had traveled all over Europe and spoke German, French, and English as well as his native Polish.

Well done, Mr. Salomon. The one thing that Reyna hates is being ignored. If this meeting turns to business, she wants to be treated as an equal. "What brings you to Philadelphia, Mr. Salomon?"

"The war! I escaped from the British twice. The first time they thought I was a spy—and I was. Spies are usually executed unless they are more valuable alive than safely dead; as, for instance, when there is a trade of prisoners to be made. In my case, they needed me to translate for their German soldiers, and afterwards I was released. However, they arrested me a second time when I encouraged the Germans to desert and helped our prisoners escape. With the help of a German soldier who didn't want to continue fighting, I got away and came to Philadelphia to help with the war effort by raising money."

"And you are here to learn about the Kittery ship?"

"That I am. I intend to find the money to pay for the modifications you and Mr. Hackett suggested. I also want to learn more about the naval officer who will be its captain."

Reyna sat quietly, listening to Jaco answer Salomon's very pointed questions about his experiences at sea, both as a merchant's son and a naval officer. Then Salomon turned to face her. "And what brings you to Philadelphia, Miss Laredo?"

"I came to study medicine; I wish to be a doctor."

Having emigrated from Germany in 1765, Salomon was familiar with European colleges that didn't admit women. His raised eyebrow added emphasis to his question. "They let you in?"

"I attend lectures dressed as a young man."

Salomon paused, taken aback, then smiled. "Good for you." He went on to ask if she had herself been affected by the war, and she gave a précis of what she had told Jaco the first night.

Hackett's arrival changed the nature of the conversation, which continued through dinner and beyond. It became technical, with much discussion of where suitable wood could be purchased, for how much, how it could be transported to the shipyard and how much longer it would take. It would be neither simple nor inexpensive to make the changes on the actual ship that were so simple and easy on paper, or to test. But Salomon assured them it was still possible. When he left, his final words to Javier were, "Tell the committee I will find the money, even if I have to take it from my own pocket."

Kittery, August 1777

In early June, a month after the meeting in May with Hyam Solomon, a courier on a small sloop made a stop in Kittery. The young Army officer handed Jaco a note which ordered him to travel back to Philadelphia. No reason was given; the order was signed by Joseph Hewes.

Four days later, he knocked on the door to his father's house in Philadelphia. The next day, the two of them walked to Hewes' house, where Jaco was handed a thick pouch. Hewes told him to open it, and, with his father as witness, they slowly counted a stack of Bank of England notes totaling £5,000.

"Mr. Salomon was true to his word. Sign this receipt, then take the money to Mr. Hackett. As you acquire the wood needed to finish the ship, pay for it out of this money. Keep a ledger and get receipts."

Slowly, the hull began to resemble a ship. The lower sections for all three masts were stepped, and the shrouds were in place. The masts' upper sections lay on the pier, ready to be hoisted in place, now that the hounds, kessel trees and tops were installed.

Jaco watched two yard workers climb the shrouds and sit on the maintop, their legs dangling in the air, and he was very glad it was not him perched at those heights. The two men sat calmly, waiting for the main topsail mast to be hoisted so they could seat it. Once on its step, the mast section would be lashed in place. As Jaco watched, the main topsail mast was positioned first, followed by the fore and then the mizzen.

Sensing someone behind him, Jaco turned around. It was Jack Shelton. His sandy brown hair was braided in a ponytail with a black leather thong at the end. Rather than shaking hands, Jaco hugged his friend, saying, "I am glad to see you! Welcome to our new ship!"

Shelton pounded Jaco on the back and grinned. "I've been waiting to say *Captain Jacinto* for a long time."

"Jack, what news do you have?"

"I met with the Navy committee last week. Hedley Garrison will be the senior midshipman; Jeffords is going to be quartermaster. Bosun Preston and Leo Gaskins are joining us. I have not yet met the other officers. Some men from *Cutlass's* and *Providence's* crews will be part of the crew, but we are also supposed to recruit from this area. Congress authorized a crew of three Navy and one Marine lieutenants, three midshipmen, 200 men including 25 Marines, but no master."

"We can do without a master if the officers are competent. Who are they?"

"The Third Lieutenant is Neil Hayes from Portsmouth, New Hampshire. The Second Lieutenant is Edmund

Radcliffe, from Boston, and the two new midshipmen are Philip Patterson and Earl Wilson. Our Marine is Lieutenant Patrick Miller, who you know from the Nassau expedition."

Shelton had grown up as a minister's son in Providence. When he'd volunteered to become a midshipman, he had been in his second year at Yale College. Most his classmates were from the elite families of Boston he considered snobbish. He took a deep breath before saying, "Radcliffe is a cousin of the Adams on the Marine Committee. Your father would only tell me that he was on the *Cabot* when it went to Nassau. He should be here sometime this week, along with the rest of the officers."

"Aye, we'll get the measure of him when he arrives. This is all good news."

Shelton looked up at the mast, then back at his captain. "Your father kept referring to this as the Kittery ship. Does it have a real name?"

"Aye, it does. It will be revealed when we place it in commission. If we keep our wits about us, we are going to be an ugly surprise for His Majesty's navy."

"God willing! Your father said this ship is being built differently. How so?"

"Come, let me show you, but you must keep it secret. The crew will be told once we leave Kittery, but only the officers will know the details."

"Aye, Captain. Your words go from your lips to God's ears."

Bristol, early September 1777

The oily, pungent smell of stain filled the closed area that, when finished, would be the captain's cabin. Smythe put down the brush and walked out onto the main deck and took a few deep breaths. Tomorrow he would help the yard workers apply the first coat of varnish to the captain's cabin and the officer's quarters. Once the stain and varnish dried, the windows could be installed and caulked. The results would be well worth the effort, and they would be well appreciated, for Davidson wanted the officers to eat all meals except breakfast with him in the cabin. The gunroom just forward of the officers' compartments was where officers and midshipmen would eat breakfast and relax when not on watch.

Smythe walked down the companionway to the berthing deck and watched yard workers mount the pulleys connecting the wheel to the rudder. Once the ship was launched and tied to a pier, the upper sections of *Puritan's* masts and the rigging would be installed. That evolution was at least a month away.

"Ahoy there, Mr. Smythe!"

Smythe recognized the annoyed tone Captain Davidson used when he did not wish to be kept waiting. Smythe looked over the side and saw his captain standing next to his carriage.

Smythe climbed down the temporary scaffolding, erected so the painters could paint the hull, then down a ladder to the ground, past *Puritan's* copper sheathing that gleamed in the afternoon sun."

"Good afternoon, sir. Welcome back to Bristol. What news have you?"

Davidson flicked a speck of imaginary dirt off his immaculate blue uniform. "Get cleaned up. I have a list of potential officers to review with you; I want to know if you vouch for any of them. And I have found where we can get a crew, so we shan't have to raid jails. What a load of codswallop if we had to take prisoners."

"Very well. Where shall we meet?"

"Plan on being at the house I rented by six and staying for supper."

Smythe brushed a lock of his blond hair from his eyes. "Yes, sir. That will give me time to wash."

"Phew! I would hope so. But you don't need to wear a uniform in this damnable heat." The footman standing by the carriage opened the door for the captain and, after closing it, took his position at the back of the cab. The driver flicked his reins, and the carriage rolled away from the docks.

At first, Smythe had wondered why such a dandy was in the Navy at all, dreading that here was another man who valued appearances over ability, family connection over actual competence. But over the course of several meetings and conversations, he had learned there was more to this officer than a well tailored uniform. Davidson was caustic at times, but he was willing to listen and would readily accept a better idea from a subordinate.

Above all, Davidson valued well-founded experience. During an earlier dinner, Davidson, who was usually guarded about his personal life, had admitted that he had never been in action. He'd spent the Seven Years War blockading French ports. He'd passed the lieutenant's exam easily, made commander four years later, and captain after three more. He'd remarked that being the third son of the Duke of Somerset had probably helped when his name was put up for promotion.

After supper, with the dishes cleared away and the tankards refilled, Captain Davidson placed three sheets of paper on the table and slid them towards Smythe's hand. "The Second Sea Lord said all these officers are unassigned for one reason or another. I do not know any of them." He sniffed and curled his lip. "However, as John Heywood remarked in his book of proverbs, beggars can't be choosers."

After the first time Davidson had quoted a proverb of Heywood's, Smythe had gone to Bristol's small circulating library and found a copy of the book. He had read through a fair bit of it but had never heard this one before. Still, he was pretty sure how it applied to their situation.

Smythe studied the list of 90 names. "Sir, I know four."

"Out with it, man. Don't hold back."

For a man who often appeared aloof, even dismissive, Davidson liked to dive into details. Smythe had learned that his captain easily gleaned what was important from what was not.

"Lieutenant Roote and Gladden were on the *Deer*. Roote is a good man, but he lost most of his left arm in the fight with *Duchess*. I wouldn't take Gladden because, unless he has changed, his heart is not bound to the sea. He tried to resign; I guess the Admiralty said no."

Davidson seemed to be appraising Smythe. "And the other two?"

"Rathburn and Hearns were midshipmen when I knew them. Both were competent; I would have thought that by now they would be lieutenants."

"Do they have potential to be good officers?"

"Rathburn yes. Hearns.... perhaps."

"Why perhaps?"

"Sir, he was shaken by what happened on the *Deer*. We got an ugly taste of the rebel's tactics, and it cost us dearly. The memory may still affect him, but he is a good man."

"Would you take a chance on either midshipman?"

"Sir, I would rather deal with men I know than men I don't, so yes. But that is only three; If you wish, I can show the list to other lieutenants supervising the construction of their ships. They might have counsel for us."

"No, I would prefer not to do that. It is a good suggestion, but I don't think the Second Sea Lord would appreciate it if this list were shown around." Davidson slid another list across the table. "These are the available masters."

Smythe scanned the names, written in alphabetical order; he tapped one. "I know Bartholomew Shilling from *Jodpur*. If we can get him, then I would do so quickly."

"Why is he available?"

"Sir, I do not know, but I can tell you this: Master Shilling should be a captain, but does not want the responsibility. He has forgotten more about ship handling than most captains know."

"Sounds like a man we can use."

"Aye, Captain. It would be my pleasure to sail with him again."

"Good. We take Shilling , Roote and the two midshipmen. I will let the Admiralty know and they can make the necessary arrangements to have them assigned to *Puritan* along with Lieutenant Bullocks. The price I paid to get this list was that I have to take him. Many people consider him to be a complete cock-up until you get into a fight with the enemy, and that's when Bullocks shines. His men love him, but senior officers hate Bullocks because he is not afraid to speak his mind and is right more often than not. I trust you will keep him in line."

Davidson paused and sipped a French wine he imported from an area north of Bordeaux. "I will arrange to man *Puritan* from sailors sitting on barracks ships in Portsmouth. The faster we get *Puritan* in commission, the faster we can claim them. The other challenge is figuring out how to get them here without having half of them desert. Someplace along the way, we'll go to the local orphanage to get our powder monkeys. If we are lucky, we can turn them into seamen as they get older. You might want to give them some schooling so they can read and write. Also, once they are on board, assign them to learn a skill from the bosun, carpenter, cook and even the quartermaster."

"Aye, sir, I will do that. By the bye sir, I think there is a way to get the crew to Bristol once we have *Puritan* in the water. Then we can put them to work helping us get fitted out."

"How do you propose to get the men from Portsmouth over to Bristol? We can't have them walk, for God's sake."

"Sir, Hillhouse has a scow they use to haul lumber we may be able use. It'll only take three or four of us to sail it around to Portsmouth. On the first trip, we can take a couple of yard hands and pay them an extra quid or so for their time. Once we get the officers here, we can get the rest of the crew ourselves. It may take two or three trips, and Hillhouse may want to charge us for the scow."

"Brilliant! I like the way you think, Smythe. Since you know Harkins, you will ask to use the scow, politely of course, once we know the day *Puritan* will be launched. If he is reluctant, I will explain the facts of life, if you take my meaning."

"Yes, sir, I do."

"Excellent. Let us toast our solution. It is much better than the bloody nest of vipers you get when you scour the streets of Bristol and take whatever scum you can cajole to make their mark on a muster."

Davidson's view of the poor made Smythe uncomfortable, but he understood the meaning of his statement. In order to man their ships, Royal Navy captains often had to stoop to devious ways to get men to sign on. One was getting them drunk. Another was paying their fines or bail in return for having bailiffs turn them over to the Royal Navy and its strict discipline. The list of officers, and Davidson's confidence that he could pull men from barracks ships, told Smythe that his captain had political connections beyond anything that he or his father could imagine.

Kittery, September 1777

Flags hung from the rigging of the Kittery ship as it rode easily next to the pier. Hanging from the flag halyard was the ensign of the Continental Navy. At the top of the mainmast, a flag with a coiled rattlesnake on a yellow background and the words "Don't Tread on Me" rippled in the light wind. The Marines had first flown it when they landed on Nassau; Hacker had allowed it to be hung on *Providence;* Jaco had flown it on *Cutlass,* and now it was flying on the new frigate.

The dignitaries—John Hewes, John Adams, Javier Jacinto, John Hackett and Elliot Simmons—sat facing the ship's crew mustered at the aft end of the main deck. Conversation amongst the ranks stopped when the Chairman of the Marine Committee walked to the quarterdeck's forward railing. The only sound was the gentle flapping of the flags and the occasional slap of a wave against the side.

"Gentlemen, I am honored to share this moment with you. I want to thank Mr. Hackett for designing this fine ship, Mr. Simmons for providing its cannon, and all the men who built a ship that is both formidable and seaworthy. Captain Jacinto, please join me."

Jaco, wearing the dark blue coat of Continental Naval officers with gold epaulets on both shoulders, climbed the steps to the quarterdeck. His chose a deliberate pace, remembering what Captain Jones and Lieutenant Struthers had said: "Don't rush about. Show you are in control, even when your mind is racing and your stomach is churning." Today, his gut was rumbling from excitement, not fear. About to turn 18, he was to take command of a frigate.

The two men shook hands, and before Adams released Jacinto's, he put his left hand on the young captain's shoulder. Adams turned to the audience. "It is my honor to officially name and place the Continental Navy *Frigate Scorpion* in commission. May the Royal Navy feel its sting."

Adams took an envelope from his coat pocket. "Captain, here are your sailing orders."

After the applause died down, Adams sat down and John Hewes bent over and picked up a long wooden box. He approached the new captain. "In appreciation of your accomplishments that led to selecting you to command *Scorpion,* the Congress would like to present you with this spyglass. May you use it in both peace and war. God bless our cause, and God bless *Scorpion.*"

Now it was Jacinto's turn to speak. "Mr. Adams, Mr. Hewes, on behalf of *Scorpion's* crew, thank you. It is my honor to take command. I promise that the Royal Navy will rue the day *Scorpion* took to the seas. We will defeat the enemy wherever and whenever we find them."

Someone amongst the crew yelled, "Three cheers for Captain Jacinto and *Scorpion!*"

In his cabin after the ceremony, Jaco's father handed him a letter from Reyna, a book called the *Nautical Almanac,* and a beautifully finished triangular oak box. On the top was a brass plaque that said P. Dolland & Son. Under the name was the date it was finished—April 7th, 1761, and a serial number.

Jaco recognized the book compiled by the British astronomer Nevil Maskelyne, based on the work of the German astronomer Tobias Mayer, who'd corrected the data on the phases of the moon from previous astronomers. Maskelyne added data on the positions of Venus and Jupiter relative to the earth. If either planet was visible through an octant or sextant, then a ship's longitude could be plotted within 30 miles.

Jaco eased open the brass latches and opened the box. Inside was a brass and wood sextant with reflecting lenses that allowed the user to take elevations of celestial bodies of up to 120 degrees, 40 more than the octant that had already been purchased for the ship.

"Thank you, *Papá*. I will enjoy using this sextant. Where did you get it?"

"Out of England via Amsterdam. The spyglass was also made by Dolland & Son and uses a new type of glass that eliminates the image and color distortion common in older spyglasses. Use both in good health!"

Bristol, late September 1777

Puritan was launched three months after its originally scheduled date. Before the chocks and wedges were knocked out so that the cradle on which the frigate rested could roll down the way, Langston turned to Smythe. "This is the most dangerous moment in a ship's life. If we don't have it balanced right, it might fall on its side before it gets into the water. Worse, once it is in the water, the bloody thing might simply sink. I've seen both happen, and when it does, there are red faces all around."

Puritan rumbled into the River Avon. The cradle, weighed down with cast iron ingots, sank enough so that when the pegs holding the trestles to the side of the ship were hammered out, it could be pulled ashore and re-used. *Puritan* came free and floated, seeming to balance herself on the water.

Next, *Puritan* was hauled to a pier to be fitted out. Its cannon had been sitting on their carriages in a shed since June. They would be the last items loaded aboard. Stepping the tops of *Puritan's* three masts and installing the rigging came first.

Every day of the fitting out, Smythe walked through *Puritan's* hold looking for leaks. It was a ritual he planned to continue. He finished inspecting the compartments on the berthing deck where the lieutenants, the master, the bosun, quartermaster, the captain of the marines and the surgeon, if they were lucky enough to have one, would live. They were ready to be occupied. Hearing the noise of a saw and hammer in the captain's cabin, Smythe went aft and found Captain Davidson watching the carpenter at work. Davidson's arms were folded, his face twisted in an expression of mild distain.

"Ah, there you are, Mr. Smythe. What do you think of the Admiralty designed tables?"

"Sir, they are sturdy and can be easily stowed."

"That is a very practical answer. So, you don't think we need one with more character?"

By character, Smythe took Davidson to mean one that was custom designed and built just for the *Puritan*. "No, sir, I don't. When you are given a larger ship to command, that will be the time for custom work. Here a table has to be small to fit; there is no room here to display a table of character."

"Ahhhhh, good point, Smythe." Davidson looked about with a considering eye.

"What do you think about having one or two of my men on board?"

Smythe realized that Davidson was talking about the butler and footman who accompanied him on his carriage. Or it might be a cook he had in mind.

"Sir, we can make room for someone who is a good cook, but unless he is a watch stander, or handle sails or mans a gun, he will only consume food, water, and space in the fo'c'sle."

Davidson didn't say anything, so Smythe continued. "Sir, if it were up to me, I would say no to a manservant. My prior captains and the officers ate what the crew ate and deemed a cook was unnecessary. The only difference between what the officers and the ratings ate was that we had wine and port.

The men drank beer and got their tot of rum every day because the water quickly gets foul."

"I take your point. But, I disagree. I will have Alastair join us. He is an excellent cook, will take care of the officer's laundry and other tasks I will assign him. Write it off to one of the privileges of a peer to make life a little bit easier on board one of His King's ships."

"Aye, aye, sir. We can give him one the compartments for midshipmen. Rathburn and Hearns can have the other."

"Good oh. Then it is sorted. I will inform Alastair and he can begin to pack what he needs and stock the pantry."

Smythe hoped that he would be dismissed so he could attend to the next item his "to do" list—inspecting the sails. They were already cut to the sail plan, but there are always differences between what is designed and what fits. And there was the minor detail of making sure the ship received all the sails in the plan.

"When do you think we should go fetch the crew?"

"Captain, I can ask Mr. Harkins for a couple of hands to sail the scow. If we leave Friday, we would drop anchor in Portsmouth Sunday afternoon. With a letter from you, we could bring our officers, warrants, and 60 to 70 of the crew."

"A weekend trip is a good idea. Inform the yard we will take them up on their gracious offer to use their scow for a few days—for free." Davidson's eyebrow raised and Smythe heard the derision in his captain's voice.

At first Harkins objected, saying the scow was unsuited for carrying a large number of people. He succumbed to Davidson's persuasive argument that His Majesty's Navy would not be pleased if a shipyard refused to assist in a time of dire need.

* * *

The scow wasn't ideal, but the hold was big enough to let 60 men hang their hammocks from the iron cargo tie downs.

Smythe was sure they would grumble about the tight quarters, but hoped they would appreciate that they were about to go to sea rather than stay in the cramped barracks ship. After delivering Captain Davidson's note to a captain at the naval base, Smythe was led by Commander Russell to H.M.S. *Essex*, a 64-gun three-decker recently converted to a barracks ship. Its masts were gone and its gun decks converted to berthing spaces. The captain's cabin was divided into smaller spaces to provide quarters for officers awaiting assignments.

Master Shilling was leaning over the bulwark and spotted Smythe and his unruly blond hair walking down the pier; he was waiting at the gangway with Roote and Rathburn by the time Smyth boarded. All three were excited to see their former shipmate, and pleased by the news they were joining *Puritan's* crew. Lieutenant Bullocks, however, was nowhere to be found.

Annoyed, Commander Russell confronted the officer on the watch, an elderly lieutenant. "Where is Lieutenant Bullocks?" he asked.

"I don't know, sir, but I suggest the commander check the local pubs. That's where he spends his time. Try the Red Lion first. It's his favorite. If he is not there, try one of the others along the street."

Smythe nodded. "Mr. Roote, you and Master Shilling pick 60 good men and get them on their way to the scow tied up at the pier. Also find Midshipman Hearns." Turning to the Royal Navy officer who led him to the barracks ship, Smythe said, "Commander Russell, we will be back next weekend to collect more men for *Puritan's* crew.

Commander Russell replied, "We will be ready to help."

Smythe turned to *Puritan's* senior midshipman, "Mr. Rathburn, you and I have a lieutenant to find."

Bullocks was not at the Red Lion, nor at the Dolphin, whose proprietor suggested they try the West India Inn. As they entered the smoky great room of that establishment, they spotted a burly lieutenant seated at a table with one arm around a woman. His blue coat had seen better days and needed cleaning as well as mending. By the description given to Smythe, this man was their missing officer.

Smythe stood in front of the drunken Bullocks, his hands clasped behind the small of his back and his feet shoulder width apart. Bullocks let go of the woman and looked Smythe up and down as if he were examining a piece of meat. Bullocks took a swig from his tankard, belched, and demanded, "What the bloody hell do you want?"

"Mr. Bullocks, I am Lieutenant Smythe, First Lieutenant of His Majesty's frigate *Puritan* to which you have been assigned. You are to come with me."

"Go fuck yourself. No one wants me."

Bullocks spoke loud enough to attract the attention of other patrons. Smythe took a step closer to Bullocks. He had to steel himself not to recoil from the sour stench of ale and body odor. "Mr. Bullocks, you either come with me or I will have the Marines waiting outside arrest you for drunkenness on duty, failure to obey an order, and whatever else I can charge you with. Instead of living on *Essex,* you will live on a prison ship where the conditions will less pleasant, and you will not be allowed to go ashore. Now, are you going to come with me, or do I call the Marines?"

"Bloody hell, man. I need to finish my drink."

"No, you don't. You've had enough. Now get up."

Bullocks belched again and put his tankard down. He wobbled as he pushed himself to a standing position. Rathburn grabbed his left arm to keep Bullocks from falling down or starting a fight.

With firm grips on each of Bullocks' ample biceps, Rathburn and Smythe led him out of the inn. As they exited, Smythe tossed two shillings to the owner, who nodded. Smythe didn't care if it was over payment; he just wanted Bullocks without any fuss.

Bullocks could barely put one foot in front of the other. Fifty feet from the inn, he wrenched his arms free, lurched into an alley, and vomited. That seemed to do him some good; by the time they reached the scow, Bullocks was sober enough to walk on his own. But Smythe didn't want to spend three days with the man in his present condition.

"Bullocks, you come with me. Rathburn, fetch his sea chest."

The base's fire station was 200 feet from where the scow was moored. In the back, Smythe handed Bullocks bar of soap. "Strip and clean yourself, or I will get some men to hold you and I will do it with a brush."

Bullocks rolled his eyes and undressed. He was hosed down by the firemen, who laughed as they sprayed him. Now somewhat cleaner, Bullocks put on dry clothes and was escorted back to the scow.

Bullocks' sea chest seemed to be uncommonly heavy. The sailors cursed and swore as they tried to hoist it onto the scow's deck. It slipped from their hands, crashed to the deck, and split open. A scattering of clothing tumbled out, and three bags of coins clinked to the deck. Rathburn scooped them up and took them to the scow's cabin. Evidently, Bullocks was the sort of officer who preferred to keep his prize money close, rather than entrust it to a bank, and spent it freely.

On board Frigate Scorpion, *late September 1777*

The sun was out but not enough to take the fall chill out of the air. *Scorpion* sailed under mainsails and jib, down the Piscataqua River. Along the shore, leaves were beginning to change color, but had not reached their full riot of red, orange, yellow, brown and green.

Once in the Atlantic, Jaco tacked the ship several times to train the crew and see how *Scorpion* handled before adding sail. Just as he expected, the longer hull, more pointed bow and tapered stern easily sliced through the water.

To compensate for the added weight of three layers of wood along her sides, *Scorpion's* armament was reduced from 15 guns a side to ten. With paired 9-pounder stern and bow chasers, she carried 24 cannon. In the Royal Navy, *Scorpion* would have been classified by size and tonnage as a sixth-rate frigate. Her speed and maneuverability made her ideal for escorting convoys, blockade duty, scouting, and most important, hunting.

Another of John Hackett's innovations was a sealed, two foot extended keel containing 10 tons of tar-covered lead ingots. It increased *Scorpion's* draft and added weight, but Hackett had calculated that the counterweight would increase the amount of sail the frigate could carry when the wind came over either beam.

As sails were added, *Scorpion* accelerated and her bow cut through the swells with ease. *Scorpion* showed its captain that it was not a plow horse, but a responsive, agile thoroughbred that liked to run fast.

With each combination of sails, Jaco let *Scorpion* run for 60 minutes, recording the course, wind direction, sea state and speed. In the strong, steady breeze coming over her port quarter, the frigate reached 14 knots with the royals, topgallants, topsails and mains on each mast sheeted home. It felt that it could go faster with more sails hung.

Jaco worked *Scorpion* north toward the south shore of a small, uninhabited island called Monhegan, whose rocky cliffs were perfect for gunnery practice. They arrived just before dark. The ship spent the first part of the night sailing slowly out into the Atlantic to give the crew a chance to rest. Just after midnight *Scorpion* reversed course and headed west toward Monhegan. After a breakfast of oatmeal, apples and bacon, Jaco mustered the crew.

"Gentlemen, *Scorpion* has sailed as we expected—fast, stable and easy to handle. Today, we will practice gunnery. *Scorpion's* long 12-pounders were cast specially for this ship. They give us longer range and are more accurate than 12-pounders with shorter barrels. However, to take advantage of their range, we have to be able to hit what we aim at! I sent Lieutenant Shelton ashore to set up canvas targets on the cliffs. I expect you to hit them. This is not a game. Fire as if the cost of the shot that does not hit the target will be taken from your pay. Crews that cannot fire at least two accurate shots every five minutes will be re-organized. The goal is three shots in five minutes. Lieutenants Radcliffe and Hayes and Midshipmen Garrison and Patterson will be watching to ensure that no shortcuts are taken."

Scorpion made four passes past the targets, and Jaco watched the results through his new telescope. The results were good, but he wanted better, so after lunch the practice resumed at a distance of 300 yards from the cliff. Shards of rock and shrapnel from the iron balls ripped the targets apart. As the gun crews aim improved, Jaco tacked *Scorpion* around so it was approximately 500 yards away. Even with the ship traveling at five knots, the iron balls hammered into the cliffs, shredding what was left of the canvas.

After that, Jaco had the crew slacken the sails and let *Scorpion* slowly sail parallel to the main coast. Dinner that night was smoked beef and boiled potatoes washed down with a ration of beer.

Jaco listened to his officers discuss their observations. By the time they'd fired two-dozen balls from each cannon, all of the gun crews were firing and reloading well within the three-shots-in-five-minutes standard he'd set. Midshipmen Garrison and Patterson were jubilant, and Lieutenant Hayes asked Jack Shelton if any other crew in the Continental Navy could fire as fast and accurately as *Scorpion*'s crew. Tomorrow, however, was another day, and different conditions would prevail. The sailing and gun drills would continue.

* * *

During the night, *Scorpion* paralleled the Maine coast, staying far enough away to avoid the islands. By nine in the morning they were back at Monhegan Island for more target practice. After the gun crews demonstrated their accuracy, it was time for the swivel guns and for the Marines to show how good they were as sharpshooters.

A small plank attached to a thin rope was tossed over the side by a sailor straddling the bowsprit. One at a time, the Marines fired until each man had fired three shots, while their commander kept track of hits and misses. Given they were firing muskets that were notoriously inaccurate beyond 50 yards, close was considered good enough. What Jaco really wanted was for the Marines to become proficient shooting from the rigging and the narrow confines of the main top platforms on each mast.

Then the swivel guns were fired, and the water around the plank erupted. When the geysers subsided, all that remained were splinters. Pleased with the day's work, Jaco set a course for Kittery, convinced *Scorpion* was almost ready to meet the Royal Navy.

CHAPTER 14

SCORPION'S STING

On board Frigate Scorpion, *October 1777*

The pleasant smell of cooked bacon permeated the captain's cabin, and the remains of a breakfast of bacon, eggs, and bread were on the table. A local apple grower had delivered a dozen barrels of freshly pressed apple cider, and Jaco was enjoying a glassful and some time alone when there was a knock on his door. In response to his "Come in," Midshipman Garrison entered.

"Sir, a courier arrived from Philadelphia and insists on personally giving you a box he has brought with him."

"Bring him along, and let's see what is so important."

A man in his late twenties was ushered in, carrying a wide, flat oak box. He put it on the table and asked, "Sir, are you Captain Jaco Jacinto?"

"I am. Who are you, sir?"

"Sir, I am Lieutenant Ralph Rangle. I work for the Marine Committee. Mr. Hewes and you father wanted me to make sure you got this set of French charts before you sailed. They are the most recent we could obtain, printed in 1775."

Rangle opened the latches so Jaco could see the contents. Each chart had a sheet of thick blue paper glued to the back and was separated from the others by a thin piece of linen. Jaco examined the top chart of the Atlantic Coast of France.

"Perfecto! Please pass my thanks on to the Marine Committee. We will put these to good use."

"Then I shall take my departure. I wish you good luck and Godspeed."

Wind pushed *Scorpion* out into the river and then into the open waters of the Atlantic. Jaco summoned the officers to the captain's cabin, and once they were all gathered around the table, he spread out a chart of the Atlantic Coast of North America. Next, he took the envelope containing *Scorpion's* sailing orders from a locked box, and pulled the flap free of the wax seal. The handwriting was neat. He read aloud:

> Captain Jacinto,
>
> Take Scorpion into the Atlantic or the Caribbean to prey on British merchant ships, and bring your prizes to a port not held by the British where they and their cargo can be sold.
>
> Your primary mission is to disrupt British commerce wherever you can by capturing or destroying its merchant ships and raiding English ports. Should Scorpion encounter any Royal Navy men-of-war, use your judgment as to whether or not you should engage.
>
> Good luck and Godspeed.
>
> John Adams
> Chairman, Marine Committee
> Second Continental Congress

Captain Jacinto picked up a pair of dividers. "Gentlemen, we sail first toward Halifax, where we are likely to find merchant ships. *Scorpion* will escort any prizes back to Boston. Once in port, the prize crew captain turns over the ship to the proper authorities and re-embarks on *Scorpion.*"

He used the dividers to mark off the route of the next part of his plan. "Since all you know how much I love cold weather..." He waited for the chuckling to die down. "... *Scorpion* will swing north to a point about 100 miles east of Halifax and then head south, where any prizes we take will be escorted to Charleston or Savannah. Each time, we will stay only long enough to take on provisions. Understood?"

Jaco looked at his officers, who nodded. "If we meet the Royal Navy, we will use our superior speed to avoid any action that involves more than one of their frigates or a ship-of-the-line. However, I consider any solitary frigate near our size fair game. Every night at dinner, we will discuss a different phase of a battle between ships, so we all understand how to handle our ship and lead the men we command."

Jaco was pleased by the seriousness of the men at the table. "Every day, we are going to have gun drills. I want the men to be able to load, run out and fire their cannon in their sleep, and we will make sure each man knows every position and action in the gun drill."

Jack Shelton uncorked the bottle of port at the far end of the table and began pouring glasses. Jaco continued.

"Once a week, I intend to dine with the crew and take their questions. They must know and trust their captain, and they must know and trust each of you. I hate flogging, because there are other ways to enforce discipline. I want the crew to respect us and perform willingly for us. I do not want them to act out of fear. A crew that respects its officers will fight much harder for their captain than a crew that fears him. Tomorrow morning, I will address the crew to tell them of our orders and our plan. Now, let us drink to our cause, to *Scorpion,* and our success. Gentlemen, raise your glasses."

* * *

First light on their eighth day in the Atlantic unveiled light gray clouds and a five-foot swell in slate-blue water. It had been a cold night; the helmsman rubbed his hands to restore circulation. One of the unique features that Jaco had asked Hackett to design was a removable u-shaped enclosure around the binnacle and the wheel. In cold weather, it would keep the wind off the man who had to maintain a steady course; in battle, its three-inch thick planks would shield the helmsman from musket balls and splinters. Even so, the night watch left a man with cold feet and numb fingers.

Jacinto's standing orders were that, unless otherwise directed, *Scorpion* sailed at night only under her mainsails and jib. Now that that the sun was full up, Midshipman Garrison sent the men aloft to take advantage of the steady wind out of the so' west.

Standing by himself on the quarterdeck, Jacinto watched carefully before scanning the sea around his ship. White caps dotted the waves, and *Scorpion's* bow sent spray as far back as the foremast. He felt *Scorpion* was playing with the waves, wanting to go faster.

The midnight sextant sighting had indicted a position of 250 miles south of Halifax. So far, they had not encountered any merchant ships.

"Sail ho!" came a call from aloft. "Three points broad on the port bow."

With his spyglass, Jaco searched the horizon but saw nothing. "What type of ship?"

"Don't know yet, Captain. I can see her royals on three masts, and that's all."

Jaco looked up and called, "Can you tell what course the ship is on?"

There was a pause, and everyone on the quarterdeck could see both lookouts pointing their glasses at the unknown ship. "Sir, she's running so' west."

"Distance?"

"I'd reckon 12 miles."

The ship was over an hour away. If they continued their current course, would *Scorpion* pass ahead or behind it? Behind would be better; he was sure *Scorpion* could run down any prize worth the taking. Passing ahead mean *Scorpion* would have to reverse course and loop around.

Jacinto looked at Simon Cox, the third quartermaster's mate, who was all of 16. Anytime he stood out in the wind, the fair skin on his cheeks face turned bright red. "Mr. Cox, hold a course of west by north."

A while later came the call, "Deck ahoy. I think the ship has spotted us. She's just set her fore staysail. It's a merchantman. She's flying the flag of the British West Indies India Company."

"Mr. Wilson, please show them our flag so they know who we are."

Soon the Gadsden flag was flying from the maintop, and the four-foot by six-foot Continental Navy ensign streamed from the aft mizzenmast stay.

"Mr. Garrison, we're going to approach from the starboard rear quarter. When we get closer, go to the bow and ask them to heave to. West Indiamen have 9-pounders, and we will not take any chances. If they refuse, we fall off, rake her from the stern, then come up on the windward side, about 500 yards away. At that range, she will be target practice. If and when she strikes, we heave to and send over a boarding party."

About a mile from the merchantman, Jaco ordered *Scorpion* cleared for action. He was expecting resistance.

"Mr. Radcliffe, please show him our sting. Load chain shot and run out. Tell the gunners not to prick the cartridges, in case the ship does not want a fight."

Those on the quarterdeck heard the rumble and felt the vibration of the wooden wheels as the 3,000-pound cannon and 600 pound carriages were wheeled across the gun deck. Jaco scanned the merchant ship *Nevis*. Two men in blue coats were studying his ship, one with a spyglass and the other with his naked eye. Two other men stood by the wheel, and the one not holding the spokes looked over his shoulder at the approaching Continental Navy ship. None of the gun ports were open, nor were there men in the rigging with muskets. *So, Captain of the* Nevis, *what game are you playing?*

"Mr. Radcliffe, fire one warning shot from our port bow chaser."

Radcliffe, standing with his torso out of the companionway, bent down and yelled the order. At the forward end of the gun deck, Midshipman Garrison had the long 9-pounder bow chaser aimed so its ball would go past the *Nevis*. The entire gun crew was grinning; they had the honor of firing the *Scorpion's* first shot at an enemy ship. A touch of glowing hemp to the pile of gunpowder filling the touchhole, a flash, then the cannon bellowed and the carriage jumped back. Wind blew gunsmoke into the gun deck. Swiftly, the gun crew cleaned and loaded the cannon.

A voice from the maintop yelled out. "Deck, ball spout forward of the port bow."

"Captain, aye." What Jaco did not see was a response. Neither of the men on *Nevis's* quarterdeck moved. "Mr. Radcliffe, pass the word to fire another shot. Perhaps our British friends didn't see the first one."

Garrison nodded to the gun captain. Again, a flash, a loud bang, and more smoke on the gun deck, but *Nevis* held course. "Mr. Radcliffe, ask Mr. Garrison to warp the bow chaser so that it bears on the *Nevis*. When it does, fire one shot at the hull."

Radcliffe bent down, and a short time later the gun boomed. Chunks of wood flew off *Nevis's* bulwark aft of the mizzenmast.

A man at the aft end of the merchantman's quarterdeck waved frantically and released the halyard to lower the flag. Its sails were let loose and flapped in the breeze; the ship started to slow and turned westward into the wind.

"Mr. Radcliffe, have the port gun crews come on the main deck. We are going fall off to come up on our prize's leeward side. Keep starboard battery ready to fire. If they fire on us, you may return fire until I give the order to cease."

Radcliffe waved an acknowledgement.

Scorpion's bow was approaching the *Nevis*. The loudest noise was the flapping of the heavy canvass on both ships and the groaning of the masts as *Scorpion* wallowed in the swells. Jack Shelton stood on the bulwark as far forward as he could get, a speaking trumpet in one hand, the other grasping a stay.

"*Nevis* standby to accept a boarding party. Have the crew muster by the foremast on the main deck."

The man in the blue frocked coat waved.

Amidships, *Scorpion's* crew was already hoisting the cutter over the side, the oars flat on the thwarts that doubled as seats. Just before it was lowered to the water, two men climbed in. Once it was in the water, two more rowers lowered themselves aboard, followed by Lieutenant Hayes and four more seamen.

The cutter was joined in the water by the 20-foot long boat; together they ferried over the 20-man prize crew and brought back *Nevis's* officers and papers.

Shelton climbed up on the quarterdeck to report. "Captain, Hayes sent back word that *Nevis* is carrying 10 tons of sugar, 48 barrels of rum, several of which we are about to liberate, and a ton of assorted spices. The captain will be over on the next boat, and he has warned his crew that any resistance will be met with force. Hayes has the key to the ship's armory. And, sir, I'd like to suggest that we bring all its powder over to *Scorpion*."

"Good idea. How long do you think it will take?" *Spices! Nevis will fetch a nice pot of prize money if we are lucky enough to get her to Boston.*

"Two hours or so, once we get our prize crew on board."

"Mr. Shelton, inform Lieutenant Hayes that we will not look for any more merchant ships, and we shall escort him to Boston. However, should we come across a frigate, *Scorpion* will engage while he is to continue to port. He is not to risk our prize getting recaptured."

* * *

Jaco was not the only one on deck watching the brilliant orange ball slowly move below the horizon, spreading a wake of light across the waves. From where he stood at the aft end of the quarterdeck, it looked as if *Scorpion* were sailing right into the setting sun. He looked astern and watched the crew of *Nevis* reef sails into a nighttime rig. On *Scorpion,* the same drill was happening; he wanted to make sure its sails were trimmed so it wouldn't run away from the slower *Nevis.*

"Sir, a quick word."

The speaker was Abner Jeffords, who was alone at the wheel. His quartermaster's mate was busy supervising hanging a lantern that *Nevis* could see. Lieutenant Radcliffe was at the forward end of the deck, watching the crew coil lines as the ship prepared for what it hoped would be an uneventful night at sea.

Speaking softly so it would be difficult for anyone else to hear, Jaco asked, "Jeffords, how are things on the berthing deck?"

"Well, Captain, there's space for 250 men, but we've only got 200 so there is extra room. Most of the lads, if that is what you're asking, are good men. Me and the others from *Cutlass* and *Providence* have told them what a good officer you are but there's a few I've got my eye on. They're all from Boston and think Mr. Radcliffe's connections will help them after the war. He's a slippery one, that Mr. Radcliffe."

"In what way?"

"He's always asking you for something, but never gives anything in return. And, he is very impressed with himself and his family's position among the wealthy of Boston. Most of the men give him a wide berth, if you know what I mean."

"I do.

Jeffords looked around so see if anyone was around them. No one was. "If there's trouble a-brewing, we—that's Landry, Lofton, Gaskins and Penway and a few others—will let you know."

I"m counting on that."

Jeffords made an adjustment to the wheel and looked aft at the ship's wake to make sure it was straight as an arrow. It was. Satisfied, he continued. "Captain, I've had the pleasure of going to sea with you since we were together on *Alfred*. Do you know what the crew called you behind your back?"

Jaco didn't know whether or not to be alarmed, so he did his best to be neutral. "No, enlighten me."

"They dubbed you Midshipman Perfecto. And then, on *Providence* you were Lieutenant Perfecto, and now you are Captain Perfecto. We've all heard you say the word, and even the laziest man aboard has seen how your standards and our drills pay off. Sir, I can't speak for every man jack on

Scorpion, but most of us would follow you through the portals of hell."

Jaco didn't know what to say. "Thank you, Jeffords. I will do my best to live up to these expectations and keep us from that particular doorway."

"I am confident you will."

Perfecto! I have accomplished one of my goals as a leader. Jaco was smiling from ear to ear as he headed to his cabin to make a journal entry.

Royal Navy Base, Portsmouth, October 1777

Captain Davidson's frigate slowly sailed up the channel, following a small sloop to where it was to anchor. With only half his crew, Davidson was being cautious.

Once *Puritan* was secure in its berth and Davidson was satisfied the frigate was not going to drift, he called out, "Put the boats in the water." Turning to his first lieutenant, he said, "Mr. Smythe, I must go ashore to report *Puritan* has arrived. I will tell the Port Captain that we are expecting the lighters to be alongside at eight a.m. with supplies. Mr. Roote and Midshipman Rathburn will go to the *Essex* and get the rest of the crew. Mr. Bullocks is not allowed to go ashore."

"Aye, aye, sir."

"One more thing, Mr. Smythe. Since your parents live across the river in Gosport, you have leave to spend nights at home. If you wish to do so, I will instruct the watch to have a boat take you to the Gosport Ferry Dock at six p.m. and be waiting for you at seven in the morning. Is that agreeable?"

"Yes, sir. It is most generous. Thank you."

"You've earned it, and don't thank me, thank your parents for living nearby!"

Captain Davidson waited impatiently while *Puritan's* pinnace was hoisted over the side and the six oarsmen took up their positions. With two sailors holding it close to the side of the ship, the two junior officers made their way down the ladder on the side of the hull. Then the 20 foot-long pinnace was pulled forward so Captain Davidson could climb down and take his position at the stern. He had a very important matter to attend to, one he felt sure would make all the difference in the world to the ship's morale.

The next day, Captain Davidson asked all the ship's officers to join him in his cabin. Waiting there was a stranger none had seen before.

"Gentlemen, this is Mr. Glass, my tailor. He is here to fit you with a new set of uniforms. He will measure you, and by the time we leave Portsmouth, each man will have four new coats, eight shirts and six sets of breeches. Do not concern yourselves with the cost; they have already been paid for. When we go to sea, we will all look like proper Royal Navy officers. Come forward, Mr. Smythe, you're first."

* * *

Darren Smythe stood by the window in the third floor bedroom he'd once shared with an older brother, looking out onto Portsmouth harbor. In the moonlight, he spotted *Puritan's* crosstrees amongst those of the ships anchored in the harbor. It, not this house, was now his home.

While he had been away, a chasm had formed between his parents, brothers, sisters and himself. There was no ill-will or bad feeling on either side; it was just their daily lives were very different. Theirs was a world of wives, children, social events, contracts and business decisions. His was a life of almost monastic discipline and enduring danger from the sea, accident, or the enemy. He'd also experienced the death of close friends, something that no one else in the family had witnessed.

Darren could talk fluently about navigation, ship handling, leading men, ship construction and repair, but these topics held little interest for the others. His stories about life on board Royal Navy ships were politely listened too, and then the adults went back to discussing potential contracts, children, and who was marrying whom amongst their friends.

His sister Emily's husband was a barrister who, among other clients, handled Smythe & Sons legal affairs. Eric, the oldest of his siblings, was an engineer and helped his father run the family business by designing medical instruments and managing the factory. Gerald, who Darren regarded as the smartest of his siblings, had a degree in chemistry and created compounds that became medicines in their apothecary.

Family was important. Darren was glad to see them and wanted to be part of their life, not merely a stranger who showed up every year or so. Deep inside, he knew that if he were asked, he would give up the navy and contribute to Smythe & Sons. He would do it, but not willingly. For as long as Darren could remember, he'd yearned to serve on His Majesty's ships.

Even when he'd doubted his ability to sail *Deer* to Bermuda, or when on the blood-stained deck of *Sorcerer* he'd surrendered a King's ship, he would not have changed his choice. It was the life he, not anyone else, knew was right for himself. Now, as a First Lieutenant, he was one step away from his goal of being the captain of his own ship, something he'd dreamed about as a little boy sitting on the rock watching the ships come and go from Portsmouth.

A conversation during dinner about the war with the rebellious colonies had brought him to this pensive moment. The question of how the war was affecting Smythe & Sons was being discussed when Emily tossed her napkin on the table and looked at Darren.

"I think this war is stupid. English boys are being killed every day in North America, and what does it get us? A few extra orders? Will those orders make a difference in whether or not we and our employees eat? No! His Majesty is wasting hundreds of thousands of pounds and mens' lives because he does not want to give British citizens the right to be represented in Parliament. I think this war is about men wanting to show how powerful they are rather than doing what's right. I say we end the war by giving the rebels a choice—their independence or the same rights every British citizen enjoys! In the end, it is we who will be taxed to pay for this stupid war that may get one of my brothers killed. Sorry, Darren, but that's how I feel."

When she finished, Darren couldn't keep from smiling—that was Emily. She had a way of getting right to the core of any topic. Emily's words reminded him of the conversations he'd had with Jaco Jacinto. He wondered where the young rebel officer was, and whether he would ever see him again.

On board Frigate Scorpion, *October 1777*

Right after leaving Boston, Jaco mustered the crew and passed around a sheet that listed the estimated payout for *Nevis,* using Captain Jones' formula.

	Share	Total Prize Pool	Number of Participants	Share
Continental Congress	1/8	£2,375	1	£2,375
Ship's Captain	1/8	£2,375	1	£2,375
Lieutenants, Surgeon, Marine Captain	1/8	£2,375	4	£593.75
Warrant officers - carpenter, Marine officers, quartermaster, bo' sun	1/8	£2,375	4	£593.75
Midshipmen, Marine sergeant, mates	1/8	£2,375	12	£197.92
Crew	3/8	£2,375	185	£38.51

Nevis prize money pool as calculated by Jaco

Assuming the cargo sold for £12,000 and the ship for £7,000, the paper showed how much each man on *Scorpion* would be due. Jaco had insisted that the men be paid in English pounds; he was not sure what the money being issued by any of the 13 colonies would be worth.The amount each seaman would receive was about 10 times his monthly pay. For the officers, it was a small fortune.

Now, replenished with barrels of dried apples and pears, casks of salt beef, pork, flour, beer and water provided by Boston merchants, they were headed south. The farther *Scorpion* sailed, the warmer it got.

At noon, the three midshipmen took turns with the sextant to fix their position, striving to match the one Lieutenant Radcliffe plotted. All put *Scorpion* 100 miles off the Virginia coast due east of the entrance to Chesapeake Bay. In his log, Jaco noted *Scorpion* was loafing along at nine knots and had not seen another ship since rounding Cape Cod.

The afternoon drill covered the steps they would take to sail the ship if the wheel were shot away. Gaskins was confident he could rig pulleys to get the rudder working in short order from either the hatch in the after hold or the one at the aft end of the berthing deck. Jaco had a question.

"Can we have the parts in place, ready to use?"

Gaskins' smile showed his missing teeth, and his words hissed out as he answered. "Aye, sssir, we can."

"Can we test it?"

"Aye, sssir, that we can do."

Jaco grinned. "Why haven't you done it, then?"

Gaskins knuckled his forehead. "Captain, it will be done before you go to sssleep."

"Before you start work, bring me a sketch. Sometime in the next day or so, we will have a drill in which we tack the ship using one of these methods."

Other officers were enjoying the sunshine. Sailors not on watch were drying or clothes, or writing letters, or whittling. Two sailors had taken out penny whistles and were having a contest to see who could play "Yankee Doodle Dandy" faster.

Jaco's plans for the next day's drills were interrupted by the shout, "Sail ho!" from the masthead. "Deck, it's a bloody forest of sails, two points forward of the starboard beam. We can see at least eight sets of sails, and three are much taller than the others."

Jaco decided he wanted to see for himself. "Mr. Shelton, I need some exercise and am going to the main top."

Halfway up, Jaco remembered why his top men all wore strips of cloth over their hands. His fingers bore small specks of the coal black, sticky pitch that covered the shrouds. Worse, the queasiness and fear of heights returned, worse than ever. He swallowed, willing his stomach to settle.

The platform on the mainmast was about 80 feet above the Atlantic, and *Scorpion* was heeled five degrees because she was sailing as close to the wind as she could. For a second, Jaco's imagination and fear took hold and showed him what it would be like to fall. Then he took hold of himself and completed the climb.

To make room on the platform, the junior lookout stepped around to the windward shroud. Jaco put one foot against the mast and kept both legs flexed to allow his body to absorb the corkscrew movement of the ship. It took all his mental strength to keep from grabbing hold of the mast and holding on as tight as he could. Then he sighted the ships.

The nearest were about eight miles away, and two were headed straight toward *Scorpion*. One was a frigate, the other was a sloop that looked like the *Sorcerer*. Farther back, the three largest ships were three-deckers and three more frigates. Jaco thanked the two sailors for spotting the ships. As he climbed down, he considered what to do next.

Do I take on the frigate and the sloop? To fight we would have to slow down, which would let the three-deckers catch up. Or do I exchange broadsides as we pass in opposite directions? A lucky shot from the frigate would slow us down. Do I let them close before I show them our heels? Or do I crowd on more sail and disappear over the horizon? With this wind, we can easily outrun their fastest ships.

Back on the quarterdeck, he turned to the ship's bosun. "Mr. Preston, call all hands. Get ready to make sail."

Once the sound of the bosun's whistle ended, he turned to Jeffords at the wheel. "Alter course two points to the port to give us a more southerly course. When we have all the sails set, we'll trim them for best speed."

Above, 18 top men, six to a mast and three on each side, stood on the foot lines beneath the royals' yards. Bo' Sun Preston put the speaking trumpet to his mouth and began to issue commands. He had a loud, booming voice and probably didn't need the trumpet to be heard.

"Free the gaskets on the royals."

The leading seamen yelled acknowledgement.

"Loose the royals, NOW!"

On deck, as the sails came down on all three masts, teams of men pulled on the sheets attached to the sails' clews to make sure the sail dropped cleanly and didn't foul the rigging.

It wasn't simultaneous, but close enough so any Royal Navy officer would admire a crew's ability to release three royals at the same time. On the deck, Preston waited until the men were off the yards before he bellowed, "Release the royals braces, NOW!"

At a suitable time, this was followed by "Haul the port and starboard royal braces on all three masts, NOW! Come on, lads, put your backs into it!"

Three pulls later, the royals' braces were stacked with the top and mainsail yards. "Port and starboard side, sheet home the royals."

Scorpion heeled over another two degrees from the added push. This caught some on the quarterdeck by surprise. To Jaco, *Scorpion* was starting to gallop; he wondered if he should add to the strain on the masts by hoisting the staysails.

"Bosun Preston, fly only the jib and the flying jib. Leave the staysails on deck in case we need them. We should already have enough canvas out to show the Royal Navy a clean pair of heels." Preston waved an acknowledgement.

By dark, the royals of the Royal Navy ships had disappeared below the horizon. Despite the danger of working on the yards at night, Jaco felt it was worth the risk to increase their distance. He waited an hour after the sun set before ordering his men to go aloft and reef the royals and topgallants, leaving their standard cruising set—main, top sails and jib.

In his log that night, Jaco noted with pride that under the royals, *Scorpion* made 12 knots. In the morning, he planned to head so' west by south toward the Turks and Caicos Islands.

On board H.M.S. Puritan, October 1777

It took *Puritan* half a day to work its way out of Portsmouth, around the Isle of Wight and into the English Channel. There the winds forced them to sail so' by so' west to a point 10 miles from the tip of France's Cotentin Peninsula and Guernsey Island before Davidson could order a course toward the Canary Islands.

With supper over, Davidson waited while Alistair poured each officer a glass of port. If Alistair, who slept in a compartment reserved for midshipmen, had a last name, none of the officers were told it. He was just Alistair, and an excellent cook who managed the officers' mess and prepared and served all their meals.

Davidson held up his glass, "Gentlemen, to our Navy and His Majesty's ship *Puritan.*"

It was Thursday, so next he said, "To the bloody war, may it mean promotions for all of us!"

With the toasts over, Davidson set his glass down deliberately on the table. "We have been ordered to proceed forthwith and report to the Commander of the West Indies Station in Port Royal for further orders. With luck we will spend the winter in fine weather."

Davidson sipped the tawny, 15 year-old port and read aloud the next sentence in his sailing orders. "'In the course of *Puritan's* voyage, should you encounter a rebel ship, you are to capture it and bring it to the nearest British port before proceeding to Port Royal.'" He let the letter float to the table. "So, gentlemen, we have a hunting license, but only if we run over a rebel ship."

Puritan's captain waited for the laughter to die down. "Our lookouts need to keep a sharp eye about them: we wouldn't want to miss any prizes. Mr. Smythe, plan a route that gets *Puritan* to Port Royal as fast as she goes."

CHAPTER 15

BATTLE IN THE BERMUDA TRIANGLE

On board Frigate Scorpion, *November 1777*

The night brought heavy rain, lightning and strong winds, and waves broke over the frigate's bows. Jaco reduced the sails to just mains and jib and let the ship run with the wind. Even so, *Scorpion* pitched and rolled so much that Jacinto ordered the fire in the ship's stove doused. Dinner was dried apples and hardtack dipped in rum washed down with beer.

Before Jaco went to bed, he resolved that, if it wasn't stormy the next day, *Scorpion* would sail under its mains, tops, topgallants and royals to dry them out. Sails that stayed wet were heavy and hard to handle; they also quickly mildewed and turned moldy.

But instead of bright sun and blue sky, dawn revealed heavy fog and very light, variable winds from the west. The jib flapped uselessly, and instead of their usual bow shape, the mains and topsails on each mast were slack. Blocks normally under tension from the ropes clacked noisily. *Scorpion* was barely making steerageway.

Jaco walked around the wet main deck, peering into the fog with the same sense of foreboding he'd felt when *Sorcerer* was stalking *Cutlass*. He'd made mistakes then and had been lucky. Now he didn't want to depend on luck.

The longer *Scorpion* was in the fog, the less he liked it. Lieutenant Radcliffe had the forenoon watch; he wasn't someone Jaco trusted with his innermost thoughts. The men he did trust—Jack Shelton, Hedley Garrison and Abner Jeffords—were sleeping after spending the night getting *Scorpion* through the storm.

"Mr. Radcliffe, have you sent our lookouts to the royals?"

"Yes, sir, I did at first light. They are still in the clouds."

"Let us keep the noise down. Pass the word, no pipes, no shouting and no bells. Our ears will have to be our eyes."

"Aye, aye, sir. And sir, before Mr. Gaskins turned in, he went through our bilges looking for leaks after the storm. He didn't find any and asked me to tell you."

"Perfecto."

The feeling that *Scorpion* was in danger wouldn't go away. Jaco grabbed the quarterdeck railing just forward of the binnacle. Anxiety tightened his grip; his hands tried to squeeze the stain out of the wood. He heard a faint rumbling that he recognized as wooden wheels being pulled over a wooden deck. *Ours, or some other ship's?* Ahead, he could see the clouds thinning a bit. *Scorpion* was about to sail into a patch of clear sky and would be an easy target.

Jaco walked over to the third lieutenant and quietly asked, "Mr. Hayes, did any of our guns come loose last night?"

"No, sir. They were all secured, and the watch checked them every half hour."

"I thought I heard the sound of gun carriages being pulled over a wooden deck just now. Listen."

Both men heard the thwack of a gunport opening. It was followed by several more. Hayes turned to Jaco with his eyes wide open. Jaco yelled, "Everyone on the quarterdeck *GET DOWN!*"

Through the railing, he could see flashes a scant 100 yards away. The first broadside slammed into the *Scorpion's* port side. One cannonball blew away the railing and Hayes who was near the wheel went down, his mid-section ripped open by a by a large splinter.

In the silence that followed, Jaco called out orders. "Clear the decks for action. Run out, load with ball, and fire as you bear at the gun flashes."

Seeing the head Marine, he yelled, "Lieutenant Miller, get your men aloft. Mr. Patterson, to the maintop to direct the swivel guns. Remember how we trained to clear quarter and main decks."

Scorpion was now bathed in partial sunlight while her enemy was still not visible. All anyone on the deck of the *Scorpion* saw were orange muzzle flashes in the fog. Trading broadsides with an unknown and unseen Royal Navy ship was Jaco's worst nightmare. So far he'd only seen gun flashes from one deck; that meant it was a frigate of some kind.

A second broadside from the British ship slammed into *Scorpion's* side. A ball took out a section of railing about 10 feet behind Jaco before blowing out a piece on the starboard side. He didn't hear any screams from wounded men; he hoped the layered planking was doing its job.

Smoke erupted from *Scorpion* as her port gun crews began their work. It would come down to who could shoot the fastest and most accurately. The only problem was, they were shooting at gun flashes, not a ship.

The hiss of a cannon ball passing close overhead caused Jaco to turn around. White smoke from *Scorpion's* port side wafting over the quarterdeck made it hard to see anything. Then Jack Shelton appeared at his side, roused by the broadsides and ready for action despite lack of sleep. Jaco asked how the bulwarks were standing up to the barrage, and Jack assured him they were still sound. Then Jaco ordered, "Tell Mr. Radcliffe to switch to chain shot as soon as we can see the damn enemy."

Shelton left, and gradually some of the fog dissipated. Jaco found himself staring at a 32-gun Royal Navy frigate. There were gaping holes in the ship's bulwark and side where *Scorpion's* 12-pound balls had hit. Guns from both ships fired as fast as they were re-loaded; his crews were getting off shots faster.

The Marines on the shrouds waited patiently for the ships to get close enough for them to use the swivel guns and their skills as marksmen. Jaco turned to Private Griffin, who was, when he came on deck, assigned as his messenger. "Go tell the swivel gunners to start firing. We're in range."

Griffin, resplendent in his green coat, ran down the deck to the mainmast, climbed halfway up and yelled at the maintop. As the young man was swinging his leg off the shroud to jump back down onto the deck, a cannon ball went through him. One leg went forward, and his hip and right leg flew over the port side of the ship. His head and upper body hung on the shroud for a second before falling over the side.

A loud crack drew Jaco's attention from the gruesome sight of the young Marine's death. The other ship's foremast tilted aft and its yards snagged in the mainmast's rigging. Chain shot had done its job.

Radcliffe stuck his head out of the companionway to get a better look at the crippled enemy ship. Jaco told him, "Go back to steel shot and aim at their gun ports."

The Bostonian's face, blackened by powder and smoke, disappeared just as a ball splintered the railing and slammed into the quartermaster's enclosure. Jaco saw the quartermaster's mate stagger back from the shattered wheel, his hands wrapped around a large wooden splinter embedded in his chest. Lacking a helm, *Scorpion* started to turn slowly into the wind and its sails began to luff.

Abner Jeffords appeared out of nowhere. "Sir, I'll get a team below to handle the rudder. We'll open the hatch forward of the binnacle so you can shout steering commands. I'll pass the word when we are ready. This is what *Scorpion* was designed for, and what we drilled."

Only one word came out of Jaco's dry mouth. "Go!"

Scorpion had been ambushed and was trading broadsides with a bigger British ship that had a dozen more guns than the *Scorpion*. Even if he suddenly had all *Scorpion's* sails set, there wasn't enough wind to get out of the way. There was only one way this fight was going to end, and that was hand-to-hand combat.

"Mr. Shelton, pass the word to Mr. Radcliffe that I want anyone on the gun deck not needed to fire our port side cannon to meet me by the forward companionway. Pass out pistols and cutlasses. That ship means to board us, but we are going to board him first."

Jaco raced to his cabin, got his sword and tomahawk, and stuffed two pistols into his belt. Back on the main deck, he saw Lieutenant Miller organizing his Marines into a boarding party. Their bayonets were already fixed.

"Mr. Shelton, take the quarterdeck and communicate through the hatch with Mr. Jeffords. Stay on this course. Veer off if the British frigate tries to hit us amidships so we take a glancing blow. I will lead the boarding party and if I should fall, you have *Scorpion*. Do not let the British take my ship! Radcliffe knows to keep his gun crews firing for as along as possible. It is your call if they are needed to repel boarders."

"But, sir—"

"No buts, Jack. This is my ship and no goddamned British frigate is going to take it from me."

Just before the British frigate struck the smaller *Scorpion*, Shelton ordered Jeffords to turn hard to starboard. *Scorpion* responded and the bowsprit of the Royal Navy frigate broke off as it struck at a slight angle. As the ships closed, a musket volley from the Royal Marines in the British ship's rigging sent several members of *Scorpion's* crew to fall screaming in pain.

Then Lieutenant Miller's Marines, hiding behind the bulwark, stood up on command and fired as they found targets. Royal Marines and sailors fell from the British ship's rigging. Some bounced off the bulwark and fell into the water, others landed on the deck.

Men on both sides tossed grapnels onto the other ship. Overhead, *Scorpion's* swivel guns spoke a second time; Jaco could hear the lead balls hiss overhead and thud into men and wood. He grabbed a stay and stood up. "Let's go, men of *Scorpion.*"

As Jaco leaped over the narrow gap between the two ships, a Royal Marine aimed his musket directly at him. Before he could fire, two musket balls slammed into his chest. He staggered backward and fired into the air. Another Royal Marine slumped forward from a musket ball in the stomach. His bayonet stuck in the wood deck as he tried to stay upright and force his mortally wounded body to function.

British sailors surged forward to defend their ship. Jaco parried one thrust with his sword, slashed, and turned the man's arm into a bloody mess. He emptied a pistol into another man, then tossed it away. The next sailor who charged him got a ball in the chest from his second pistol before Jaco dropped it. Then, with his sword in right hand and his tomahawk in his left, he waded into the crowd of men.

Every move he made was a variation of those his father had taught him. Parry with the sword, strike with the tomahawk. Catch the blade of his adversary's sword with the tomahawk and stab with the sword. Spin and slide to the side to make himself smaller.

Blood from a tomahawk blow that severed an artery in a sailor's neck splashed onto Jaco's shirt and sleeve. Suddenly it got very quiet and Jaco looked around. The deck was littered with dead and wounded men.

Lieutenant Patrick Miller came to his side, his sword dripping blood. "Sir, I think we have won the day."

"Not so fast, Mr. Miller. I don't think they have given up just yet."

Behind Miller, a blood-spattered Hedley Garrison was organizing the men in a line as they reloaded their muskets and pistols. A sailor handed Jaco his two pistols. "Sir, you might need these again. They are reloaded.

Dead Royal Navy sailors and Marines lay on the aft deck alongside members of his crew. No one was on the quarterdeck, nor were any Royal Marines left in the rigging. *Where was the rest of the crew?*

"Garrison, secure the forward companionway as well as the center hatch." Three men, hearing the order, had started forward when there was a yell from under the quarterdeck.

"Sir, would you step aside, you are in the way." Jaco turned around and saw two rows of muskets. Miller had the first row of Marines kneeling, and the second row standing behind them.

British sailors emerged from the aft companionway, the door under the quarterdeck, and the grating just forward of the mizzenmast. They spread out and started to level their weapons at *Scorpion's* sailors and Marines.

"Steady, men, steady." Miller sounded as if he was on the parade ground. "Front row, fire."

The volley was ragged, but most of the first row of British sailors staggered and fell. "Second row, fire."

Once all the muskets were discharged, Miller pointed his sword to the *Scorpion's* masts and yelled, "Your turn, gentlemen!"

Musket balls rained down on the British.

Wanting to stop the carnage, Jaco yelled to the men he faced, "Surrender or we will kill all of you!"

"Bloody hell you will!" A sailor rose up from the gun deck, swinging the business end of his musket around to aim a shot at Jaco. He was not fast enough. Jaco raised and fired his pistol into the man's face. The musket flew to the side and went off, sending its ball into the port bulwark.

Jaco shouted, "Strike, damn you! There has been enough killing."

A voice came from under the quarterdeck. "I agree. We surrender. His Majesty's Ship *Coburg* is yours." Slowly, men lowered weapons. The speaker came forward and held a sword flat in both hands. "I am Quentin Reed, *Coburg's* First Lieutenant. And you are?"

"Captain Jaco Jacinto of the Continental Navy Frigate *Scorpion.*"

After accepting the sword, Jaco looked around him. Do you have a surgeon aboard?"

"Aye, and he has much work to do."

"My surgeon and men will help you care for your wounded after they deal with mine. Have your sailmaker prepare the dead for burial. While they do that, you and I are going to inspect your ship."

On the gun deck, half of *Coburg's* cannon were blown off their carriages. There were gaping holes in the planking where balls from his long twelves had punched through the side. Dead men lay everywhere, their blood brighter than the dull red paint of the gun deck.

Below, the bilges were filling with water. Jacinto ordered Reed to have the wounded brought up on deck. Gaskins was already on board and stood patiently behind his captain. He looked sad as he reported, "Sssir, thiss ship won't make it. It iss not worth trying to ssave."

"Can you save the wheel? *Scorpion* needs a new one."

Gaskins smiled. "I'll have a look, ssir. And I'll sssee to ssalvaging what we can from the magazine."

Of *Coburg's* crew of 240 men, 73 were dead, 15 wouldn't live more than a few days, and 32 had survivable wounds. *Scorpion* had 19 dead, five of whom had been killed on the gun deck when a ball from the *Coburg* struck their cannon and sent shards of iron across the gun deck.

While Reed's crew prepared their comrades for burial, Jaco had his men free *Scorpion* from the *Coburg*. Despite being hit from close range, none of *Scorpion's* bulwarks had given way. The British frigate's boats, which had been towed behind it during the fight, were used to ferry the wounded to the *Scorpion*. The boats would replace *Scorpion's,* which were splintered from *Coburg's* first two broadsides.

In the afternoon, Reed read the Royal Navy's burial service. One by one, 73 canvas-shrouded bodies slid into the water. Then Jaco did the same for *Scorpion's* dead.

With *Scorpion* crowded with prisoners, Jaco had only one course—head for Charleston. He'd just given the order to Quartermaster Jeffords to get underway when Lieutenant Radcliffe came to his side.

"Captain, why Charleston? It is only 70 miles from British-held Savannah. Hampton, Virginia, or even Philadelphia would be much safer. The difference in sailing time is not that great. Besides, Hampton has a foundry, and we could replace our 12-pounders there. I don't think we can get replacements in Charleston."

Jaco turned to face his second lieutenant. "Every hour we have the British sailors on board, we are in danger. Charleston is closest, and it has standard 12-pounders."

Radcliffe sneered. "Is there another reason? Maybe it is because Charleston is your home town."

Clasping his hands behind his back, Jaco squared himself in front of Edmund Radcliffe, who was a head taller and 50 pounds heavier. "Watch your mouth, Mr. Radcliffe. I do not like what you are implying. If you ever again question my judgment or imply I make decisions based on what is good for me rather than what is the best for this ship and its crew, I will consider it insubordination. And if necessary, I will place you in irons until we get to a port where you can be tried by court martial."

Radcliffe took a step forward to loom over his shorter captain. "I'm surprised you are not challenging me to a duel. Isn't that what *southern* gentlemen like to do?" Jaco's cold stare was answered by a similar look from Radcliffe.

"Dueling is not the answer, Radcliffe, but if you force me into one, you will regret it. Now don't you have duties to attend too?" Radcliffe scowled and turned away.

Jaco turned and watched *Coburg's* wheel being lowered to a boat.

Bosun Preston and four others were the last men on *Coburg*. The ship's lanterns were lined on each deck as they piled canvas and splintered wood on all three of its decks. Rum was poured on the piles. Preston ordered the four sailors into the boat. He lit each pile before he was rowed under darkening skies back to the *Scorpion*. The Royal Navy frigate was settling and burning as *Scorpion* sailed into the night.

On board H.M.S. Puritan, *November 1777*

Puffy clouds dotted the sky, and the frigate was making seven knots under what her captain decreed was her standard set of canvas—mains, tops and topgallants. He also allowed his officers to stand watches in their shirts rather than the lightweight coats he'd had made for them in England. Captain Davidson was about to order the first of the afternoon's drills when, as his journal noted, a lookout spotted a semi-submerged hulk at 1:29 p.m.

Darren Smythe looked through the brass tube of the Dolland, and thought of Horrocks. Jodpur's captain had bought the expensive, superior instrument with prize money because it had better glass than what was in Royal Navy standard spyglasses. Horrocks was right. The images were clearer and sharper.

Davidson immediately ordered *Puritan* to heave to. While most of the crew stood on the deck grimly surveying the blackened hulk, a boarding party led by Smythe was sent to inspect the ship. Rounding the stern, the lieutenant saw the burned paint and the ship's name—*H.M.S. Coburg*.

Smythe stood in shin-deep water on *Coburg's* gun deck and examined holes in rotted planking that looked identical to what Handley had found on *Jodpur*. The jagged gaps left by flying splinters made him sick; good men had died as a result of shoddy construction. Gun carriages were knocked on their side and cannon were lying on the deck.

Coburg's charred mizzenmast and single mainsail spar looked like a lonely crucifix marking the death of the frigate. Smythe concluded the victor had set the ship afire, assuming that it would burn until its magazine exploded. Just before he left to go back to the *Puritan,* Smythe pried out three links of chain embedded in the stump of the mainmast. His conclusion was that the rebel ship had gone after *Coburg's* rigging at some point in the battle, not knowing how much damage its solid shot was doing.

Back on *Puritan*, the aristocratic Davidson listened carefully to Smythe's analysis and then tapped his chart. "We're less than 100 miles from Bermuda, where you will give your report to the Admiral. I will strongly suggest that your notes be sent post haste to my father's friend, the First

Sea Lord, Sir Hugh Palliser. I am sure he will be interested in your findings."

"Yes, sir. I will convert my notes into a formal report."

Later, Davidson would note in his log that Smythe returned to *Puritan* at 3:06 p.m. There was nothing he could do to salvage *Coburg*. He noted the position in his log, thinking that if any other Royal Navy ship came across *Coburg*, it should be a reminder not to take the rebels lightly. He did not include this thought in his log.

Charleston, November 1777

Scorpion's sudden arrival caused a stir in South Carolina's largest city. Many of its citizens lined the docks to see the frigate, some of whom, Jaco suspected, were Loyalists who would send riders to British-held Savannah. Knowing this, Jaco wanted to minimize the time they spent in port. By the time the frigate anchored, several boats were headed her way, one of which held the head of the town's garrison.

Jaco welcomed General Moultrie and Philip Wood, the port captain, to come on board. When they arrived on the main deck, the 154 survivors from *H.M.S. Coburg's* were sitting quietly in five rows. Between the day of the fight and the day *Scorpion* anchored, 13 more of *Coburg's* crew had been buried at sea.

Wood didn't recognize *Scorpion's* 18 year-old captain until Jaco reminded him who he was. Then Wood rubbed his mouth to hide a smile. "And where did you get this lot?"

"They're what is left of the crew of *H.M.S. Coburg,* a 32-gun frigate. We lost 19 good men."

"What happened to the *Coburg*?"

"We sunk it. I have its logs, its flag and its bell in my cabin." He didn't want to say that *Scorpion's* wheel came from *Coburg*.

"We'll take your prisoners. Do you want them paroled?"

"That's not for me to decide. Just treat them with honor. They fought well to defend their ship."

"I will make arrangements to get those who don't want to join our cause to Savannah, but first, I think the town will want to celebrate."

Jaco pointed to his cabin as way of saying he didn't want to talk in front of the British prisoners. When they were private, he asked Wood, "Do you have a packet taking reports to the Congress?"

"One is readying to leave today. Why?"

"I'd like to send my report before we make some repairs."

Captain Wood nodded. "What do you need?"

"Supplies, two 12-pounders, and shipwrights to help my crew make repairs."

"That we can provide. Or, why don't you take on some supplies here, then take *Scorpion* to Hampton, Virginia to finish outfitting? With the British now occupying Philadelphia, the Congress is meeting in York, Pennsylvania. You can tell the courier to send any reply from the Committee to you in Hampton. That will shorten the time for their response, and you will clear our harbour before the British can retaliate. Tell me, Captain Jacinto, how long have you been at sea?

"We left Maine in early September."

"So you have not heard about the victory at Saratoga."

"No, sir. What happened?"

"British General Burgoyne invaded New York from Canada. He came through the Lake Champlain valley where Generals Gates and Benedict Arnold defeated him. We captured over 6,000 prisoners."

"Sir, when was this?"

"Last October."

"That is all the French needed."

"Captain Jacinto, what do you mean by that?"

"I was told that in the dispatches I carried from France to Philadelphia when I was captain of the *Cutlass*, the French King told Benjamin Franklin that we needed to win another major victory against the British Army before France would declare war on Britain."

"Ah."

Just then, General Moultrie entered. "Captain Jacinto," he demanded, "what type of cannon does *Scorpion* have? I've not seen the like of them before."

"They are specially made long 12-pounders. We can hit an enemy ship at over 500 yards."

"Interesting. But why so few? A ship this size is meant to carry more guns, is it not?"

Jaco explained to Captain Wood and General Moultrie the modifications made to the Kittery ship, then said, "*Scorpion* was designed for twenty-four normal 12-pounders. The long twelves are much heavier, so we carry only twenty. Two of our guns were damaged in the fight, so we are down to 18."

Moultrie eyed the captured bell and flag of *Coburg*, folded neatly on Jaco's desk. "Captain Jacinto, we hope you will honor us with your company tonight at supper. There is much to discuss."

* * *

There were two people Jaco wanted to see—Reyna, and his mother, in that order. However, family comes first, so... his mother, then Reyna. Unfortunately, they would have to be short visits, for he was to dine with Captain Wood and General Moultrie. He'd already sent Midshipman Garrison to personally deliver a note to Reyna, saying he would come calling after his official supper. There was just enough time to visit home before then.

A little after 8:30 p.m., Jaco knocked on the front door of the Laredo house. The night sky was alight with stars, a trees rustled in a faint breeze. A Negro servant opened the door and looked at him quizzically in the dim light. "Who may you be?"

He recognized the woman who had been with the Laredo's household for as long as he could remember. "Annie, it is me, Jaco Jacinto!"

"Ahhhhh! I didn't recognize you. You're all growed up. Come into the parlor and I will get Mrs. Laredo."

Adah Laredo was followed by a grinning Reyna. Jaco stood until both women seated themselves. Then he took a chair facing Reyna's mother, who greeted him and said, "It is good to see you, Jaco. However, just because there is a war going on, it doesn't mean that my family will suspend the requirement for good manners and behavior. Normally, I would ask that you not come calling at this hour. Tonight, I will make an exception."

"Thank you, ma'am."

Adah Laredo stood up to leave, and Jaco rose politely. "I expect you to be out the door at eleven."

Jaco nodded. "Yes, ma'am, I will." Then he said, "But I intend to come back when my duties permit."

Adah smiled. "I expect that you will, and you are always welcome."

* * *

Now that they were in port, Lieutenant Radcliffe put into action a plan he'd conceived while at sea. It rankled Radcliffe that he—a proper Bostonian—had not been given command of *Scorpion*. Under his command, *Scorpion* would have cruised between New York and Halifax, taking more prizes like *Nevis*. The prize money would have made him wealthy. Instead, the soft southerner had sailed south—to be warm!

The fact that he was only the Second Lieutenant, not *Scorpion's* First Lieutenant, added fuel to Radcliffe's ire. He still seethed from the confrontation with his captain after *Coburg* was captured.

If they had sailed to Philadelphia, he could have shared what was in his journal with John Adams and John Hopkins. Now they risked being blockaded in Charleston. But he had another arrow he could fire at Jacinto.

The next day, while the other officers were busy supervising repairs, he wrote a letter to his father to give to John Adams. Then he went ashore to arrange for the supplies *Scorpion* needed and left the letter for the next packet to Boston. Once *Scorpion* returned to Philadelphia, it would have a new captain. A proper, Bostonian captain. Himself. *And if the Marine Committee doesn't take action to relieve Jacinto, the next time* Scorpion *goes to sea, I will find an opportunity to take command.*

But to Lieutenant Radcliffe's disgust, no sooner were supplies taken on then Captain Jacinto ordered sail for Hampton, Virginia. On the one hand, Radcliffe was relieved that *Scorpion* would be away from Charleston; on the other hand, the reply from his father and John Adams would miss him and have to be forwarded.

* * *

Three days later, just after *Scorpion's* repairs were completed at the Hampton harbour, a courier arrived from the Marine Committee in York. He brought Jaco a pouch and conveyed the instructions that it was to be delivered to France as soon as possible. He also handed over *Scorpion's* new sailing orders.

CHAPTER 16

GOLDEN PRIZE

On board Frigate Scorpion, *December 1777*

Pushed by a strong westerly wind, *Scorpion* rushed down the Chesapeake Bay toward the Atlantic, safely away from the pier in Hampton, Virginia. Jaco's plan was to reach the Atlantic Ocean just before dark and disappear into the blackness to avoid any Royal Navy frigates that might be lurking outside the bay's entrance. To this end, even though *Scorpion* was blacked out and showing no lanterns, Jaco was sailing her at top speed so she would be hard to follow and harder to catch.

A locked box in his cabin contained documents signed by key members of the Continental Congress, outlining what help they requested from the French. His sailing orders read:

Captain Jacinto,

Scorpion is to make best possible speed to Brest and deliver the documents to the American mission. If your ship should be in danger of capture, these documents must be destroyed so they do not fall into British hands.

Once the documents are delivered, replenish your supplies and commence commerce raiding around the British Isles. Your mission is to disrupt British commerce wherever you can by capturing or destroying its merchant ships and raiding its ports. Prizes are to be taken to Amsterdam, Brest or Saint-Nazaire where they will be sold.

The French or Dutch governments will retain one quarter of the prize money to help pay for the support given to our cause. Your crew will divide the remaining three-quarters according to the official formula. We leave when to return up to you.

Good luck and Godspeed.

John Adams

Chairman, Marine Committee

Due to the urgency of Scorpion's mission, Jaco kept the topgallants, tops and main sails set all the way across the Atlantic, even at night. The frigate seemed to enjoy running at high speed day after day. He trusted the sturdy New England oak trees that formed *Scorpion's* masts. They were strong enough to withstand the pressure from the wind and Royal Navy cannon balls. They were perfecto!

Port Royal, December 1777

With *Puritan* at anchor and taking on provisions, Captain Davidson made his official visit to the Commander of the West Indies Station. The flagship, a three-decker with 74 guns, rode easily at anchor, accompanied by three frigates and two sloops.

After the usual pleasantries, Davidson summarized the report Smythe had prepared. The portly rear admiral's head nodded up and down, and he repeatedly wiped sweat off his brow.

"Captain, this is not good for our Navy. We cannot have our ships poorly built or it will be the end of us all."

"Yes, sir, I agree."

"This war is not going well, even though we occupy the rebel's capital and their largest city. The bloody bastards just don't know when to quit. The latest from the Admiralty says that France and the Dutch are about to enter the war on the side of the rebels. Lord only knows what the Spanish intend to do. Since most of the rebel ships down here are small privateers, the Admiralty is convinced that the dozen sloops and small frigates I have here suffice to protect our convoys. I've been ordered to send my fifth-rate frigates back to Britain for blockade duty off France. That includes *Puritan*. I assume it will take a few days for you to take on food and fresh water, then I'm afraid, you'll have to head back to England as fast as you can."

"What about the frigate that took the *Coburg?*"

"Unless that ship comes into the Caribbean, it is the North American Station's problem, not mine. If it comes my way, then I'll have to deal with it. Let me know when you are ready, and I will have your official sailing orders delivered. Please don't stay in Port Royal longer than is necessary."

Davidson knew the conversation was over. They were headed back to England in at most four or five days. This back-and-forthing was, he mused, an inordinate waste of time and resources. If only there were some way of conveying news and orders more efficiently! Well, while they were here there was at least the opportunity to take on fresh supplies, including such fruits as would not be available in England.

Brest, December 1777

Radcliffe completed his purser duties for the resupplying of *Scorpion,* then made his way to the house of the agent of the Continental Congress. Samuel Gardner, a fellow Bostonian from one of Massachusetts' leading families, lived in Brest to manage his family's trading interests. When the war began, he'd set up and managed the courier service between Franklin's mission in Paris and Brest. The riders who made the four-day, 360-mile journey were fellow Colonials who spoke fluent French and had lived in France.

Gardner made Edmund Radcliffe welcome. While they'd never met, both families knew of each other. They were from the Massachusetts colony's upper crust, dubbed, a century later, "the Boston Brahmins" by Oliver Wendell Holmes.

Ostensibly, Radcliffe was there to report that all the supplies he'd ordered had arrived at the pier and were of satisfactory quality. He politely refused Gardner's offer of a drink or something to eat, explaining that they were under orders to depart as swiftly as possible. Then he held out a folded sheet of paper sealed with blue wax. "Mr. Gardner, please make sure this letter goes in the next pouch to the Congress. My cousin, John Adams, is on the Marine Committee. He will be most interested in its contents."

Gardner promised to forward the letter with the next courier pouch.

The following day, *Scorpion* sailed into the Atlantic. The cold wind coming off the North Atlantic rattled the windows of the captain's cabin. It made standing on the quarterdeck, even bundled in a wool blanket, unpleasant. The wooden shield provided some protection for the officer on watch and the quartermaster, but after four hours, one went below thoroughly chilled.

Jaco had mounted the *Coburg's* bell on the port side of the aft bulkhead of his cabin; he tapped it to bring the officers' meeting to order. "Gentlemen, it is time for the second part of our mission. Within days, the Royal Navy will know a 24-gun Continental Navy frigate sailed from Brest. King George will not be happy, once we announce ourselves by taking a few prizes in his home waters."

Jack Shelton slid a 'blueback' chart of England and the North Sea onto the table. The French-made charts got their nickname from the stiff, light blue paper glued to the back of each map. Glasses were placed to weigh down the corners. "We have three areas where we can hunt—the Celtic Sea off Brest where we are right now, the Irish Sea, and the North Sea."

Jaco used the tip of his long hunting knife to point to the water between Ireland and Great Britain. "The Irish Sea, particularly in the northern end, is small; once we get in, it will be hard to sneak out. The Royal Navy could easily overwhelm us. For now, I've ruled it out as a hunting ground."

The knife moved south to the area west of Brest known as the Celtic Sea. "Royal Navy ships headed to Portsmouth and merchant ships en route to London and other ports on England's east coast come through these waters. If chased, we can easily run to Brest with any prizes. However, once France declares war, these waters will be swarming with Royal Navy frigates, and we can expect them to blockade Brest, Cherbourg and Le Harve along with as many of the other ports as they can. Once they spot us, we will have to fight several of their ships."

Jaco put the tip of the knife between the Dutch and England coasts. "The North Sea is full of merchant ships, and we can take our prizes to Amsterdam. To escape, we can go north around Scotland or come back through the English Channel. Gentleman, *this* is where *Scorpion* is going hunting."

Lieutenant Radcliffe leaned over the chart. "Sir, if I may say so, I believe the Celtic Sea would be our best option because we can always run into the Atlantic to get away."

"True, Mr. Radcliffe, the Celtic Sea offers a quick escape. However, I am betting that the Royal Navy is already planning to send ships to patrol French Atlantic ports, so if we hunt in the Celtic Sea, we will have a hard time getting our prizes into any major French port. And escorting prizes across the Atlantic this time of year would be difficult and risky."

Lieutenant Radcliffe folded his arms. He'd made his point. As he expected, his captain had rejected his idea, something he would be sure to mention in his next letter to the Marine Committee.

Jaco had one last point to make. "Prizes taken in the North Sea will sail for Amsterdam, and the prize captains will be given a letter of introduction from my father to give to the Dutch East India Company. He is their agent in Charleston and regularly corresponds with the leaders of the company. My father has a written commitment that the Dutch East India Company will give us a fair price for our prizes and do so more quickly than the French." Now for the reassignments. This was exactly why he had ordered officers to take over for each other during drills.

"With Hayes' death, Midshipman Garrison, you are now Lieutenant Garrison and *Scorpion's* Third Lieutenant. With that appointment, Mr. Garrison, you are also the ship's gunner. Midshipman Patterson, in a fight, I want you on the maintop. Midshipman Wilson, you are to help Mr. Radcliffe with the gun deck. Both of you did well against *Coburg*."

After hearing the ayes, Jaco moved on to the last point. "Gentlemen, we want to find large merchantmen to take as prizes. If we spot a small ship, I will make a determination whether to take it as a prize, sink it, or leave it alone. We were lucky in that we were able to sign on men in Charleston to replace those we lost, so we have enough men for one or two prize crews. I'd rather not squander them on small captures. As fast as we can, we are going to put any prisoners ashore. *Scorpion* is a warship, not a transport. While I do not fear any Royal Navy frigate up to 36 guns, we are here as a commerce raider, not to take on the Royal Navy. If we have to fight one to escape, we will do so by using our superior speed and sailing abilities. But until we know France is at war with the British, we don't have a friendly shipyard where we can go for major repairs, so a clean escape is preferable. Any questions?"

Several of the officers asked detailed questions about the coasts and ports of these northern waters, studying the chart as they listened to Jaco's explanations. When all were answered, Jaco smiled and said, "And now, gentlemen, I have excellent news. just before we left Brest, Mr. Radcliffe bought smoked beef, French cheese, wine and beer for everyone on board. Let's enjoy a good dinner before we head into the English Channel."

* * *

Dawn broke with a bright sun and crystal blue sky. Temperature was, according to the frigate's thermometer, a bearable 45 degrees. It was a pleasant switch from the gray overcast, slate-blue seas and cold rain of the past three days that made sailing in the North Sea miserable. Despite being in one of the most traveled bodies of water, *Scorpion* could have been alone in another world.

Nevertheless, Jaco believed they were ideally positioned to find prizes. Ostend, 30 miles to the east, was part of the Catholic Netherlands and part of the Holy Roman Empire. Six of its member states—Anhalt-Zerbst, Ansbach-Bayreuth, Brunswick, Hannover, Hesse and Waldeck—had sent troops to fight with the British Army in North America. Ostend, therefore, was not a port in which *Scorpion* would seek refuge. It was, however, a port which merchant ships frequented. The entrance to the Thames River estuary and London, the center of the British Empire, was 50 miles to the west. *Scorpion* was headed to Kingsgate, a spit of land jutting into the English Channel where *Scorpion* would reverse course and sail to a point two miles off the Belgian coast.

Kingsgate was still 30 miles away when the lookout on the foremast sang out, "Sail ho! One point off the starboard bow. It's a big merchantman."

Jaco yelled back, "How far?"

"Five miles."

"Why didn't you see it before?"

"Sir, she's shortened sail to just her tops and mains and is low in the water."

As *Scorpion* closed on the merchantman, small fishing boats appeared on the horizon. While they were not a threat, they could complicate any actions *Scorpion* might want to take. Jaco started issuing instructions.

"Mr. Shelton, clear for action and load with solid shot. No drums or whistles and don't run out until I give the order. I don't want to rip up any rigging which we would then have to repair. We shall come up on her windward side about 200 feet away, show our colors and ask her to strike."

Jaco faced his Second Lieutenant and looked him in the eye as he spoke. He assumed that the man would do his duty, and he needed to make sure the Bostonian knew his intent. "Mr. Radcliffe, have the port gun crews on the deck to help maneuver until we get parallel and start closing, then I will tell you to have them man their guns. On my command, open the starboard gun ports to show our British friends our sting. If she shoots first, fire until ordered to stop or she strikes. I don't think it will come to that, but this close to home, who knows what a captain nearing the end of a long voyage will dare. The last thing I want is to have our gunfire alert everyone in southern England that we are here!"

"Aye, aye, sir." Radcliffe's tone was neither sarcastic nor defensive. He simply acknowledged his orders.

So far, Radcliffe had proven to be a capable and loyal officer, but Jaco didn't trust him. In a private moment before he left, his father had told him of Adams' persistent attempts to give Radcliffe command of *Scorpion*. Still, Jaco was determined not to let his personal dislike color his judgment of the man. Before his Second Lieutenant left the quarterdeck, Jaco offered an olive branch. "One last thing. Mr. Radcliffe, this is your prize to take to Amsterdam. If you have to fire, don't tear it up too badly, because you may damage her cargo." Giving Radcliffe captaincy of the prize minimized the risk of him not performing in battle.

Radcliffe allowed himself to smile. Once a lieutenant was made acting captain, however briefly, promotion was virtually guaranteed. This fat prize and his cousin's patronage were about to ensure his future.

Jaco continued issuing orders. "Mr. Patterson, go to the main top and load our swivel guns. We may need a blast from them to convince the captain to strike. Mr. Preston, get ready to slacken sail on my command so we don't sail past and give them an opportunity to turn and rake our stern."

As *Scorpion* approached the rear quarter of the merchantman, named *Madras,* the men on its quarterdeck waved. In all their experience of sailing these waters, frigates, even small ones, were British.

Jaco went to the forward railing of the quarterdeck. "Bosun, let's bring *Scorpion* about. Loosen sheets for all the sails. Ready on the braces. Gentlemen, let us do this smartly and show them how a Continental Navy ship is handled. Helm a-lee. Mr. Jeffords, you may turn the wheel... now!"

Scorpion's bow responded. With the sails flapping, Jaco called out, "Raise the tacks and sheets."

The frigate was now on a parallel course to *Madras*. The jib floated between the forward stay and the foremast. "All sails haul. Mr. Preston, please show our friends on *Madras* our sailing skills. Sheet home the jib."

Scorpion quickly caught up to *Madras* and Jaco waited until the bowsprit of *Scorpion* approached amidships of *Madras*. "Mr. Radcliffe, show *Madras* our sting. Bosun Preston, show them our colors."

With that, Jaco walked to the starboard side of the quarterdeck, speaking trumpet in hand. "*Madras, Madras,* this is the Continental Navy *Frigate Scorpion.* We intend to capture you as a prize, either peacefully or with a fight. Please strike your colors, or be fired upon."

A stocky man in a blue coat looked over the railing of the *Madras* at the businesslike long twelves and determined that resistance was futile. The Union Jack fluttered down.

"Slack sail to slow so we may board," Jaco continued. "Please have your crew muster in the fo'c'sle. No man will be harmed unless he resists."

The two ships slowed and two of *Scorpion's* boats were slung over the side. "Mr. Radcliffe, a word before you depart to take over your new command."

Jaco held out an envelope with wax seals from the Continental Congress and one from an agent of the Dutch East India Company. "Here is the letter from my father. Send back an inventory of what the ship is carrying. When you are ready, bend on as much sail as you think *Madras* can handle and head for Amsterdam. We will sail on your port rear quarter. With good luck, in two days time we should be much richer men drinking excellent Dutch beer."

Jaco was watching the transfer of the crew when Lieutenant Radcliffe came to the railing of *Madras*. "Captain, could you come over? The captain wishes to speak with you."

Waiting for Jacinto at the ladder of *Madras* was Lieutenant Radcliffe and *Madras's* captain, who introduced himself. "Captain Jacinto, I am Captain Hall. Would you please join me in my cabin where we can talk privately?"

"Very well, but I'd like Lieutenant Garrison to join us." Jaco had brought Garrison along because he had a keen, inquisitive mind and a knack for asking questions that made everyone in the wardroom think. If nothing else, he would be another witness to what was said.

Hall's eyebrows rose when he looked at the lanky Garrison, who was barely 17. *Little does he know I am only a year older,* Jaco thought, amused. Hall nodded, and the three men walked to the cabin, while Radcliffe continued to oversee the taking of the prize.

As the last to enter, Garrison closed the door to Captain Hall's cabin, where a tall, aristocratic man waited.

"Captain Jacinto, this is Lord Stafford. He is a director of the British East India Company and a member of the House of Lords. I apologize for not having him on deck earlier, but under the circumstances...." Hall let his voice trail off. Lord Stafford stepped forward, a man confident of getting his way.

Stafford had his hands clasped behind his back and spoke as he would to a commoner who worked for him. "Captain Jacinto, I understand you intend to take *Madras* as a prize to some foreign port. That is your right, but I am prepared to give you a Bank of England draft for £15,000 sterling to keep the *Madras* from being sold as a prize. I hope you know what a draft is. That is quite a bit more than it would be worth if auctioned in France. You can exchange it for gold and silver at a Dutch bank."

Jaco ignored the man's imperious tone. "Lord Stafford, I know what a draft is; before the war I worked in my father's import/export business. However, I am not interested in a draft on the Bank of England. It would be very hard to explain to my crew that a piece of paper is worth the same as a ship they can see and touch."

"I'll double the offer to £30,000 pounds." Lord Stafford spoke flatly, his gaze intent upon the young captain before him. He was used to getting his way and had to control his anger at being told no by a man half his age and a rebel to boot.

"Thank you, but no. Captain Hall, please give Lieutenant Harrison your journal, the ship's papers and its manifest. Mr. Harrison may look young, but he has been through this drill several times and knows what he is reading."

Lord Stafford interrupted. "I'll triple it. A draft of £45,000 Sterling is yours if you let us go."

Jaco shook his head as if to say, "I am not accepting your offer, and as captain of the *Scorpion* I have important tasks to perform."

There was a rap on the door. It was Lieutenant Radcliffe. Jaco turned to the two Englishmen. "Good day, gentlemen, I think this discussion is over."

Radcliffe looked pleased. "Sir, we have a solution to our prisoner problem."

Jaco followed his lieutenant to the railing. He could see *Scorpion's* sailors aiming muskets over the side. A mast with a luffing lateen sail stuck 20 feet above the top of *Madras'* bulwark.

"And that is?"

"A scow carrying a load of coal came up and asked if they could help. Rather than capture it, I think we should put *Madras's* crew on board and let it sail off into the sunset."

"*Perfecto!* Mr. Radcliffe, that is a brilliant idea. Do so. Have you searched the ship?"

"No, not yet."

"Take care of the prisoner transfer, then bring over 25 sailors to handle *Madras*. Lieutenant Garrison and I will have a look into the holds."

As they entered the forward hold bearing lanterns, Jacinto turned to Garrison. "Why would a member of the House of Lords and a director of the British East India Company offer us £45,000 for this ship? Was he attempting to ransom himself? Or are they hiding something? We need to find out, and quickly."

Opening the hatch to the forward hold, the pleasant aroma of cardamom, tamarind, curry, and cumin was strong enough to taste. Crates packed with spices filled the forward hold; they would be worth a fortune, but not £45,000.

The aft hold held sturdily built boxes lashed to the hull, covered with sailcloth. Garrison peeled the canvas back. Each box had "Property of the Bank of England" painted on the top.

Garrison found a heavy iron bar with a flattened tip in the carpenter's compartment. Both men hung their lanterns on pegs, then Jaco jammed the heavy iron bar into a gap between the top and the sides of the top box and pushed down.

Iron nails groaned and gave way. Jaco slid the bar along the seam and levered out the plank. He brushed back the sawdust and found himself looking at a gold ingot with the imprint of the Bank of England.

This *is what Lord Stafford was hiding.*

Jaco went to the second row of crates and opened the top one. In it, he found more gold bars. "Mr. Garrison, hammer these back in place, and be quick about it. Then replace the cover. Not a word about this until we reach Amsterdam. Once we are safely in Dutch waters, we will transfer these crates to the *Scorpion*. There is enough gold here to fund our revolution. I will inform Mr. Radcliffe to anchor away from the port until we can transfer the crates. Once they are on board *Scorpion,* I will tell him what we transferred."

Portsmouth, January 1778

Bright winter sun warmed *Puritan's* quarterdeck as the ship rocked at anchor. It was a pleasant change from the cold, drab overcast that had greeted the frigate when they reached port on New Year's Day. Smythe enjoyed the midday sunshine; it would cool quickly once the sun dropped below the horizon.

When Darren saw a pinnace flying the flag of the port admiral rowing hard toward the *Puritan,* he leaned over the bulwark and called down. "Good afternoon, Lieutenant, I am Lieutenant Smythe. What brings you out to the *Puritan* in such a hurry?"

The lieutenant bobbed his head. "Respects to Captain Davidson. Admiral Arthur would like him to come to his office immediately. It is, I am told, a matter of great importance that cannot wait. My orders are to bring Captain Davidson with me."

"Wait here. I'll go fetch him."

After listening to Smythe, Captain Davidson lifted his coat off a peg behind his desk. "Someone must have blotted his copybook and we may be asked to rewrite it! So, let's go see what Admiral Arthur thinks is so vital. I hope it not an order to rush off and blockade some French port. I've had enough of that nonsense for a lifetime!"

Waiting in Admiral Arthur's office were two men who looked as if they'd spent the night in a coal bin. The lieutenant who'd brought them moved to take a seat at a small writing desk in the corner of the large office.

Admiral Arthur came forward with his hand extended. "Captain Davidson, thank you for coming on such short notice. I think, after you hear what these two men have to say, your orders are going to be to your liking. May I present Lord Stafford, Director of the British East India Company and member of the House of Lords. This is Captain Davidson, the Duke of Somerset."

The two "royals" warmly shook hands, comfortable with a fellow peer of the realm. Smythe watched the two members of the nobility shake hands. *The rest of us, including Admiral Arthur, are just commoners. I wonder who is higher in the peerage?*

Admiral Arthur continued. "And this, gentlemen, is Captain Hall, of the British East India Company ship *Madras*."

Again, there was a shaking of the hands. Davidson presented his first lieutenant. "This is Lieutenant Smythe, my number one."

Before they sat down, a young midshipman came in with a fresh pot of tea and cups, along with a decanter of port and glasses. After each man was served his preference, Admiral Arthur nodded to Lord Stafford. "Lord Stafford, please tell Captain Davidson and Lieutenant Smythe what you told me."

Succinctly, Stafford described the taking of the *Madras*. During his description of the transport in a coal scow, Smythe had to school himself not to laugh at Lord Stafford's obvious chagrin. He suspected that the glint in Captain Davidson's eye was wry amusement at a fellow lord's plight. At the conclusion, Stafford simply it was imperative that the Royal Navy recapture *Madras* and her cargo. He did not explain why.

Davidson waited. He took a sip of his tea and put the cup and the saucer down gently on the table to give himself time to phrase a delicate question. Context was important.

"Lord Stafford, pirates and our enemies have been taking our ships for centuries. These rebels are just the latest lot. The Navy and I are sorry for the company's loss, but what is so special about *Madras's* cargo that we must rush about looking for it?"

Smythe thought that Davidson had put it nicely. Good. If his captain hadn't asked the question he would have, and damn the fallout.

Lord Stafford looked at Admiral Arthur, who gave him a "You need to tell him" look. Stafford tossed back his glass of port, visibly steeled himself, and answered.

"*Madras* was carrying eight tons of Bank of England gold. The company had insured it with Lloyds for one point one million pounds Sterling."

"Oh, my...." was all that Davidson could say. His words hung in the air.

Captain Hall, not wanting to be blamed for the loss of *Madras,* broke the silence. "Two Royal Navy frigates escorted us until we cleared the Straits of Dover and started working our way west toward the Thames River. Despite my pleas that their escort duty was not yet finished, they peeled off at first light and headed for Chatham Dockyard on the River Medway."

Smythe was sure that Admiral Arthur was wondering under whose orders the two frigates were sailing. He suspected their careers might end soon. He decided it was time to get some useful intelligence. "Captain Hall, would you describe the rebel ship, please?"

Hall, glad he was relieved of the burden of reporting the loss of his ship, answered readily enough. "It was a three-masted frigate named *Scorpion*. Its main battery was, I believe, twenty 12-pounders. Their muzzles came quite a ways out of the side of the ship. I saw long nines in the bow and stern, so she carries 24 guns."

"How big was *Scorpion?*"

"It is slightly smaller than a Royal Navy fifth-rater."

Smythe thought that sounded incorrect. *Why would the rebels equip a ship sent into these waters with only 24 cannon when they know most of our frigates carry 36?*

Suddenly, his mind flashed to the wreck of the *Coburg*. Maybe it had encountered *Scorpion*.

"Captain Hall, did you meet the captain of the *Scorpion*?"

"Aye, both his lordship and I spoke with him. He is a menacing looking fellow with a black hair and coal-black eyes. Kind of what one would think a bloody pirate would look like."

"Did you get the man's name?"

"That I did. Has one of those hard to pronounce foreign names." Hall struggled to pronounce the unfamiliar syllables. "Hay Sento is the way he said it."

Smythe forced himself not to react. "How well was his ship handled?"

"He brought alongside *Madras* in a manner that would make any Royal Navy captain proud, I'll say that. His crew knew what they were doing."

Both Admiral Arthur and Lord Stafford were silent during this exchange. Captain Davidson looked at his first lieutenant and was about to ask a question when Admiral Arthur spoke.

"Captain Davidson, how soon can you be at sea?"

"I have food and water for two, maybe three weeks. Given that limitation, I can leave immediately with the tide tonight."

"I will take care of getting you what I can in the way of more provisions today. I am giving you command of a small squadron that will include two 20-gun frigates with 9-pounders, *H.M.S. Hussar* and *H.M.S. Griffin,* along with two ketch rigged sloops, *H.M.S. Happy* and *H.M.S. Savage* that each have twelve 6-pounders. They should be fast enough to catch the rebel frigate."

"Ah, good, we will have eyes upon the water. Please ask their captains to come on board *Puritan* at 3 p.m. so we can plan how to catch the *Scorpion*."

"My flag lieutenant will do that."

"In that case, gentlemen, we shall depart so we can get our ship ready to go sea." Captain Davidson rose and exchanged additional courtesies with Lord Stafford.

Davidson waited until he and Darren were standing on the pier about to go down the stone steps to a boat. Then he put his hand on Smythe's shoulder to turn him so they were face to face. "You know this rebel captain, don't you?"

"I do, sir. His name is Jaco Jacinto and he was the captain of the *Cutlass* when it captured the *Sorcerer*. We spent hours talking on the way to Brest. He is a very capable officer and will make our task very difficult."

"Do you consider him a friend?"

"Yes, sir, I do. I'd be lying if I didn't admit it. But trust me, sir, I understand he is also our enemy, and I can assure you I will do my duty."

Davidson gazed over the waters as he processed Smythe's admission. He trusted Smythe. He also knew that sometimes deeper loyalties altered the course of battle. Didn't Homer describe Trojan and Achaean warriors exchanging armor as a pledge not to attack one another? He had be sure that Smythe was an asset, not a liability.

CHAPTER 17

MORE THAN A WEE BIT O' BURNIN'

On board H.M.S. Puritan, *January 1778*

From the quarterdeck, Darren Smythe could not see the ships in, as Captain Davidson put it, their little fleet. Assuming each was in position, *Hussar* on the port side and *Griffin* on the starboard beam should be just visible to the lookouts. Outboard of the frigates were the sloops—*Happy* to the starboard of *Griffin,* and *Savage* to the port of *Hussar.* Davidson estimated this formation gave the squadron a 70-mile wide search horizon.

Since Smythe had first-hand knowledge of their quarry, Davidson had directed Smythe to lay out their strategy in a meeting before they sailed. *Puritan's* First Lieutenant had addressed the four other captains, saying, "Gentlemen, Captain Davidson and I hazard that *Scorpion* is most likely to head to Amsterdam. Our goal is to intercept *Scorpion* and *Madras* before they reach port. If we are too late for that, we shall catch him coming out. So speed and alert lookouts are of the essence."

Roger Ulster, captain of the *Hussar,* waved his hands in a limp-wristed manner. "Why don't you think this Jacinto chap will run for Brest? He can dump the *Madras* there and head to America."

"Because he would have to run through an English Channel chock full of Royal Navy ships while escorting a ship that is much slower. I believe his priority is getting *Madras'* and its extremely valuable cargo sold as soon as he can."

Smythe then had moved on to the subject of *Scorpion*'s captain.

"Sirs, you need to be aware that Captain Jacinto is a capable adversary. He outmaneuvered *Sorcerer,* which was larger, more heavily armed, and had the advantage of surprise. I also suspect that *Scorpion* defeated our 32-gun frigate *Coburg.* If you meet him in battle, do not assume that *Scorpion* will behave like a French or Spanish ship."

Now, as he scanned the waters for any sign of *Scorpion*, Smythe wondered how to marshal *Puritan*'s resources for an encounter with a fast, heavily armed frigate, commanded by an intelligent and daring officer—a man he knew and liked.

On board Frigate Scorpion, *January 1778*

Scorpion and *Madras* anchored 200 feet apart in the Zuider Zee. It took six hours using boats from both ships to move the 160 crates of gold bars, each weighing just over 100 pounds, from *Madras* into *Scorpion's* aft hold.

Relieved of her precious cargo, *Madras* sailed *Madras* to the Dutch East India Company anchorage. *Scorpion* anchored farther out to await the return of its prize crew. It could, if need be, depart quickly.

Leaving Lieutenant Jack Shelton in charge of *Scorpion* and Midshipman Patterson in command of *Madras,* Lieutenant Radcliffe and Midshipman Garrison went with their captain to the home of Luuk Visser, a director of the Dutch West India Company, whom Jaco had met as a boy.

Luuk Visser welcomed the three men into his house and served plates of crusty bread, cheese, smoked herring and hot chocolate. Jaco told their host about the *Madras* and its cargo of spices, but not the gold. Visser volunteered to inspect the *Madras* right away. The Dutch East India and

West India Companies, he explained, always needed good ships, and getting one as a prize was cheaper than building one new. "As for the cargo, the company will buy it, assuming it isn't spoiled."

"It isn't. The aroma of spices fills the ship."

"Ah," Visser said delightedly, rubbing his hands, "that is most promising. Let us set out and see what you have brought."

Jaco did his best to hide his anxiety during Visser's inspection. He was gambling that he had at least a two-day head start on the Royal Navy, which would want nothing more than to reclaim the gold and sink the ship responsible for its loss. As captain, he had a difficult choice to make: wait for payment, or leave immediately with the gold. Certainly the gold was paramount, but Jaco felt an obligation to his men. Eventually, the Continental Congress would get the prize money and pay it out, but by then many of the crew would have finished their enlistment and so wouldn't get their share. Remembering how faithfully his men had trained on sails and guns to be ready for battle, he resolved to finalize the sale of *Madras*.

He waited on *Madras'* quarterdeck with Radcliffe and Visser while Garrison and two of Visser's men inspected the ship and its cargo. When the men came on deck, Visser walked forward to intercept them, and a rapid conversation in Dutch followed that Jaco didn't understand. *If I am going to deal with Dutch merchants, I had better learn their language.* There was a lot of head bobbing and arm waving. At the end, there were vigorous nods, and Visser walked back to where the Americans were standing. "We'll take the ship and its cargo. We just need to negotiate the price. Come, let us go to our office so we can conclude our business."

The Dutch East India Company offices were, by South Carolinian standards, opulent. The walls of each room were lined with brightly colored silk tapestries from India, and Visser's office had a painting signed by Rembrandt. The furniture was made from polished teak with inlays of mahogany and rosewood.

Visser led the three Americans to the large room with paintings by Vermeer and Steen, where Jan Van der Klerk, another director of the company, joined them. Another platter of Dutch cheeses, smoked fish and crusty bread was brought in, along with a pitcher of beer.

"Captain Jacinto," said Visser, "before we begin, I do have one question. What was in *Madras's* aft hold?"

"Military stores that are valuable to our cause. We transferred those to *Scorpion.*" There was no way Jaco was going to mention gold.

"Ah. Well then, we are prepared to make a generous offer of £13,000 Sterling for *Madras* and its cargo."

"We believe the cargo is worth much more. We'd like £17,000 Sterling."

Visser eyed the young man before him. He was very much like his father, as shrewd and fair a trader as Visser had ever met. "£15,000 Sterling. That is high as we will go."

That number was in line with what Lord Stafford had offered. *Perfecto!* "We accept."

"How do you wish to be paid? We can provide chests full of coins, or a draft."

"Silver and gold coins. That is something that my crew will understand."

Van der Klerk nodded. "We will deliver it this afternoon."

At ten minutes to five in the afternoon, Jaco boarded *Scorpion's* cutter. It took four of the sailors to shift the two heavy wooden boxes containing the equivalent of £15,000 pounds sterling in Dutch guilders. "Be careful, lads," Jaco warned them cheerfully, "those chests contain all your prize money for *Madras.* So row carefully; we wouldn't want to capsize and lose them."

* * *

Dawn was still several hours away when *Scorpion* began to slowly work its way through the darkness toward the entrance to the Zuider Zee. A strong nor' west wind forced them to tack back and forth before the ship passed through the gap between the islands of Vlieland and Terschelling. Despite Radcliffe's dire prediction that the Royal Navy would be waiting for them, first light revealed nothing more menacing than a merchant ship waiting for *Scorpion* to clear the channel.

Once in the North Sea, Jaco ordered a course of west by south that was as close to the wind line as *Scorpion* could sail. When the lookouts reported they could no longer see Vlieland and the horizon was clear, Jaco tacked again to head nor' nor' east.

At dinner, Edmund Radcliffe openly questioned why *Scorpion* was paralleling the Dutch coast. He passionately laid out his reasons why *Scorpion* should head straight to Boston or Philadelphia via the English Channel, confident *Scorpion* could outrun any English ship. The gold, he insisted, was much more important than disrupting British commerce. He urged Jaco to turn *Scorpion* around and sail through the Straits of Dover and past the Royal Navy base at Portsmouth during the night, maintaining that the channel was the shortest and fastest route into the Atlantic.

Jaco let Radcliffe talk on, observing the reactions of the other officers.

Garrison waited until Radcliffe finished, then spoke up. "Edmund, what about the Royal Navy? By now, they have ships patrolling off every major French port and in the channel looking for *Scorpion.* How do you propose to avoid them? Even if we can outsail any one of them we risk being surrounded, and we don't have enough ammunition to sink them all!"

There was a round of chuckles around the table. But the more *Scorpion's* officers questioned Radcliffe, the more argumentative he became. Jaco put six glasses in a row and filled each one with port as a way to stop the conversation. When each man had a glass, Jaco raised his. "Gentlemen, a toast to our cause."

The other officers raised their glasses. "Our cause."

Next, Jaco pulled a rolled blueback chart from the chart rack and bolted to the starboard bulwark. It held the charts for the area in which *Scorpion* was sailing. The rest were kept in the original box.

"Gentlemen, despite what is in our hold, we still have the third task of our original orders to accomplish. The first was getting the documents to Brest. That is done.The second was to take prizes. That we have accomplished! The third is to disrupt British commerce. The gold in our hold does not, I say *does not* change those orders."

Again, Jaco watched the reactions of his officers. "Right now, if Lord Stafford has any influence and has his way, every ship in the Royal Navy based in southern England that can sail is looking for *Scorpion*. They will send ships to watch Brest, Cherbourg, Le Harve, St. Nazaire, and all the other French Atlantic ports, and probably the Dutch ones as well. If we show up, they will descend on us like a pack of wolves. Trying to sneak through the English Channel, which is long and narrow and full of British frigates, would be difficult. No matter when a ship enters, Mr. Radcliffe, even with favorable winds, it takes two full days to transit to the Celtic Sea. Going through under cover of a single night is not possible. Garrison is correct. A single frigate could drive us into the arms of a first or second rater. That is not a chance I am willing to take with this ship, with you, the crew, or with the gold."

He tapped the chart. "So, here is what we are going to do. It gives us the best chance to escape and allows *Scorpion* to accomplish our third task." With a pair of dividers, he touched the name of a town in Scotland. "We are going to conduct two raids and burn as many ships as we can. The first target is Aberdeen." The dividers moved toward the top of the chart. "From there, we will go north, pass through Pentland Firth, and raid Stornoway. This will force the Royal Navy to send ships north, which takes time and requires many ships to patrol because it is a large area. We then slip into the Atlantic west of Ireland. This time of the year, there is more darkness than day, which will make it harder for them to spot us. But remember, our lookouts will be at a disadvantage, for our masts are not as tall as a larger ship's." He looked around the table and saw grim faces. *Scorpion* was now the hunted, and what their captain laid out made sense.

"Captain, won't the gold make Scorpion hard to handle?" Garrison asked, and several others looked as though this had been a concern of theirs as well. Once again, Garrison was willing to ask the hard questions. But according to the watch, even with the gold on board *Scorpion* had not lost speed. The gold, by Jaco's math, represented 1.2% of his ship's displacement. Every day, they consumed provisions—beer, water, food—and the ship got lighter. The gold, stored low in the ship, offset this.

"We have eight weeks of food on board, which is more than enough to make it back home. As we eat and drink, we get lighter. The gold, low in our hold, will help keep us stable. *It will not slow us down.*"

He was not finished. "We will not take any more prizes until we are out into the Atlantic heading south. Then, if we stumble on one, we make a decision as to whether or not we take it. I will tell the crew tomorrow morning and put it in the my journal and the ship's log that the families of the men who are captured or killed will still get their man's full share of prize money when it is paid out."

Jaco paused, and Radcliffe broke the silence. "I still think we should go through the channel. It is the best and safest course of action. If asked, I think the majority of the crew will agree with me."

"And, Mr. Radcliffe, you know this how?"

"From the men who sailed on *Madras* and others with whom I have spoken. They want to get home as fast as possible and collect their prize money."

"So you polled them, as if this was an election, did you?"

"I did. They agree with me, and they will follow me."

Jaco took a sip of his port and forced himself not to react. The thought that he could charge his second lieutenant with sedition, possibly planning a mutiny, passed through his head. Instead, he would take his case to the crew. He already had a separate log noting when Radcliffe had been insubordinate. Shelton and Midshipman Garrison had initialed his notes as accurate. Tonight there would be another entry, also witnessed.

So far, he was lucky in that the crew was not openly divided. Based on what Jeffords and Gaskins were telling him, only a few sided with Radcliffe. Now it seemed that Radcliffe was trying to expand his following.

* * *

Jaco knocked on the door to the gunroom while the officers were eating breakfast. As the captain, he could have walked in, but this was the officers' mess, and as a matter of courtesy, he always asked permission to enter.

Scorpion's captain spoke calmly. "Just after the forenoon watch comes on, I will have the entire crew muster on the gun deck so I can address them. Mr. Jeffords will be at the wheel; Mr. Radcliffe, you will be on the quarterdeck with him. Mr. Garrison will be the lookout. Everyone else will be on the gun deck. No shirkers."

"Why, may I ask?" That was Mr. Radcliffe.

"Because the crew needs to know of our plan. If we have the misfortune to be surprised by the Royal Navy, I want every man of our crew to already know how we plan to evade or confront opposition. That will save precious time." He did not add, *And should any of us fall to shot or musket fire, they will still know how to carry on.*

* * *

The men who were on the second dog watch had moved to the gun deck. Already, it was dark outside and the berthing deck was lit by a few lanterns hung from the center of the ribs supporting the gun deck. Without them, it would have been pitch black.

For those not on watch, it was quiet time to sit and talk with their friends on the crew. Abner Scruggles, who was from South Boston, was holding court, as he usually did, in one of the eight-man messes toward the aft end of the berthing deck. "I say it is bloody madness, given the gold in our hold, to conduct another raid. We need to get home, get our prize money and go have a drink or two.

Colin Gentry, besides being a gunner's mate, was the leading topman for the foremast, which meant he was the senior seaman on the mast when they were furling or letting sails loose. He listened intently. Scruggles continued. "I say our fine southern captain is leading us into a trap that will get many of us killed so he can have a bigger share of the prize money!"

Before Gentry could say something, Lofton Newton spoke up. "That just goes to show you don't understand the prize money formula, Scruggles, and worse, you think we're all as block-headed as you. Captain Jacinto's amount is fixed no matter how big or small the crew is. *If* half the crew was killed and *you* were one of the survivors, your share would double, so shut up. None of us want to oblige you."

Allen Hendricks, one of Scruggles' fellow Bostonians, chimed in. "Once we raid Aberdeen, we'll have the whole bloody Royal Navy chasing us. I fear this will not end well. I don't want to be stuck on one of their ruddy prison ships."

Scruggles nodded, "Aye, there's that. We wouldn't be freezin' our arses off if another officer was in charge."

Gentry slid off his sea chest and walked to over to stand in front of Scruggles and his friend Hendricks. "And who may that be?"

Scruggles hooted. "Mr. Radcliffe, of course! He's a proper Bostonian who knows what to do, not like this South Carolina bumpkin we have as a captain. So far, he's been lucky. I do fear his luck is about to run out. There's some of us who think so." Allen Hendricks nodded emphatically.

Gentry, now joined by Lofton Newton, looked at both Hendricks and Scruggles. His voice was calm and not threatening, even though both men had just indicated they would follow Radcliff if he led a mutiny. "This is the fourth ship I have sailed on where Captain Jacinto was an officer. I've watched him grow from a midshipman to one of the best captains around. Mr. Radcliffe has done nothing since joining this crew but complain. I suggest you mind your p's and q's and do your jobs as Captain Jacinto and First Lieutenant Shelton order. Listening to Mr. Radcliff might lead to you dancing from the end of a rope."

On board H.M.S. Puritan, *January 1778*

Puritan and the other ships wallowed in the waves under rare, bright sunshine to allow all five captains to convene on *Puritan*. The ships were five miles off the Dutch island of

Vlieland. In recognition of Davidson's appointment as the commodore of the squadron and *Puritan's* status as flagship, a white pennant with a red cross fluttered from the top of the mainmast.

Three days ago, Davidson had ordered Lieutenant Bayard Hill, commanding officer of the sloop *H.M.S. Savage,* to proceed at best possible speed to Amsterdam to gather what intelligence he could, while the remaining ships patrolled the two main entrances to the Zuider Zee. Once *Savage* was seen coming out, Davidson ordered Rathburn to hoist the signal, *"Captains, repair on board flagship."* It was time to find out if Hill had learned something useful.

Lieutenant Hill was in his late 20s. A long scar ran vertically down his cheek made by a French officer's sword when he was a midshipman boarding the French 74-gun *Courageux* at the Battle of Cape Finisterre. He faced the assembled officers and gave his report.

"Gentlemen, *Scorpion* left the Zuider Zee yesterday, and *Madras* is now flying the flag of the Dutch East India Company. According to the representative of the British East India Company, *Madras's* cargo of spices has already been sold." At this news, there was a murmur of dismay around the table. More than one officer shook his head, and Smythe heard a muttered, "Damn! One day too late."

Hill raised his voice and continued. "But there was no talk of gold. I asked around carefully. If gold bars had traded hands in Amsterdam, I would have heard of it! I conclude, gentlemen, that the gold is still aboard *Scorpion*, and we are only a day behind."

"Did you learn where *Scorpion* was headed?"

"A captain of a British East India Company ship saw the *Scorpion* passing Vlieland Island headed west."

Captain Davidson smacked his hand on the table. "Brilliant! Mr. Smythe, you know the man. What say you?"

Smythe thought hard. *What would I do if I were Jacinto?* "Commodore, the captain of *Scorpion* must know he is being hunted. If he sails directly down the English Channel, he runs the greatest risk of being intercepted by our ships. Now the captain reported seeing Scorpion sailing *west*, not south. That is suggestive. I suspect Captain Jacinto thinks he will run into far fewer Royal Navy ships if he goes north and slips between the Orkneys and the Shetland Islands."

Captain Davidson looked around the table. All the eyes were on him, not Smythe. It was his decision to make.

If I take the squadron north and bring Scorpion *to heel or gather convincing information that the Yankee frigate had taken that route, there will be no question I made the right decision, whether or not we actually catch the bloody rebel ship. If Scorpion went south, there is indeed a good chance it will be intercepted and captured. And if my decision is questioned, I could force a board of inquiry based on the fact that Smythe admitted Jacinto was a friend. That would clear my name and my career would continue. Smythe's would be over. For his sake, I hope he is right.*

Davidson stood up. "Gentlemen, we go north. *Savage* and *Happy* will sail at best speed and gather what information they can. Stay within sight of each other. If you spot *Scorpion*, determine its course, then one ship can follow and the other head back to the flagship. Do not engage unless the rebel forces the issue. *Griffin* and *Hussar*, keep my lights in sight during the night. In the morning, we will spread out as before. Our base course will be direct to the gap between the Orkneys and the Shetland Islands. Gentlemen, if there are no questions, I suggest we get on with our business and catch this rebel bastard."

Lieutenant Hill picked up his glass and held it up. "To our success."

Each of the grim-faced men repeated "Success!" and drained their glasses.

On board Frigate Scorpion

Jaco directed *Scorpion* to a point north and east of Aberdeen so it would arrive at Aberdeen's harbor around 10 p.m. By coming from this direction, the lookouts should be able spot any patrolling British frigate and have the wind gage that would allow *Scorpion* to run or engage. The route gave Jaco time to take a quick nap. When he came back on the quarterdeck, the sun was setting. Garrison had the watch and Jeffords was at the wheel. Normal watch teams had two quartermasters, who swapped positions at each ringing of the bell. The one not at the wheel could offer suggestions about the trim of the sails to reduce the amount of weather helm—the amount the wheel is turned toward the wind—to keep the boat on course. After a quick conversation with Garrison, Jaco walked to the upwind corner of the quarterdeck. Unknown to Jaco, the crew referred to this spot as "*Perfecto* Corner."

The bell rang. Jeffords finished his turn at the wheel and walked to where Jaco was scanning the sea with his spyglass. "Beggin' the captain's pardon, may I have a word, sir?"

Jaco turned to his senior quartermaster. "What's on your mind?"

"It is about what you told the crew this morning. All but a few of the crew is right with you, sir. You can ask Gaskins and Penway; they and their mates will tell you the same thing. They're confident you'll get us home in one piece. Many know you from *Alfred, Providence,* and *Cutlass,* and that's why they are on this ship. All you need to do is tell them why, like you did this morning, and they will shut down any complaints they hear, right enough."

There were many implications to what Jeffords said. Now was the time to ask the hard question. "How many oppose the course of action we are taking?"

"Twelve, maybe fifteen. All of *them* are from Boston and the towns around. They think if they support Radcliffe, he will use his connections with other wealthy Boston families on their behalf after the war. In Marblehead, we call the Radcliffes, Adams, Boylstons, Gardners and the rest the Boston Bullies, because they take advantage of hard-working fishermen like my father. They want their fish cheaper and they direct their banks to charge us usurious interest rates. As far as I am concerned, they can all go to hell!"

"Do you know who the seamen are?"

"Aye, that I do. So does Gaskins, and Penway. They tolerate Mr. Radcliffe because he is the Second Lieutenant, but I know 12-year-old boys who know more about sailing than he does."

"And the crew, what do they think of Mr. Radcliffe?"

"Most think he is a pompous bastard who is out for himself, not the men he leads."

Alarm bells were going off in Jaco's head. "Would Penway, Gaskins and you sign a statement attesting to what you just told me?"

"Aye, sir. I was hoping you would ask us to do just that. If you write it and read it to us, I'm sure they would make their mark. So will others like Gentry and Lofton."

"Do you mind if I have Mr. Shelton witness your statement?"

"That would be a good thing, sir."

"Abner, I cannot thank you enough for confiding in me. Please pass on the same sentiments to Penway and Gaskins. Tell them we'll get their words on paper in a day or so. In the meantime, we have a job to do, during which I will do my best to neutralize Mr. Radcliffe, for all our sakes."

"Aye, sir. To my way of thinking, that would be good."

* * *

Scorpion glided to a halt in the darkness, just before 10 p.m. The loudest noise was the splashing of its anchor. By the time the ship stopped moving, both cutters were hung out on the main and foremast stays and tackles, then lowered into the water. A 20-foot boat, also liberated from *Coburg,* was the third and last to be lowered. The temperature had already dropped to near freezing, and the light wind caused men to shiver.

Midshipman Wilson sat in the stern of one cutter, and Midshipman Patterson had the tiller on the second. The recently promoted Lieutenant Garrison had command of the long boat and was the raid's commander. Once each boat was rigged with a single triangular sail and a working jib, two-dozen torches made from sailcloth dipped in pitch were handed down to each boat, along with muskets and pistols. A bucket with a coil of lit slow match was the last item to be passed down.

Light from lamps along the piers silhouetted the ships tied to the quays and made it easy to navigate. Garrison's long boat led. Once inside the mouth, he headed up the River Dee, the southernmost prong. Patterson tacked his boat to sail into the north fork, while Wilson headed into the middle one. Each boat went to the far end, past where the ships were anchored or tied up, before tacking 180 degrees. As they headed back to the *Scorpion,* the boats zigzagged from one side to the other. At each ship, a sailor stopped the motion of the boat so one of his shipmates could put a lit torch onto the racks of belaying pins on either side of where the shrouds were fastened to the hull. The pitch-covered rigging flared, and fire quickly worked its way up the rigging to the canvas sails.

Wilson tossed his last torch into an open gunport of a frigate slightly smaller than *Scorpion*. It must have landed on something flammable, for flames whooshed out and joined the fire eating up the rigging. There was a shout, and several men peered over the side and pointed at his cutter. A man with a musket leaned over and fired. The ball made a splash in the water near where Wilson sat in the stern. One of the sailors grabbed a musket to return fire, but Wilson held out his hand. "Landry, don't waste the powder! Let us all row to get more speed!"

When the three boats met at the entrance to the River Dee, two 20-gun frigates, four large and six smaller merchantmen were burning. Men peering out the open gun ports of *Scorpion* and those on watch could see the sails of their returning boats sails silhouetted against the red-orange flames that lit up the sky.

One of the mates Jeffords was training as a helmsman had been born and raised near Aberdeen. Now his parents ran a small inn on Long Island. Lachlan Stewart liked to whittle the shapes of sea creatures out of bits of wood, crooning to himself as he fashioned fish, whales, or gulls. He spoke with a strong Scottish accent; often Jaco had to ask him to repeat what he said. Now Stewart stood at the quarterdeck railing, just aft of Perfecto Corner. The fires in Aberdeen's harbor lit up the western sky, casting enough light to create shadows on the dark water.

"Cap'n, thar's more than a wee bit-o-burnin' going on. Burnin' their bloody ships will give the damn Southrons something to remember *Scorpion* by!"

"Lachlan, what is a Southron?"

"it is what we Scots call the English. Another word is sassenach, which is Gaelic, and if I were to you call you one of these names, sir, it would not be a compliment."

"I see."

As soon as the returning boats were alongside and tied to the lines that would be used to hoist them aboard, Bosun Preston ordered the men at the capstan to start raising the anchor. Jaco ordered the jib raised and sheeted home, so the nor' west wind would push the ship's bow away from land. Then *Scorpion's* braces for the main and topsails were pulled around so the sails would fill. Before retiring to the captain's cabin, Jaco ordered. "Mr. Shelton, please make sure each member of the crew gets my thanks and two tots of rum for a job well done."

Jaco noted in his log that they got underway at 2:54 in the morning, and that *Scorpion* had been at anchor less than five hours. Dawn wouldn't be until almost nine, giving them five hours to escape into the darkness.

It was now time to figure out how to stop a potential mutiny.

On board H.M.S. Savage, *January 1778*

A layer of high, thin clouds filtered the brightness of the sun and reduced the glare from the water. *Savage's* lookout had spotted a pillar of smoke rising from Aberdeen's harbor. With a sense of foreboding, Lieutenant Hill kept *Savage* or course for the Scottish port. Through his spyglass, he could see there was not one, but at least six columns of oily black smoke.

"Deck, there's a small sloop one point off the port bow headed our way." Two of the men on the boat were waving vigorously.

Hill turned to his bosun and quartermaster. "Get all hands on deck. Once we find out what this is about, we'll fall off and get underway." He leaned over the bulwark as the sloop drew close. Below were four men, all grimy and dirty; probably, Hill thought, from fighting the fires.

"Are you the captain?" one called up.

"Aye, I am Lieutenant Hill, commander of His Majesty's Sloop *Savage.*"

"I am Commander Gaffney from His Majesty's Frigate *Leaf,* 20 guns. Last night a raider burned my ship, the 24-gun frigate *H.M.S. Pine,* and four merchant ships to the waterline. Another dozen ships have fire damage to their rigging. There are now no Royal Navy frigates capable of sailing in eastern Scotland."

"Do you know the name of the ship?"

"No, but I would give my life to put my ship alongside and blast it to hell!"

"So would I, Commander Gaffney, so would I. Do you know when the ship left and where it was headed?"

Gaffney shook his head. "They appeared like a ghost after dark, and departed sometime in the wee hours."

"Thank you, sir. *Savage* is part of the squadron hunting a rebel ship that may have conducted this attack. We must get underway."

Gaffney waved as he pulled in the sheet controlling the mainsail boom. "Good luck, and catch the bastards."

"That, sir, is what we intend to do."

The sloop fell off as the wind filled its sails. With the small boat safely away, Hill turned to his quartermaster and bosun. "Well, it seems the young lieutenant Smythe guessed right. We will make our best speed back to the squadron, and we'll tell the commodore that *Scorpion* passed this way."

On board Frigate Scorpion, *January*

The very strong wind through Pentland Firth varied from west by so' west to west nor' west and was icy cold. Dark, low scudding clouds and driving rain made the conditions worse. For three hours, *Scorpion* tacked back and forth along the mouth, beating against the wind and the 10-knot current.

Twice, the frigate started into Pentland Firth's five-mile wide entrance. Because it could not sail closer than 60 degrees to the wind line, *Scorpion* had to retreat into the North Sea rather than risk being driven onto the rocks by the strong current and the wind.

Soaking wet and chilled by the rain, Jaco was miserable and frustrated. They'd wasted a half a day trying to get through the firth. Going around to the north of Hollandstoun Island would add a day to their transit to Stornoway. Dusk was a few hours away and he had to make a decision. Every day *Scorpion* was in these waters, the danger of being caught by the Royal Navy increased.

"Deck ahoy! I have two sails three points astern."

"Can you make out what type of ship?"

The lookout had been a seaman on the *Cutlass*. Now Colin Gentry was one of *Scorpion's* leading top men. "By the cut of the sails, I would say ketch rigged Royal Navy sloops."

Jaco cupped his hands and looked toward the mainmast. "Any other ships with them?"

A few seconds passed. "None I can see."

Lightly armed sloops can sail even closer to the wind than Scorpion *can. They might even be faster! Are they scouts for a squadron?* "How far away?"

"Five miles at most."

"Let me know if they change course or signal."

"Captain, what do you make of them?" Lieutenant Radcliffe had joined him on the quarterdeck.

"They're not firing flares, which tells me that whomever they are scouting for is well behind them. That is good for us."

"How so?"

"Call the officers to the quarterdeck and I'll explain."

Soon Lieutenants Shelton, Radcliffe and Garrison, Marine Lieutenant Miller, and Midshipmen Wilson and

Patterson were huddled in the port rear corner of the quarterdeck. The delay gave Jaco time to flesh out his plan.

"Gentlemen, the winds and currents are against us, so we are not chancing the Pentland Firth again. Instead, we are going to put those two sloops out of action so they cannot summon their friends, then go around the northern tip of Hollandstoun Island. It will delay our raid on Stornoway by a day, maybe two. If, as we approach Stornoway, we see a British frigate, we slip away instead of raiding."

Jack Shelton had a grin on his face. "The bloody Brits won't be expecting this."

"Aye, Jack, that's my thinking. If they run, we chase them until dark and then go on our way."

Radcliffe, who had his arms crossed, drawled, "Wouldn't we be better off just losing them during the night? It would be safer, given what is in our hold."

"Yes and no. If they are part of a squadron, their mission is probably to have one shadow us while the other runs back to his friends. I intend to make sure that does not happen. That way, any other ships won't know where to look for us. "

On board H.M.S. Savage, *the same day*

Lieutenant Bayard Hill studied the mystery ship through his spyglass. It matched Captain Hall's description of the *Scorpion*. They had found their prey! Hill signaled *Happy,* "Enemy in sight."

When his counterpart acknowledged, he signaled, "Follow me until dark, am pursuing."

Another acknowledgement. Their orders were to find and follow. That task was accomplished. Now, he had to learn where *Scorpion* was headed before he could send *Happy* back for *Puritan, Hussar* and *Griffin*. He didn't want the rebel to escape in the night, and wondered how far to the south Commodore Davidson was.

On board Frigate Scorpion

The two sloops were about half a mile apart and closing. Jaco turned to his third lieutenant. "Mr. Garrison, call the watch. We're going to wear the ship to so' so' east to head toward them. When we are steady up on our new course, beat to quarters. Keep the Marines on the main deck, and do not load or run out until I give the word."

Jaco had a plan with several options. Time and the British captains actions would tell him which one to execute.

On board H.M.S. Savage

The rebel frigate was now headed directly towards *Savage* and *Happy*. Hill realized *Scorpion* meant to do battle with the two sloops. *I don't need to follow, I need to run toward* Griffin, Hussar *and* Puritan. *and hope the rebel captain takes the bait. But if I tun too soon, Scorpion might flee. If I wait too long to turn, the rebel ship could rake my sloop. Commodore Davidson, I hope you are where you are supposed to be!*

Hill turned to the second quartermaster. "Signal *Happy* to come about when we do."

"Aye, aye sir."

Hill waited until the signal was acknowledged before giving his next order. "Quartermaster, stand by to come to starboard on my command."

"Aye aye, sir."

"Helm a-lee. New course so' by east."

The six-foot waves were tossing *Savage* around. If he pulled the sails in for maximum speed, he risked demasting his ship.

Once *Scorpion* closed with his ship, it would be time for his next move.

On board Frigate Scorpion

Jaco watched through his spyglass as the two Royal Navy sloops came about and tacked in opposite directions, east and west. He was calculating how much ground *Scorpion* gained as the two sloops slowed, turned through the wind, and re-trimmed their sails, when he heard the nasal voice and Boston accent of Lieutenant Radcliffe.

"You do realize those sloops are running because just over the horizon several frigates are waiting, do you not, Captain?"

"Maybe. But I am betting that *Scorpion* is still faster than any British frigate. They'll have a hard time finding us after dark."

"You are risking every man jack on this ship, to say nothing of the gold, just to prove a foolish point."

"And, Mr. Radcliffe, what point may that be?"

"That you think you are smarter and better than they are."

Jaco leaned forward with his hands on the railing and decided to ignore his second lieutenant's comment. "Mr. Radcliffe, we have beaten to quarters. Shouldn't you be on the gun deck?"

Once Radcliffe left, Jaco walked to the bow of the main deck. It gave him time to let his anger at Radcliffe fade. It also gave a different view of the two sloops through his spyglass. He could now read their names, and on *Savage* he saw a solitary figure in a royal blue coat gazing back at his ship. The man looked to be about his size and had blond hair. It was not Darren Smythe, but Jaco wondered if Smythe knew this officer.

Suddenly, a flash of fire lit the sky above *Savage*. Smoke followed a tongue of flame that rose 500 feet in the air, then exploded in a red flash. The muted bang reached *Scorpion* as the red ball of fire burned out and dropped toward the water.

At first Jaco though it might have been a problem with a gun exploding, but then he realized it was a flare, a signal to ships beyond the horizon of *Scorpion's* lookouts. Or, was it a bluff to dissuade him from pursuing?

To help relieve the tension, Jaco walked to the forward end of the main deck. Cold spray soaked Jaco as he stood just aft of the bowsprit. Walking back to the quarterdeck, Jaco modified his plan of action.

"Mr. Shelton, pass the word to Mr. Radcliffe to load ball and aim at their hulls."

"Aye, aye, sir. Do you think they will try to fight?"

"I am counting on them continuing to run. Have Mr. Preston get enough men on deck to handle our sails and still leave enough to man both batteries."

On board H.M.S. Savage

Hill looked back at the onrushing rebel frigate. It would be dark in less than two hours, but that, unfortunately, would be enough time for that damnably fast frigate to overtake *Savage* and get a clear shot up his stern. He had not realized just how fast the rebel ship could go.

We should have turned sooner. If I don't want to be eaten, it is time to make a move. But how to I stop Scorpion without sending all that gold to the bottom of the Atlantic? Damn!

Turning to the senior midshipman, Hill ordered, "Signal *Happy,* turn 90 degrees to starboard on my signal. Then stand by to come about to port."

On board Frigate Scorpion,

When he saw the jib and foresails of the *Savage* begin to flap, Jaco smiled to himself. *Savage* was well into its tack when *Happy* began to turn. With six-foot seas and a strong wind, *Scorpion* had the advantage; it was not as affected by the waves due to its design and larger size. Both Royal Navy ships would lose speed from the change in direction. Suddenly he frowned. The sloops were diverging. They were forcing him to choose one.

With the wind coming over her starboard beam and all the sail *Scorpion* was carrying, she was heeled over so that the muzzles of the port battery aimed at the water and the starboard guns pointed at the sky. *It is,* Jaco thought, *time to take advantage of our long twelves and do the unexpected.*

His next move was all about timing—when to slacken sail to level the ship, yet keep enough steerageway so *Scorpion* didn't get rolled by the waves or turn into the wind. His objective was to engage both sloops, one right after the other. "Mr. Preston, on my command, loosen all the staysails, top sails, topgallants and royals. Let them luff if you have too. Mr. Jeffords, keep us steady on course."

Next he addressed Garrison and Radcliffe, standing just forward of the quarterdeck. "We're not going to tack to chase one or the other. Instead, we're going slow down, level the ship, and give our gun crews a chance to fire into each sloop. Because these two sloops are going in opposite directions we will shoot at *Savage,* the one on the port side, first because it is further away. Then we shoot at *Happy* on the starboard side. They will be well within range of our long twelves at under 400 yards. Aim carefully. I know the men can do it, and now's the time to prove their skills. Have a second ball and powder cartridge by the guns. When I give the order to fire, your gunners are free to fire as they bear." Both men nodded. Garrison went down the forward companionway; Radcliffe descended aft.

Now it was all about judging how much his greyhound of the sea would slow down. On the port side, *Savage* was 300 yards away and starting to accelerate. The sloop on the starboard side, *Happy,* was closer at just over 200. By the time they crossed its stern, it would be about 300 yards away.

The number one long 12 on the port side bellowed, and a geyser of water rose on the port side of the port sloop. Then the number two gun fired, and chunks of wood flew into the air, along with the barrel of a six-pounder that soared drunkenly before it crashed onto *Savage's* deck.

Number three fired, followed by number one again. Jaco tried to keep track of the shots, but it became impossible.

What Jaco didn't know was that a 12-pound ball from the port number one gun had smashed through *H.M.S. Savage's* transom, taking a chunk out of its mizzenmast before hammering into the sloop's iron stove. The oven shattered, sending hot coals into the hammocks in the netting along the bulwark. Smoke from burning canvas started trailing the wounded sloop.

Savage's bow rose over a swell, then plunged down. The movement was enough to dislodge the mizzenmast, and its stays weren't enough to hold it in place. The mast toppled, and part of the sail fell into the water. *Savage* slewed to the left and, dragged by the sail acting as a sea anchor, slowed. Another ball pulped the helmsman and carried away the wheel before it blew a hole in the bulwark near the bow.

On *Happy,* Lieutenant Liam Justin saw the smoke rising from *Savage's* lower deck, and while he wanted to help his friend, he was about to have problems of his own. Smoke billowed out from the starboard side of *Scorpion* and his ship shuddered as if it had hit a submerged rock. Three 12-pound cannon balls pummeled his ship, sending splinters and debris flying everywhere.

Five of his 6-pounders were knocked out of action. Another iron ball deflected off a barrel, went down through the deck and out the side just above the waterline.

* * *

Once past the two sloops, Jaco kept *Scorpion* so' by so' east. The light was nearly gone. The flames from the burning *Savage* lit the horizon when Jaco tacked *Scorpion* back around to head nor' nor' east.

Jack Shelton came over to stare at the glow; he heard his captain muttered, "Poor buggers"

Seeing Shelton, Jaco nodded. "Lets get out of here. Tonight we sail under our topgallants as well as our tops and mains. We need speed to put distance between ourselves and their friends."

On board H.M.S. Puritan

It was just before dark when lookouts spotted a smudge of smoke against the horizon. Not long after, the wind carried the pungent smell of burning wood, canvas, pitch, rope and paint. *Puritan* approached the two damaged sloops and coasted to a stop.

Puritan's cutter was quickly lowered over the side with Midshipman Rathburn in the stern. When he climbed over *Savage's* gunwale, he found Lieutenant Justin had brought *Happy* alongside and lashed the sloops together so he could use *Happy's* pumps to help fight the fire.

"Mr. Justin, what happened?"

"No time, sir! Get your sailors up here on the deck and lend a hand. We must get the dead and wounded over to *Happy* before the fires get to *Savage's* magazine."

"Aye, aye." Rathburn went to the gunwale and ordered the seaman to tie up the boat and help out.

Of the 50 officers and men on the *Savage,* 26 were dead or seriously wounded, including its captain, Lieutenant Hill. Another half dozen had splinter wounds that would eventually heal if they didn't become infected.

On board Frigate Scorpion, *mid-January 1778*

All the lookouts could see was grey-blue sea and more grey-blue sea. *Scorpion* was headed so' west by south west of the Orkney Islands. The icy wind coming off Greenland had subsided, and the day had warmed to a relatively balmy 45 degrees under a winter sun that was already starting to set. Long swells worked the frigate as it headed through them at an angle. The bow was rising and falling, and each fall sent a wave of spray over the forward third the ship. On the quarterdeck, Jaco and the watch team were using their knees to absorb the movement of the ship, but even the most seasoned one had to occasionally grab part of the ship to keep from falling over.

Scorpion was making 10 knots through the long swells under what Jaco deemed the best combination of sails—jib, foresail, mains, tops and topgallants—that gave a good turn of speed and minimized the strain on the rigging and masts. Could he add more sails? Yes, but in this part of the world winter storms came up quickly. Snow and freezing rain could soak the rigging and sails, making the ship top-heavy. Handled wrong, a sodden ship with ice covered rigging would capsize.

Jaco returned to his cabin to study the chart of local waters. Spinning the divider in his hand, he debated whether or not *Scorpion* should make one more raid before heading home. He still didn't know if *Happy* and *Savage* were part of a larger, more powerful squadron, but it was likely they were. He refused to believe that the Royal Navy was so arrogant that they would send only two sloops armed with 6-pounders to hunt him down. If so, where were the rest of the ships? Had they stopped to assist the stricken sloops? He sat at the desk to consider his options.

Jaco had his hands clasped behind his head when there was a knock at his door. The door cracked open and the Marine on guard said, "Sir, it is Lieutenant Shelton."

"Send him in."

Shelton's cheeks were red from the cold. "You look like you were deep in thought. I am sorry to interrupt." Jaco waved his hand. "I was, and I still don't have a plan I like."

"It is getting late. Do you want to shorten sail, as we normally do?"

"No." Jaco surprised himself with how fast the answer came out of his mouth.

"I'll tell the watch."

Jaco waved his hand as if to say, *Sit*. Shelton nodded and took the chair next to his captain.

"Here's what I want to do." Jaco pointed to the chart. "I want to raid Stornoway to give the Royal Navy more to think about, then sail around the north side of the Isle of Lewis before heading so' west of Ireland. There the current is warm and we can sail with a favorable wind until we reach the Trade Winds. But we don't know who is in front or behind us. My fear is that we are only day ahead of a Royal Navy squadron of unknown composition. A raid might allow them to overtake us. What am I missing, Jack?"

"Jaco, the Royal Navy doesn't have a God's eye view of the ocean; they're guessing just like we are!" Shelton picked up the pair of dividers lying on the chart. "If we continue to be unpredictable, we will avoid the Royal Navy. If we can't, we should still be able to outrun their ships. And if it comes to a fight with a Royal Navy frigate that happens to intercept us, I'm not afraid, and neither is the crew. You shouldn't be either."

Jaco leaned forward and looked at the chart. "I am betting the squadron chasing us believes we went through the Pentland Firth, heading for the Atlantic and home."

Jack grinned. "That would be the *sensible* thing to do.

"Then it is decided. We're going to Stornoway tonight."

"Edmund Radcliffe won't like it."

"Too bad. All I ask that he does his duty."

"Captain, I don't trust him."

"Nor do I, so in any action I need to keep him in front of me. Make sure he is not armed. If he objects... clap him in irons."

The ship's first lieutenant looked at his captain so their eyes met.

"Garrison, Wilson and Patterson don't like or trust Radcliffe either. They think he is a cancer."

"I do too, Jack. But to use a Christian analogy, for the remainder of this voyage, Edmund Radcliffe is our cross to bear."

On board H.M.S. Puritan, *mid-January, 1778*

Smythe finished his inspection of the remaining stores in the frigate's hold. As he came up the companion way to the gun deck, Alistair was waiting. "Sir, the captain would like a word."

Seeing Alistair followed by the ship's First Lieutenant, the Marine guard at the door rapped lightly, then opened it. Davidson waved Smythe in. Lieutenant Bullocks was studying a chart and barely glanced up.

"Well, Smythe, thanks to Mr. Bullocks' knowledge of the Pentland Firth and its currents, we're now west of the Orkneys. Where do you guess this Jacinto chap is headed?"

Smythe was surprised by Davidson's tone and word usage. Until the night before, he'd referred to Jacinto as *the rebel* or *bloody bastard*. The civility in his tone caught him off guard. *Was it a sign of respect?*

"Home. Back to America."

"Carrying a million one in pounds sterling of the King's gold will make you do that. But which way?"

Darren looked down at the chart and pondered. "I doubt he will go south through The Little Minch and into the

Atlantic or the Irish Sea, because he will expect those waters to be full of our ships. I think he is done capturing prizes and will go around Ireland."

"Makes sense, Smythe. But I hear some hesitation in your voice."

"Sir, something tells me that Jaco, I mean Captain Jacinto, would like to stab us again: another hit and run raid, but I don't know where."

"Look at the chart."

Smythe studied it, then slowly tapped a finger on the paper. "I'd pick Stornoway. It's isolated, and he could be in and out in a few hours, just like Aberdeen. That would be in keeping with his aggressive style."

Davidson calibrated the dividers on a meridian of longitude and walked off the distance. "It is a logical choice. We only have three ships now, and I want to keep us together so if we do meet up with this rebel fellow we can overpower him. We'll take up position 20 miles north of Islay in a line 12 miles apart. This way, if your friend goes into Stornoway and comes out to the north, we'll catch him. If not, it will be a pleasant journey for us south through the Irish Sea and around to Portsmouth."

"Splendid strategy, sir."

"It will only be splendid if it works. Plot us a course, and I will signal *Hussar* and *Griffin*."

On board Frigate Scorpion, January 15th, 1778

Scorpion was blacked out as it made its way around the Fye Peninsula to the entrance of Stornoway's harbor. There were very few lights from the small Scottish fishing village, but enough to give *Scorpion's* crew a frame of reference. Jaco addressed the crews of the two boats already in the water.

"Gentlemen, you know the drill. Burn as many as you can, then come swiftly back to *Scorpion*. This is our last raid to remind King George of the Continental Navy's reach. I promise you two things. One, we will head for home as soon as you are back on board. And two, we will get out of this damn cold! Now, let's get on with it."

Later, with the crews returned and *Scorpion* underway again, Jaco updated his log. Two pails, each with a red-hot 12-pound cannon ball, hung from the ceiling over the table, warming his cabin. Jaco's quill pen scratched noisily on the paper:

7:08 p.m.—dropped anchor outside Stornoway, Scotland.

7:46 p.m.—two boats launched with 9 men each.

9:47 p.m.—counted 13 fires in the harbor.

10:53 p.m.—boats returned and hoisted aboard. Patterson, Wilson plus 16 sailors all safely back on board. Extra tot of rum issued to crew. Six large fishing schooners, five sloops and two scows burned.

11:09 p.m.—weighed anchor.

11:18 p.m.—course nor' east set under jib, tops, topgallants and mains. Winds from nor' nor' west. Taking *Scorpion* around northern tip of Isle of Lewis to get to the Atlantic.

11:23 p.m.—ordered watch to change course to west so' west at first light and stay out of sight of land. Headed home.

The log was now three inches thick, filled with diagrams and notes that would become the basis of his report to the Marine Committee.

Chapter 18

Three Versus One

On board Frigate Scorpion, *8:52 a.m., January 16th, 1778*

It was a short night for Jaco. He crawled out of his bunk a little after seven. The cannon balls in the iron pails had long given up what heat they'd stored. His breath formed clouds in the cold.

Over his two layers of underwear, he pulled on a wool sweater the he could wear under a heavy wool coat to keep his torso warm. It was his feet that always got cold; even with wool lining in his boots, the cold seeped through.

Jaco looked out the windows. Stars sparkled overhead in the fading darkness. The ringing of the ship's bell told him it was eight in the morning. Sunrise was still more than an hour away.

The berthing deck was pleasantly warm, if a bit stuffy, and there were smiles all around the mess tables as Jaco stopped to chat with crew members coming off watch. Everyone knew a port in North America was, with luck, only three weeks away.

Two men at one table, however, had sullen looks. Jaco recognized them as members of what Penway referred to as "Radcliffe's Fellows". Rather than say something that might lead to a confrontation, Jaco acknowledged their presence with a wave and chatted with other members of the crew.

Cold air slapped Jaco in the face as soon as he stepped onto the main deck. The moon and the stars were fading as the sky in the east began to lighten. According to Jack Shelton, who was on watch, Scorpion was 20 miles nor' nor' east of the Isle of Lewis. Jaco had just been given the position when the lookout called, "Sail ho! Three points on the port bow."

Jaco moved to the foremast and called up, "How far, and what kind of ship?"

"'Bout ten miles to the west; can't tell what kind of ship yet."

Jaco's gut warned him it was a frigate, probably more than one. Ten minutes later, through the clear lenses of his Dolland spyglass, he spotted the trapezoidal shape of a sail on a square-rigged ship colored yellow-white by the early morning sun.

The lookout called out, "Deck, the ship three points on the port bow is about nine miles away. Second ship two points off the starboard bow at about eight miles. By their looks, both are frigates and headed our way."

"Let me know if they alter course." *They are looking into the rising sun and may not have spotted us. At least not yet.*

Jaco worked out the geometry of the coming engagement, as well as the tactics *Scorpion* might use to keep the Royal Navy from cornering his ship. Then he sent Mr. Patterson to call all the officers, along with Bosun Penway and Quartermaster Jeffords, to join him on the quarterdeck.

Jaco sawing Radcliffe studying the Royal Navy frigates through a spyglass before he joined the group, the last to do so. When he arrived, there was fire in his eyes, and his voice grated as he spoke.

"Damn you to hell, Jacinto! Your refusal to sail directly home from Amsterdam, your foolish decision to conduct another raid, contrary to all common sense and my counsel, has drawn us into a trap! We should have never gone to Stornoway. It gave the Royal Navy time to catch us."

"Calm down, Edmund. These ships could have been waiting here to block our escape route. How, when and why they arrived here is not important. What does matter is that, based on our relative positions, we have the advantage."

"You want to take on two British frigates in a battle?" Radcliffe practically screamed. "Have you lost your mind? You are going to lose the gold and get us all killed! It all could have been prevented if we'd gone straight home, *as I suggested!*"

Jaco's tone got a little harsher and colder. Being polite and professional wasn't working. "Mr. Radcliffe, allow me to explain—"

Radcliffe cut him off and shouted, "You should have never been given this captaincy! You should be relieved, and if Mr. Shelton had any balls he would have done so by now! You are risking everything because you wanted to conduct a second raid when common sense said run for home. I swear to God that If I survive this battle, I will make it my business to have you court-martialed for stupidity."

Scorpion's captain took one step forward. "Radcliffe, I have had enough of your insubordination. We are at war and some of us may die. It is my job to make sure that as few sailors as possible on *Scorpion* are hurt. You have two choices. Either listen to what I have to say and then do your duty, or spend the rest of your time on board in irons in the hold chained to a rib."

The bosun and quartermaster mates on watch could hear every word Radcliffe shouted.

"Goddamn you, Jacinto! I should have taken over this ship when you decided to raid Aberdeen—"

Jaco's hand shot out and grabbed Radcliffe's arm. "And what? Finish your sentence, Lieutenant Radcliff. That is an order."

Radcliffe said nothing.

"You've not been afraid to speak your mind before. And head for home, was that what you were about to say?"

Radcliffe nodded.

"You give me no choice. In front of your fellow officers as my witnesses, Lieutenant Edmund Radcliffe, I am placing you under arrest for insubordination and plotting a mutiny." Turning to the Lieutenant Miller, "Take Mr. Radcliffe to the orlop deck and put him in irons. Mr. Radcliffe will be the first man we have had to hold there. If he resists, feel free to run him through."

The time it took Miller and two of his Marines to escort a struggling Lieutenant Radcliffe to the hold let Jaco finish formulating his plan. He was counting on the Royal Navy to follow its doctrine.

A grim-faced Lieutenant Miller returned to the quarterdeck. "Sir, Mr. Radcliffe had to be subdued by force. He will survive, but he will have a nasty headache when he awakens and finds himself down where he belongs, with the rats in the bilge."

Jaco nodded in acknowledgement, thinking that a blow to the head might knock some sense into the man. Under the Articles of War, what Radcliffe had just said was enough to get him flogged, or worse, hung.

Realizing he had to say something, Jaco said, "We will deal formally with Mr. Radcliffe after this action. Now, let us get back to the matter at hand. Mr. Miller, I don't want any of your Marines in the rigging, other than to man the swivel guns in the maintops. They are to stay on the deck to help Bosun Preston's sailors handle the sails. *Scorpion* is going to maneuver and shoot like the Royal Navy has never seen before!"

On board H.M.S. Puritan, *8:58 a.m.*

Darren Smythe studied the rebel frigate through Horrocks' spyglass, wondering how many Royal Navy captains considered their opponent to be a friend. He was excited and at the same time afraid for Jacinto, because he knew first hand the mortality rate for captains in battles.

Captain Davidson's voice sounded almost jovial. "Well, Mr. Smythe, we're about to test *Scorpion's* mettle and see if your rebel friend is all he is cracked up to be. What do you think Jacinto will do?"

"Sir, if I were Captain Jacinto, I would try to get past our three ships and outrun us. Once night comes, he can disappear."

"That is exactly what we must prevent."

On board Frigate Scorpion, *9:09 a.m.*

Pushed by a steady wind, *Scorpion's* bow cut through the slate-grey water that was the calmest Jaco had seen since they'd been in these waters. It was, he thought, as if God's had decided not to interfere with the fight.

"Mr. Jeffords, Mr. Preston, on my command, stand by to fall off to a course of nor' east. Hoist our colors and the Gadsden flag. No sense hiding who we are."

The nearer British frigate maintained its course for over a minute after *Scorpion* turned. Jaco's eye estimated the enemy ship was making eight knots, and during the delay it covered at least 700 feet. The Royal Navy ensign came into view as the frigate turned to port to parallel *Scorpion's* course. By the time it finished the turn it was 500 yards away and well within range of *Scorpion's* long twelves, but at the edge of the British frigate's 9-pounders.

It was time. Jaco nodded to Lieutenant Garrison on the main deck. "Fire as you bear."

Garrison ducked and yelled to his gun captains, "Port battery, fire as you bear as long as you have a target."

Both ships fired almost at the same time. Tongues of flame shot out from *Scorpion's* long twelves. Gray-white smoke rippled down the deck of the British ship and obscured Jaco's view. Some enemy balls sent up spouts of water short of his ship. Others sounded like sledgehammers hitting a hollow log when they smacked into *Scorpion's* hull. Others made a popping sound as they pierced sails.

The rumble of gun trucks on the deck could be heard on the quarterdeck. *Scorpion's* long twelves belched fire and smoke again. Acrid smoke filled Jaco's nostrils. When he finally could see the British frigate, there were gaps in its bulwark, just above its gun deck. *Scorpion's* gun crews had practiced for hours, and the training was paying off.

On board H.M.S. Griffin, *9:15 a.m.*

Captain Sam Westown felt *H.M.S. Griffin* shudder each time his ship was hit. At this range their own guns should be smashing the rebel frigate, but throwing rocks would do as much damage as his 9-pounders were causing. All he could see were a half-dozen holes in the rebel's mainsails. The ship's hull appeared unscathed.

Griffin, however, had taken a fearful pounding. Three of his cannon on the starboard side were out of action. One ball had smashed through the hull and splintered three casks of beef before stopping. One of his midshipmen, bloodied by splinters, went to inspect the hold for leaks and came back with the offending ball. It smelled like cooked salt beef.

As he saw *Scorpion's* bow come to port, Westown knew what was coming. His best course, he decided, was to tack

Griffin to close to a range where his guns would be more effective.

Westown could tell his ship was hurt by the way it sluggishly responded to his order to wear the ship to port. Not only had its hull taken a pounding, so had its rigging. Stays, halyards and braces floated in the wind. Instead of closing the gap, the distance between the ships widened, favoring the long guns of the rebel.

Plumes of flame spewed out from *Scorpion's* port side guns as soon as *Griffin* came parallel. The ship's beak disappeared in cloud of splinters, but *Griffin's* surviving gun crews fired back. Westown thought his eyes were playing tricks on him when he saw a ball hit *Scorpion* straight on, bounce off the hull and splash in the sea.

Griffin staggered as more 12-pound balls struck its side. When the bowsprit dropped into the water with a loud crack, Westown decided he had to save his ship and his men from an icy, watery grave. He'd done his duty; it was time to save his ship.

On board H.M.S. Puritan, *9:31 a.m.*

Davidson stared at *Scorpion* as it emerged from the smoke, seemingly unscathed. The two frigates were sailing in opposite directions, and if nothing changed *Puritan* and *Scorpion* would exchange broadsides as the rebel ship passed down his ship's starboard side. To prolong the battle, he would have to reverse course and try to run *Scorpion* down from the rear, using his bow chasers to fire up the rebel's arse. But if the frigate had long stern chasers, the return fire could be devastating.

Or he could turn to starboard to cross the bow of *Scorpion* and force the rebel ship toward *Hussar*. If *Scorpion* turned with him, they'd fight it out, broadside to broadside. If *Scorpion* turned away, he would reverse course and harry the frigate right into *Hussar,* 10 miles to the north and closing under full sail.

Davidson studied *Griffin* through his spyglass. "Mr. Smythe, I fear your friend has taken the measure of *Griffin.*"

"Aye, sir," was all Darren could say.

They were about to take on *Scorpion,* and *Puritan* might get battered just as badly.

Davidson took a step toward the wheel. "Mr. Shilling, stations to wear ship to starboard. We're going to cross the bow of this damned rebel and teach him a lesson or two."

On board Frigate Scorpion, *9:30 a.m.*

Jaco saw the second British frigate tack to his port side and thought, *Thank you. You turned too soon.* Now rather than a running gun battle with the British ship on his starboard side, blocking his route to the Atlantic, he was given an escape route and could get behind the British frigate.

"Mr. Jeffords, Mr. Preston, we're going to fall off to a course of nor' east."

"Aye, aye, sir. We're ready when you are."

Garrison came up on deck, his face blackened with smoke, and Jaco yelled out, "Good work! Load ball. We're about to have some more target practice on British oak."

Garrison waved and disappeared down the aft companion way.

"Mr. Jeffords, ease off your helm to starboard. Course nor' east. Mr. Preston, get your men to haul the yards around.

On board H.M.S. Puritan, *9:38 a.m.*

To no one in particular, Davidson said aloud, "You bloody rebel bastard. You don't want to fight me!"

Smythe scanned *Scorpion*'s quarterdeck through Horrocks' spyglass and located Jacinto, who was easily recognizable. He was standing by the railing, looking over at *Puritan* through a spyglass of his own. *May God spare both of us.*

"Mr. Smythe, what do you estimate the range is?"

"Between 600 and 700 yards. Maximum range for our 12-pounders, and our carronades aren't very accurate beyond 200. Sir, if you want to get a good look at your enemy, Captain Jacinto is on his quarterdeck."

Davidson put his glass to his eye and found Jacinto just as the number one gun on *Scorpion's* port side belched fire and smoke. The ball didn't fall short into the water. It smacked into *Puritan's* hull, causing the ship to vibrate from the impact.

Roote had already ordered the gun captains to fire as soon as they had a target. Elevation screws had the barrels raised up almost as far as they could go. On his command, *Puritan*'s guns roared defiance.

From the quarterdeck, Smythe watched for *Puritan's* balls to strike, but other than a new hole in its mizzen main sail, he saw no damage. *What?* There were no telltale spouts on the water from balls that had fallen short. He was sure *Puritan's* gunners had hit the rebel ship!

Scorpion's long guns fired again, and six balls struck *Puritan*. Each time, the frigate shuddered. The bulwark between the main and mizzen masts took a direct hit and erupted in a hail of deadly splinters. Despite the pounding, her gun crews fired another broadside. This time Smythe clearly saw two balls strike *Puritan's* hull—and rebound. The rest fell short.

Smythe felt his stomach constrict in a most unusual way, as if it were a hedgehog trying to curl itself into a ball. *Damn!*

What is that ship's hull made from? Iron? Smythe hoped he'd live long enough to make a report.

On board Frigate Scorpion, *9:40 a.m.*

Scorpion's number ten gun on the port side fired for the third time. Jaco yelled down to Bosun Preston, "We're going to tack to port. Stand by."

Once acknowledged, Jaco turned to his quartermaster, "Mr. Jeffords, helm a-lee. Steady up on nor' nor' west."

To Garrison on the main deck, Jaco yelled out, "Mr. Garrison, with a little luck we will rake the stern of this British fellow, and before they can come about we will be off."

Jeffords had Preston release the sheets on the jib, and *Scorpion's* bow started to come around. Jaco was judging the distance to the stern of the bigger British frigate when one of the lookouts called out, "Deck, ahoy! Man-o-war two points abeam on the starboard bow!"

"How far?"

"Three or four miles. Looks like she is headed right for us."

That ship is 20 minutes away. I will deal with him once we get this broadside off.

Through his spyglass, Jaco looked at the new ship. Then he looked at the one coming up on his port side and read the name: *Puritan.* Two men were on the quarterdeck looking at him through spyglasses. One was the captain. The other was Smythe!

Darren, I hope to God you survive my broadside. Unfortunately, you know as well as I do that there will be no quarter until one of us hauls down our flag, and so far neither of us has a reason to do so.

On board H.M.S. Puritan, 9:50 a.m.

Davidson ran to the forward end of the quarterdeck. "Stand by to come about to starboard. Mr. Shilling, unless you want the rebels to rake this ship, helm a-lee NOW!!! Deck there, release the jib and foresail sheets. Be quick about it. We need to get our stern away from the enemy."

Puritan slowed noticeably as it turned through the wind. To Darren Smythe, it seemed to take forever. Seeing his one-armed friend appear out of the aft companionway to the gun deck, Smythe yelled, "Mr. Roote, I fear we are going to take another pounding. Fire as your starboard battery bears."

Scorpion's first ball hit just forward of where the officers' slept. It tore a chunk of wood out of the bulwark before embedding itself in the far side. *Puritan* shuddered as five more balls hit. The only question in Davidson's mind was how to hurt *Scorpion* in return.

Puritan's captain shouted, "Mr. Rathburn, signal *Hussar:* 'Ram enemy if possible'. Once you get an acknowledgement, go to the gun deck and see what damage has been done. Mr. Smythe, we have to get *Puritan's* house in order so we can continue the chase. And before this year is over, I want to know what type of bloody cannon that rebel ship has, and how that hull is built to be impervious to our bloody shot!"

On board Frigate Scorpion, 9:58 a.m.

With *Puritan* behind him and trying to regain its speed after tacking, Jaco fixed his eyes on the oncoming British frigate. The steady bearing meant only one thing: it intended to ram *Scorpion* to keep it from escaping.

Garrison came up on the quarterdeck to report and to see for himself what the situation was. "Captain, guns are all in good shape. We have a few splinter wounds from a ball that hit the edge of a gunport, but my starboard battery is itching to fire their guns."

"Tell them to get ready; their chance is coming."

Jaco estimated he had six or seven minutes to make a decision as to whether he would veer to the west and away from the third frigate or turn nor' east to pass wide and come up his stern. Jaco looked aft. *Puritan* was trailing *Scorpion* and had cut the corner. For the first time in the battle, Jaco thought he might have to fight it out with more than one Royal Navy ship at the same time. He debated whether to send topmen aloft to fire down on the decks of the British ships, but felt an odd reluctance to do so. Right now, smart, fast sailing and shot were more important, and he needed every hand on the ropes or at the guns.

Shelton joined Garrison and Jaco on the starboard quarterdeck to get a look at the oncoming frigate.

"Gentlemen, what do you make of our situation? So far, we've out-sailed and out-shot the Royal Navy, but I'm running out of tricks. Do you have any ideas?"

"I do, Captain." Garrison's voice was full of confidence. "We keep going and let this new ship think they are going to grapple. Unless they planned the intercept perfectly, that ship will have to keep adjusting its course. We wait to alter our course until it is inside 400 yards, cross its bow, hammer it, and wear back off to this course. I'll damn near guarantee at that range that my gunner's will get off two shots and will bring one of her masts down."

"What about *Puritan*, the ship behind us?"

"After raking this new ship, we head due north until two or three hours after dark, then come around to the so' west. Damaged as she is, I don't think *Puritan* can catch us unless the newcomer slows us down or forces us to grapple."

On board H.M.S. Hussar, 10:07 a.m.

Captain Roger Ulster knew cannon fire when he heard it. When dawn broke, *Puritan* was out of sight of even his best lookouts, so Ulster turned so' east toward the sound of battle.

As his ship bore down, he counted three sets of sails. One was barely moving. Another was headed east, trailed by *Puritan,* which was signaling. Davidson wanted Ulster to ram *Scorpion.*

Ulster's terse commands kept adjusting the course to maintain constant bearing as it closed on the rebel frigate. *Hussar* was galloping along at eight knots, which was as fast as it could go under the canvas she was carrying and on its present tack.

Through his spyglass, Ulster scrutinized *Scorpion* for the telltale signs that it had been in a fight. He was puzzled; other than holes in its sails, it appeared unhurt.

The bearing from *Hussar* relative to *Scorpion* was no longer constant. Instead of two points of the port bow, it was now less than one, meaning *Scorpion* might pass in front of his ship. The rebel frigate was sailing faster than he had allowed for. To intercept, *Hussar* needed to wear to starboard to compensate, or fall off and try to rake the rebel's stern. His orders were to ram. He hoped *Hussar* survived long enough for *Puritan* to close the gap.

On board Frigate Scorpion, 10:10 a.m.

Ulster was not the only one who noticed the change in bearing. Jaco leaned over the quarterdeck railing to call out, "Mr. Preston, pull around our topgallants and royals. I don't think they are perfectly stacked. We need a little more speed."

Preston looked up and put the back of his hand to his forehead. Less than a minute later, *Scorpion's* upper yards creaked around.

"Mr. Garrison!"

"Aye, sir!"

"Can you pull out the ball and put in chain shot?"

"How close are we going to be, sir?"

"Damned close, probably inside 200 yards."

"We'll double shot. It is simpler than reloading. We'll aim at the top of the bulwarks. This way the balls will send splinters flying around and the chain shot will cut up the Britisher's rigging."

"I want you to bring a mast down. Two extra tots of rum to the gun crews if they can do it."

"Sir, are we going to tack?"

"Not unless he falls off to cross our stern. If he makes that move, we fall off to port; and if he catches us, we trade broadsides. It will be our 12-pounders against his nines, so I'll take that chance."

On board H.M.S. Hussar, 10:11 a.m.

Roger Ulster had an impending sense of doom that he'd felt only once before, during the Seven Years War. Memories of being the Second Lieutenant on a 36-gun frigate taking on a 60-gun French fourth-rater raced through his mind. In the end, his ship had won, but it had been turned into a splintered wreck.

The move made by the captain of the *Scorpion* reminded him of Lieutenant Smythe's warning—this rebel was no Frenchman! Seeing *Hussar* was about to be raked from the bow, he ordered his quartermaster to turn starboard and try to maintain the constant bearing so he could ram *Scorpion*. He yelled at his second lieutenant to fire when his guns came to bear on the closing frigate.

Scorpion spat fire first, and he heard a screech overhead, followed by a twang as the shrouds for the foremast parted.

Hussar's guns fired as they came to bear. Ulster stared with disbelief when he was sure that not one, but *all* of *Hussar's* 9-pound cannon balls bounced off *Scorpion's* hull.

Scorpion's mix of sold and chain shot sent chunks of wood flying or whistled overhead, followed by the pops of stays, shrouds and halyards parting. He was still staring at the *Scorpion's* intact hull when he heard a loud crack. The upper section of the mainmast slowly toppled to the deck, bringing with it the upper two sections of the foremast.

Scorpion stopped firing and sailed on. All Ulster could do was watch the rebel frigate sail into the distance.

On board H.M.S. Puritan, 2:38 p.m.

It was hours after the engagement, nightfall was approaching, and *Puritan's* lookouts could no longer see *Scorpion*. There were lowering clouds on the horizon that promised a cold rain.

The dark skies matched Davidson's mood. He'd failed. *Scorpion* would vanish into the Atlantic, and chasing the fast rebel frigate was futile.

After a gloomy supper, Davidson pulled on his oilskin and stepped outside. A driving rain was pelting *Puritan*. With his permission, Smythe had sent the watch below to the gun deck so they didn't have to weather the cold soaking the helmsmen; those on the quarterdeck would have to endure.

Smythe's curly blond hair was flat against his skull, and two locks made curlicues on his forehead. He stood next to an equally bedraggled and chilled quartermaster's mate at the wheel.

Davidson looked to the west and saw what he thought was a clearing sky. "Mr. Smythe, why don't you have someone relieve you so you can dry out and get warm?"

Smythe's teeth chattered. "W-why should others s-stand the watch for me? It is m-my t-turn, and b-bad luck that the weather is as foul as it is. Eight bells for this watch will r-ring soon enough, and Mr. Roote will relieve me. Then I will g-go below and t-try to get warm."

"After you put dry clothes on, come to my cabin. We have to discuss our next move."

Smythe's teeth had finally stopped chattering when he knocked on Captain Davidson's door. At the word "Enter," the red-coated Marine on guard opened the latch.

Davidson came around the table and handed Smythe a glass holding three fingers of an amber liquid. "Drink this. It is a 24-year-old scotch from a brewery on Islay I save for important occasions—and emergencies. It will take away some of the chill, as well as the sick feeling that today the Royal Navy met its match. Your friend Jacinto took our measure in spades. We are lucky that the butcher's bill is not worse than it is. *Griffin* and *Hussar* will make it home, but they will need extensive repairs. *Puritan* was lucky by comparison. However, we too need some time dockside for repairs."

"Thank you, sir. My father enjoys a taste of scotch every so often. I've not had one in long time. Captain, we did what we could, but the fox got away and we don't have the hounds to catch him."

"Yes, and he is taking the cargo of gold back to North America as fast as he can sail." Both men took a swig, and Darren took a second. The liquor warmed his insides.

Davidson slid an unfolded piece of paper across the table. "Read this. I think it summarizes your observations about *Scorpion's* cannon."

The letter was addressed to the First Lord of the Admiralty and precisely detailed the capabilities of the rebel guns—they were more accurate, longer ranged, and struck harder. Smythe put the letter down and slid it back to his captain.

"It says what is needed. I fear that if the rebels can equip more ships with these guns and build hulls like *Scorpion's,* they will give our navy a hard time."

"My thoughts exactly." Davidson took a sip of scotch. "Smythe, what do you think we should do? Continue the chase or go home with our tail between our legs? A bloody rebel captain just out-sailed and out-fired three of His Majesty's ships. It is damned embarrassing."

"Sir, we did our best." Smythe remembered one of Heywood's proverbs. "'Every dog has his day.' I don't like it anymore than you do. In answer to your question, we should head home."

"That is the only conclusion I can draw as well. As soon as this wretched rain stops, I will have the watch alter course. And then, once we are headed in the right direction, I will order an extra tot for all the hands." Davidson held up his glass and smiled.

"I tell you, Smythe, we need more captains with tactical and sailing skills like your friend Jacinto in the King's Navy. But if you ever repeat what I just said, I will have you strung up from the highest yardarm in the Royal Navy."

Chapter 19

Battle With the Bird

On board Frigate Scorpion, *January 1778*

Dawn brought sun instead of the grey clouds and cold rain that *Scorpion* had sailed through during the night run west of Ireland. The better weather did nothing to brighten Jaco's mood. He'd let the crew celebrate last night with extra rum and beer, while he updated his log and wrote reports.

With *Scorpion* sailing easily under fair skies and steady wind, it was time to put into action the plan he'd conceived with his officers.

Right after breakfast, Patrick Miller's Marines, armed with loaded muskets and fixed bayonets, began a patrol of the deck. The eleven sailors whom Gaskins, Jeffords and Penway had identified as "Radcliffe's Fellows" were brought to the captain's cabin, where Shelton, Garrison and the captain waited.

Jaco closed the door behind the last man and walked around to face them. "Gentlemen, you are here because your shipmates believe that if Lieutenant Radcliffe tried to take over this ship, you would help him. That is called a mutiny. Lieutenants Shelton and Garrison and I are going to walk out of my cabin and give you five minutes to decide who will tell me what Lieutenant Radcliffe planned and what he offered you." *Scorpion's* captain picked up an hourglass marked in five minute intervals. "If you do not tell me what Mr.

Radcliffe planned, two things will happen. One, I will note in the log that you have forfeited your prize money, which will be more than £300 sterling per man paid in gold and silver coins. Two, you will join Mr. Radcliffe in the hold until we return to Philadelphia, where you will be tried for planning a mutiny. Under the Articles of War, if convicted, you will be flogged or hung."

He paused for a few seconds. "Five minutes, gentlemen. Five minutes should be enough to make the decision of your lives."

Standing by the closed door, counting the minutes, Jaco could hear the men arguing. The sound of the latch caused the speaking to stop abruptly. No one said a word as he walked to the stern of his cabin. He turned and faced them. "Gentlemen, what have you decided?"

Abner Scruggles, gun captain and topman, looked left and right. "Sir, we just listened to what Lieutenant Radcliffe had to say."

"Don't lie to me. Several of your shipmates who will testify at your court martial overheard Mr. Radcliffe and you discussing how to take over the ship and immediately sail it to Boston. Now, Scruggles, would you like to try again?"

Scruggles hung his head. Another man took a half-step forward. "Sir, I am Allen Hendricks, leading topman for the mizzenmast, and also a gun captain. When we clear for action, I man one of the swivel guns in the mizzen maintop. Lieutenant Radcliffe asked me to spray our quarterdeck if we got close to a Royal Navy ship or into a boarding action. He didn't tell me to kill you, but it was clear that he wanted Captain Jacinto and First Lieutenant Shelton to be wounded or killed."

Jaco felt as if he had been stabbed. This really hurt, not physically, but emotionally. A man he trusted to do his job against the enemy was willing to kill him. He struggled to control his anger.

"Did Mr. Radcliffe offer you any incentive?"

"Oh, yes, sir. He said that if there were fewer officers and he was in command, he would double our share of prize money."

"Anything else?"

"Aye. If we joined his crew when he made captain, we would all be warrants or even officers."

"I see. Did he tell you how he could make that happen?"

Hendricks paused, then answered, "He said he has friends on the Marine Committee who would give us commissions."

"Thank you." Jaco looked at the other men in the room. "Is what Hendricks said true?"

"Aye, sir," said a man in the first row. "Hendricks is telling the truth. Radcliffe showed us a piece of paper that has numbers on it and pointed to our share of the prize money if he took command."

The other men added more details. Several admitted that the only thing that had stopped them from following Radcliffe's plans was they suspected that the other sailors were keeping a watchful eye on them.

Jaco looked each man in the eye, then said, "Each of you will dictate a statement to Mr. Shelton so it is in your words. Then you will sign it or make your mark, and I will sign it as well. Mr. Shelton and Mr. Garrison will sign as witnesses. The statements will not be used against you, but will be presented at Mr. Radcliffe's court martial, if there is one, as evidence he was planning a mutiny. When we are done here, you will rejoin the crew as if nothing happened. What you tell your shipmates is your business; however, I suggest that if you say anything, tell the truth, or they may take matters into their own hands. Let me tell you, many of your shipmates are very unhappy that you were willing to jeopardize their lives and their prize money. If you refuse to follow an order, you will be arrested and join Mr. Radcliffe in the hold to face charges. If that occurs, you will lose your share of prize money and may be flogged. Is that clear?"

There were eleven ayes.

Once the statements were completed and signed, it was time to bring Lieutenant Radcliffe up from the hold. He was dirty and grimy and smelled like a bilge rat. Jaco thought the odor befitted him.

After the action with the three Royal Navy frigates, Garrison had searched Radcliffe's compartment and found Radcliffe's journal, several sheets that showed calculations of prize money, and a list of the men who would get double shares. The journal revealed that he had been keeping an account of the times he disagreed with Captain Jacinto's actions, along with a detailed plan on how he would take over the frigate. It was clear Radcliffe had been planning a mutiny.

Jaco debated whether or not to have the manacles around Radcliffe's wrists and ankles removed; given the gravity of the situation, he decided to leave them on to send a message.

With his officers standing next to him, Jaco addressed the man. "Edmund Radcliffe, when we return, I will recommend that you be court-martialed for planning a mutiny. We have your diary, which alone is enough evidence to convict you, and statements from the men you approached. You are lucky I don't hold the trial on board *Scorpion*."

Radcliffe sneered. "Jacinto, you don't have the balls. Your career is over. You will be relieved of command as soon as we dock."

Jaco refused to take the bait. "Because of the seriousness of the charges, you will continue to be confined in the forward hold, allowed on the main deck three times a day to walk for 30 minutes. You will continue to eat alone and be held incommunicado. Any attempt to communicate with a member of the crew without either Lieutenant Shelton's or my permission will be dealt with harshly. Remember, with the evidence I have, I could try, convict and hang you before we get home. Do not give me a reason to do so."

Once Radcliffe was escorted back to the hold, Jaco mustered the crew on the gun deck and explained what had just happened. Looking at their faces, he saw that most had already guessed what had gone on in the captain's cabin.

* * *

For two weeks, the crew endured cold, rain and low clouds. Fortunately, the winds were out of the west, making it easy to sail south. By the time the ship reached 15 degrees west latitude, the temperature was in the 60s and Jaco ordered a course toward North America. *Scorpion* was being pushed by the Trade Winds coming out of Africa.

His standing orders for the watch teams were to avoid any ships. Jaco was tired; dealing with Radcliffe had drained him more than he realized.

Most of the crew seemed cheerful enough. In the afternoons, Jaco encouraged his sailors to gather on the main deck. Those who could play musical instruments gave impromptu concerts. Shanties such as "Ben's Gone Away", "Polly on the Short" and "Fare Thee Well, My Dearest Nancy" were sung. One enterprising gunner composed a song about the cruise called "Perfecto Prize".

Penway reported that Radcliffe's Fellows were a subdued lot. It appeared to Landry and others in the messes that they were trying to rejoin the crew which had, for the most part, shunned them.

Early one afternoon came the call, "Deck, sail ho, one point of the starboard bow. It looks like a schooner."

Wanting something to do, Jaco climbed the masthead to have a look. Halfway up he began feeing queasy and light-headed, and questioned his decision to go on the ratlines in the first place.

Looking through the narrow circle of his spyglass's field of view, he recognized *Cutlass*. Her captain was pushing the schooner as fast as it could go. Jaco came down the windward shroud, yelling for Midshipman Patterson to make the recognition signal and then hoist the Continental Navy flag and the Gadsden flag.

Next, he ordered *Scorpion* to come about. If *Cutlass* ran he would let it go, figuring that *Cutlass* had fallen into British hands. If it stopped, there might be some news.

"Sir, the schooner is asking what ship we are."

"Tell them, and give them my name as the captain. And ask them to heave to so we can talk."

In a neat bit of maneuvering, *Cutlass* tacked around and hove to less than 100 feet downwind from *Scorpion*. Jaco called over the short distance, "Who is in command of the *Cutlass*?"

"Sir, Lieutenant Ralph Reed. I took over *Cutlass* after you went to *Scorpion.*"

"Congratulations! What news do you have?"

"I am carrying reports of victories in Pennsylvania and New Jersey. The British are retreating out of New Jersey, and the French are with us. Where are you headed?"

"Not sure. Is Philadelphia still occupied by the British?"

"Yes, but not for long. The British are retreating to New York. Good luck, sir."

"Good luck to you. The British are all over the French ports. Keep a sharp eye out."

Cutlass fell off and headed east, and *Scorpion* resumed its westbound course.

Raider of the Scottish Coast

Philadelphia, March 1778

Jaco let *Scorpion* charge up the Delaware Bay like a horse headed for the barn and a bucket of oats. Passing Wilmington, he had the top sails furled and, with the wind from the west, came up the channel without having to tack. *Scorpion* passed the spot where the ship would dock and tacked to port. With the sails slackened, under Jeffords's expert guidance at the helm, *Scorpion* nosed into the pier with a gentle bump.

The frigate had been spotted coming up the river and the Marine Committee alerted, so five of its members were waiting on the pier. Jaco invited them to his cabin, where Jack Shelton was waiting. The two chests full of guilders sat on the table next to a crate from the hold, covered by a cloth.

Jaco served each man a glass of madeira taken from the *Madras,* and they toasted their cause. The Congressmen were polite, but their expressions told him they were anxious to ask questions, and curious as to what was in chest and the crate.

John Adams, Chairman of the Marine Committee, looked around the cabin. "Where is Mr. Radcliffe?" Rather than dance around the issue, Jaco met and held Adams' eye. From the journal, he knew Radcliffe had sent along letters from Brest and Amsterdam that were not complimentary. "He is being held in irons on the orlop deck, charged with planning a mutiny. I have sworn statements from the crew members he tried to recruit, witnessed by my officers, as well as a log, also witnessed by my officers, detailing the discipline problems I had with Mr. Radcliffe. There is also his journal, in which he wrote out his plans to take over *Scorpion*. I had more than enough evidence to hold a court martial while we were at sea, convict and hang him." Jaco looked at both Stephen Hopkins and John Adams, who had shocked looks on their faces.

"However, I decided to turn the evidence and Mr. Radcliffe over to the Marine Committee, and you, gentlemen, may decide what to do. None of my officers or mates, nor most of the crew, wish to serve on a ship with him ever again."

Stephen Hopkins cleared his throat, then spoke in a gravelly voice. "You know there are always two sides to a story like this."

Jaco held his gaze. "I have sworn statements from eleven sailors describing the inducements Mr. Radcliffe offered them to turn against their captain *during a battle.* His plan was that they should use the mizzentop swivel gun to kill Mr. Shelton, Quartermaster Jeffords and myself. I think it is pretty clear that Edmund Radcliffe wanted to take command of *Scorpion* and was willing to commit murder to do so."

Adams looked apoplectic and Hopkins clenched his fists. Jaco addressed the other members of the committee, gesturing to the chest. "I am willing to continue discussing Mr. Radcliffe's disgusting behavior, but I have something to show you that is far more important. Would you gentlemen like to know what is in the chests and in the box? If you will allow me—"

Hopkins interrupted. "Is that pirate booty?"

Jaco stared at him coldly. "No, sir, this is prize money paid to the Continental Congress for a cargo of spices and a British East India Company cargo ship called the *Madras.* It was captured by *Scorpion,* and, sir, I do not appreciate your inference that we are pirates."

"That's what the British call you."

"I don't give a damn what His Majesty or the captains of his ships call us. We are not pirates. We are a frigate in a very young navy that is short of ships, cannons, ammunition and men. We are authorized to take prizes, and that is what we did."

The older man looked at Jaco, then down at the unopened chest. "I am sorry I offended you. It was a feeble attempt at humor from someone who has been running from the bloody British Army all winter."

"And I apologize for my strong reaction, but it has been a long voyage. Since delivering the courier's packet, we took the *Madras,* damaged five Royal Navy ships, and raided two ports in Scotland."

Jaco flipped off the iron hasp and opened the lid to the chest. "Gentlemen, this is the payment for the sale of the *Madras* and part of its cargo. In it, there is the equivalent of £15,000 pounds Sterling in gold and silver Dutch guilders. Seven-eighths of this goes to the crew of *Scorpion.* My report has a sheet with the payout. Every man jack on this ship has earned a princely sum."

He let the men look at the coins that glistened in the sunlight shining through the stern windows. Then Jaco tapped the top of the cloth-covered box. "We brought the rest of *Madras's* cargo back with us. I apologize for only taking one prize, but I think you will agree this one was worth it."

With that, Jaco put on a pair of linen gloves, while Jack Shelton pulled the cloth off the crate, revealing the Bank of England logo branded onto the lid. Carefully, Jaco lifted the lid and picked up a gold bar.

"In *Scorpion's* hold are 1,600 of these bars. Eight tons in all. I hope you have a safe place to store 160 of these crates. This should go a long way to funding our cause. In addition to the prize money from the sale of *Madras,* my crew is entitled to divide 10 percent of the value of the gold, which is worth about one million, one hundred thousand pounds Sterling."

His father was quick to answer. "We do have a safe place. The First Bank of the United States has a vault where we can store it. And, you are right, there is enough money to pay our Army and Navy."

An hour later, 16 wagons and 50 soldiers arrived at the pier. The crates were quickly unloaded and the wagons trundled off.

Once the cargo was gone, Javier Jacinto came back on board, accompanied by John Hewes. The chest of guilders was still sitting on the table.

Javier looked at his son, who looked as if he were 40, not almost 19. Jaco had dark bags under his eyes and his face was lined. Seeing this made what he had to say more painful.

"Son, we need your report and recommendations for promotions, and we have another mission for you."

Jaco went the back of the cabin, opened a box and handed Hewes the oilskin pouch containing his report. The he said, "Father, the crew of the *Scorpion,* and that includes me, needs shore leave. The ship needs two new long twelves and some repairs. And I have a request to make."

Javier Jacinto looked somber. "And that is?"

Jaco looked first to Hewes, and then his father, and spoke as a son speaking to a parent, not as an officer speaking to his superior. "Father, I would like to go back to Charleston. There is some unfinished business I have to attend to."

"With Reyna?"

Jaco's reaction must have given him away. He simply nodded.

"She is a beautiful and wonderful woman. You intend to propose?"

"I do."

"Do you think she will accept?"

"I do."

"And I am sure she will wait for you."

"Father, how do you know that?"

"Her father and I are good friends, and she confides in him. Let us work on getting you and your crew some time off while we refit and re-provision *Scorpion*. Obviously, we now have the money."

There was an uncomfortable silence that none of the men in the cabin wanted to break. Finally, Jaco asked, "Father, Mr. Hewes, what is it you want me to do?

Mr. Hewes leaned forward. "You father says you speak French fluently. As far as I know, you are the only captain besides Jones who does. We are expecting a French fleet to arrive sometime in July. General Washington and the Marine Committee want to propose to the French fleet commander that you to be our liaison officer to his staff."

"What about *Scorpion?*"

"We have not decided who should be its new captain. Do you have a recommendation?"

"If not me, then Jack Shelton. Sir, how would it be if *Scorpion* were assigned to the French fleet? It could be used as a scout for them; we know the waters along our coast. As its captain, I could also be on the French Admiral's staff."

"The current thought is that you would be on the French flagship. There are members of the Marine Committee who want to see what other captains can do with *Scorpion.*"

"As in officers like Mr. Radcliffe?"

Hewes didn't say a word.

That bastard Edmund Radcliffe has been campaigning with his family friends who are in the Continental Congress, as well as with Adams and Hopkins to get command of Scorpion. *Wait until they read what is in my report.*

"Sir, Lieutenant Jack Shelton deserves a command and would be the one most respected by the crew. He also has experience bringing prizes home. And I should warn you: most of the crew will walk away rather than serve under Mr. Radcliffe. However, if Mr. Shelton and the rest of my officers are retained, we could convince most of the crew to re-enlist. Be sure to mention that to any Committee members who advocate for Radcliffe."

Portsmouth, April 1778

Repairing and re-provisioning started immediately upon *Puritan's* return to Portsmouth. The Admiralty also ordered a formal enquiry into the seizure of the *Madras* and Davidson's battle with *Scorpion*. Davidson realized that, despite rank and patronage, his career was on the line. After Davidson, Darren Smythe was asked to appear and he spent an hour answering questions from Admiral Arthur and four captains.

When he started to describe *Scorpion's* superior cannon, Captain Brighton curtly cut him off. "That is not a subject for this board, nor should it concern lieutenants."

The rebuff led to an ugly silence that was broken when Admiral Arthur asked a question about Jacinto. When it was over, Smythe was relieved to be dismissed, and returned directly to *Puritan*. When he told Davidson about Brighton's reaction, his captain said, "Brighton refused to accept the facts about *Scorpion's* guns and he was not pleased when I suggested that if he ever went to sea and had to face them himself, he might form a different opinion. Do not worry about the board. I told them that you performed in an exemplary manner."

"Thank you, sir."

* * *

The board of inquiry concluded privately that the less said about *Scorpion* publicly, the better. Captain Davidson was ordered to Portsmouth to take command of a new, first rate 90-gun ship of the line. His replacement, Captain Everett Martingdale, was to take command of *Puritan*.

From Darren's perspective, the two men were as different as they could be. While Davidson was patrician and aristocratic, he also genuinely cared for his sailors. Martingdale was short, with dark hair and a large nose, and a brooding, caustic personality. When Admiral Clayton introduced Smythe as *Puritan's* First Lieutenant, Martingdale ignored him. Squaring to face to the admiral, he said, "Sir, as *Puritan's* captain it is my right to choose my own officers."

Darren tried not to react. He wanted to leave the room.

Admiral Clayton responded immediately. "Captain Martingdale, the Royal Navy is stretched very thin and there are no spare officers, particularly of Mr. Smythe's quality."

Martingdale grunted. "Admiral, if you will excuse me, I have my baggage to look after. Davidson, shall we do the change over tomorrow morning, say at nine?"

"I am Your Grace, the Duke of Somerset to you, Martingdale. Nine will be fine. I shall have a boat alongside the flagship at half past eight."

Martingdale bowed slightly. "Very well, *Your Grace*."

Neither Admiral Clayton nor Captain Davidson said anything until they were sure Martingdale was out of earshot.

"Captain Davidson, please accept my apologies for Captain Martingdale's rude behavior. Rumor has it the Mediterranean Fleet commander doesn't want Martingdale, so they sent him to Portsmouth. He has friends in Parliament who put pressure on the Admiralty. Your posting to a ship-of-the-line created an opening."

Davidson turned to his young lieutenant. "Smythe, I am sorry that you will have to be this man's number one. Do your duty and I will protect you, as will Admiral Clayton. In the meantime, try to minimize the damage he causes."

The admiral was more specific. "Martingdale likes to have men flogged. He claims it is good for morale.

"Admiral, Captain, I will try not to let you down."

"Young man, your duty is to your crew. Do not let *them* down."

* * *

Once established on *Puritan*, Martingdale made it clear that he would dine alone. His servant and cook was a man named Justin Hale, who was assigned to sleep with the midshipmen.

They were three days out of Portsmouth, headed to Port Royal, when Martingdale spotted two men having a good laugh. "You there, by the mainmast, what is so bloody funny about coiling a line?"

The man who was laughing turned to face his captain and fell suddenly silent.

"Have you lost your voice?"

The man spoke softly. "No."

Other men on the main deck moved away from the sailor.

"Speak up, man. What did you say."

"I said no."

"No what?"

"No, sir."

"You were laughing at your captain, weren't you? You made a joke about me!"

The man hesitated, not knowing what to say. The pause gave Martingdale the opening he needed. "So you do not deny it? That is an offense under Article 21 of the Articles of War. Master at Arms, hold that man for punishment. What's your name?

"O'Bannion, sir." He spat out the last word angrily.

An hour later, Martingdale noted in his log that Seaman Sean O'Bannion was guilty of mocking a superior officer and was assigned a punishment of four lashes to be executed immediately.

The drums rolled and all hands were mustered to witness punishment. Martingdale announced the offense and the punishment. The he leaned over the railing. "O Bannion, do you have anything to say?"

O'Bannion bellowed. "The joke, sir, is on you for giving me four lashes for being a happy sailor."

Martingdale flushed. "Give him two more for impertinence and insubordination. Go on, Bosun, do your duty, and don't go easy on him, or you too will feel the lash."

Smythe stood one step behind and one step to the right, horrified by what his captain had just done. Martingdale hadn't consulted him or any of the other officers. *Now I know why this man was a pariah in the Mediterranean Squadron. How long will I have to endure serving with him?*

After the lashes were administered, another bosun tossed sea water on the man's lacerated back before he was taken to the surgeon's cockpit to recover. Martingdale dismissed the crew. As he passed Smythe on the way to his cabin, he said loudly, "That will send a message to the crew not to trifle with me. They *will* do what I say, when I say it. And they will show proper respect at all times."

Smythe didn't respond. He could sense the mood on the ship changing as the crew brooded about what the monster who now led them might do next.

* * *

Puritan took on provisions in Port Royal, then headed to its patrol station off the French Naval base at Martinique. After the flogging, Darren only spoke to Martingdale when spoken to, or when he needed to have a question answered about what Martingdale wanted done. In the wardroom, all the officers knew how unhappy the sailors were with their captain. Smiles on the berthing deck disappeared as morale plummeted, and sailors did only what was specifically ordered, nothing more.

One day, out of old habit, Darren made a suggestion on trimming the sails to get more speed out of *Puritan*. He'd forgotten the first rule of dealing with the captain he'd privately dubbed "Mad Martinet Martingdale." He dared not write or speak the sobriquet, but it made dealing with a man who was the perfect example of how not to be the captain of a Royal Navy frigate somewhat bearable.

Martingdale shouted back, "Damn your eyes! Mr. Smythe, I expect my officers to speak to me only when told to speak. If I do not address you, you are to hold your tongue!"

Martingdale was not on the quarterdeck when Smythe turned the watch over to Master Shilling, who whispered to Darren, "Please defend me at my court martial if I kill that bastard."

The smiling faces that Darren used to see as made his rounds around *Puritan* had turned openly sullen. The experienced seamen had seen the likes of Martingdale before. They knew it was only a matter of time before someone was again hauled up on a real or specious charge and flogged. The other officers did their best to avoid Martingdale. Captain Brown kept the Marines off to themselves as much as possible.

Now Smythe saw his job as protecting his fellow officers and sailors from Mad Martinet Martingdale. He wondered if doing so would cost him his own career, or even his life.

Basse Terre was empty, and Martingdale was impatient to find French warships or prizes. He didn't want to tack back and forth between Guadeloupe and Martinique, so *Puritan* patrolled the French held islands in the Lesser Antilles, looking for the French Caribbean fleet.

With the weather in the 80s and a bright blue sky dotted with puffy clouds it was a pleasant day for a sail, but nobody was enjoying it.

* * *

Thirty-five miles from Martinique's northern tip, *Puritan's* lookouts spotted a French frigate a scant mile ahead. Through the narrow field of view of the brass spyglass that had belonged to Captain Horrocks, Smythe watched French sailors shorten sail. The frigate's name—*Oiseau*—translated to bird. Already, it was towing its boats so they wouldn't be splintered by cannon balls. Smythe wondered what other preparations the French captain had ordered.

Martingdale strode about the quarterdeck, resplendent in his blue uniform coat and gold epaulets, his fine appearance marred only by the sweat dripping down his forehead and cheeks. Every man on deck was sweating profusely in the heat, even the sailors in cotton shirts and breeches.

Martingale had ordered his officers to wear uniforms on duty, even though it was common for officers of the Royal Navy to dress as befitted the climate in these waters. Smythe, knowing the captain rarely left his cabin, usually wore what the sailors did; it made inspections easier and was was much more comfortable than the heavy wool of the Navy uniforms designed for the cold climate of the North Atlantic. In a private conversation with Martingale, Smythe had cautiously suggested that allowing the officers of the watch to wear informal dress would preserve their uniforms for official occasions. In a sarcastic voice, Martingale had replied that, while his first lieutenant might choose to dress like a common sailor when he climbed ratlines or checked the bilge for leaks, he expected his officers to wear the uniform of their rank when they were on display.

By now Smythe knew Martingdale's adherence to the Royal Navy's fighting instructions. Martingdale would shorten sail, so that when they came alongside the *Oiseau* there would be little ship handling to do while the ships traded broadsides. Smythe was afraid the French 24-pounder carronades would rip *Puritan* apart. The more Smythe thought about it, the more he didn't like the idea of trading broadsides. Why not take advantage of *Puritan's* speed and maneuverability?

"Captain, a word about the coming action, sir."

"Yes, Mr. Smythe, what is it?" Martingdale's angry tone conveyed *'What do you know about fighting the French?'*

"Sir, I would respectfully like to offer an alternative to trading broadsides that would take advantage of *Puritan's* sailing qualities and her crew's capabilities."

Martingdale looked at his first lieutenant. When he'd first met Smythe, he'd wanted to write a letter to the Admiralty demanding a more seasoned second in command; but as he'd observed the young officer, who had not yet turned 20, he'd realized the man was competent beyond his years. It was the only reason he would listen to a suggestion from Smythe. Martingdale's tone was, as usual, caustic, terse, and annoyed. "And what do you propose?"

"We continue with our sails set as they are. I suspect *Oiseau's* captain is letting us catch up because he either has a nasty surprise for us, or his bottom is so fouled he cannot get away. Trading broadsides lets his 24-pounder carronades do their dirty work. Therefore, before we come alongside to trade broadsides, we cross astern of *Oiseau* to rake her with both solid and chain shot. At close range, our carronades will tear up the French ship. Then, as we pass, we can either tack back across her stern and do it again, or come down *Oiseau's* port side for a broadside."

"Why would we go to all that trouble?"

"Because, sir, the solid shot will disable some of her guns and the chain shot will, at the very least, make *Oiseau* harder to handle, or even bring down a mast. Since we are faster and more maneuverable, we can tack back and forth until we cripple her and then have a clear advantage when we come alongside to take her."

When he answered, Martingdale's voice was sarcastic and loud. "It seems to be an awful lot of mucking about to get into a fight."

"Sir, the end result will be less damage to *Puritan,* a more valuable prize for you, and fewer of our sailors will be injured."

The captain's tone was curt. "If it doesn't work, then what?"

"We trade broadsides in the traditional manner."

"Mr. Smythe, are you telling me that the Royal Navy's *proven tactics* are wrong, and that you won't dare to go toe to toe with a French frigate? Are you a coward?" The last words were spoken in a sneer.

"No, sir, not at all. It is just that I have learned there are tactical alternatives that are less costly to a ship and its crew."

"Noted. Carry on. "

Smythe realized that Martingdale had given him the courtesy of hearing his suggestion, but had already decided what he was going to do. It was a decision that would no doubt get many of *Puritan's* sailors wounded or killed—one of whom might be *Puritan's* first lieutenant.

As Smythe passed the binnacle, Quartermaster Shilling kept his head straight ahead. He must have heard every word of the exchange.

"Smythe!" Martingdale called after him. "We are about to engage the enemy. You will attire yourself as befits an officer of His Majesty's Navy!"

Smythe acknowledged with a loud, obsequious "Aye, sir!" and headed below to change into his heavy woolen uniform.

Then he joined Lieutenant Roote for an inspection of the gun deck.

The empty left sleeve of Roote's uniform was neatly pinned to the front of his coat. Beads of sweat covered his face.

"Well, Darren, I guess we're going to have another go at the Frenchies. Don't worry, we'll give a good account of ourselves down here."

"I know you will." Smythe strode forward, trying to show that he was not afraid. The sand spread on the decks to keep them from getting slippery with blood crunched underfoot.

"Mr. Hearns, are you ready?"

"We are, sir. As soon as the captain gives the word, we'll give the bloody Frenchies hell."

Smythe nodded and gripped the railing of the forward companionway, not for balance, but to keep his hands from shaking. He, like Captain Martingdale, would be exposed to musket fire from the French Marines, canister from swivel guns and small cannon, and shot from *Oiseau's* 24-pound carronades, as well as its 12-pounders.

Emerging into the bright sunlight on the main deck, Smythe approached the crew of the forward-most swivel gun. They were focused on the *Oiseau,* now only 300 yards ahead. The gun captain put the back of his hand to his forehead. "Mr. Smythe, we'll sweep the quarterdeck first and then the rigging to get rid of their Marines."

"Aye, that should do the trick. Take your time and aim. Accuracy, even with canister, is more important than speed."

Smythe started aft, looking at the tops of each mast. While they were clearing for action, he told the Marines manning the swivel guns to focus on the French carronade crews. Midshipman Rathburn waved from the main top, where Marines operated the two swivel guns. Martingdale had ordered the majority of the Marines to fire from behind the bulwarks at the French ship's Marines in their rigging and then, if needed, join a boarding party.

Just before he climbed up the ladder to the quarterdeck, Smythe took a deep breath. Then he walked over to Martingdale. "Sir, the men are ready."

The captain nodded curtly. "*Puritan* will carry the day. I want to take *Oiseau* back to Port Royal as a prize."

"Aye, sir, that would be a wonderful outcome." *I hope I live to see it.*

With both ships running with the wind over their starboard quarters, even the rigging was quiet as *Puritan* closed the last few hundred feet. "Mr. Smythe, pass the word to Mr. Roote to open fire as soon his guns bear."

"Aye aye, sir."

Smythe was starting down the quarterdeck ladder when Roote stuck his head out of the aft companionway. "Mr. Roote, you may fire as your guns bear."

Roote waved, ducked down, and the forward swivel gun barked. Smythe saw wood fly from the railings around *Oiseau's* quarterdeck, and then there were fewer men standing than before. Seconds later, the first 12-pounder on the port side belched smoke and flame. Even though he knew it was coming, Smythe flinched in surprise.

Oiseau's cannon began their return fire. Its stern 24-pound carronade fired, and fragments of wood flew into the air as the ball tore into *Puritan's* beak where the bowsprit was mounted to the hull. Smythe saw the three men on the forward swivel gun reloading. Some were dripping blood.

For a moment, the exchange of gunfire and cannon balls were concentrated at the forward end of *Puritan* and the aft end of *Oiseau*. As *Puritan* advanced, more cannon were brought to bear by both ships. Flashes of flame were followed by billowing smoke as guns from both ships fired, less than

200 yards apart. The white smoke was rent by tongues of red-orange flame.

Smythe felt French 12-pound balls hammer *Puritan's* side. The sound of wood being sheared mixed with the screams of wounded men coming from both ships. The men manning *Puritan's* forward swivel gun disappeared in a mist of blood, body parts, and wood as a cannon ball pulverized them.

As the ships drew even, the firing got closer to the men on the quarterdecks. *Oiseau's* forward deck-mounted carronade bellowed again. A section of the starboard bulwark just aft of the mainmast disappeared in a deadly spray of splinters. The 24-pound ball punched out a section on the port bulwark before sending up a plume of water 100 feet from *Puritan's* starboard side.

Smythe saw the French sailors on *Oiseau's* foretop point their swivel gun at *Puritan's* deck. His feet felt as if they were nailed to the planking. He saw the flash and then smoke as the gun fired. He heard a sucking hollow sound and felt needles sticking into his side and legs.

Turning, he saw Captain Martingdale stagger back and fall to the deck, with three dark spots in his chest. The quartermaster's mate next to the wheel was down with a ball in his belly, and the bosun was staring at his left leg that was a pulped mass of blood. Shilling's blue coat was splattered with blood as he took the wheel.

Smythe ran to his captain. As he knelt down, several musket balls zinged overhead. Martingdale stared up at him, blinked, and gasped. Blood rose and bubbled from his mouth. "Smythe, I'm done for.... Don't lose my ship!"

"That I won't, sir."

Smythe stood up and yelled to several sailors on the main deck. "Take the captain to the surgeon!"

The French aft 24-pounder roared again, and the aft railing on the quarterdeck disappeared in flurry of splinters. Smoke from the canon hung in a choking haze and made it hard to see, but Smythe spotted the distinctive, hulking form of Lieutenant Bullocks. He was supposed to be in the magazine. *What was he doing up here?* Smythe screamed at the third lieutenant, "Mr. Bullocks, tell Mr. Roote to switch to chain shot, and send 20 men from the starboard battery to the main deck to help you with the sails."

I'm now in command and we will change tactics. I hope it is not too late.

Bullocks waved and descended the companionway to the gun deck. Smythe went over to Shilling, who was still at the wheel. Musket balls coming from the French rigging hissed by before they smacked into the deck or railing. Both ships rocked from the impact and recoil of cannon fire, making it difficult for snipers to aim.

"I'm going to have the men pull in all the sails and see if we can get ahead of the *Oiseau*. Once we are clear, we are going cross the Frenchman's bow and rake her. If we can't, the Frenchman will ram us amidships and we can board her. One way or the other we are going end this madness of trading broadsides."

We'll need some speed to get in front. The French frigate doesn't have enough speed to tack; if he tries, they may wind up coming to a stop. If Oiseau *tries to cross my stern, we tack to port and sail away, then use our superior speed to re-engage.*

Bullocks came up from the gun deck. Smythe cupped his hands and yelled, "Pull in the sheets for all the sails and sheet them home. Do it smartly!"

Bullocks nodded and started directing the sailors. He looked like a man possessed as he ran back and forth encouraging the men. Musket balls took divots out of the deck wherever he went. Occasionally a man would fall, but *Puritan* began pull forward of the French frigate.

The cannon fire ended as *Puritan's* stern passed the bow of the *Oiseau*. In the quiet, Smythe went to the forward end of the quarterdeck and called down for Roote.

Midshipman Rathburn's powder-covered face came up above the deck. "Mr. Roote fell, sir. We've got the ship's boys filling the gaps."

"We are going to cross the bow of the *Oiseau*. Double load chain shot. Aim at the rigging, and fire as the guns bear."

Oiseau's rigging was hardly touched, and men were loosening the partially reefed sails so it could speed up and maneuver.

You French bastard, you realize what I am trying to do. Smythe gripped the hilt of his sword tightly with his left hand. "Mr. Shilling, on my command, I want you to come about to port so we cross *Oiseau's* bow. I don't give a damn what the course is." Turning to the main deck, Smythe ordered, "Mr. Bullocks, if you will, get men to man the braces. Once we cross, I want to keep moving so the Frenchman cannot ram us."

Bullocks yelled, "Aye, aye!" Two dozen more men came up from the gun deck, joining those already standing by the sheets and braces for each mast. The burly Bullocks seemed fearless as he walked up and down the deck, setting them to work to make sure that all the sheets and braces were still connected. For the ones that were severed, he sent men into the rigging with sections of rope to make repairs.

Looking at *Oiseau*, Smythe realized it was all a matter of timing. He waited a few more seconds to let *Puritan* gain more speed before he yelled, "Now, Mr. Shilling, now! Helm a-lee to port. Mr. Bullocks, haul on the braces. Jib and foremast first, and then get the rest around. Do it smartly, we don't need perfection, just keep the wind on the sails."

Slowly, *Puritan* responded to the helm. "Haul, Mr. Bullocks, get them to haul!" The yards for the foremast creaked around.

"Now get the main and mizzen masts done."

With the yards almost perpendicular to the direction *Puritan* was sailing, the frigate started to slowly accelerate. The first gun went off, followed by the rest in rapid succession. Smythe didn't count, but he estimated they got more than a dozen shots off.

The wind that had been steady and gentle at the beginning of the fight was now very light and *Puritan* was not gaining speed. *Oiseau* would be able to ram them.

Damn you, Martingdale. If you had listened to me, you and Roote wouldn't be dead, and Puritan *wouldn't have taken the pounding she endured.*

Smythe was holding onto the port rail when he heard a loud crack. He looked up, fearing one of *Puritan's* masts had failed under the strain. They were all intact; he turned to the *Oiseau*. The top of its mainmast had toppled over, followed by the top of its foremast. As they came down, men thudded onto the deck. Others fell screaming into the water.

Puritan's guns that could still aim at *Oiseau* fired, but the French frigate's momentum would still let it ram, or worse, cross *Puritan's* stern.

On the main deck, Bullocks was waiting by the main mast with groups of sailors with their hands already on the lines for the braces and sheets.

Smythe looked at the sails. There was very little wind, but he had to get the ship away from *Oiseau* before both frigates were in irons. "Mr. Bullocks, loosen the sheets and braces for all masts. Mr. Shilling, turn port now!!!"

The French captain had anticipated *Puritan's move*. His men were cutting away the rigging and masts and heaving them over the side, and as soon as Shilling committed

Puritan to the turn he ordered his helmsman to turn his ship to port to ram the Royal Navy frigate.

"Mr. Bullocks, pass the word to Mr. Rathburn to keep the port battery firing as long as his guns bear. Dog all the other gun ports. The rest of the gun crews need to come to the main deck to repel boarders."

Looking up, Smythe spotted Midshipman Hearns in the main top. "Hearns! Do your best. I don't want a Frenchman alive forward of its main mast."

Private Blanchard, the young Marine who was assigned as a guard to *Puritan's* captain, handed Smythe two pistols. "Sir, you'll need these. They're primed and loaded."

"Master Shilling, ease off the helm so *Oiseau* hits us at an angle."

"Aye, aye."

Smythe noticed that Shilling's coat had much more blood on it than before. "Mr. Shilling, are you wounded?"

"Aye, but I will stay at the wheel until we take *Oiseau*." Briefly, his eyes met Darren's. "My captain knows what he is about."

Overhead, the swivel guns barked. Smythe saw the French ship's bowsprit break off as it hit *Puritan's* bulwark. *Oiseau's* bow slid down the side, pushing 12-pounders back into *Puritan* and tearing off gun ports. Out of a hatch on the *Oiseau's* fo'c'sle, two grapnels arced out, trailing a quarter-inch-thick line. From the bow chaser gun ports, French sailors hauled in the lines to pull the two ships together.

For a few seconds, there were no cannon, muskets or swivel guns fired from either ship. There were no targets on the deck of the *Oiseau* for *Puritan's* Marines, who crouched along the bulwark waiting for a Frenchman to appear.

Bullocks stood up on the bulwark, waving his cutlass and yelling over his shoulder. "Men of the *Puritan*, let's take this bloody Frenchman!"

The burly lieutenant jumped down onto the deck of the French ship, followed by a surge of Royal Navy sailors and Marines. In the maintop, Hearns yelled through a speaking trumpet, "Englishmen, get down!"

Some men hesitated, others flattened themselves as a row of French Marines emerged from underneath the sheltered entrance to the captain's cabin. The swivel guns on the *Puritan's* main mast barked. As French Marines went down, they were replaced by others. Royal Marines behind the bulwarks on the *Puritan* aimed their muskets. Captain Brown waved his sword. "Marines, fire!"

The muskets went off almost simultaneously. "Now, show them cold British steel. Charge!" Brown climbed over the bulwarks of the two ships and ran down *Oiseau's* main deck, followed by two-dozen Marines and many British sailors.

Smythe looked around. Something was odd. He spotted two French sailors climbing over the side, coming from a gunport. He ran to the edge of the quarterdeck and fired his pistol at the first man, who screamed as he fell backwards into the water. Dashing to the main deck, he waited until the second man got a hand on the top of the bulwark and brought his cutlass down on the man's arm just above the wrist. The severed hand fell onto *Puritan's* main deck and the man screamed as he frantically hung on with his remaining hand. Smythe hammered him on the head with the barrel of the empty pistol, and the Frenchman fell backward into the water.

More French sailors came over the side, and Smythe shoved his second pistol in the belly of one and pulled the trigger. The blast and the ball sent the man backward with his mid section ripped apart. He slashed at others with his cutlass. He was joined by men from the gun deck. A contingent of sailors under the command of Midshipman

Rathburn dealt with French sailors trying to come through the gun ports.

Musket and pistol fire was replaced by the clanging sound of cutlasses and swords. Suddenly, Smythe heard someone yell, *"Arrêter, arrêter!!! Nous nous rendon. Nous sommes finis!!!"* Stop, stop!!! We surrender. We are finished.

The French sailors raised their hands, and suddenly the only sounds were the groans of the wounded. Smythe climbed onto the bulwark of the *Puritan,* feeling horribly exposed. *"Où est votre captaine?"* Where is your captain?

"Il est mort. Je suis Lieutenant Jean Rouen et je suis responsable." He is dead. I am Lieutenant Jean Rouen and I am in charge.

Smythe asked if Rouen spoke English and was relieved when he said, "But of course." Smythe then ordered all the able-bodied French sailors and Marines to put their arms in a pile by the mizzenmast and gather on the bow of their ship. The he called for Lieutenant Bullocks.

Captain Brown came up to Smythe. "Sir, I'm sorry to report that Mr. Bullocks didn't make it." Over Brown's shoulder, Darren could see Bullocks slumped over, a pike stuck in his belly.

"Captain Brown, search the prisoners and gather the French wounded on the gun deck. I want their butcher's bill. If they have a surgeon, bring him forward."

A grim Midshipman Rathburn came over to Smythe. "Sir, I'll take a look at the *Oiseau* and see if we can sail her."

Smythe nodded and, seeing Mr. Hearns said, "Have the carpenter check *Puritan,* and find out how many of our men are dead or wounded."

Rathburn looked at Smythe and saw splinters protruding from the bloody coat and breeches. "Sir, you are wounded. I'll have the surgeon see to you."

"No, have him tend to the seriously wounded. He can pull the splinters our later, or I will do it."

Ehausted and numb, Smythe walked to the quarterdeck. Martingdale was still lying where he'd fallen, the front of his uniform coat darkened with blood. Smythe knelt down and picked up his limp right hand. It was still warm, probably from the sun.

"Captain, I didn't lose your ship."

CHAPTER 20

ELUSIVE PRIZES

On board H.M.S. Puritan, *April 1778*

The stench from dead bodies pervaded the frigate. From the orlop deck, the sickening smell of infected wounds wafted up to the berthing and gun decks. Even on the main deck, it was hard to ignore.

While some of the Smythe's crew worked on getting *Oiseau* ready to sail, others helped prepare the dead for burial. *Puritan* had lost its captain, two lieutenants, and 37 sailors. Another 31 were wounded, some of whom would not live much longer. Of *Oiseau's* crew, 71 were killed and 55 were wounded. Jean Rouen and two midshipmen were *Oiseau's* only surviving officers.

Smythe inspected where six 24-pound balls had smashed through *Puritan's* gun deck bulwarks. For more than a foot around each hole, the wood was shattered. He pulled down two large splinters that were stuck like spears in the overhead.

After talking to Hearns, he learned the men in *Puritan's* maintop had decimated the crews manning the Frenchman's 24-pound carronades with a rain of canister from their swivel guns. Their deadly work had saved *Puritan* from more of the deadly shot fired from the French carronades.

Work stopped on both ships for the funerals. Wind began to gust, and dark clouds on the western horizon were headed their way. *Puritan* and *Oiseau* were in for a rough night.

Before the rain arrived, Smythe signaled *Oiseau* to shorten sail on its mizzenmast—the only mast that survived the fight intact—and *Puritan* did the same. Smythe kept the more maneuverable *Puritan* leeward and a quarter mile away. In the morning, he was relieved to see both ships had survived the squall and were still sailing close.

Smythe was determined to bring *Oiseau* to a British base. The closest one was Barbados—170 miles to the east so' east. He was studying the chart when there was a knock on the door.

Midshipman Hearns, now *Puritan's* acting first lieutenant, entered. "Sir, Master Shilling is resting comfortably in his compartment. The surgeon thinks he will survive.

This was good news. Shilling had lost a lot of blood from several wounds that, individually, would not have been serious, but added together were.

Midshipman Rathburn was on the *Oiseau* as its captain, with 40 of *Puritan's* crew and half of its Marines to keep watch on the French sailors crowded into the orlop deck. Given a chance, the Frenchmen would try to take back their ship. Smythe's order to Rathburn was that they must not be allowed to do so.

"Sir," Midshipman Hearns said, "*Oiseau* is signaling. It is taking on water."

Smythe followed the midshipman to the quarterdeck. "Mr. Hearns, signal *Oiseau* to slacken sail and that I will come aboard. Get a cutter ready."

Oiseau was down at the bow. Had the damage been caused by *Puritan's* 12-pounders, or by *Oiseau's* bow ramming the *Puritan?* He didn't think the ships had hit that hard. *Could it be sabotage?*

With what he'd learned from Commanders Handley and Langston about a ship's construction running through his head, Smythe climbed *Oiseau's* ladder to where Midshipman Rathburn waited.

"A word in private, Mr. Rathburn."

"Aye, sir. The captain's cabin is private."

Inside, Smythe waited until Rathburn closed the door. "Any chance the prisoners caused the problem?"

"No, sir, we locked them on the berthing deck, with the hatches open so they get some fresh air. They cannot get into the hold."

"And the pumps?"

"Sir, the Frenchmen are working the pumps. Right now, they are barely keeping up with the water. We moved the food to the gun deck."

"Show me, and then we'll have a chat with Lieutenant Rouen."

Holding a lantern over his head, Smythe climbed down into the hold. The water was knee deep, and rats scurried along the ribs. As he sloshed forward, Smythe spotted a waterfall coming from between two planks on the port side near the bow, about where *Oiseau* had rammed *Puritan.* He could see where an attempt had been made to re-caulk the seam and wedge in timbers to push the planks back into place.

"Mr. Rathburn, who did this?"

"The French carpenter. Apparently, it started leaking during the fight and he got it stopped. Then the storm last night worked the hull, and the leak got worse. We've tried to repair it, but as you see, we were not very successful."

"Get our man down here immediately along with the French carpenter, and see what they can do."

"Sir, both men told me that if we try to plug it more, it will make the leak worse or dislodge other planks. The planks are stove in and the rib is broken."

"Then bring Lieutenant Rouen to the captain's cabin and let's have a chat."

"Aye, sir."

The interval, as he waited in *Oiseau's* cabin for Rathburn to return with the French officer, gave Smythe time to think through a plan. Anger at losing his prize, no matter how justified, was not going to help. A knock on the door put an end to his pacing.

"Monsieur Lieutenant Smythe, you wanted to see me." The man's English was excellent, even with his French accent.

"Monsieur Rouen, does *Oiseau* have a history of leaks?"

"*Non.* Not bad ones. The ship has not been in a yard for three years. We were going to stop in Martinique to take on supplies before we headed for France, where the ship was to be careened and its bottom cleaned. With a fouled bottom we could not outrun you, so we had no choice but to fight."

"Is your carpenter competent?

"He has kept *Oiseau* afloat for two years."

"Did you order him to do a poor repair?"

"Of course not! I do not want to go swimming anymore than you do."

Darren couldn't help smile at the answer. "I assume you have seen the leak."

"I have. My carpenter says it is it is only a matter of time before the pegs holding the planks fail."

"You realize that unless we get it stopped, your men are going spend 10 days crammed into a hold on the *Puritan*. I cannot give your men a chance to take over my ship."

"Please do not treat us like criminals. You have my word that we will not try to take your ship. For us, this war is over.

I tell you, we are not anxious to return to France. We do not like our king."

This took Smythe aback. "Well then, muster your men and their sea chests on the main deck. We'll transfer the wounded first."

Philadelphia, April 1778

For the Americans, Independence Hall was the seat of power. It is where the First and now the Second Continental Congress met, made decisions, spent money, and dictated strategy. Now that the Articles of Confederation were ratified, its status as the ruling body of the United States of America was official.

Captain Jaco Jacinto, a few weeks before his nineteenth birthday, had the responsibility to win battles. When *Cutlass* or *Scorpion* were at sea, Jaco could not send a messenger to the Continental Congress asking for advice. Hundreds or thousands of miles away from Philadelphia, Jacinto had nothing but his sailing orders to guide life-and-death decisions. He and he alone was responsible for his ship's success or failure. The longer *Scorpion* was at sea, the heavier this responsibility became.

Back in port, rather than stay with his father, Jaco slept aboard *Scorpion*. Half of the crew had been given liberty, and his staying on board his ship allowed another officer to go ashore. He wasn't worried about men deserting, because the prize money for *Madras* had yet to be paid out. In his report, he'd calculated the prize money for each category using the same formula used by John Paul Jones. His share was £1,875 for *Madras* and her cargo of spices, and £2,375 for *Nevis*. his one-eighth share of the 10% of the £1,100,000 in gold £13,750. The total was £18,000, which would make him very, very rich. But, he was not in the Continental Navy for money; his family had plenty. He was a naval officer because he believed in independence from Britain.

Jaco had delivered his cruise report, including diagrams from journals depicting each naval action, to the Marine Committee two days after *Scorpion* docked. The matter of Edmund Radcliffe was much more complicated. The Second Lieutenant had been moved from *Scorpion* to a small house, where he was held under house arrest until such time as the Continental Congress decided what to do with him.

The delay let John Adams and Stephen Hopkins maneuver in order to forestall what threatened to be an embarrassing court martial of the son of a prominent Boston family. The resulting compromise was that Jaco would be questioned before the entire Continental Congress and Radcliffe would be sent back to Boston pending some as yet to be determined legal action.

The night before the hearing, Mr. Hewes and Jaco's father spent several hours with Jaco in his cabin on *Scorpion,* discussing what the members of Congress might ask. All three of them suspected that Congressman Adams would attempt to discredit Jaco as a way to exonerate Edmund Radcliffe. Such a move would also be an attempt to embarrass Mr. Hewes for his choice of a captain who made poor decisions. They were convinced that Adams wanted to force both John Hewes and Javier Jacinto to resign from the Marine Committee.

It was like a Shakespearean play, Javier said, and they had to let all five acts play out. Act I had been the selection of Jaco as *Scorpion's* captain. The voyage that delivered a fortune in gold was Act II. Act III was Radcliffe's plans to lead a mutiny. The negotiations that caused the delay in determining whether or not Radcliffe would be court-martialed was Act IV. Jaco's appearance before the entire Continental Congress, and the votes that followed his appearance, was Act V.

The day of the hearing, Jaco arrived a half-hour early. Alvin Harper, who assisted the Georgia delegation, met him at the door and explained that the meeting would be conducted in the room where the members of the Continental Congress gathered. There was podium at the far end, and in the center of the floor there was a chair and a small table covered with a green cloth. That, Harper explained, was where Jaco would sit.

Harper, a native of Savannah, spoke with a soft, Georgia accent. "I am the law clerk preparing the charges against Lieutenant Radcliffe. In my opinion, we need to hang Radcliffe to send a message to the arrogant Bostonians who think it furthers their interests to put incompetent men in positions of command. If Congress sends Radcliffe to Boston for trial, under the Articles of Confederation, we, the Continental Congress, do not have the power to ask for extradition. But I am afraid there are many in Congress who are jealous of your success. Georgia, South and North Carolina, Maryland and Virginia stand with your father and Mr. Hewes. It is the men from Massachusetts, Connecticut, New York and New Jersey who do not like you because you are a southerner and you succeeded where their men failed."

Just then the door opened from within. Harper gestured towards the doorway and said, "Captain..."

As Jaco passed, Harper whispered. "Good luck!"

Jaco waited until he was announced, then entered, looking straight at the podium where John Adams stood. He strode to the table and placed his hat on it. He did not sit down. Instead, he stood ramrod-straight with his hands clasped behind his back. *This is worse than being shot at by British cannons.*

John Adams intoned, "Mr. Jacinto, thank you for coming." He spread his hands out on both sides. "We, the Second Continental Congress, would like to hear about your recent voyage and ask you questions. Some members of Congress don't think it was as conducted in the best possible manner."

In the silence that followed, Jaco answered. "Sir, unless I have been relieved of my duties, I am still a captain and in command of the Continental Navy frigate *Scorpion*. Is that not true?"

Adams looked at him crossly. He did not like being challenged, particularly by a man as young as Jacinto. "Yes, for the moment, you are still *Scorpion's* captain."

"*Perfecto!*" Jaco turned so he faced each man in the room before speaking. It was time to seize the initiative. "And I would like to confirm that the Marine Committee selects captains based on how well they perform their duties and the successes their ships achieve. Do you, Mr. Adams, sir, not agree?"

Adams nodded. As he saw it, the young man was about to hang himself with his own arrogance. If he did, it would make his job that much simpler.

"Mr. Adams, sir, I did not hear your answer. Do you, or do you not agree?"

"Yes, I do." *You are not showing the proper respect for your betters, to say nothing of your elders. That too will play into sinking your ship, young man.*

"Good! At least we agree on something." No one laughed, but several men cleared their throats, and Jaco saw two congressmen rub their faces in a way that suggested they were hiding smiles. Even though he was a tireless advocate of independence, Adams was not universally liked.

My first shots were fired. Now, Mr. Adams, I am going to rake you from the bow. "Then the Congress needs to consider all the evidence. Under my leadership, *Scorpion* defeated and sunk His Majesty's Ship *Coburg,* a 32-gun frigate that was bigger and more heavily armed than

Scorpion. We did it in such a manner that only a few members of my crew were killed or wounded. *Scorpion* took messages to France in record time. Previously, the record time had been set by *Cutlass,* under my command. Once *Scorpion* left France, my sailing orders read, and I quote from my orders signed by Mr. Adams—'disrupt British commerce wherever you can *by capturing or destroying its merchant ships and raiding its ports.'* We captured *Madras,* a British West India cargo ship that was carrying eight tons of gold worth £1,100,000 sterling. Let me repeat the value of the gold—£1,100,000 sterling. We now have that gold to back our currency. Before this voyage, the Continental Dollar was only backed by patriotism and faith in our cause."

This last shot hit home. Jaco sensed a shift in the room as Congressmen digested what he said. Last night, he had been able to go to sleep only after he decided he was going to put the naysayers on the defensive.

He used his forefinger to tap the table as he continued. "After transferring the gold to *Scorpion,* I was faced with a difficult set of decisions, centered around how to dispose of *Madras,* and how to collect the prize money which the Continental Navy uses to pay our men, build ships, buy food, guns, powder and shot. We sold *Madras* and its cargo of spices in Amsterdam for the equivalent of £15,000 Sterling in Dutch gold and silver guilders. When we arrived in Philadelphia, Mr. Stephen Hopkins referred to the chest of silver guilders as pirates' booty. I took exception to his remark because *Scorpion* is not a privateer hunting ships for money. It is Continental Navy ship built to wage war against the British. So, Mr. Hopkins and Mr. Adams, the gold and the prize money from *Madras* is to be used to fund our cause, and my crew members given their rightful share. As we speak, Continental Navy ships are tied to piers because there has been no money to pay for crews or provisions. With the cargo *Scorpion* captured, we now have that money."

As Mr. Adams opened his mouth, Jaco held up his hand as if to say, 'I am not finished.' He looked around the room. Those who wanted him relieved of command looked down, not wanting him to see their faces, or they glared at him. He now knew who the enemy were. Others stared at the ceiling. Most members were listening intently to what he had to say.

"But taking one British ship, no matter how valuable its cargo, does not disrupt England's commerce. England has plenty of gold. We would have to take a dozen prizes like *Madras* to have an effect. What I decided to do next was to conduct raids to send a message to the British that *no place on their island is safe from the Continental Navy*. My raids will cause Lloyds to raise insurance rates, which makes shipping British cargo around the world more expensive. More raids like mine will make shipping insurance prohibitively expensive. *That*, gentlemen, is how one disrupts English commerce."

A member of the delegation from Connecticut interrupted. "Captain Jacinto, don't you agree that your youth and enthusiasm overcame your best judgment to bring the gold and *Scorpion* home sooner?"

"No, sir, I do not. The decision was a sensible one because it made *Scorpion's* movements unpredictable as it executed its orders. A more direct route would have taken *Scorpion* through waters that are heavily guarded. We would most certainly have been captured."

The delegate from Connecticut persisted. "Yet you still ran into a Royal Navy squadron."

"Yes, we did, but it was a much smaller one that if we had gone through the English Channel past its main base. We defeated three ships with very little damage to *Scorpion* and only a few casualties. May I remind you that the Royal Navy has almost 500 ships, so the chances of *Scorpion* meeting Royal Navy frigates in the English Channel and Celtic Sea s are very high. Our movements were designed to minimize the chances of having to fight superior numbers of larger, heavily armed ships."

A member of the Maryland delegation who had been sitting quietly, with his hands folded in his lap, now stood up. "I find the second-guessing of Captain Jacinto to be preposterous. None of us were on his ship. None of us were faced with the choices he was forced to make, including dealing with an unhappy officer who was planning a mutiny to seize command for himself. We have Captain Jacinto to thank for desperately needed funds, such as we have been unable to raise despite all our best efforts. So, I say, questioning Captain Jacinto further—"

Angrily, John Adams interrupted. "I beg your pardon, sir. Edmund Radcliffe is an *honorable* man who disagreed with his captain's decisions."

The gentleman from Maryland responded, "The documents I and many others have seen, Mr. Adams, tell a much more sordid story. Captain Jacinto had every right to hang Radcliffe. So I would like Captain Jacinto to tell his version of events."

"Hear, hear!" resounded through the chamber, and Jaco waited until the voices subsided.

Jaco tightened the clasp his hands behind his back to keep them from shaking. He took a deep breath and chose his words carefully.

"*Scorpion* out-sailed and out-fought the Royal Navy every time we met them *under my leadership.*"

His hands came out from behind his back so it looked as if he was holding a large, imaginary bowl. "All of this and much more is detailed in my report given to the Marine Committee. It is similar to the reports written independently by all of my officers, except one who disagreed with my actions. His name is Lieutenant Edmund Radcliffe. I have delivered a report on Lieutenant Radcliffe's performance to the Marine Committee recommending that he be tried by court martial for sedition and planning a mutiny. All eleven of the other men involved in his plot have made their mark on sworn statements, detailing what Mr. Radcliffe told them about his plans. Officers, warrants and seamen have come forward voluntarily and signed statements that describe Radcliffe's efforts to sow dissension amongst the crew. He was not successful because the crew had faith in my leadership and judgement.

"The Marine Committee has Radclffe's journal, in which he outlines his plans to take over *Scorpion. These plans included the murder of his fellow officers.* If I had not put him in irons, he would have enacted those plans in the heat of battle. It is a credit to my crew that they knew about the men recruited by Mr. Radcliffe and made sure they did not succeed. Under the Articles of War, I could have tried Mr. Radcliffe and the eleven men for planning a mutiny, and, if convicted, had each of them hung or shot. Instead, I chose to hold Mr. Radcliffe in irons until we returned home. Those who previously said they would help Radcliffe have agreed to testify against him. I leave it up to the Congress to decide what to do with Mr. Radcliffe, who has already forfeited his share of the prize money."

Another congressman stood up. Jaco believed he was from Rhode Island. "I think Captain Jacinto made a very commendable decision regarding Edmund Radcliffe. We, the Continental Congress and the Marine Committee, can evaluate the evidence and decide how to proceed."

Jaco turned around so that he could look at all the men he'd identified as supporting John Adams and Stephen Hopkins. They glared at him, eyes flashing scorn and even hate. "Thank you, sir. Since we are looking at what actually occurred, not what should or might have been, the facts and the results say I made right decisions."

Jaco took a deep breath. "I suspect some of you may have read letters from Lieutenant Radcliffe criticizing my decisions. All of my officers had plenty of opportunities to question my plans and offer suggestions during meetings. Mr. Radcliffe participated in those discussions. Sadly, he also planned a mutiny. Lieutenant Radcliffe's plans represent more than mere ambition and professional jealousy. They were *treasonous*."

John Adams' face went white. In the hush that followed, Jaco's voice sounded once more. "I believe my performance as the Captain of the *Scorpion* met the standards expected of me. The best testament to whether or not I am a good or bad captain is *Scorpion's* re-enlistment rate. It is close to one hundred per cent. *Scorpion's* crew wants to continue serving under my command, and this is the best indicator of my competence as a captain. Thank you, gentlemen, for permitting me to speak."

There was silence in the hall for about five seconds. Then a representative from New Hampshire, whom Jaco remembered from *Scorpion's* commissioning, stood up clapping; he was joined by congressmen from all but four delegations. Reluctantly, the members from the New York, New Jersey, Connecticut and Massachusetts stood up, but did not clap.

Mr. Hewes walked to the podium, and John Adams took his seat. "Thank you, Captain Jacinto. Let the record show that the majority of the Congress supports your decisions and actions. Unless anyone has an objection, this hearing is over. The Marine Committee will revoke Mr. Radcliffe's commission and decide whether or not a court martial will be held."

Raider of the Scottish Coast

On board H.M.S. Puritan, *May 1778*

On the last boat that brought *Oiseau's* crew to *Puritan,* Smythe left enough French powder to blow a large hole in the ship's bottom to ensure that, unlike *Coburg, Oiseau* would sink. Rathburn poured the fuse to the kegs and walked around the *Oiseau* lighting piles of sailcloth, hemp and pitch placed around the frigate. Just before he climbed down into the boat to be rowed back to *Puritan,* he lit the pile canvas sprinkled with gunpowder to start the fire on the gun deck.

The French crew was allowed to watch the end of their ship from *Puritan's* main deck. Black smoke from *Oiseau's* funeral pyre rose high into the sky. There was a rumble, a flash, and smoke billowed out of the open gun ports and companionways. The mizzenmast teetered for a few seconds, then crashed to the deck.

Oiseau's stern rose out of the smoke and then sank. Five minutes later, the top of the mainmast disappeared below the surface of the Caribbean.

After he gave the orders to set a course for Port Royal, Smythe stared at the spot where *Oiseau* sank, wondering if he and his men would ever earn any more prize money. He turned away, thankful he was still alive.

Charleston, May 1778

It was a lovely spring day, and after services Jaco escorted Reyna from the synagogue on Hassel Street to her house. Her parents and his mother trailed far enough behind to give them privacy, yet remain close enough to be chaperones.

The group enjoyed lunch at the Laredo's house, and afterwards Reyna and Jaco went to the gazebo in the large, shaded back yard. They sat side by side on the wide seat of the swing.

Since arriving via sloop on May 5th, Jaco had called on Reyna every morning. Each day, they did something different. One day it was a sail around the harbor. Another day, they went for a ride in the country, escorted by two armed men. Friday, they took a long chaperoned walk along the harbor. Jaco had noted that it wasn't as crowded as it used to be, but there were still many ships being readied for sea.

Jaco was very interested in how Reyna's apprenticeship, now with two doctors in Charleston, was progressing.

She told him that at some point in the near future, she would be the first female doctor in the city, even though she had not been to medical school. From talking to friends Jaco had heard that already many Charlestonians preferred her over other doctors. But despite her knowledge and letters of recommendation, the University of Pennsylvania again had rejected her application.

Reyna was infuriated that women could not attend medical school; it meant she could never officially earn the title of doctor. It was one of the many things she wanted to change after the war.

As they walked along, Reyna reached out and touched Jaco's arm. "When are you leaving?"

"Sometime around the end of the month. I am awaiting my orders."

"Are you still going to be the captain of the *Scorpion?*"

"That is being worked out."

"You can't tell me more?"

"No." *I don't know what I will be doing, other than it is some sort of role with the French Navy.*

The silence was uncomfortable. It was the same question his mother and Reyna's parents had asked. It was one for which he had no answer, other than he was in the Navy until the war ended or he was invalided out.

Jaco had come to Charleston with a purpose; it was now or never. He took her hand and blurted out, "Reyna, I love you. We both know we are meant for each other. Will you marry me?"

It didn't come out the way he wanted, but there it was. Direct and to the point, the way he hoped Reyna would like.

Reyna smiled and looked down before she looked at Jaco. "I will marry you when this war is over."

Jaco could barely contain his excitement. "So the answer is yes?"

"Yes. We are now officially engaged, which means you cannot have any girlfriends in Philadelphia or Boston or wherever you go."

"I don't now and won't ever."

"Good."

"Shall we go tell your parents?"

"They already know my answer. We have been waiting for you to ask."

Reyna smiled at his astonished expression. "Let's go tell your mother!"

The End

Cast of Main Characters by Ship

CONTINENTAL NAVY

Frigate Alfred
Jacinto, Jaco—3rd Midshipman
Jones, John Paul—First Lieutenant
Lodge, James—2nd Midshipman
Nicholas, Samuel—Marine Captain
Penway, David—Bosun
Reasoner, Harry—Gunner
Saltonstall, Dudley—Captain
Shelton, Jack—Topman, Quartermaster Mate
Struthers, Greg—Second Lieutenant

Sloop Providence
Bentley, John—Marine Lieutenant Marine
Garrison, Hedley—3rd Midshipman
Gaskins, Leo—Ship's carpenter
Hacker, Hoysted,—Captain after Jones
Hastings, Dwight—Bosun
Henderson, Dudley—Leading Seaman
Hitchcock, Levi—Sailmaker
Jacinto, Jaco—2rd LT
Jones, John Paul—Captain
James, Benjamin—First Lieutenant under Hoysted
Jeffords, Abner—1st Quartermaster Mate
Shelton, Jack—2nd Midshipman
Swain, Geoffrey—Quartermaster

Schooner Cutlass
Dupuis, Henri—First Lieutenant
Garrison, Hedley—2nd Midshipman
Gunderson, Jake—Carpenter's Mate
Jeffords, Abner—Quartermaster
Jacinto, Jaco—Lieutenant and CO
Preston, Bradley—Bosun
Shelton, Jack—Second Lieutenant

Frigate Scorpion
Radcliffe, Edmund—Second Lieutenant
Cox, Simon—3rd QM mate
Garrison, Hedley—1st Midshipman
Gaskins, Leo—Ship's Carpenter
Hayes, Neil—Third Lieutenant
Jeffords, Abner—Quartermaster
Miller, Patrick—Marine Lieutenant
Patterson, Philip—2nd Midshipman
Preston, Bradley—Bosun
Shelton, Jack—First Lieutenant
Wilson, Earl—3rd Midshipman

ROYAL NAVY

H.M.S. Deer
Crenshaw, Albert—1st Midshipman
Gaines,—Surgeon
Gladden, Brandon—First Lieutenant
Hyde, Everett—Master
O'Hare, Sean—3rd Midshipman
Roote, Ian—Second Lieutenant
Smythe, Darren—2nd Midshipman
Tillerson—Captain

H.M.S. *Jodpur*
Griffin, Andrew—First Lieutenant
Blackwell, Nigel—Second Lieutenant
Hearns, Alan—1st Midshipman
Horrocks, Reginald—Captain
O'Hare, Sean—3rd Midshipman
Shilling, Bartholomew—Master
Smythe, Darren—Third Lieutenant

H.M.S. *Puritan*
Bullocks, Earl—Third Lieutenant
Brown, Harvey—Marine Captain
Davidson, Stacey—Captain
Hearns, Alan—Second Midshipman
Rathburn, Drew—First Midshipman
Roote, Ian—Second Lieutenant
Smythe, Darren—First Lieutenant
Shilling, Bartholomew—Master

Royal Navy Ship Rating System

There was not a standardized and formal rating system for Royal Navy ships until 1677. Samuel Pepys, known for his detailed diary of his life and times, was at the time the Secretary of the Admiralty and as such created the rating system show below that became the "standard" for sailing ships and did not go away until wooden sailing ships were replaced by those made from iron and steel and powered by steam.

Rating	Type Ship	Number of Gun Decks	Number of Cannon in Its Main Battery
First Rater	Ship of the Line	3	100—120
Second Rater	Ship of the Line	3	90—98
Third Rater	Ship of the Line	3	64—80
Fourth Rater	Ship of the Line	2	48—60
Fifth Rater	Frigate	2	32—44
Sixth Rater	Frigate	1	20—28
Other	Sloop of War, Brig	1	16—18

SHIPS OF THE RAIDER OF THE SCOTTISH COAST

American Ships

	Alfred (real)	*Cutlass* (fictional)	*Providence* (real)	*Scropion* (fictional)
Type	Frigate	Schooner	Sloop	Frigate
Rigging	Square rigged with 3 masts	Lateen rigged with 2 masts	Single mast with square rigged top sail	Square rigged with three masts
Displace-ment	440 tons	~ 80 tons	~ 100 tons	600 tons
Length	140'	65'	65'	155'
Beam	32'	18'	20'	28'
Max Speed	10 knots	14 knots	12 knots	14 knots
Crew (officers and men)	220	35	65	200
Main Arma-ment	Twenty 9-pounders, Ten 6-pounders	Ten 6-pounders, Four swivel guns	Twelve 6-pounders, Forteen swivel guns	Twenty long 12-pounders Four long 9-pounders

Royal Navy Ships

	Coburg (fictional	Deer (fictional)	Jodpur (fictional)	Puritan (fictional)	Sorcerer (fictional)
Type	Frigate	Frigate	Frigate	Frigate	Sloop
Class Based On	Lowestoffe	Alarm	Modified Richmond	Amazon	Bonetta
Rigging	Square rigged with 3 masts	Square rigged with 3 masts	Square rigged with 3 masts	Square rigged with 3 masts	Square rigged with 3 masts
Displacement	717 tons	683 tons	677 tons	689 tons	220 tons
Length	130'	125'	127'	126'	85'
Beam	35'	35'	34'	35'	24'
Speed	11 knots	11 knots	11 knots	11 knots	12 knots
Crew	220	220	210	220	100
Armament	Twenty 12-pounders, Six 6-pounders, 12 swivel guns	Twenty-six 12 pounders Six 6-pounders, Twelve swivel guns	Twenty-six 12 pounders Six 6-pounders Twelve swivel guns	Twenty-six 12- pounders Six 18-pound carronades Six 6-pounders	Ten 6-pounders 12 swivel guns

FRENCH SHIP

	Oiseau (fictional)
Type	Frigate
Class	Charmante
Rigging	Square rigged with 3 masts
Displacement	840 tons
Length	140'
Beam	28'
Speed	10 knots
Crew	270
Armament	Twenty-six 12- pounders Twelve 6-pounders, Four 24-pound carronades

Timing of Watches and Ship's Bells

During the Age of Sail, clocks were expensive and ships rarely had more than two. To keep everyone informed of the time in the ship's routine, the ship's day was divided into six, four-hour watches. The exception is that the Dog Watches are split to allow the crew to eat dinner.

0000 (midnight)—0400—Middle Watch
0401—0800—Morning Watch
0801—1200—Forenoon Watch
1201—1600—Afternoon Watch
1601—1800—First Dog Watch
1800—2000—Second Dog Watch
2000—0000—First Watch

So, to let everyone know what time it was, the ship's bell was wrung every thirty minutes during the watch in a standard, recognizable pattern.

- 30 (.5 hour) minutes into the watch—1 bell
- 60 (1.0 hour) minutes into the watch—2 bells
- 90 minutes (1.5 hours) into the watch—2 bells, pause and 1 bell
- 120 minutes (2.0 hours) into the watch—2 bells, pause, 2 bells
- 150 minutes (2.5 hours) into the watch—2 bells, pause, 2 bells, pause 1 bell
- 180 minutes (3.0 hours) into the watch—2 bells, pause, 2 bells, pause, 2 bells
- 210 minutes (3.5 hours) into the watch—2 bells, pause, 2 bells, pause, 2 bells, pause, 1 bell

- 240 minutes (4.0 hours) into the watch—2 bells, pause, 2 bells, pause, 2 bells, pause, 2 bells.

Therefore, when a sailor of this era says it is six bells into the First watch, he means it is three hours into a watch that began at 2000 or 8 p.m., and it is now 2300 or 11 p.m.

About the Author

Marc Liebman

Marc retired as a Captain after twenty-four years in the Navy and is a combat veteran of Vietnam, the Tanker Wars of the 1980s and Desert Shield/Storm. He is a Naval Aviator with just under 6,000 hours of flight time in helicopters and fixed-wing aircraft. Captain Liebman has worked with the armed forces of Australia, Canada, Japan, Thailand, the Republic of Korea, the Philippines and the U.K.

He has been a partner in two different consulting firms advising clients on business and operational strategy, business process re-engineering, sales and marketing. Marc has also been the CEO of an aerospace and defense manufacturing company as well as an associate editor of a national magazine and a copywriter for an advertising agency.

Marc's latest career is as a novelist and six of his books— *Cherubs 2, Big Mother 40, Render Harmless, Forgotten, Inner Look* and *Moscow Airlift* have been published. A seventh—*The Simushir Island Incident*—will be released in

2020. *Big Mother 40* was ranked by the readers who buy books on Amazon as one of the top 100 war novels. *Forgotten* was a 2017 Finalist in Historical Fiction in the Next Generation Indie Book Awards, a Finalist in Fiction in the 2017 Literary Excellence Awards, and was rated as Five Star by Readers Favorites. *Inner Look* was also rated Five Star by Readers Favorites.

The Liebmans live near Aubrey, Texas. Marc is married to Betty, his lovely wife of 49+ years. They spend a lot of time visiting their four grandchildren.

IF YOU ENJOYED THIS BOOK
Please write a review.
This is important to the author and helps to get the word out to
others
Visit

PENMORE PRESS
www.penmorepress.com

BELLERAPHON'S

CHAMPION

BY

JOHN DANIELSKI

Deep within each man, lies the secret knowledge of whether he is a stalwart or a coward. Three years an un-blooded Royal Marine, 1st Lieutenant Thomas Pennywhistle will finally "meet the lion," protecting HMS Bellerophon at the Battle of Trafalgar.

Not only will Pennywhistle be responsible for the lives of 72 marines aboard Bellerophon but their direction will fall entirely on his shoulders since his fellow Marine officers consist of a boy, a card shark, and a dying consumptive. If he has what it takes to command, it will take everything he's got.

In the course of battle, he will encounter marvels and terrors; from valiant foes to women performing miracles, from the skill of acrobats to the luck of the ship's cat, from a dead man still full of fight to a coward who has none. He and his marines will meet enemy élan will with trained volleys and disciplined bayonets. Most of all, he will meet himself; discovering just how dark his true nature really is.

Europe will be changed forever by Trafalgar, and so will Pennywhistle.

PENMORE PRESS
www.penmorepress.com

A Sloop of War

by

Philip K.Allan

This second novel in the series of Lieutenant Alexander Clay novels takes us to the island of Barbados, where the temperature of the politics, prejudices and amorous ambitions within society are only matched by the sweltering heat of the climate. After limping into the harbor of Barbados with his crippled frigate *Agrius* and accompanied by his French prize, Clay meets with Admiral Caldwell, the Commander in Chief of the island. The admiral is impressed enough by Clay's engagement with the French man of war to give him his own command.

The *Rush* is sent first to blockade the French island of St Lucia, then to support a landing by British troops in an attempt to take the island from the French garrison. The crew and officers of the *Rush* are repeatedly threatened along the way by a singular Spanish ship, in a contest that can only end with destruction or capture. And all this time, hanging over Clay is an accusation of murder leveled against him by the nephew of his previous captain.

Philip K Allan has all the ingredients here for a gripping tale of danger, heroism, greed, and sea battles, in a story that is well researched and full of excitement from beginning to end.

PENMORE PRESS
www.penmorepress.com

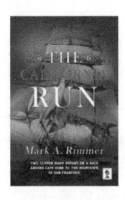

The California Run

by

Mark A. Rimmer

New York, 1850. Two clipper ships depart on a race around Cape Horn to the boomtown of San Francisco, where the first to arrive will gain the largest profits and also win a $50,000 wager for her owner.

Sapphire is a veteran ship with an experienced crew. Achilles is a new-build with a crimped, mostly unwilling crew. Inside Achilles' forecastle space reside an unruly gang of British sailors whose only goal is to reach the gold fields, a group of contrarily reluctant Swedish immigrants whose only desire is to return to New York and the luckless Englishman, Harry Jenkins, who has somehow managed to get himself crimped by the equally as deceitful Sarah Doyle, and must now spend the entire voyage working as a common sailor down in Achilles' forecastle while Sarah enjoys all the rich comforts of the aft passenger saloon.

Despite having such a clear advantage, Sapphire's owner has also placed a saboteur, Gideon, aboard Achilles with instructions to impede her in any way possible. Gideon sets to with enthusiasm and before she even reaches Cape Horn Achilles' chief mate and captain have both been murdered. Her inexperienced 2nd Mate, Nate Cooper, suddenly finds himself in command of Achilles and, with the help of the late captain's niece, Emma, who herself is the only experienced navigator remaining on board, they must somehow regain control over this diverse crew of misfits and encourage them onwards and around the Horn.

PENMORE PRESS
www.penmorepress.com

Fortune's Whelp
by
Benerson Little

Privateer, Swordsman, and Rake:

Set in the 17th century during the heyday of privateering and the decline of buccaneering, *Fortune's Whelp* is a brash, swords-out sea-going adventure. Scotsman Edward MacNaughton, a former privateer captain, twice accused and acquitted of piracy and currently seeking a commission, is ensnared in the intrigue associated with the attempt to assassinate King William III in 1696. Who plots to kill the king, who will rise in rebellion—and which of three women in his life, the dangerous smuggler, the wealthy widow with a dark past, or the former lover seeking independence—might kill to further political ends? Variously wooing and defying Fortune, Captain MacNaughton approaches life in the same way he wields a sword or commands a fighting ship: with the heart of a lion and the craft of a fox.

PENMORE PRESS
www.penmorepress.com

Penmore Press

Challenging, Intriguing, Adventurous, Historical and Imaginative

www.penmorepress.com

CPSIA information can be obtained
at www.ICGtesting.com
Printed in the USA
BVHW081205030820
585345BV00002B/2